HECTOR H

NOBODY'S BOY
(Sans Famille)

&

NOBODY'S GIRL
("En Famille")

**TRANSLATED FROM THE FRENCH BY
FLORENCE CREWE-JONES**

®2018 Neo Books (Neoeditorialbooks@gmail.com). This book is a product of its time, and it does not necessarily reflect the same views on race, gender, sexuality, ethnicity, and interpersonal relations as it would if it was written today.

HECTOR HENRY MALOT 1
  Translated from the French by Florence Crewe-Jones 1
    HECTOR MALOT 5
BOOK ONE. NOBODY'S BOY 7
  (Sans Famille) 7
  INTRODUCTION 7
    CHAPTER I. MY VILLAGE HOME 8
    CHAPTER II. MY ADOPTED FATHER 13
    CHAPTER III. SIGNOR VITALIS' COMPANY 19
    CHAPTER IV. THE MATERNAL HOUSE 27
    CHAPTER V. EN ROUTE 32
    CHAPTER VI. MY DÉBUT 35
    CHAPTER VII. CHILD AND ANIMAL LEARNING 41
    CHAPTER VIII. ONE WHO HAD KNOWN A KING 45
    CHAPTER IX. ARRESTED 49
    CHAPTER X. HOMELESS 55
    CHAPTER XI. ANOTHER BOY'S MOTHER 69
    CHAPTER XII. THE MASTER'S CONSENT 76
    CHAPTER XIII. WEARY DREARY DAYS 80
    CHAPTER XIV. THE DEATH OF PRETTY-HEART 92
    CHAPTER XV. FAITHFUL FRIENDS 101
    CHAPTER XVI. THE PADRONE 104
    CHAPTER XVII. POOR VITALIS 113
    CHAPTER XVIII. NEW FRIENDS 119
    CHAPTER XIX. DISASTER 125
    CHAPTER XX. MATTIA 134
    CHAPTER XXI. MEETING OLD FRIENDS 143
    CHAPTER XXII. IMPRISONED IN A MINE 147
    CHAPTER XXIII. ONCE MORE UPON THE WAY 158
    CHAPTER XXIV. FRIENDSHIP THAT IS TRUE 162
    CHAPTER XXV. MOTHER, BROTHERS AND SISTERS 176
    CHAPTER XXVI. BITTER DISAPPOINTMENT 182
    CHAPTER XXVII. A DISTRESSING DISCOVERY 186
    CHAPTER XXVIII. A MYSTERIOUS STRANGER 197
    CHAPTER XXIX. IN PRISON 199
    CHAPTER XXX. ESCAPE 205
    CHAPTER XXXI. HUNTING FOR THE SWAN 210
    CHAPTER XXXII. FINDING A REAL MOTHER 213
    CHAPTER XXXIII. THE DREAM COME TRUE 218
BOOK TWO. NOBODY'S GIRL 222
  ("En Famille") 222
  INTRODUCTION 222

CHAPTER I. PERRINE AND PALIKARE	223
CHAPTER II. GRAIN-OF-SALT IS KIND	234
CHAPTER III. "POOR LITTLE GIRL"	247
CHAPTER IV. A HARD ROAD TO TRAVEL	250
CHAPTER V. STORMS AND FEARS	257
CHAPTER VI. THE RESCUE	264
CHAPTER VII. MARAUCOURT AT LAST	267
CHAPTER VIII. GRANDFATHER VULFRAN	273
CHAPTER IX. ONE SLEEPLESS NIGHT	278
CHAPTER X. THE HUT ON THE ISLAND	287
CHAPTER XI. WORK IN THE FACTORY	289
CHAPTER XII. NEW SHOES	298
CHAPTER XIII. STRANGE HOUSEKEEPING	301
CHAPTER XIV. A BANQUET IN THE HUT	308
CHAPTER XV. AURELIE'S CHANCE	313
CHAPTER XVI. GRANDFATHER'S INTERPRETER	318
CHAPTER XVII. HARD QUESTIONS	323
CHAPTER XVIII. SECRETARY TO M. VULFRAN	329
CHAPTER XIX. SUSPICION AND CONFIDENCE	335
CHAPTER XX. THE SCHEMERS	342
CHAPTER XXI. LETTERS FROM DACCA	348
CHAPTER XXII. A CABLE TO DACCA	354
CHAPTER XXIII. GRANDFATHER'S COMPANION	360
CHAPTER XXIV. GETTING AN EDUCATION	367
CHAPTER XXV. MEDDLING RELATIVES	374
CHAPTER XXVI. PAINFUL ARGUMENTS	379
CHAPTER XXVII. THE BLIND MAN'S GRIEF	383
CHAPTER XXVIII. AN UNRESPECTED FUNERAL	387
CHAPTER XXIX. THE ANGEL OF REFORM	391
CHAPTER XXX. GRANDFATHER FINDS PERRINE	397
CHAPTER XXXI. THE GRATEFUL PEOPLE	400

HECTOR MALOT

HECTOR-HENRI MALOT, the son of a notary public, was born at La Brouille (Seine-Inferieure), March 20, 1830. He studied law, intending to devote himself also to the Notariat, but toward 1853 or 1854 commenced writing for various small journals. Somewhat later he assisted in compiling the 'Biographie Generale' of Firmin Didot, and was also a contributor to some reviews. Under the generic title of 'Les Victimes d'Amour,' he made his debut with the following three family-romances: 'Les Amants (1859), Les Epoux (1865), and Les Enfants (1866).' About the same period he published a book, 'La Vie Moderne en Angleterre.'

Malot has written quite a number of novels, of which the greatest is 'Conscience,' crowned by the French Academy in 1878.

His works have met with great success in all countries. They possess that lasting interest which attends all work based on keen observation and masterly analysis of the secret motives of human actions.

The titles of his writings run as follows: 'Les Amours de Jacques (1868); Un Beau Frere (1869); Romain Kalbris (1864), being a romance for children; Une Bonne Afaire, and Madame Obernin (1870); Un Cure de Province (1872); Un Mariage sons le Second Empire (1873); Une Belle Mere (1874); L'Auberge du Monde (1875-1876, 4 vols.); Les Batailles du Mariage (1877, 3 vols.); Cara (1877); Le Docteur Claude (1879); Le Boheme Tapageuse (1880, 3 vols.); Pompon, and Une Femme d'Argent (1881); La Petite Soeur, and Les Millions Honteux (1882); Les Besogneux, and Paulette (1883); Marichette, and Micheline (1884.); Le Lieutenant Bonnet, and Sang Bleu (1885); Baccara, and Zyte (1886); Viceo Francis, Seduction, and Ghislaine (1887); Mondaine (1888); Mariage Riche, and Justice (1889); Mere (1890), Anie (1891); Complices (1892); Conscience (1893); and Amours de Jeunes et Amours de Vieux (1894).'

About this time Hector Malot resolved not to write fiction any more. He announced this determination in a card published in the journal, 'Le Temps,' May 25, 1895—It was then maliciously stated that "M. Malot his retired from business after having accumulated a fortune." However, he took up his pen again and published a history of his literary life: Le Roman de mes Romans (1896); besides two volumes of fiction, L'Amour dominateur (1896), and Pages choisies (1898), works which showed that, in the language of Holy Writ, "his eye was not dimmed nor his natural force abated," and afforded him a triumph over his slanderers.

EDOUARD PAILLERON de l'Academie Francaise.

BOOK ONE.
NOBODY'S BOY

(SANS FAMILLE)

INTRODUCTION

"Nobody's Boy," published in France under the title "Sans Famille," has become justly famous as one of the supreme juvenile stories of the world. In the midst of its early popularity, it was crowned by the Academy as one of the masterpieces of French literature. A few years later, it was followed by "En Famille," which is published by us as a companion story under the title "Nobody's Girl."

"Nobody's Boy" is a human document of child experiences that is fascinating reading for young and old. Parents, teachers and others, who are careful to have children read inspiring books, will welcome this beautiful story of Hector Malot, as among the best for them to recommend.

Such digressions in the original, as do not belong to the heart of the story, have been eliminated, so that the lost boy's experiences continue as the undisturbed interest, on through to the happy conclusion.

Loyal friendship and honest conduct are the vital ideals of this story, and the heart interest is eloquent with noble character.

THE PUBLISHERS.

CHAPTER I. MY VILLAGE HOME

I was a foundling. But until I was eight years of age I thought I had a mother like other children, for when I cried a woman held me tightly in her arms and rocked me gently until my tears stopped falling. I never got into bed without her coming to kiss me, and when the December winds blew the icy snow against the window panes, she would take my feet between her hands and warm them, while she sang to me. Even now I can remember the song she used to sing. If a storm came on while I was out minding our cow, she would run down the lane to meet me, and cover my head and shoulders with her cotton skirt so that I should not get wet.

When I had a quarrel with one of the village boys she made me tell her all about it, and she would talk kindly to me when I was wrong and praise me when I was in the right. By these and many other things, by the way she spoke to me and looked at me, and the gentle way she scolded me, I believed that she was my mother.

My village, or, to be more exact, the village where I was brought up, for I did not have a village of my own, no birthplace, any more than I had a father or mother—the village where I spent my childhood was called Chavanon; it is one of the poorest in France. Only sections of the land could be cultivated, for the great stretch of moors was covered with heather and broom. We lived in a little house down by the brook.

Until I was eight years of age I had never seen a man in our house; yet my adopted mother was not a widow, but her husband, who was a stone-cutter, worked in Paris, and he had not been back to the village since I was of an age to notice what was going on around me. Occasionally he sent news by some companion who returned to the village, for there were many of the peasants who were employed as stone-cutters in the city.

"Mother Barberin," the man would say, "your husband is quite well, and he told me to tell you that he's still working, and to give you this money. Will you count it?"

That was all. Mother Barberin was satisfied, her husband was well and he had work.

Because Barberin was away from home it must not be thought that he was not on good terms with his wife. He stayed in Paris because his work kept him there. When he was old he would come back and live with his wife on the money that he had saved.

8

One November evening a man stopped at our gate. I was standing on the doorstep breaking sticks. He looked over the top bar of the gate and called to me to know if Mother Barberin lived there. I shouted yes and told him to come in. He pushed open the old gate and came slowly up to the house. I had never seen such a dirty man. He was covered with mud from head to foot. It was easy to see that he had come a distance on bad roads. Upon hearing our voices Mother Barberin ran out.

"I've brought some news from Paris," said the man.

Something in the man's tone alarmed Mother Barberin.

"Oh, dear," she cried, wringing her hands, "something has happened to Jerome!"

"Yes, there is, but don't get scared. He's been hurt, but he ain't dead, but maybe he'll be deformed. I used to share a room with him, and as I was coming back home he asked me to give you the message. I can't stop as I've got several miles to go, and it's getting late."

But Mother Barberin wanted to know more; she begged him to stay to supper. The roads were so bad! and they did say that wolves had been seen on the outskirts of the wood. He could go early in the morning. Wouldn't he stay?

Yes, he would. He sat down by the corner of the fire and while eating his supper told us how the accident had occurred. Barberin had been terribly hurt by a falling scaffold, and as he had had no business to be in that particular spot, the builder had refused to pay an indemnity.

"Poor Barberin," said the man as he dried the legs of his trousers, which were now quite stiff under the coating of mud, "he's got no luck, no luck! Some chaps would get a mint o' money out of an affair like this, but your man won't get nothing!"

"No luck!" he said again in such a sympathetic tone, which showed plainly that he for one would willingly have the life half crushed out of his body if he could get a pension. "As I tell him, he ought to sue that builder."

"A lawsuit," exclaimed Mother Barberin, "that costs a lot of money."

"Yes, but if you win!"

Mother Barberin wanted to start off to Paris, only it was such a terrible affair ... the journey was so long, and cost so much!

The next morning we went into the village and consulted the priest. He advised her not to go without first finding out if she could be of any use. He wrote to the hospital where they had taken Barberin, and a few days later received a reply saying that Barberin's wife was not to go, but that she could send a certain sum of money to her husband, because he was going to sue the builder upon whose works he had met with the accident.

Days and weeks passed, and from time to time letters came asking for more money. The last, more insistent than the previous ones, said that if there was no more money the cow must be sold to procure the sum.

Only those who have lived in the country with the peasants know what distress there is in these three words, "Sell the cow." As long as they have their cow in the shed they know that they will not suffer from hunger. We got butter from ours to put in the soup, and milk to moisten the potatoes. We lived so well from ours that until the time of which I write I had hardly ever tasted meat. But our cow not only gave us nourishment, she was our friend. Some people imagine that a cow is a stupid animal. It is not so, a cow is most intelligent. When we spoke to ours and stroked her and kissed her, she understood us, and with her big round eyes which looked so soft, she knew well enough how to make us know what she wanted and what she did not want. In fact, she loved us and we loved her, and that is all there is to say. However, we had to part with her, for it was only by the sale of the cow that Barberin's husband would be satisfied.

A cattle dealer came to our house, and after thoroughly examining Rousette,—all the time shaking his head and saying that she would not suit him at all, he could never sell her again, she had no milk, she made bad butter,—he ended by saying that he would take her, but only out of kindness because Mother Barberin was an honest good woman.

Poor Rousette, as though she knew what was happening, refused to come out of the barn and began to bellow.

"Go in at the back of her and chase her out," the man said to me, holding out a whip which he had carried hanging round his neck.

"No, that he won't," cried mother. Taking poor Rousette by the loins, she spoke to her softly: "There, my beauty, come ... come along then."

Rousette could not resist her, and then, when she got to the road, the man tied her up behind his cart and his horse trotted off and she had to follow.

We went back to the house, but for a long time we could hear her bellowing. No more milk, no butter! In the morning a piece of bread, at night some potatoes with salt.

Shrove Tuesday happened to be a few days after we had sold the cow. The year before Mother Barberin had made a feast for me with pancakes and apple fritters, and I had eaten so many that she had beamed and laughed with pleasure. But now we had no Rousette to give us milk or butter, so there would be no Shrove Tuesday, I said to myself sadly.

But Mother Barberin had a surprise for me. Although she was not in the habit of borrowing, she had asked for a cup of milk from one of the neighbors, a piece of butter from another, and when I got home about midday she was emptying the flour into a big earthenware bowl.

"Oh," I said, going up to her, "flour?"

"Why, yes," she said, smiling, "it's flour, my little Remi, beautiful flour. See what lovely flakes it makes."

Just because I was so anxious to know what the flour was for I did not dare ask. And besides I did not want her to know that I remembered that it was Shrove Tuesday for fear she might feel unhappy.

"What does one make with flour?" she asked, smiling at me.

"Bread."

"What else?"

"Pap."

"And what else?"

"Why, I don't know."

"Yes, you know, only as you are a good little boy, you don't dare say. You know that to-day is Pancake day, and because you think we haven't any butter and milk you don't dare speak. Isn't that so, eh?

"Oh, Mother."

"I didn't mean that Pancake day should be so bad after all for my little Remi. Look in that bin."

I lifted up the lid quickly and saw some milk, butter, eggs, and three apples.

"Give me the eggs," she said; "while I break them, you peel the apples."

While I cut the apples into slices, she broke the eggs into the flour and began to beat the mixture, adding a little milk from time to time. When the paste was well beaten she placed the big earthenware bowl on the warm cinders, for it was not until supper time that we were to have the pancakes and fritters. I must say frankly that it was a very long day, and more than once I lifted up the cloth that she had thrown over the bowl.

"You'll make the paste cold," she cried; "and it won't rise well."

But it was rising well, little bubbles were coming up on the top. And the eggs and milk were beginning to smell good.

"Go and chop some wood," Mother Barberin said; "we need a good clear fire."

At last the candle was lit.

"Put the wood on the fire!"

She did not have to say this twice; I had been waiting impatiently to hear these words. Soon a bright flame leaped up the chimney and the light from the fire lit up all the kitchen. Then Mother Barberin took down the frying pan from its hook and placed it on the fire.

"Give me the butter!"

With the end of her knife she slipped a piece as large as a nut into the pan, where it melted and spluttered. It was a long time since we had smelled that odor. How good that butter smelled! I was listening to it fizzing when I heard footsteps out in our yard.

Whoever could be coming to disturb us at this hour? A neighbor perhaps to ask for some firewood. I couldn't think, for just at that moment Mother Barberin put her big wooden spoon into the bowl and was pouring a spoonful of the paste into the pan, and it was not the moment to let one's thoughts wander. Somebody knocked on the door with a stick, then it was flung open.

"Who's there?" asked Mother Barberin, without turning round.

A man had come in. By the bright flame which lit him up I could see that he carried a big stick in his hand.

"So, you're having a feast here, don't disturb yourselves," he said roughly.

"Oh, Lord!" cried Mother Barberin, putting the frying pan quickly on the floor, "is it you, Jerome."

Then, taking me by the arm she dragged me towards the man who had stopped in the doorway.

"Here's your father."

CHAPTER II. MY ADOPTED FATHER

Mother Barberin kissed her husband; I was about to do the same when he put out his stick and stopped me.

"What's this?... you told me...."

"Well, yes, but it isn't true ... because...."

"Ah, it isn't true, eh?"

He stepped towards me with his stick raised; instinctively I shrunk back. What had I done? Nothing wrong, surely! I was only going to kiss him. I looked at him timidly, but he had turned from me and was speaking to Mother Barberin.

"So you're keeping Shrove Tuesday," he said. "I'm glad, for I'm famished. What have you got for supper?"

"I was making some pancakes and apple fritters."

"So I see, but you're not going to give pancakes to a man who has covered the miles that I have."

"I haven't anything else. You see we didn't expect you."

"What? nothing else! Nothing for supper!" He glanced round the kitchen.

"There's some butter."

He looked up at the ceiling, at the spot where the bacon used to hang, but for a long time there had been nothing on the hook; only a few ropes of onions and garlic hung from the beam now.

"Here's some onions," he said, knocking a rope down with his big stick; "with four or five onions and a piece of butter we'll have a good soup. Take out the pancakes and fry the onions in the pan!"

"Take the pancakes out of the frying pan!"

Without a word, Mother Barberin hurried to do what her husband asked. He sat down on a chair by the corner of the fireplace. I had not dared to leave the place where his stick had sent me. Leaning against the table, I looked at him.

He was a man about fifty with a hard face and rough ways. His head leaned a little bit towards his right shoulder, on account of the wound he had received, and this deformity gave him a still more forbidding aspect.

Mother Barberin had put the frying pan again on the fire.

"Is it with a little bit of butter like that you're going to try and make a soup?" he asked. Thereupon he seized the plate with the butter and threw it all into the pan. No more butter ... then ... no more pancakes.

At any other moment I should have been greatly upset at this catastrophe, but I was not thinking of the pancakes and fritters now. The thought that was uppermost in my mind was, that this man who seemed so cruel was my father! My father! Absently I said the word over and over again to myself. I had never thought much what a father would be. Vaguely, I had imagined him to be a sort of mother with a big voice, but in looking at this one who had fallen from heaven, I felt greatly worried and frightened. I had wanted to kiss him and he had pushed me away with his stick. Why? My mother had never pushed me away when I went to kiss her; on the contrary, she always took me in her arms and held me tight.

"Instead of standing there as though you're made of wood," he said, "put the plates on the table."

I nearly fell down in my haste to obey. The soup was made. Mother Barberin served it on the plates. Then, leaving the big chimney corner, he came and sat down and commenced to eat, stopping only from time to time to glance at me. I felt so uncomfortable that I could not eat. I looked at him also, but out of the corner of my eye, then I turned my head quickly when I caught his eye.

"Doesn't he eat more than that usually?" he asked suddenly.

"Oh, yes, he's got a good appetite."

"That's a pity. He doesn't seem to want his supper now, though."

Mother Barberin did not seem to want to talk. She went to and fro, waiting on her husband.

"Ain't you hungry?"

"No."

"Well then, go to bed and go to sleep at once. If you don't I'll be angry."

My mother gave me a look which told me to obey without answering. But there was no occasion for this warning. I had not thought of saying a word.

As in a great many poor homes, our kitchen was also the bedroom. Near the fireplace were all the things for the meals—the table, the pots and pans, and the sideboard; at the other end was the bedroom. In a corner stood

Mother Barberin's big bed, in the opposite corner, in a little alcove, was my bed under a red figured curtain.

I hurriedly undressed and got into bed. But to go to sleep was another thing. I was terribly worried and very unhappy. How could this man be my father? And if he was, why did he treat me so badly?

With my nose flattened against the wall I tried to drive these thoughts away and go to sleep as he had ordered me, but it was impossible. Sleep would not come. I had never felt so wide awake.

After a time, I could not say how long, I heard some one coming over to my bed. The slow step was heavy and dragged, so I knew at once that it was not Mother Barberin. I felt a warm breath on my cheek.

"Are you asleep?" This was said in a harsh whisper.

I took care not to answer, for the terrible words, "I'll be angry" still rang in my ears.

"He's asleep," said Mother Barberin; "the moment he gets into bed he drops off. You can talk without being afraid that he'll hear."

I ought, of course, to have told him that I was not asleep, but I did not dare. I had been ordered to go to sleep, I was not yet asleep, so I was in the wrong.

"Well, what about your lawsuit?" asked Mother Barberin.

"Lost it. The judge said that I was to blame for being under the scaffold." Thereupon he banged his fist on the table and began to swear, without saying anything that meant anything.

"Case lost," he went on after a moment; "money lost, all gone, poverty staring us in the face. And as though that isn't enough, when I get back here, I find a child. Why didn't you do what I told you to do?"

"Because I couldn't."

"You could not take him to a Foundlings' Home?"

"A woman can't give up a little mite like that if she's fed it with her own milk and grown to love it."

"It's not your child."

"Well, I wanted to do what you told me, but just at that very moment he fell ill."

"Ill?"

"Yes. Then I couldn't take him to that place. He might have died."

15

"But when he got better?"

"Well, he didn't get better all at once. After that sickness another came. He coughed so it would have made your heart bleed to hear him, poor little mite. Our little Nicolas died like that. It seemed to me that if I sent him to the Foundlings' Home he'd died also."

"But after?... after?"

"Well, time went on and I thought that as I'd put off going I'd put it off a bit longer."

"How old is he now?"

"Eight."

"Well then, he'll go now to the place where he should have gone sooner, and he won't like it so well now."

"Oh, Jerome, you can't ... you won't do that!"

"Won't I? and who's going to stop me? Do you think we can keep him always?"

There was a moment's silence. I was hardly able to breathe. The lump in my throat nearly choked me. After a time Mother Barberin went on:

"How Paris has changed you! You wouldn't have spoken like that to me before you went away."

"Perhaps not. But if Paris has changed me, it's also pretty near killed me. I can't work now. We've got no money. The cow's sold. When we haven't enough to feed ourselves, have we got to feed a child that don't belong to us?"

"He's mine."

"He's no more yours than mine. Besides, he ain't a country boy. He's no poor man's child. He's a delicate morsel, no arms, no legs."

"He's the prettiest boy in the village!"

"I don't say he ain't pretty. But sturdy, no! Do you think you can make a working man out of a chit with shoulders like his? He's a city child and there's no place for city children here."

"I tell you he's a fine boy and as intelligent and cute as a little cat, and he's got a good heart, and he'll work for us...."

"In the meantime we've got to work for him, and I'm no good for much now."

"If his parents claim him, what will you say?"

"His parents! Has he got any parents? They would have found him by now if he had. It was a crazy thing for me to think that his parents would come and claim him some day and pay us for his keep. I was a fool. 'Cause he was wrapped up in fine clothes trimmed with lace, that wasn't to say that his parents were going to hunt for him. Besides, they're dead."

"Perhaps they're not. And one day they may come...."

"If you women ain't obstinate!"

"But if they do come?"

"Well, we've sent him to the Home. But we've said enough. I'll take him to-morrow. I'm going 'round to see François now. I'll be back in an hour."

The door was opened and closed again. He had gone. Then I quickly sat up in bed and began to call to Mother Barberin.

"Say! Mamma!"

She ran over to my bed.

"Are you going to let me go to the Foundlings' Home?"

"No, my little Remi, no."

She kissed me and held me tight in her arms. I felt better after that and my tears dried on my cheeks.

"You didn't go to sleep, then?" she asked softly.

"It wasn't my fault."

"I'm not scolding you. You heard what he said, then?"

"Yes, you're not my mamma, but ... he isn't my father."

The last words I had said in a different tone because, although I was unhappy at learning that she was not my mother, I was glad, I was almost proud, to know that he was not my father. This contradiction of my feelings betrayed itself in my voice. Mother Barberin did not appear to notice.

"Perhaps I ought to have told you the truth, but you seemed so much my own boy that I couldn't tell you I was not your real mother. You heard what Jerome said, my boy. He found you one day in a street in Paris, the Avenue de Breuteuil. It was in February, early in the morning, he was going to work when he heard a baby cry, and he found you on a step. He looked about to call some one, and as he did so a man came out from behind a tree and ran away. You cried so loud that Jerome didn't like to put you back on the step again. While he was wondering what to do, some more men came along, and they all decided that they'd take you to the police station. You wouldn't stop crying. Poor mite, you must have been cold. But then, when they got you warm at the station house, you still cried, so they thought you were hungry, and they got you some milk. My! you were hungry! When you'd had enough they undressed you and held you before the fire. You were a beautiful pink boy, and all dressed in lovely clothes. The lieutenant wrote down a description of the clothes and where you were found, and said that he should have to send you to the Home unless one of the men liked to take charge of you. Such a beautiful, fine child it wouldn't be difficult to bring up, he said, and the parents would surely make a search for it and pay any one well for looking after it, so Jerome said he'd take it. Just at that time I had a baby the same age. So I was well able to feed both you two mites. There, dearie, that was how I came to be your mother."

"Oh, Mamma, Mamma!"

"Yes, dearie, there! and at the end of three months I lost my own little baby and then I got even more fond of you. It was such a pity Jerome couldn't forget, and seeing at the end of three years that your parents hadn't come after you, he tried to make me send you to the Home. You heard why I didn't do as he told me?"

"Oh, don't send me to the Home," I cried, clinging to her, "Mother Barberin, please, please, don't send me to the Home."

"No, dearie, no, you shan't go. I'll settle it. Jerome is not really unkind, you'll see. He's had a lot of trouble and he is kind of worried about the future. We'll all work, you shall work, too."

"Yes, yes, I'll do anything you want me to do, but don't send me to the Home."

"You shan't go, that is if you promise to go to sleep at once. When he returns he mustn't find you awake."

She kissed me and turned me over with my face to the wall. I wanted to go to sleep, but I had received too hard a blow to slip off quietly into slumberland. Dear good Mother Barberin was not my own mother! Then what was a real mother? Something better, something sweeter still? It wasn't possible! Then I thought that a real father might not have held up his stick to me.... He wanted to send me to the Home, would mother be able to prevent him?

In the village there were two children from the Home. They were called "workhouse children." They had a metal plaque hung round their necks with a number on it. They were badly dressed, and so dirty! All the other children made fun of them and threw stones at them. They chased them like boys chase a lost dog, for fun, and because a stray dog has no one to protect it. Oh, I did not want to be like those children. I did not want to have a number hung round my neck. I did not want them to call after me, "Hi, Workhouse Kid; Hi Foundling!" The very thought of it made me feel cold and my teeth chatter. I could not go to sleep. And Barberin was coming back soon!

But fortunately he did not return until very late, and sleep came before he arrived.

CHAPTER III. SIGNOR VITALIS' COMPANY

That night I dreamed that I had been taken to the Home. When I opened my eyes in the early morning I could scarcely believe that I was still there in my little bed. I felt the bed and pinched my arms to see if it were true. Ah, yes, I was still with Mother Barberin.

She said nothing to me all the morning, and I began to think that they had given up the idea of sending me away. Perhaps she had said that she was determined to keep me. But when mid day came Barberin told me to put on my cap and follow him. I looked at Mother Barberin to implore her to help me. Without her husband noticing she made me a sign to go with him. I obeyed. She tapped me on the shoulder as I passed her, to let me know that I had nothing to fear. Without a word I followed him.

It was some distance from our house to the village—a good hour's walk. Barberin never said a word to me the whole way. He walked along, limping. Now and again he turned 'round to see if I was following. Where was he taking me? I asked myself the question again and again. Despite the reassuring sign that Mother Barberin had made, I felt that something was going to happen to me and I wanted to run away. I tried to lag behind, thinking that I would jump down into a ditch where Barberin could not catch me.

At first he had seemed satisfied that I should tramp along just behind him, on his heels, but he evidently soon began to suspect what I intended to do, and he grabbed me by the wrist. I was forced to keep up with him. This was the way we entered the village. Every one who passed us turned round to stare, for I looked like a bad dog held on a leash.

As we were about to pass the tavern, a man who was standing in the doorway called to Barberin and asked him to go in. Barberin took me by the ear and pushed me in before him, and when we got inside he closed the door. I felt relieved. This was only the village tavern, and for a long time I had wanted to see what it was like inside. I had often wondered what was going on behind the red curtains, I was going to know now....

Barberin sat down at a table with the boss who had asked him to go in. I sat by the fireplace. In a corner near me there was a tall old man with a long white beard. He wore a strange costume. I had never seen anything like it before. Long ringlets fell to his shoulders and he wore a tall gray hat ornamented with green and red feathers. A sheepskin, the woolly side turned inside, was fastened round his body. There were no sleeves to the skin, but through two large holes, cut beneath the shoulders, his arms were thrust, covered with velvet sleeves which had once been blue in color. Woolen gaiters reached up to his knees, and to hold them in place a ribbon was interlaced several times round his legs. He sat with his elbow resting on his crossed knees. I had never seen a living person in such a quiet calm attitude. He looked to me like one of the saints in our Church. Lying beside him were three dogs—a white spaniel, a black spaniel, and a pretty little gray dog with a sharp, cute little look. The white spaniel wore a policeman's old helmet, which was fastened under its chin with a leather strap.

While I stared at the man in wonder, Barberin and the owner of the tavern talked in low voices. I knew that I was the subject of their talk. Barberin was telling him that he had brought me to the village to take me to the mayor's office, so that the mayor should ask the Charity Home to pay for my keep. That was all that dear Mother Barberin had been able to do, but I felt that if Barberin could get something for keeping me I had nothing to fear.

The old man, who without appearing, had evidently been listening, suddenly pointed to me, and turning to Barberin said with a marked foreign accent:

"Is that the child that's in your way?"

"That's him."

"And you think the Home is going to pay you for his keep?"

"Lord! as he ain't got no parents and I've been put to great expense for him, it is only right that the town should pay me something."

"I don't say it isn't, but do you think that just because a thing is right, it's done?"

"That, no!"

"Well, then I don't think you'll ever get what you're after."

"Then he goes to the Home, there's no law that forces me to keep him in my place if I don't want to."

"You agreed in the beginning to take him, so it's up to you to keep your promise."

"Well, I ain't going to keep him. And when I want to turn him out I'll do so."

"Perhaps there's a way to get rid of him now," said the old man after a moment's thought, "and make a little money into the bargain."

"If you'll show me how, I'll stand a drink."

"Order the drinks, the affair's settled."

"Sure?

"Sure."

The old man got up and took a seat opposite Barberin. A strange thing, as he rose, I saw his sheepskin move. It was lifted up, and I wondered if he had another dog under his arm.

What were they going to do with me? My heart beat against my side, I could not take my eyes off the old man.

"You won't let this child eat any more of your bread unless somebody pays for it, that's it, isn't it?"

"That's it ... because...."

"Never mind the reason. That don't concern me. Now if you don't want him, just give him to me. I'll take charge of him."

"You? take charge of him!"

"You want to get rid of him, don't you?"

"Give you a child like him, a beautiful boy, for he is beautiful, the prettiest boy in the village, look at him."

"I've looked at him."

"Remi, come here."

I went over to the table, my knees trembling.

"There, don't be afraid, little one," said the old man.

"Just look at him," said Barberin again.

"I don't say that he is a homely child, if he was I wouldn't want him. I don't want a monster."

"Ah, now if he was a monster with two ears, or even a dwarf...."

"You'd keep him, you could make your fortune out of a monster. But this little boy is not a dwarf, nor a monster, so you can't exhibit him: he's made the same as others, and he's no good for anything."

"He's good for work."

"He's not strong."

"Not strong, him! Land's sakes! He's as strong as any man, look at his legs, they're that solid! Have you ever seen straighter legs than his?"

Barberin pulled up my pants.

"Too thin," said the old man.

"And his arms?" continued Barberin.

"Like his legs ... might be better. They can't hold out against fatigue and poverty."

"What, them legs and arms? Feel 'em. Just see for yourself."

The old man passed his skinny hand over my legs and felt them, shaking his head the while and making a grimace.

I had already seen a similar scene enacted when the cattle dealer came to buy our cow. He also had felt and pinched the cow. He also had shaken his head and said that it was not a good cow, it would be impossible to sell it again, and yet after all he had bought it and taken it away with him. Was the old man going to buy me and take me away with him? Oh, Mother Barberin! Mother Barberin!

If I had dared I would have said that only the night before Barberin had reproached me for seeming delicate and having thin arms and legs, but I felt that I should gain nothing by it but an angry word, so I kept silent.

For a long time they wrangled over my good and bad points.

"Well, such as he is," said the old man at last, "I'll take him, but mind you, I don't buy him outright. I'll hire him. I'll give you twenty francs a year for him."

"Twenty francs!"

"That's a good sum, and I'll pay in advance."

"But if I keep him the town will pay me more than ten francs a month."

"I know what you'd get from the town, and besides you've got to feed him."

"He will work."

"If you thought that he could work you wouldn't be so anxious to get rid of him. It is not for the money that's paid for their keep that you people take in lost children, it's for the work that you can get out of them. You make servants of them, they pay you and they themselves get no wages. If this child could have done much for you, you would have kept him."

"Anyway, I should always have ten francs a month."

"And if the Home, instead of letting you have him, gave him to some one else, you wouldn't get anything at all. Now with me you won't have to run for your money, all you have to do is to hold out your hand."

He pulled a leather purse from his pocket, counting out four silver pieces of money; he threw them down on the table, making them ring as they fell.

"But think," cried Barberin; "this child's parents will show up one day or the other."

"What does that matter?"

"Well, those who've brought him up will get something. If I hadn't thought of that I wouldn't have taken him in the first place."

Oh! the wicked man! How I did dislike Barberin!

"Now, look here, it's because you think his parents won't show up now that you're turning him out," said the old man. "Well, if by any chance they do appear, they'll go straight to you, not to me, for nobody knows me."

"But if it's you who finds them?"

"Well, in that case we'll go shares and I'll put thirty down for him now."

"Make it forty."

"No, for what he'll do for me that isn't possible."

"What do you want him to do for you? For good legs, he's got good legs; for good arms, he's got good arms. I hold to what I said before. What are you going to do with him?"

Then the old man looked at Barberin mockingly, then emptied his glass slowly:

"He's just to keep me company. I'm getting old and at night I get a bit lonesome. When one is tired it's nice to have a child around."

"Well, for that I'm sure his legs are strong enough."

"Oh, not too much so, for he must also dance and jump and walk, and then walk and jump again. He'll take his place in Signor Vitalis' traveling company."

"Where's this company?"

"I am Signor Vitalis, and I'll show you the company right here."

With this he opened the sheepskin and took out a strange animal which he held on his left arm, pressed against his chest. This was the animal that had several times raised the sheepskin, but it was not a little dog as I had thought. I found no name to give to this strange creature, which I saw for the first time. I looked at it in astonishment. It was dressed in a red coat trimmed with gold braid, but its arms and legs were bare, for they really were arms and legs, and not paws, but they were covered with a black, hairy skin, they were not white or pink. The head which was as large as a clenched fist was wide and short, the turned-up nose had spreading nostrils, and the lips were yellow. But what struck me more than anything, were the two eyes, close to each other, which glittered like glass.

"Oh, the ugly monkey!" cried Barberin.

A monkey! I opened my eyes still wider. So this was a monkey, for although I had never seen a monkey, I had heard of them. So this little tiny creature that looked like a black baby was a monkey!

"This is the star of my company," said Signor Vitalis. "This is Mr. Pretty-Heart. Now, Pretty-Heart,"—turning to the animal—"make your bow to the society."

The monkey put his hand to his lips and threw a kiss to each of us.

"Now," continued Signor Vitalis, holding out his hand to the white spaniel, "the next. Signor Capi will have the honor of introducing his friends to the esteemed company here present."

The spaniel, who up till this moment had not made a movement, jumped up quickly, and standing on his hind paws, crossed his fore paws on his chest and bowed to his master so low that his police helmet touched the ground. This polite duty accomplished, he turned to his companions, and with one paw still pressed on his chest, he made a sign with the other for them to draw nearer. The two dogs, whose eyes had been fixed on the white spaniel, got up at once and giving' each one of us his paw, shook hands as one does in polite society, and then taking a few steps back bowed to us in turn.

"The one I call 'Capi,'" said Signor Vitalis, "which is an abbreviation of *Capitano* in Italian, is the chief. He is the most intelligent and he conveys my orders to the others. That black haired young dandy is Signor Zerbino, which signifies 'the sport.' Notice him and I am sure you will admit that the name is very appropriate. And that young person with, the modest air is Miss Dulcie. She is English, and her name is chosen on account of her sweet disposition. With these remarkable *artistes* I travel through the country, earning my living, sometimes good, sometimes bad, ... it is a matter of luck! Capi!..."

The spaniel crossed his paws.

"Capi, come here, and be on your best behavior. These people are well brought up, and they must be spoken to with great politeness. Be good enough to tell this little boy who is looking at you with such big, round eyes what time it is."

Capi uncrossed his paws, went up to his master, drew aside the sheepskin, and after feeling in his vest pocket pulled out a large silver watch. He looked at the watch for a moment, then gave two distinct barks, then after these two decisive sharp barks, he uttered three little barks, not so loud nor so clear.

The hour was quarter of three.

"Very good," said Vitalis; "thank you, Signor Capi. And now ask Miss Dulcie to oblige us by dancing with the skipping rope."

Capi again felt in his master's vest pocket and pulled out a cord. He made a brief sign to Zerbino, who immediately took his position opposite to him. Then Capi threw him one end of the cord and they both began to turn it very gravely. Then Dulcie jumped lightly into the rope and with her beautiful soft eyes fixed on her master, began to skip.

"You see how intelligent they are," said Vitalis; "their intelligence would be even more appreciated if I drew comparisons. For instance, if I had a fool to act with them. That is why I want your boy. He is to be the fool so that the dogs' intelligence will stand out in a more marked manner."

"Oh, he's to be the fool...." interrupted Barberin.

"It takes a clever man to play the fool," said Vitalis, "the boy will be able to act the part with a few lessons. We'll test him at once. If he has any intelligence he will understand that with me he will be able to see the country and other countries besides; but if he stays here all he can do is to drive a herd of cattle in the same fields from morning to night. If he hasn't any intelligence he'll cry and stamp his feet, and then I won't take him with me and he'll be sent to the Foundlings' Home, where he'll have to work hard and have little to eat."

I had enough intelligence to know this, ... the dogs were very funny, and it would be fun to be with them always, but Mother, Mother Barberin!... I could not leave her!... Then if I refused perhaps I should not stay with Mother Barberin.... I might be sent to the Home. I was very unhappy, and as my eyes filled with tears, Signor Vitalis tapped me gently on the cheek.

"Ah, the little chap understands because he does not make a great noise. He is arguing the matter in his little head, and to-morrow...."

"Oh, sir," I cried, "let me stay with Mother Barberin, please let me stay."

I could not say more, for Capi's loud barking interrupted me. At the same moment the dog sprang towards the table upon which Pretty-Heart was seated. The monkey, profiting by the moment when every one was occupied with me, had quickly seized his master's glass, which was full of wine, and was about to empty it. But Capi, who was a good watch dog, had seen the monkey's trick and like the faithful servant that he was, he had foiled him.

"Mr. Pretty-Heart," said Vitalis severely, "you are a glutton and a thief; go over there into the corner and turn your face to the wall, and you, Zerbino, keep guard: if he moves give him a good slap. As to you, Mr. Capi, you are a good dog, give me your paw. I'd like to shake hands with you."

The monkey, uttering little stifled cries, obeyed and went into the corner, and the dog, proud and happy, held out his paw to his master.

"Now," continued Vitalis, "back to business. I'll give you thirty francs for him then."

"No, forty."

A discussion commenced, but Vitalis soon stopped it by saying:

"This doesn't interest the child, let him go outside and play."

At the same time he made a sign to Barberin.

"Yes, go out into the yard at the back, but don't move or you'll have me to reckon with."

I could not but obey. I went into the yard, but I had no heart to play. I sat down on a big stone and waited. They were deciding what was to become of me. What would it be? They talked for a long time. I sat waiting, and it was an hour later when Barberin came out into the yard. He was alone. Had he come to fetch me to hand me over to Vitalis?

"Come," he said, "back home."

Home! Then I was not to leave Mother Barberin?

I wanted to ask questions, but I was afraid, because he seemed in a very bad temper. We walked all the way home in silence. But just before we arrived home Barberin, who was walking ahead, stopped.

"You know," he said, taking me roughly by the ear, "if you say one single word of what you have heard to-day, you shall smart for it. Understand?"

CHAPTER IV. THE MATERNAL HOUSE

"Well," asked Mother Barberin, when we entered, "what did the mayor say?"

"We didn't see him."

"How! You didn't see him?"

"No, I met some friends at the Notre-Dame café and when we came out it was too late. So we'll go back to-morrow."

So Barberin had given up the idea of driving a bargain with the man with the dogs.

On the way home I wondered if this was not some trick of his, returning to the house, but his last words drove all my doubts away. As we had to go back to the village the next day to see the mayor, it was certain that Barberin had not accepted Vitalis' terms.

But in spite of his threats I would have spoken of my fears to Mother Barberin if I could have found myself alone for one moment with her, but all the evening Barberin did not leave the house, and I went to bed without getting the opportunity. I went to sleep thinking that I would tell her the next day. But the next day when I got up, I did not see her. As I was running all round the house looking for her, Barberin saw me and asked me what I wanted.

"Mamma."

"She has gone to the village and won't be back till this afternoon."

She had not told me the night before that she was going to the village, and without knowing why, I began to feel anxious. Why didn't she wait for us, if we were going in the afternoon? Would she be back before we started? Without knowing quite why, I began to feel very frightened, and Barberin looked at me in a way that did not tend to reassure me. To escape from his look I ran into the garden.

Our garden meant a great deal to us. In it we grew almost all that we ate—potatoes, cabbages, carrots, turnips. There was no ground wasted, yet Mother Barberin had given me a little patch all to myself, in which I had planted ferns and herbs that I had pulled up in the lanes while I was minding the cow. I had planted everything pell mell, one beside the other, in my bit of garden: it was not beautiful, but I loved it. It was mine. I arranged it as I wished, just as I felt at the time, and when I spoke of it, which happened twenty times a day, it was "My garden."

Already the jonquils were in bud and the lilac was beginning to shoot, and the wall flowers would soon be out. How would they bloom? I wondered, and that was why I came to see them every day. But there was another part of my garden that I studied with great anxiety. I had planted a vegetable that some one had given to me and which was almost unknown in our village; it was Jerusalem artichokes. I was told they would be delicious, better than potatoes, for they had the taste of French artichokes, potatoes, and turnips combined. Having been told this, I intended them to be a surprise for Mother Barberin. I had not breathed a word about this present I had for her. I planted them in my own bit of garden. When they began to shoot I would let her think that they were flowers, then one fine day when they were ripe, while she was out, I would pull them up and cook them myself. How? I was not quite sure, but I did not worry over such a small detail; then when she returned to supper I would serve her a dish of Jerusalem artichokes! It would be something fresh to replace those everlasting potatoes, and Mother Barberin would not suffer too much from the sale of poor Rousette. And the inventor of this new dish of vegetables was I, Remi, I was the one! So I was of some use in the house.

With such a plan in my head I had to bestow careful attention on my Jerusalem artichokes. Every day I looked at the spot where I had planted them, it seemed to me that they would never grow. I was kneeling on both knees on the ground, supported on my hands, with my nose almost touching the earth where the artichokes were sown, when I heard Barberin calling me impatiently. I hurried back to the house. Imagine my surprise when I saw, standing before the fireplace, Vitalis and his dogs.

I knew at once what Barberin wanted of me. Vitalis had come to fetch me and it was so that Mother Barberin should not stop me from going that

Barberin had sent her to the village. Knowing full well that I could expect nothing from Barberin, I ran up to Vitalis.

"Oh, don't take me away. Please, sir, don't take me away." I began to sob.

"Now, little chap," he said, kindly enough, "you won't be unhappy with me. I don't whip children, and you'll have the dogs for company. Why should you be sorry to go with me?"

"Mother Barberin!..."

"Anyhow, you're not going to stay here," said Barberin roughly, taking me by the ear. "Go with this gentleman or go to the workhouse. Choose!"

"No, no. Mamma! Mamma!"

"So, you're going to make me mad, eh!" cried Barberin. "I'll beat you good and hard and chase you out of the house."

"The child is sorry to leave his mamma, don't beat him for that. He's got feelings, that's a good sign."

"If you pity him he'll cry all the more."

"Well, now to business."

Saying that, Vitalis laid eight five franc pieces on the table, which Barberin with a sweep of his hand cleared up and thrust into his pocket.

"Where's his bundle?" asked Vitalis.

"Here it is," said Barberin, handing him a blue cotton handkerchief tied up at the four corners. "There are two shirts and a pair of cotton pants."

"That was not what was agreed; you said you'd give some clothes. These are only rags."

"He ain't got no more."

"If I ask the boy I know he'll say that's not true. But I haven't the time to argue the matter. We must be off. Come on, my little fellow. What's your name?"

"Remi."

"Well, then, Remi, take your bundle and walk along beside Capi."

I held out both my hands to him, then to Barberin. But both men turned away their heads. Then Vitalis took me by the wrist. I had to go.

Ah, our poor little house! It seemed to me when I passed over the threshold that I left a bit of my body there. With my eyes full of tears I looked around, but there was no one near to help me. No one on the road, and no one in the field close by. I began to call:

"Mamma ... Mother Barberin!"

But no one replied to my call, and my voice trailed off into a sob. I had to follow Vitalis, who had not let go of my wrist.

"Good-by and good luck," cried Barberin. Then he entered the house. It was over.

"Come, Remi, hurry along, my child," said Vitalis. He took hold of my arm and I walked side by side with him. Fortunately he did not walk fast. I think he suited his step to mine.

We were walking up hill. As I turned I could still see Mother Barberin's house, but it was getting smaller and smaller. Many a time I had walked this road and I knew that for a little while longer I should still see the house, then when we turned the bend, I should see it no more. Before me the unknown, behind me was the house, where until that day I had lived such a happy life. Perhaps I should never see it again! Fortunately the hill was long, but at last we reached the top. Vitalis had not let go his hold.

"Will you let me rest a bit?" I asked.

"Surely, my boy," he replied.

He let go of me, but I saw him make a sign to Capi and the dog understood. He came close to me. I knew that Capi would grab me by the leg if I attempted to escape. I went up a high grassy mound and sat down, the dog beside me. With tear-dimmed eyes I looked about for Mother Barberin's cottage. Below was the valley and the wood, and away in the distance stood the little house I had left. Little puffs of yellow smoke were coming out of the chimney, going straight up in the sky, and then on towards us. In spite of the distance and the height, I could see everything very clearly. On the rubbish heap I could see our big fat hen running about, but she did not look as big as usual; if I had not known that it was our hen, I should have taken her for a little pigeon. At the side of the house I could see the twisted pear tree that I used to ride as a horse. In the stream I could just make out the drain that I had had so much trouble in digging, so that it would work a mill made by my own hands; the wheel, alas! had never turned, despite all the hours I had spent upon it. I could see my garden. Oh, my dear garden!...

Who would see my flowers bloom? and my Jerusalem artichokes, who would tend them? Barberin, perhaps, that wicked Barberin! With the next step my garden would be hidden from me. Suddenly on the road which led to our house from the village, I saw a white sunbonnet. Then it disappeared behind some trees, then it came in view again. The distance was so great that I could only see a white top, like a spring butterfly. It was going in and out amongst the trees. But there is a time when the heart sees better and farther than the sharpest eyes. I knew it was Mother Barberin. It was she. I was sure of it.

"Well," asked Vitalis, "shall we go on now?"

"Oh, sir, no, please no."

"Then it is true what they say, you haven't any legs, tired out already. That doesn't promise very good days for us."

I did not reply, I was looking....

It *was* Mother Barberin. It was her bonnet. It was her blue skirt. She was walking quickly as though she was in a hurry to get home. When she got to our gate she pushed it open and went quickly up the garden path. I jumped up at once and stood up on the bank, without giving a thought to Capi, who sprang towards me. Mother Barberin did not stay long in the house. She came out and began running to and fro, in the yard, with her arms stretched out.

She was looking for me. I leaned forwards and, at the top of my voice, I cried:

"Mamma! Mamma!" But my cry could not reach her, it was lost in the air.

"What's the matter? Have you gone crazy?" asked Vitalis.

I did not reply; my eyes were still fixed on Mother Barberin. But she did not look up, for she did not know that I was there above her. She went round the garden, then out into the road, looking up and down. I cried louder, but like my first call it was useless. Then Vitalis understood, and he also came up on the bank. It did not take him long to see the figure with the white sunbonnet.

"Poor little chap," he said softly to himself.

"Oh," I sobbed, encouraged by his words of pity, "do let me go back." But he took me by the wrist and drew me down and onto the road.

"As you are now rested," he said, "we'll move on."

I tried to free myself, but he held me firmly.

"Capi! Zerbino," he said, looking at the dogs. The two dogs came close to me; Capi behind, Zerbino in front. After taking a few steps I turned round. We had passed the bend of the hill and I could no longer see the valley nor our house.

CHAPTER V. EN ROUTE

Because a man pays forty francs for a child that is not to say that he is a monster, and that he intends to eat the child. Vitalis had no desire to eat me and although he bought children he was not a bad man. I soon had proof of this. We had been walking in silence for some time. I heaved a sigh.

"I know just how you feel," said Vitalis; "cry all you want. But try and see that this is for your own good. Those people are not your parents; the wife has been good to you and I know that you love her, that is why you feel so badly. But she could not keep you if the husband did not want you. And he may not be such a bad chap after all; he is ill and can't do any more work. He'll find it hard to get along...."

Yes, what he said was true, but I had only one thought in my mind, perhaps I should never again see the one I loved most in the world.

"You won't be unhappy with me," he continued; "it is better than being sent to the Home. And let me tell you, you must not try to run away, because if you do Capi and Zerbino would soon catch you."

Run away—I no longer thought of doing so. Where should I go? This tall old man perhaps would be a kind master after all. I had never walked so far at a stretch. All around us were barren lands and hills, not beautiful like I had thought the world would be outside of my village.

Vitalis walked with big regular strides, carrying Pretty-Heart on his shoulder, or in his bag, and the dogs trotted close to us. From time to time Vitalis said a word of friendship to them, sometimes in French, sometimes in a language that I did not understand. Neither he nor the animals seemed to get tired. But I ... I was exhausted. I dragged my limbs along and it was as much as I could do to keep up with my new master. Yet I did not like to ask him to let me stop.

"It's those wooden shoes that tire you," he said, looking down at me. "When we get to Ussel, I'll buy you some shoes."

These words gave me courage. I had always longed for a pair of shoes. The mayor's son and the inn-keeper's son wore shoes, so that on Sunday when they came to church they seemed to slide down the stone aisles, while we other country boys in our clogs made a deafening noise.

"Is Ussel far?"

"Ah, that comes from your heart," said Vitalis, laughing. "So you want to have a pair of shoes, do you? Well, I'll promise you them and with big nails, too. And I'll buy you some velvet pants, and a vest and a hat. That'll make you dry your tears, I hope, and give you legs to do the next six miles."

Shoes with nails! I was overcome with pride. It was grand enough to have shoes, but shoes with nails! I forgot my grief. Shoes with nails! Velvet pants! a vest! a hat! Oh, if Mother Barberin could see me, how happy she would be, how proud of me! But in spite of the promise that I should have shoes and velvet pants at the end of the six miles, it seemed impossible that I could cover the distance.

The sky, which had been blue when we started, was now filled with gray clouds and soon a fine rain commenced to fall. Vitalis was covered well enough with his sheepskin and he was able to shelter Pretty-Heart, who, at the first drop of rain, had promptly retired into his hiding place. But the dogs and I had nothing to cover us, and soon we were drenched to the skin. The dogs from time to time could shake themselves, but I was unable to employ this natural means, and I had to tramp along under my water-soaked, heavy garments, which chilled me.

"Do you catch cold easily?" asked my new master.

"I don't know. I don't remember ever having a cold."

"That's good. So there is something in you. But I don't want to have it worse for you than we are obliged. There is a village a little farther on and we'll sleep there."

There was no inn in this village and no one wanted to take into their homes an old beggar who dragged along with him a child and three dogs, soaked to the skin.

"No lodgings here," they said.

And they shut the door in our faces. We went from one house to another, but all refused to admit us. Must we tramp those four miles on to Ussel without resting a bit? The night had fallen and the rain had chilled us through and through. Oh, for Mother Barberin's house!

Finally a peasant, more charitable than his neighbors, agreed to let us go into his barn. But he made the condition that we could sleep there, but must have no light.

"Give me your matches," he said to Vitalis. "I'll give you them back tomorrow, when you go."

At least we had a roof to cover us from the storm.

In the sack which Vitalis had slung over his back he took out a hunch of bread and broke it into four pieces. Then I saw for the first time how he maintained obedience and discipline in his company. Whilst we had gone from door to door seeking shelter, Zerbino had gone into a house and he had run out again almost at once, carrying in his jaws a crust. Vitalis had only said:

"Alright, Zerbino ... to-night."

I had thought no more of this theft, when I saw Vitalis cut the roll; Zerbino looked very dejected. Vitalis and I were sitting on a box with Pretty-Heart between us. The three dogs stood in a row before us, Capi and Dulcie with their eyes fixed on their master. Zerbino stood with drooping ears and tail between his legs.

"The thief must leave the ranks and go into a corner," said Vitalis in a tone of command; "he'll go to sleep without his supper."

Zerbino left his place, and in a zigzag went over to the corner that Vitalis indicated with his finger. He crouched down under a heap of hay out of sight, but we heard him breathe plaintively, with a little whine.

Vitalis then handed me a piece of bread, and while eating his own he broke little pieces for Pretty-Heart, Capi and Dulcie. How I longed for Mother Barberin's soup ... even without butter, and the warm fire, and my little bed with the coverlets that I pulled right up to my nose. Completely fagged out, I sat there, my feet raw by the rubbing of my clogs. I trembled with cold in my wet clothing. It was night now, but I did not think of going to sleep.

"Your teeth are chattering," said Vitalis; "are you cold?"

"A little."

I heard him open his bag.

"I haven't got much of a wardrobe," he said, "but here's a dry shirt and a vest you can put on. Then get underneath the hay and you'll soon get warm and go to sleep."

But I did not get warm as quick as Vitalis thought; for a long time I turned and turned on my bed of straw, too unhappy to sleep. Would all my days now be like this, walking in the pouring rain; sleeping in a loft, shaking with cold, and only a piece of dry bread for supper? No one to love me; no one to cuddle me; no Mother Barberin!

My heart was very sad. The tears rolled down my cheeks, then I felt a warm breath pass over my face. I stretched out my hand and my finger touched Capi's woolly coat. He had come softly to me, stepping cautiously on the straw, and he smelt me: he sniffed gently, his breath ran over my cheek and in my hair. What did he want? Presently he laid down on the straw, quite close to me, and very gently he commenced to lick my hand. Touched by this caress, I sat up on my straw bed and throwing my arms round his neck kissed his cold nose. He gave a little stifled cry, and then quickly put his paw in my hand and remained quite still. I forgot my fatigue and my sorrows. I was no longer alone. I had a friend.

CHAPTER VI. MY DÉBUT

We started early the next morning. The sky was blue and a light wind had come up in the night and dried all the mud. The birds were singing blithely in the trees and the dogs scampered around us. Now and again Capi stood up on his hind paws and barked into my face, two or three times. I knew what he meant. He was my friend. He was intelligent, and he understood every thing, and he knew how to make you understand. In his tail only was more wit and eloquence than in the tongue or in the eyes of many people.

Although I had never left my village and was most curious to see a town, what I most wanted to see in that town was a boot shop. Where was the welcome shop where I should find the shoes with nails that Vitalis had promised me? I glanced about in every direction as we passed down the old streets of Ussel. Suddenly my master turned into a shop behind the market. Hanging outside the front were some old guns, a coat trimmed with gold braid, several lamps, and some rusty keys. We went down three steps and found ourselves in a large room where the sun could never have entered since the roof had been put on the house. How could such beautiful things as nailed shoes be sold in such a terrible place? Yet Vitalis knew, and soon I had the pleasure of being shod in nailed shoes which were ten times as heavy as my clogs. My master's generosity did not stop there. He bought me a blue velvet coat, a pair of trousers, and a felt hat.

Velvet for me who had never worn anything but cotton! This was surely the best man in the world, and the most generous. It is true that the velvet was creased, and that the woolen trousers were well worn, and it was difficult to guess what had been the original color of the felt hat, it had been so soaked with rain; but dazzled by so much finery I was unconscious of the imperfections which were hidden under their aspect.

When we got back to the inn, to my sorrow and astonishment, Vitalis took a pair of scissors and cut the two legs of my trousers to the height of the knees, before he would let me get into them. I looked at him with round eyes.

"That's because I don't want you to look like everybody else," he explained. "When in France I'll dress you like an Italian; when in Italy, like a French boy."

I was still more amazed.

"We are *artistes*, are we not? Well, we must not dress like the ordinary folk. If we went about dressed like the country people, do you think anybody would look at us? Should we get a crowd around us when we stop? No! Appearances count for a great deal in life."

I was a French boy in the morning, and by night I had become an Italian. My trousers reached my knees. Vitalis interlaced red cords all down my stockings and twisted some red ribbon all over my felt hat, and then decorated it with a bunch of woolen flowers.

I don't know what others thought of me, but to be frank I must admit that I thought I looked superb; and Capi was of the same opinion, for he stared at me for a long time, then held out his paw with a satisfied air. I was glad to have Capi's approval, which was all the more agreeable, because, during the time I had been dressing, Pretty-Heart had seated himself opposite to me, and with exaggerated airs had imitated every movement I had made, and when I was finished put his hands on his hips, threw back his head, and laughed mockingly.

It is a scientific question as to whether monkeys laugh or not. I lived on familiar terms with Pretty-Heart for a long time, and I know that he certainly did laugh and often in a way that was most humiliating to me. Of course, he did not laugh like a man, but when something amused him, he would draw back the corners of his mouth, screw up his eyes, and work his jaws rapidly, while his black eyes seemed to dart flames.

"Now you're ready," said Vitalis, as I placed my hat on my head, "and we'll get to work, because to-morrow is market day and we must give a performance. You must play in a comedy with the two dogs and Pretty-Heart."

"But I don't know how to play a comedy," I cried, scared.

"That is why I am going to teach you. You can't know unless you learn. These animals have studied hard to learn their part. It has been hard work for them; but now see how clever they are. The piece we are going to play is called, 'Mr. Pretty-Heart's Servant, or The Fool is not Always the One You Would Think.' Now this is it: Mr. Pretty-Heart's servant, whose name is Capi, is about to leave him because he is getting old. And Capi has promised his master that before he leaves he will get him another servant. Now this successor is not to be a dog, it is to be a boy, a country boy named Remi."

"Oh...."

"You have just come from the country to take a position with Mr. Pretty-Heart."

"Monkeys don't have servants."

"In plays they have. Well, you've come straight from your village and your new master thinks that you're a fool."

"Oh, I don't like that!"

"What does that matter if it makes the people laugh? Well, you have come to this gentleman to be his servant and you are told to set the table. Here is one like we shall use in the play; go and set it."

On this table there were plates, a glass, a knife, a fork, and a white tablecloth. How could I arrange all those things? As I pondered over this question, leaning forward with hands stretched out and mouth open, not knowing where to begin, my master clapped his hands and laughed heartily.

"Bravo!" he cried, "bravo! that's perfect. The boy I had before put on a sly expression as much as to say, 'See what a fool I can make of myself'; you are natural; that is splendid."

"But I don't know what I have to do."

"That's why you are so good! After you do know, you will have to pretend just what you are feeling now. If you can get that same expression and stand just like you are standing now, you'll be a great success. To play this part to perfection you have only to act and look as you do at this moment."

"Mr. Pretty-Heart's Servant" was not a great play. The performance lasted not more than twenty minutes. Vitalis made us do it over and over again, the dogs and I.

I was surprised to see our master so patient. I had seen the animals in my village treated with oaths and blows when they could not learn. Although the lesson lasted a long time, not once did he get angry, not once did he swear.

"Now do that over again," he said severely, when a mistake had been made. "That is bad, Capi. I'll scold you, Pretty-Heart, if you don't pay attention."

And that was all, but yet it was enough.

"Take the dogs for an example," he said, while teaching me; "compare them with Pretty-Heart. Pretty-Heart has, perhaps, vivacity and intelligence, but he has no patience. He learns easily what he is taught, but he forgets it at once; besides he never does what he is told willingly. He likes to do just the contrary. That is his nature, and that is why I do not get angry with him; monkeys have not the same conscience that a dog has; they don't understand the meaning of the word 'duty,' and that is why they are inferior to the dog. Do you understand that?"

"I think so."

"You are intelligent and attentive. Be obedient, do your best in what you have to do. Remember that all through life."

Talking to him so, I summoned up courage to ask him about what had so astonished me during the rehearsal: how could he be so wonderfully patient with the dogs, the monkey, and myself?

He smiled.

"One can see that you have lived only with peasants who are rough with animals, and think that they can only be made to obey by having a stick held over their heads. A great mistake. One gains very little by being cruel, but one can obtain a lot, if not all, by gentleness. It is because I am never unkind to my animals that they are what they are. If I had beaten them they would be frightened creatures; fear paralyzes the intelligence. Besides, if I gave way to temper I should not be what I am; I could not have acquired this patience which has won their confidence. That shows that who instructs others, instructs himself. As I have given lessons to my animals, so I have received lessons from them. I have developed their intelligence; they have formed my character."

I laughed. This seemed strange to me.

"You find that odd," he continued; "odd that a dog could give a lesson to a man, yet it is true. The master is obliged to watch over himself when he undertakes to teach a dog. The dog takes after the master. Show me your dog and I'll tell you what you are. The criminal has a dog who is a rogue. The burglar's dog is a thief; the country yokel has a stupid, unintelligent dog. A kind, thoughtful man has a good dog."

I was very nervous at the thought of appearing before the public the next day. The dogs and the monkey had the advantage over me, they had played before, hundreds of times. What would Vitalis say if I did not play my part well? What would the audience say? I was so worried that, when at last I dropped off to sleep, I could see in my dreams a crowd of people holding their sides with laughter because I was such a fool.

I was even more nervous the next day, when we marched off in a procession to the market place, where we were to give our performance. Vitalis led the way. Holding his head high and with chest thrown out, he kept time with his arms and feet while gayly playing his fife. Behind him came Capi, carrying Pretty-Heart on his back, wearing the uniform of an English general, a red coat and trousers trimmed with gold braid and helmet topped with a plume. Zerbino and Dulcie came next, at a respectful distance. I brought up the rear. Our procession took up some length as we had to walk a certain space apart. The piercing notes of the fife brought the people running from their houses. Scores of children ran behind us, and by the time we had reached the square, there was a great crowd. Our theater was quickly arranged. A rope was fastened to four trees and in the middle of this square we took our places.

The first numbers on the program consisted of various tricks performed by the dogs. I had not the slightest notion what they did. I was so nervous and taken up in repeating my own part. All that I remember was that Vitalis put aside his fife and took his violin and played accompaniments to the dogs' maneuvers; sometimes it was dance music, sometimes sentimental airs.

The tricks over, Capi took a metal cup between his teeth and began to go the round of the "distinguished audience." When a spectator failed to drop a coin in, he put his two fore paws upon the reluctant giver's pocket, barked three times, then tapped the pocket with his paw. At this every one laughed and shouted with delight.

"If that ain't a cunning spaniel! He knows who's got money and who hasn't!"

"Say, out with it!"

"He'll give something!"

"Not he!"

"And his uncle left him a legacy! The stingy cuss!"

And, finally, a penny was dug out of a deep pocket and thrown into the cup. During this time, Vitalis, without saying a word, but with his eyes following Capi, gayly played his violin. Soon Capi returned to his master, proudly carrying the full cup.

Now for the comedy.

"Ladies and gentlemen," said Vitalis, gesticulating with his bow in one hand and his violin in the other, "we are going to give a delightful comedy, called 'Mr. Pretty-Heart's Servant, or the Fool is not Always the One You Would Think.' A man of my standing does not lower himself by praising his plays and actors in advance. All I have to say is look, listen, and be ready to applaud."

What Vitalis called a delightful comedy was really a pantomime; naturally it had to be for the very good reason that two of its principals, Pretty-Heart and Capi, could not speak, and the third, myself, was incapable of uttering two words. However, so that the audience would clearly understand the play, Vitalis explained the various situations, as the piece progressed. For instance, striking up a warlike air, he announced the entrance of General Pretty-Heart, who had won his high rank in various battles in India. Up to that day General Pretty-Heart had only had Capi for a servant, but he now wished to have a human being as his means allowed him this luxury. For a long time animals had been the slaves of men, but it was time that such was changed!

While waiting for the servant to arrive, the General walked up and down, smoking his cigar. You should see the way he blew the smoke into the onlookers' faces! Becoming impatient, he began to roll his eyes like a man who is about to have a fit of temper. He bit his lips, and stamped on the ground. At the third stamp I had to make my appearance on the scene, led by Capi. If I had forgotten my part the dog would have reminded me. At a given moment he held out his paw to me and introduced me to the General. The latter, upon noticing me, held up his two hands in despair. What! Was that the servant they had procured for him. Then he came and looked pertly up into my face, and walked around me, shrugging his shoulders. His expression was so comical that every one burst out laughing. They quite understood that the monkey thought I was a fool. The spectators thought that also. The piece was made to show how dense was my stupidity, while every opportunity was afforded the monkey to show his sagacity and intelligence. After having examined me thoroughly, the General, out of pity, decided to keep me. He pointed to a table that was already set for luncheon, and signed to me to take my seat.

"The General thinks that after his servant has had something to eat he won't be such an idiot," explained Vitalis.

40

I sat down at the little table; a table napkin was placed on my plate. What was I to do with the napkin?

Capi made a sign for me to use it. After looking at it thoughtfully for a moment, I blew my nose. Then the General held his sides with laughter, and Capi fell over with his four paws up in the air, upset at my stupidity.

Seeing that I had made a mistake, I stared again at the table napkin, wondering what I was to do with it. Then I had an idea. I rolled it up and made a necktie for myself. More laughter from the General. Another fall from Capi, his paws in the air.

Then, finally overcome with exasperation, the General dragged me from the chair, seated himself at my place, and ate up the meal that had been prepared for me.

Ah! he knew how to use a table napkin! How gracefully he tucked it into his uniform, and spread it out upon his knees. And with what an elegant air he broke his bread and emptied his glass!

The climax was reached when, luncheon over, he asked for a toothpick, which he quickly passed between his teeth. At this, applause broke out on all sides, and the performance ended triumphantly.

What a fool of a servant and what a wonderful monkey!

On our way back to the inn Vitalis complimented me, and I was already such a good comedian that I appreciated this praise from my master.

CHAPTER VII. CHILD AND ANIMAL LEARNING

Vitalis' small group of actors were certainly very clever, but their talent was not very versatile. For this reason we were not able to remain long in the same town. Three days after our arrival in Ussel we were on our way again. Where were we going? I had grown bold enough to put this question to my master.

"Do you know this part of the country?" he asked, looking at me.

"No."

"Then why do you ask where we are going?"

"So as to know."

"To know what?"

I was silent.

"Do you know how to read?" he asked, after looking thoughtfully at me for a moment.

"No."

"Then I'll teach you from a book the names and all about the towns through which we travel. It will be like having a story told to you."

I had been brought up in utter ignorance. True, I had been sent to the village school for one month, but during this month I had never once had a book in my hand. At the time of which I write, there were many villages in France that did not even boast of a school, and in some, where there was a schoolmaster, either he knew nothing, or he had some other occupation and could give little attention to the children confided to his care.

This was the case with the master of our village school. I do not mean to say that he was ignorant, but during the month that I attended his school, he did not give us one single lesson. He had something else to do. By trade he was a shoe-maker, or rather, a clog maker, for no one bought shoes from him. He sat at his bench all day, shaving pieces of beech wood into clogs. So I learnt absolutely nothing at school, not even my alphabet.

"Is it difficult to read?" I asked, after we had walked some time in silence.

"Have you got a hard head?"

"I don't know, but I'd like to learn if you'll teach me."

"Well, we'll see about that. We've plenty of time ahead of us."

Time ahead of us! Why not commence at once? I did not know how difficult it was to learn to read. I thought that I just had to open a book and, almost at once, know what it contained.

The next day, as we were walking along, Vitalis stooped down and picked up a piece of wood covered with dust.

"See, this is the book from which you are going to learn to read," he said.

A book! A piece of wood! I looked at him to see if he were joking. But he looked quite serious. I stared at the bit of wood. It was as long as my arm and as wide as my two hands. There was no inscription or drawing on it.

"Wait until we get to those trees down there, where we'll rest," said Vitalis, smiling at my astonishment. "I'll show you how I'm going to teach you to read from this."

When we got to the trees we threw our bags on the ground and sat down on the green grass with the daisies growing here and there. Pretty-Heart, having got rid of his chain, sprang up into a tree and shook the branches one after the other, as though he were making nuts fall. The dogs lay down beside us. Vitalis took out his knife and, after having smoothed the wood on both sides, began to cut tiny pieces, twelve all of equal size.

"I am going to carve a letter out of each piece of wood," he said, looking up at me. I had not taken my eyes off of him. "You will learn these letters from their shapes, and when you are able to tell me what they are, at first sight, I'll form them into words. When you can read the words, then you shall learn from a book."

I soon had my pockets full of little bits of wood, and was not long in learning the letters of the alphabet, but to know how to read was quite another thing. I could not get along very fast, and often I regretted having expressed a wish to learn. I must say, however, it was not because I was lazy, it was pride.

While teaching me my letters Vitalis thought that he would teach Capi at the same time. If a dog could learn to tell the hour from a watch, why could he not learn the letters? The pieces of wood were all spread out on the grass, and he was taught that with his paw he must draw out the letter for which he was asked.

At first I made more progress than he, but if I had quicker intelligence, he had better memory. Once he learnt a thing he knew it always. He did not forget. When I made a mistake Vitalis would say:

"Capi will learn to read before you, Remi."

And Capi, evidently understanding, proudly shook his tail.

I was so hurt that I applied myself to the task with all my heart, and while the poor dog could get no farther than pulling out the four letters which spelled his name, I finally learned to read from a book.

"Now that you know how to read words, how would you like to read music?" asked Vitalis.

"If I knew how to read music could I sing like you?" I asked.

"Ah, so you would like to sing like me," he answered.

"I know that would be impossible, but I'd like to sing a little."

"Do you like to hear me sing, then?"

"I like it more than anything. It is better than the nightingales, but it's not like their song at all. When you sing, sometimes I want to cry, and sometimes I want to laugh. Don't think me silly, master, but when you sing those songs, I think that I am back with dear Mother Barberin. If I shut my eyes I can see her again in our little house, and yet I don't know the words you sing, because they are Italian."

I looked up at him and saw the tears standing in his eyes; then I stopped and asked him if what I had said hurt him.

"No, my child," he said, his voice shaking, "you do not pain me; on the contrary, you take me back to my younger days. Yes, I will teach you to sing, little Remi, and, as you have a heart, you also will make people weep with your songs."

He stopped suddenly, and I felt that he did not wish to say more at that moment. I did not know the reason why he should feel sad.

The next day he cut out little pieces of wood for the music notes the same as he had for the letters. The notes were more complicated than the alphabet, and this time I found it much harder and more tedious to learn. Vitalis, so patient with the dogs, more than once lost patience with me.

"With an animal," he cried, "one controls oneself, because one is dealing with a poor dumb creature, but you are enough to drive me mad!" He threw up his hands dramatically.

Pretty-Heart, who took special delight in imitating gestures he thought funny, mimicked my master, and as the monkey was present at my lessons every day, I had the humiliation to see him lift his arms in despair every time I hesitated.

"See, Pretty-Heart is even mocking you," cried Vitalis.

If I had dared, I would have said that he mocked the master just as much as the pupil, but respect, as well as a certain fear, forbade me.

Finally, after many weeks of study, I was able to sing an air from a piece of paper that Vitalis himself had written. That day my master did not throw up his hands, but instead, patted me on the cheek, declaring that if I continued thus I should certainly become a great singer.

CHAPTER VIII. ONE WHO HAD KNOWN A KING

Our mode of traveling was very simple: We went straight ahead, anywhere, and when we found a village, which from the distance looked sufficiently important, we began preparations for a triumphal entry. I dressed the dogs, and combed Dulcie's hair; stuck a plaster over Capi's eye when he was playing the part of an old grouchy man, and forced Pretty-Heart into his General's uniform. That was the most difficult thing I had to do, for the monkey, who knew well enough that this was a prelude to work for him, invented the oddest tricks to prevent me from dressing him. Then I was forced to call Capi to come to my aid, and between the two of us we finally managed to subdue him.

The company all dressed, Vitalis took his fife and we went in marching order into the village. If the number of people who trooped behind us was sufficient, we gave a performance, but if we had only a few stragglers, we did not think it worth our while to stop, so continued on our way. When we stayed several days in a town, Vitalis would let me go about alone if Capi was with me. He trusted me with Capi.

"You are traveling through France at the age when most boys are at school," he once said to me; "open your eyes, look and learn. When you see something that you do not understand, do not be afraid to ask me questions. I have not always been what you see me now. I have learnt many other things."

"What?"

"We will speak of that later. For the present listen to my advice, and when you grow up I hope you will think with a little gratitude of the poor musician of whom you were so afraid when he took you from your adopted mother. The change may not be bad for you after all."

I wondered what my master had been in the days gone by.

We tramped on until we came to the plains of Quercy, which were very flat and desolate. There was not a brook, pond, or river to be seen. In the middle of the plain we came to a small village called Bastide-Murat. We spent the night in a barn belonging to the inn.

"It was here in this village," said Vitalis, "and probably in this inn, that a man was born who led thousands of soldiers to battle and who, having commenced his life as a stable boy, afterwards became a king. His name was Murat. They called him a hero, and they named this village after him. I knew him and often talked with him."

"When he was a stable boy?"

"No," replied Vitalis, laughing, "when he was a king. This is the first time I have been in this part of the country. I knew him in Naples, where he was king."

"You have known a king!"

The tone in which I said this must have been rather comical, for my master laughed heartily.

We were seated on a bench before the stable door, our backs against the wall, which, was still hot from the sun's rays. The locusts were chanting their monotonous song in a great sycamore which covered us with its branches. Over the tops of the houses the full moon, which had just appeared, rose gently in the heavens. The night seemed all the more beautiful because the day had been scorchingly hot.

"Do you want to go to bed?" asked Vitalis, "or would you like me to tell you the story of King Murat?"

"Oh, tell me the story!"

Then he told me the story of Joachim Murat; for hours we sat on the bench. As he talked, the pale light from the moon fell across him, and I listened in rapt attention, my eyes fixed on his face. I had not heard this story before. Who would have told me? Not Mother Barberin, surely! She did not know anything about it. She was born at Chavanon, and would probably die there. Her mind had never traveled farther than her eyes.

My master had seen a king, and this king had spoken to him! What was my master in his youth, and how had he become what I saw him now in his old age?...

We had been tramping since morning. Vitalis had said that we should reach a village by night where we could sleep, but night had come, and I saw no signs of this village, no smoke in the distance to indicate that we were near a house. I could see nothing but a stretch of plains ahead of us. I was tired, and longed to go to sleep. Vitalis was tired also. He wanted to stop and rest by the roadside, but instead of sitting down beside him, I told him that I would climb a hill that was on the left of us and see if I could make out a village. I called Capi, but Capi also was tired, and turned a deaf ear to my call; this he usually did when he did not wish to obey me.

"Are you afraid?" asked Vitalis.

46

His question made me start off at once, alone.

Night had fallen. There was no moon, but the twinkling stars in the sky threw their light on a misty atmosphere. The various things around me seemed to take on a strange, weird form in the dim light. Wild furze grew in bushes beside some huge stones which, towering above me, seemed as though they turned to look at me. The higher I climbed, the thicker became the trees and shrubs, their tops passing over my head and interlacing. Sometimes I had to crawl through them to get by. Yet I was determined to get to the top of the hill. But, when at last I did, and gazed around, I could see no light anywhere; nothing but strange shadows and forms, and great trees which seemed to hold out their branches to me, like arms ready to enfold me.

I listened to see if I could catch the bark of a dog, or the bellow of a cow, but all was silent. With my ear on the alert, scarcely breathing so as to hear better, I stood quiet for a moment. Then I began to tremble, the silence of this lonely, uncultivated country frightened me. Of what was I frightened? The silence probably ... the night ... anyhow, a nameless fear was creeping over me. My heart beat quickly, as though some danger was near. I glanced fearfully around me, and then in the distance I saw a great form moving amongst the trees. At the same time I could hear the rustling of branches. I tried to tell myself that it was fear that made me fancy I saw something unusual. Perhaps it was a shrub, a branch. But then, the branches were moving and there was not a breath of wind or a breeze that could shake them. They could not move unless swayed by the breeze or touched by some one.

Some one?

No, this great, dark form that was coming towards me could not be a man—some kind of animal that I did not know, or an immense night bird, a gigantic spider, hovering over the tops of the trees. What was certain, this creature had legs of unusual length, which brought it along with amazing bounds. Seeing this, I quickly found my own legs, and rushed down the hill towards Vitalis. But, strange to say, I made less haste going down than I had in climbing up. I threw myself into the thick of the thistles and brambles, scratching myself at every step. Scrambling out of a prickly bush I took a glance back. The animal was coming nearer! It was almost upon me!

Fortunately, I had reached the bottom of the hill and I could run quicker across the grass. Although I raced at the top of my speed, the Thing was gaining upon me. There was no need for me to look behind, I knew that it was just at the back of me. I could scarcely breathe. My race had almost exhausted me; my breath came in gasps. I made one final effort and fell sprawling at Vitalis' feet. I could only repeat two words:

"The beast! the beast!"

Above the loud barking of the dogs, I heard a hearty peal of laughter. At the same time my master put his hands on my shoulders and forced me to look round.

"You goose," he cried, still laughing, "look up and see it."

His laugh, more than his words, brought me to my senses. I opened one eye, then the other, and looked where he was pointing. The apparition, which had so frightened me, had stopped and was standing still in the road. At the sight of it again, I must confess, I began to shake, but I was with Vitalis and the dogs were beside me. I was not alone up there in the trees.... I looked up boldly and fixed my eyes on the Thing.

Was it an animal or a man? It had the body, the head, and arms like a man, but the shaggy skin which covered it, and the two long thin legs upon which it seemed to poise, looked as though they belonged to an animal.

Although the night was dark, I could see this, for the silhouette of this dark form stood out against the starry sky. I should have remained a long time undecided as to what it was, if my master had not spoken to it.

"Can you tell me if we are far from the village?" he asked, politely.

He was a man, then, if one could speak to him! What was my astonishment when the animal said that there were no houses near, but an inn to which he would take us. If he could talk, why did he have paws?

If I had had the courage, I would have gone up to him to see how his paws were made, but I was still somewhat afraid, so I picked up my bag and followed my master, without saying a word.

"You see now what scared you so," Vitalis said, laughing, as we went on our way.

"But I don't know what it is, yet. Are there giants in this part of the country, then?"

"Yes, when men are standing on stilts."

Then he explained to me that the Landais, so as to get over the marshy plains, and not sink in up to their hips, stride about the country on stilts.

What a goose I had been!

CHAPTER IX. ARRESTED

I had a pleasant remembrance of Pau, the beautiful winter resort where the wind scarcely ever blew. We stayed there the whole winter, for we were taking in quite a lot of money. Our audience consisted mostly of children, and they were never tired if we did give the same performance over and over again. They were children of the rich, mostly English and American. Fat little boys, with ruddy skins, and pretty little girls with soft eyes almost as beautiful as Dulcie's. It was from these children that I got a taste for candy, for they always came with their pockets stuffed with sweets which they divided between Pretty-Heart, the dogs, and myself. But when the spring approached our audience grew smaller. One by one, two by two, the little ones came to shake hands with Pretty-Heart, Capi, and Dulcie. They had come to say good-by. They were going away. So we also had to leave the beautiful winter resort and take up our wandering life again.

For a long time, I do not know how many days or weeks, we went through valleys, over hills, leaving behind the bluish top of the Pyrenees, which now looked like a mass of clouds.

Then one night we came to a great town with ugly red brick houses and with streets paved with little pointed stones, hard to the feet of travelers who had walked a dozen miles a day. My master told me that we were in Toulouse and that we should stay there for a long time. As usual, the first thing we did was to look about for a suitable place to hold the next day's performance. Suitable places were not lacking, especially near the Botanical Gardens, where there is a beautiful lawn shaded with big trees and a wide avenue leading to it. It was in one of the sidewalks that we gave our first performance.

A policeman stood by while we arranged our things. He seemed annoyed, either because he did not like dogs, or because he thought we had no business there; he tried to send us away. It would have been better if we had gone. We were not strong enough to hold out against the police, but my master did not think so. Although he was an old man, strolling about the country with his dogs, he was very proud. He considered that as he was not breaking the law, he should have police protection, so when the officer wanted to send us away, he refused to leave.

Vitalis was very polite; in fact he carried his Italian politeness to the extreme. One might have thought that he was addressing some high and mighty personage.

"The illustrious gentleman, who represents the police authority," he said, taking off his hat and bowing low to the policeman, "can he show me an order emanating from the said authority, which states that it is forbidden for poor strolling players, like ourselves, to carry on their humble profession on a public square?"

The policeman replied that he would have no argument. We must obey.

"Certainly," replied Vitalis, "and I promise that I will do as you order as soon as you let me know by what authority you issue it."

That day the officer turned on his heels, and my master, with hat in hand, body bent low, smilingly bowed to the retreating form.

But the next day the representative of the law returned, and jumping over the ropes which inclosed our theater, he sprang into the middle of the performance.

"Muzzle those dogs," he said roughly to Vitalis.

"Muzzle my dogs!"

"It's an order of the law, you ought to know that!"

The spectators began to protest.

"Don't interrupt!"

"Let him finish the show, cop!"

Vitalis then took off his felt hat, and with his plumes sweeping the ground, he made three stately bows to the officer.

"The illustrious gentleman representing the law, does he tell me that I must muzzle my actors?" he asked.

"Yes, and be quick about it!"

"Muzzle Capi, Zerbino, and Dulcie," cried Vitalis, addressing himself more to the audience than to the officer; "how can the great physician, Capi, known throughout the universe, prescribe a cure for Mr. Pretty-Heart, if the said physician wears a muzzle on the end of his nose?"

The children and parents began to laugh. Vitalis encouraged by the applause, continued:

"And how can the charming nurse, Dulcie, use her eloquence to persuade the patient to take the horrible medicine which is to relieve him of his pains if I am forced to carry out this cruel order of the law? I ask the audience if this is fair?"

The clapping of hands and shouts of laughter from the onlookers was answer enough. They cheered Vitalis and hooted the policeman and, above all, they were amused at the grimaces Pretty-Heart was making. He had taken his place behind the "illustrious gentleman who represented the law," and was making ridiculous grimaces behind his back. The officer crossed his arms, then uncrossed them and stuck his fists on his hips and threw back his head, so did the monkey. The onlookers screamed with laughter.

The officer turned round suddenly to see what amused them, and saw the monkey striking his own attitude to perfection. For some moments the monkey and the man stared at each other. It was a question which would lower his eyes first. The crowd yelled with delight.

"If your dogs are not muzzled to-morrow," cried the policeman, angrily shaking his first, "you'll be arrested. That's all."

"Good-day, until to-morrow, Signor," said Vitalis, bowing, "until to-morrow...."

As the officer strode away, Vitalis stood with his body almost bent to the ground in mock respect.

I thought that he would buy some muzzles for the dogs, but he did nothing of the kind, and the evening passed without him even mentioning his quarrel with the policeman. I decided at last to broach the subject myself.

"If you don't want Capi to tear off his muzzle to-morrow during the performance," I said, "I think it would be a good thing to put it on him beforehand, and let him get used to it. We can teach him that he must keep it on."

"You think I am going to put one of those things on their little noses?"

"The officer is down on us."

"You are only a country boy. Like all peasants you are afraid of a policeman.

"Don't worry," he added, "I'll have matters arranged to-morrow so that the policeman can't have me arrested, and at the same time so that the dogs won't be uncomfortable. On the other hand, the public shall be amused a bit. This officer should be the means of bringing us some more money and, in the bargain, play the comic rôle in the piece that I shall prepare for him. Now, to-morrow, you are to go there alone with Pretty-Heart. You will arrange the ropes, and play a few pieces on your harp, and when you have a large audience the officer will arrive on the scene. I will make my appearance with the dogs. Then the farce will commence."

I did not at all like going alone the next day, but I knew that my master must be obeyed.

As soon as I got to our usual place I roped off an inclosure and commenced to play. The people came from all parts and crowded outside the ropes. By now I had learnt to play the harp and sing very well. Amongst other songs, I had learnt a Neapolitan *canzonetta* which was always greatly applauded. But to-day I knew that the crowd had not come to pay tribute to my talent. All who had witnessed the dispute with the officer the day before were present, and had brought their friends with them. The police are not liked at Toulouse, and the public were curious to see how the old Italian would come out, and what significance was attached to his parting words, "Until to-morrow, Signor." Several of the spectators, seeing me alone with Pretty-Heart, interrupted my song to ask if the "old Italian" was coming.

I nodded. The policeman arrived. Pretty-Heart saw him first. He at once put his clenched hands on his hips and began trotting around in a ridiculously important manner. The crowd laughed at his antics and clapped their hands. The officer glared at me angrily.

How was it going to end? I was rather ill at ease. If Vitalis were there he could reply to the officer. But I was alone. If he ordered me away, what should I say?

The policeman strode back and forth outside the ropes, and when he passed near me, he had a way of looking at me over his shoulder that did not reassure me.

Pretty-Heart did not understand the seriousness of the situation, so he gleefully strutted along inside the ropes, side by side with the officer, mimicking his every movement. As he passed me, he also looked at me over his shoulder in such a comical manner that the people laughed still louder.

I thought the matter had gone far enough, so I called Pretty-Heart, but he was in no mood to obey, and continued his walk, running and dodging me when I tried to catch him. I don't know how it happened, but the policeman, probably mad with rage, thought that I was encouraging the monkey, for he quickly jumped the ropes. In a moment he was upon me, and had knocked me to the ground with one blow. When I opened my eyes and got to my feet Vitalis, who had sprung from I don't know where, stood before me. He had just seized the policeman's wrist.

"I forbid you to strike that child," he cried, "what a cowardly thing to do!"

For some moments the two men looked at each other. The officer was purple with rage. My master was superb. He held his beautiful white head high; his face expressed indignation and command. His look was enough to make the policeman sink into the earth, but he did nothing of the kind. He wrenched his hand free, seized my master by the collar and roughly pushed him before him. Vitalis stumbled and almost fell, but he drew himself up quickly and with his free hand struck the officer on the wrist. My master was a strong man, but still he was an old man, and the policeman was young and robust. I saw how a struggle would end. But there was no struggle.

"You come along with me," said the officer, "you're under arrest."

"Why did you strike that child?" demanded Vitalis.

"No talk. Follow me."

Vitalis did not reply, but turned round to me.

"Go back to the inn," he said, "and stay there with the dogs. I'll send word to you."

He had no chance to say more, for the officer dragged him off. So ended the performance that my poor master had wanted to make amusing. The dogs at first had followed their master, but I called them back, and accustomed to obey, they returned to me. I noticed that they were muzzled, but instead of their faces being inclosed in the usual dog-muzzle, they simply wore a pretty piece of silk fastened round their noses and tied under their chins. Capi, who was white, wore red; Zerbino, who was black, wore white, and Dulcie, who was gray, wore blue. My poor master had thus carried out the order of the law.

The public had quickly dispersed. A few stragglers remained to discuss what had happened.

"The old man was right."

"He was wrong."

"Why did the cop strike the boy? He did nothing to him; never said a word."

"Bad business. The old fellow will go to jail, for sure!"

I went back to the inn, depressed. I had grown very fond of my master, more and more every day. We lived the same life together from morning till night, and often from night to morning, when we had to sleep on the same bed of straw. No father could have shown more care for his child than he showed for me. He had taught me to read, to sing, and to write. During our long tramps he gave me lessons, first on one subject then on another. On very cold days he shared his coverings with me, on hot days he had always helped me carry the bags, and the various things which I was supposed to carry. And when we ate he never served me the worst piece, keeping the best for himself; on the contrary, he shared it equally, the good and the bad. It is true, he sometimes pulled my ears more roughly than I liked, but if I needed the correction, what of that? In a word, I loved him, and he loved me. For how long would they send him to prison? What should I do during that time? How should I live?

Vitalis was in the habit of carrying his money on him, and he had not had time to give me anything before he was dragged off. I had only a few sous in my pocket. Would it be enough to buy food for Pretty-Heart, the dogs, and myself? I spent the next two days in agony, not daring to leave the inn. The monkey and the dogs were also very downcast. At last, on the third day, a man brought me a letter from him. Vitalis wrote me that on the following Saturday he was to be tried for resisting police authority, and for attacking an officer.

"I was wrong to get into a temper," he wrote. "This may cost me dearly, but it is too late now. Come to the court, you will learn a lesson." Then he gave me some advice, and sent his love to me, telling me to caress the animals for him.

While I was reading the letter, Capi, standing between my feet, put his nose to the paper, and sniffed it. I could see by the way he wagged his tail that he knew it had come from his master. This was the first time in three days that he had showed any signs of joy.

I got to the court early on Saturday morning. Many of the people who had witnessed the scene with the policeman were present. I was so scared at being in court, that I got behind a large stove and squeezed up as small as I could against the wall. Some men who had been arrested for robbery, others for fighting, were tried first. All said that they were innocent, but all were found guilty. At last Vitalis was brought in. He sat down on a bench between two policemen. What he said at first, and what they asked him, I scarcely knew, my emotion was so great. I stared at Vitalis; he stood upright, his white head thrown back. He looked ashamed and worried. I looked at the judge.

"You gave blows to the officer who arrested you," said the judge.

"Not blows, your Honor," said Vitalis, "I only struck once. When I got to the place where we were to give our performance, I was just in time to see the officer fell a child to the ground with a blow, the little boy who is with me."

"The child is not yours."

"No, but I love him as my own son. When I saw him struck I lost my temper and seized the policeman's arm so that he could not strike again."

"You struck him?"

"When he laid his hands on me I thought of him only as a man, not as a police officer."

The officer then said what he had to say.

Vitalis' eyes roamed around the room. I knew that he was looking to see if I were there, so I decided to come out of my hiding place, and elbowing through the crowd of people, I came and stood beside him. His face lit up when he saw me. Presently, the trial ended. He was sentenced to two months' imprisonment and a fine of one hundred francs. Two months' prison! The door through which Vitalis had entered was opened. Through my tears I saw him follow a policeman, and the door closed behind him. Two months' separation!

Where should I go?

CHAPTER X. HOMELESS

When I returned to the inn with heavy heart and red eyes, the landlord was standing in the yard. I was going to pass him to get to my dogs, but he stopped me.

"Well, what about your master?" he asked.

"He is sentenced."

"How long?"

"Two months' prison."

"How much fine?"

"One hundred francs."

"Two months ... one hundred francs," he repeated two or three times.

I wanted to go on, but again he stopped me.

"What are you going to do these two months?"

"I don't know, sir."

"Oh, you don't know. You've got some money to live on and to buy food for your animals, I suppose."

"No, sir."

"Then do you count on me keeping you?"

"No, sir, I don't count on any one."

That was true. I did not count upon any one.

"Your master already owes me a lot of money," he continued. "I can't board you for two months without knowing if I shall be paid. You'll have to go."

"Go! Where shall I go, sir?"

"That's not my business. I'm nothing to you. Why should I keep you?"

For a moment I was dazed. The man was right. Why should he give me shelter?

"Come, take your dogs and monkey and get out! Of course, you must leave your master's bag with me. When he comes out of jail, he'll come here to get it, and then he can settle his account."

An idea came to me.

"As you know he will settle his bill then, can't you keep me until then, and add what I cost to it?"

"Ah, ah! Your master might be able to pay for two days' lodging, but two months! that's a different thing."

"I'll eat as little as you wish."

"And your dogs and monkey! No, be off! You'll pick up enough in the villages."

"But, sir, how will my master find me when he comes out of prison? He'll come to look for me here."

"All you've got to do is to come back on that day."

"And if he writes to me?"

"I'll keep the letter."

"But if I don't answer him?..."

"Oh, stop your talk. Hurry up and get out! I give you five minutes. If I find you here when I come out again I'll settle you."

56

I knew it was useless to plead with him. I had to "get out." I went to the stables to get the dogs and Pretty-Heart, then strapping my harp on my shoulder I left the inn.

I was in a hurry to get out of town, for my dogs were not muzzled. What should I say if I met a policeman? That I had no money? It was the truth; I had only eleven sous in my pocket. That was not enough to buy muzzles. They might arrest me. If Vitalis and I were both in prison, whatever would become of the animals? I felt the responsibility of my position.

As I walked along quickly the dogs looked up at me in a way I could not fail to understand. They were hungry. Pretty-Heart, whom I carried, pulled my ear from time to time to force me to look at him. Then he rubbed his stomach in a manner that was no less expressive than the looks the dogs cast at me. I also was hungry. We had had no breakfast. My eleven sous could not buy enough for dinner and supper, so we should have to be satisfied with one meal, which, if we took it in the middle of the day, would serve us for two.

I wandered along. I did not care where I went; it was all the same to me, for I did not know the country. The question of finding a place in which to sleep did not worry me; we could sleep in the open air.... But to eat!

We must have walked for about two hours before I dared to stop, and yet the dogs had looked up at me imploringly and Pretty-Heart had pulled my ear and rubbed his stomach incessantly. At last I felt that I was far enough away from the town to have nothing to fear. I went into the first bakery that I came across. I asked for one pound and a half of bread.

"You'd do well to take a two-pound loaf," said the woman. "That's not too much for your menagerie. You must feed the poor dogs."

Oh, no, it was not too much for my menagerie, but it was too much for my purse. The bread was five sous a pound; two pounds would cost ten sous. I did not think it wise to be extravagant before knowing what I was going to do the next day. I told the woman in an offhand manner that one pound and a half was quite enough and politely asked her not to cut more. I left the shop with my bread clutched tightly in my arms. The dogs jumped joyfully around me. Pretty-Heart pulled my hair and chuckled with glee.

We did not go far. At the first tree that we saw I placed my harp against the trunk and sat down on the grass. The dogs sat opposite me, Capi in the middle, Dulcie at one side, Zerbino on the other. Pretty-Heart, who was not tired, stood up on the watch, ready to snatch the first piece that he could. To eke out the meal was a delicate matter. I cut the bread into five parts, as near the same size as possible, and distributed the slices. I gave each a piece in turn, as though I were dealing cards. Pretty-Heart, who required less food than we, fared better, for he was quite satisfied while we were still famished. I took three pieces from his share and hid them in my bag to give the dogs later. Then, as there still remained a little piece, I broke it and we each had some; that was for dessert.

After the meal I felt that the moment had come for me to say a few words to my companions. Although I was their chief, I did not feel that I was too much above them not to wish them to take part in the grave situation in which we found ourselves.

Capi had probably guessed my intentions, for he sat with his big, intelligent eyes fixed on me.

"Yes, Capi," I said, "and you, Dulcie, Zerbino and Pretty-Heart, my friends, I've bad news for you. We shan't see our master for two whole months."

"Ouah," barked Capi.

"It's bad for him and it's also bad for us, for we depend on him for everything, and now he's gone, we haven't any money."

At the mention of the word money, which he perfectly understood, Capi rose on his hind paws and commenced to trot round as though he were collecting money from the "distinguished audience."

"I see you want to give a performance, Capi," I continued; "that's good advice, but should we make anything? That's the question. We have only three sous left, so you mustn't get hungry. You've all to be very obedient; that will make it easier for us all. You must help me all you can, you dogs and Pretty-Heart. I want to feel that I can count on you."

I would not make so bold as to say that they understood all I said, but they got the general idea. They knew by our master's absence that something serious had happened, and they had expected an explanation from me. If they did not understand all that I said to them, they were at least satisfied that I had their welfare at heart, and they showed their satisfaction by the attention they gave me.

Attention? Yes, on the part of the dogs only. It was impossible for Pretty-Heart to keep still for long. He could not fix his mind upon one subject for more than a minute. During the first part of my discourse he had listened to me with the greatest interest, but before I had said twenty words, he had sprung up into a tree, the branches of which hung over our heads, and was now swinging himself from branch to branch. If Capi had insulted me in like manner, my pride would certainly have been hurt; but

I was never astonished at anything Pretty-Heart might do. He was so empty-headed. But after all, it was quite natural that he should want to have a little fun. I admit that I would like to have done the same. I would have gone up that tree with pleasure, but the importance and dignity of my present office did not permit me any such distractions.

After we had rested a while I gave the sign to start. We had to find a place somewhere to lie down for the night and gain a few sous for our food for the next day. We walked for one hour, then came in sight of a village. I quickly dressed my troop, and in as good marching order as possible we made our entry. Unfortunately, we had no fife and we lacked Vitalis' fine, commanding presence. Like a drum major, he always attracted the eye. I had not the advantage of being tall, nor was I possessed of a wonderful head. Quite the reverse, I was small and thin and I must have worn a very anxious look. While marching I glanced to the right and to the left to see what effect we were producing. Very little, I regret to say. No one followed us. Upon reaching the small square upon which was a fountain shaded with trees, I took my harp and commenced to play a waltz. The music was gay, my fingers were light, but my heart was heavy.

I told Zerbino and Dulcie to waltz together. They obeyed me at once and commenced to whirl round, keeping time. But no one put themselves out to come and see us, and yet in the doorways I saw several women knitting and talking. I continued to play, Zerbino and Dulcie went on with their waltz. Perhaps if one decided to come over to us, a second would come, then more and more.

I played on and on, Zerbino and Dulcie went round and round, but the women in the doorways did not even look over at us. It was discouraging. But I was determined not to be discouraged. I played with all my might, making the cords of my harp vibrate, almost to breaking them. Suddenly a little child, taking its first steps, trotted from his home and came towards us. No doubt the mother would follow him, and after the mother a friend would come, and we should have an audience, and then a little money.

I played more softly so as not to frighten the baby, and also to entice him to come nearer. With hands held out and swaying first on one foot, then on the other, he came on slowly. A few steps more and he would have reached us, but at that moment the mother looked round. She saw her baby at once. But instead of running after him as I had thought she would, she called to him, and the child obediently turned round and went back to her. Perhaps these people did not like dance music; it was quite possible.

I told Zerbino and Dulcie to lie down, and I began to sing my *canzonetta*. Never did I try so hard to please.

I had reached the end of the second line, when I saw a man in a round jacket, and I felt that he was coming towards me. At last! I tried to sing with even more fervor.

"Hello, what are you doing here, young rogue?" he cried.

I stopped, amazed at his words, and watched him coming nearer, with my mouth open.

"What are you doing here, I say?"

"Singing, sir."

"Have you got permission to sing on a public square in our village?"

"No, sir."

"Well, be off; if you don't I'll have you arrested."

"But, sir...."

"Be off, you little beggar."

I knew from my poor master's example what it would cost me if I went against the town authorities. I did not make him repeat his order; I hurried off.

Beggar! That was not fair. I had not begged; I had sung. In five minutes I had left behind me this inhospitable, but well guarded, village. My dogs followed me with their heads lowered, and their tails between their legs. They certainly knew that some bad luck had befallen us. Capi, from time to time, went ahead of us and turned round to look at me questioningly with his intelligent eyes. Any one else in his place would have questioned me, but Capi was too well bred to be indiscreet. I saw his lip tremble in the effort he made to keep back his protests.

When we were far enough away from the village, I signed to them to stop, and the three dogs made a circle round me, Capi in the middle, his eyes on mine.

"As we had no permission to play, they sent us away," I explained.

"Well, then?" asked Capi, with a wag of his head.

"So then we shall have to sleep in the open air and go without supper."

At the word "supper" there was a general bark. I showed them my three sous.

"You know that is all we have. If we spend those three sous to-night, we shall have nothing left for breakfast to-morrow. So, as we have had something to-day, it is better to save this." And I put my three sous back in my pocket.

Capi and Dulcie bent their heads resignedly, but Zerbino, who was not so good, and who besides was a gourmand, continued to growl. I looked at him severely.

"Capi, explain to Zerbino, he doesn't seem to understand," I said to faithful *Capitano*.

Capi at once tapped Zerbino with his paw. It seemed as though an argument was taking place between the two dogs. One may find the word argument too much, when applied to dogs, but animals certainly have a peculiar language of their kind. As to dogs, they not only know how to speak, they know how to read. Look at them with their noses in the air or, with lowered head, sniffing at the ground, smelling the bushes and stones. Suddenly they'll stop before a clump of grass, or a wall, and remain on the alert for a moment. We see nothing on the wall, but the dog reads all sorts of curious things written in mysterious letters which we do not understand.

What Capi said to Zerbino I did not hear, for if dogs can understand the language of men, men do not understand their language. I only saw that Zerbino refused to listen to reason, and that he insisted that the three sous should be spent immediately. Capi got angry, and it was only when he showed his teeth that Zerbino, who was a bit of a coward, lapsed into silence. The word "silence" is also used advisedly. I mean by silence that he laid down.

The weather was beautiful, so that to sleep in the open air was not a serious matter. The only thing was to keep out of the way of the wolves, if there were any in this part of the country.

We walked straight ahead on the white road until we found a place. We had reached a wood. Here and there were great blocks of granite. The place was very mournful and lonely, but there was no better, and I thought that we might find shelter from the damp night air amongst the granite. When I say "we," I mean Pretty-Heart and myself, for the dogs would not catch cold sleeping out of doors. I had to be careful of myself, for I knew how heavy was my responsibility. What would become of us all if I fell ill, and what would become of me if I had Pretty-Heart to nurse?

We found a sort of grotto between the stones, strewn with dried leaves. This was very nice. All that was lacking was something to eat. I tried not to think that we were hungry. Does not the proverb say, "He who sleeps, eats."

Before lying down I told Capi that I relied upon him to keep watch, and the faithful dog, instead of sleeping with us on the pine leaves, laid down like a sentinel at the entrance of our quarters. I could sleep in peace, for I knew that none would come near without me being warned by Capi. Yet, although, at rest on this point, I could not sleep at once. Pretty-Heart was asleep beside me, wrapped up in my coat; Zerbino and Dulcie were stretched at my feet. But my anxiety was greater than my fatigue.

This first day had been bad; what would the next day be? I was hungry and thirsty, and yet I only had three sous. How could I buy food for all if I did not earn something the next day? And the muzzles? And the permission to sing? Oh, what was to be done! Perhaps we should all die of hunger in the bushes. While turning over these questions in my mind, I looked up at the stars, which shone in the dark sky. There was not a breath of wind. Silence everywhere. Not the rustle of a leaf or the cry of a bird, nor the rumble of a cart on the road. As far as my eye could see, stretched space. How alone we were; how abandoned! The tears filled my eyes. Poor Mother Barberin! poor Vitalis.

I was lying on my stomach, crying into my hands, when suddenly I felt a breath pass through my hair. I turned over quickly, and a big soft tongue licked my wet cheek. It was Capi who had heard me crying and had come to comfort me as he had done on the first day of my wanderings. With my two hands I took him by the neck and kissed him on his wet nose. He uttered two or three little mournful snorts, and it seemed to me that he was crying with me. I slept. When I awoke it was full day and Capi was sitting beside me, looking at me. The birds were singing in the trees. In the distance I could hear a church bell ringing the Angelus, the morning prayer. The sun was already high in the sky, throwing its bright rays down to comfort heart and body.

We started off, going in the direction of the village where we should surely find a baker: when one goes to bed without dinner or supper one is hungry early in the morning. I made up my mind to spend the three sous, and after that we would see what would happen.

Upon arriving in the village there was no need for me to ask where the baker lived; our noses guided us straight to the shop. My sense of smell was now as keen as that of my dogs. From the distance I sniffed the delicious odor of hot bread. We could not get much for three sous, when it costs five sous a pound. Each of us had but a little piece, so our breakfast was soon over.

We *had* to make money that day. I walked through the village to find a favorable place for a performance, and also to note the expressions of the people, to try and guess if they were enemies or friends. My intention was not to give the performance at once. It was too early, but after finding a place we would come back in the middle of the day and take a chance.

I was engrossed with this idea, when suddenly I heard some one shouting behind me. I turned round quickly and saw Zerbino racing towards me, followed by an old woman. It did not take me long to know what was the matter. Profiting by my preoccupation, Zerbino had run into a house and stolen a piece of meat. He was racing alone, carrying his booty in his jaws.

"Thief! thief!" cried the old woman; "catch him! Catch all of 'em!"

When I heard her say this, I felt that somehow I was guilty, or at least, that I was responsible for Zerbino's crime, so I began to run. What could I say to the old woman if she demanded the price of the stolen meat? How could I pay her? If we were arrested they would put us in prison. Seeing me flying down the road, Dulcie and Capi were not long following my example; they were at my heels, while Pretty-Heart, whom I carried on my shoulder, clung round my neck so as not to fall.

Some one else cried: "Stop thief!" and others joined in the chase. But we raced on. Fear gave us speed. I never saw Dulcie run so fast; her feet barely touched the ground. Down a side street and across a field we went, and soon we had outstripped our pursuers, but I did not stop running until I was quite out of breath. We had raced at least two miles. I turned round. No one was following us. Capi and Dulcie were still at my heels, Zerbino was in the distance. He had stopped probably to eat his piece of meat. I called him, but he knew very well that he deserved a severe punishment, so instead of coming to me, he ran away as fast as he could. He was famished, that was why he had stolen the meat. But I could not accept this as an excuse. He had stolen. If I wanted to preserve discipline in my troop, the guilty one must be punished. If not, in the next village Dulcie would do the same, and then Capi would succumb to the temptation. I should have to punish Zerbino publicly. But in order to do that I should have to catch him, and that was not an easy thing to do.

I turned to Capi.

"Go and find Zerbino," I said gravely.

He started off at once to do what I told him, but it seemed to me that he went with less ardor than usual. From the look that he gave me, I saw that he would far rather champion Zerbino than be my envoy. I sat down to await his return with the prisoner. I was pleased to get a rest after our mad race. When we stopped running we had reached the bank of a canal with shady trees and fields on either side.

An hour passed. The dogs had not returned. I was beginning to feel anxious when at last Capi appeared alone, his head hanging down.

"Where is Zerbino?"

Capi laid down in a cowed attitude. I looked at him and noticed that one of his ears was bleeding. I knew what had happened. Zerbino had put up a fight. I felt that, although Capi had obeyed my orders, he had considered that I was too severe and had let himself be beaten. I could not scold him. I could only wait until Zerbino chose to return. I knew that sooner or later he would feel sorry and would come back and take his punishment.

I stretched myself out under a tree, holding Pretty-Heart tight for fear he should take it into his head to join Zerbino. Dulcie and Capi slept at my feet. Time passed. Zerbino did not appear. At last I also dropped off to sleep.

Several hours had passed when I awoke. By the sun I could tell that it was getting late, but there was no need for the sun to tell me that. My stomach cried out that it was a long time since I had eaten that piece of bread. And I could tell from the looks of the two dogs and Pretty-Heart that they were famished. Capi and Dulcie fixed their eyes on me piteously; Pretty-Heart made grimaces. But still Zerbino had not come back. I called to him, I whistled, but in vain. Having well lunched he was probably digesting his meal, cuddled up in a bush.

The situation was becoming serious. If I left this spot, Zerbino perhaps would get lost, for he might not be able to find us; then if I stayed, there was no chance of me making a little money to buy something to eat. Our hunger became more acute. The dogs fixed their eyes on me imploringly, and Pretty-Heart rubbed his stomach and squealed angrily.

Still Zerbino did not return. Once more I sent Capi to look for the truant, but at the end of half an hour he came back alone. What was to be done?

Although Zerbino was guilty, and through his fault we were put into this terrible position, I could not forsake him. What would my master say if I did not take his three dogs back to him? And then, in spite of all, I loved Zerbino, the rogue! I decided to wait until evening, but it was impossible to remain inactive. If we were doing something I thought we might not feel the pangs of hunger so keenly. If I could invent something to distract us, we might, for the time being, forget that we were so famished. What could we do?

I pondered over the question. Then I remembered that Vitalis had told me that when a regiment was tired out by a long march, the band played the gayest airs so that the soldiers should forget their fatigue. If I played some gay pieces on my harp, perhaps we could forget our hunger. We were all so faint and sick, yet if I played something lively and made the two poor dogs dance with Pretty-Heart the time might pass quicker. I took my instrument, which I had placed up against a tree and, turning my back to the canal I put my animals in position and began to play a dance.

At first neither the dogs nor the monkey seemed disposed to dance. All they wanted was food. My heart ached as I watched their pitiful attitude. But they must forget their hunger, poor little things! I played louder and quicker, then, little by little, the music produced its customary effect. They danced and I played on and on.

Suddenly I heard a clear voice, a child's voice, call out: "Bravo." The voice came from behind me. I turned round quickly.

A barge had stopped on the canal. The two horses which dragged the boat were standing on the opposite bank. It was a strange barge. I had never seen one like it. It was much shorter than the other boats on the canal, and the deck was fashioned like a beautiful veranda, covered with plants and foliage. I could see two people, a lady, who was still young, with a beautiful sad face, and a boy about my own age, who seemed to be lying down. It was evidently the little boy who had called out "Bravo!"

I was very surprised at seeing them. I lifted my hat to thank them for their applause.

"Are you playing for your own pleasure?" asked the lady, speaking French with a foreign accent.

"I am keeping the dogs in practice and also ... it diverts their attention."

The child said something. The lady bent over him.

"Will you play again?" she then asked, turning round to me.

Would I play? Play for an audience who had arrived at such a moment! I did not wait to be asked twice.

"Would you like a dance or a little comedy?" I asked.

"Oh, a comedy," cried the child. But the lady said she preferred a dance.

"A dance is too short," said the boy.

"If the 'distinguished audience' wishes, after the dance, we will perform our different rôles."

This was one of my master's fine phrases. I tried to say it in the same grand manner as he. Upon second thought, I was not sorry that the lady did not wish for a comedy, for I don't see how I could have given a performance; not only was Zerbino absent, but I had none of the "stage fittings" with me.

I played the first bars of a waltz. Capi took Dulcie by the waist with his two paws and they whirled round, keeping good time. Then Pretty-Heart danced alone. Successively, we went through all our repertoire. We did not feel tired now. The poor little creatures knew that they would be repaid with a meal and they did their best. I also.

Then, suddenly, in the midst of a dance in which all were taking part, Zerbino came out from behind a bush, and as Capi and Dulcie and Pretty-Heart passed near him, he boldly took his place amongst them.

While playing and watching my actors, I glanced from time to time at the little boy. He seemed to take great pleasure in what we were doing, but he did not move. He looked as though he was lying on a stretcher. The boat had drifted right to the edge of the bank, and now I could see the boy plainly. He had fair hair. His face was pale, so white that one could see the blue veins on his forehead. He had the drawn face of a sick child.

"How much do you charge for seats at your performance?" asked the lady.

"You pay according to the pleasure we have given you."

"Then, Mamma, you must pay a lot," said the child. He added something in a language that I did not understand.

"My son would like to see your actors nearer."

I made a sign to Capi. With delight, he sprang onto the boat.

"And the others!" cried the little boy.

Zerbino and Dulcie followed Capi's example.

"And the monkey!"

Pretty-Heart could have easily made the jump, but I was never sure of him. Once on board he might do some tricks that certainly would not be to the lady's taste.

"Is he spiteful?" she asked.

"No, madam, but he is not always obedient, and I am afraid that he will not behave himself."

"Well, bring him on yourself."

She signed to a man who stood near the rail. He came forward and threw a plank across to the bank. With my harp on my shoulder and Pretty-Heart in my arms I stepped up the plank.

"The monkey! the monkey!" cried the little boy, whom the lady addressed as Arthur.

I went up to him and, while he stroked and petted Pretty-Heart, I watched him. He was strapped to a board.

"Have you a father, my child?" asked the lady.

"Yes, but I am alone just now."

"For long?"

"For two months."

"Two months! Oh, poor little boy. At your age how is it that you happen to be left all alone?"

"It has to be, madam."

"Does your father make you take him a sum of money at the end of two months? Is that it?"

"No, madam, he does not force me to do anything. If I can make enough to live with my animals, that is all."

"And do you manage to get enough?"

I hesitated before replying. I felt a kind of awe, a reverence for this beautiful lady. Yet she talked to me so kindly and her voice was so sweet, that I decided to tell her the truth. There was no reason why I should not. Then I told her how Vitalis and I had been parted, that he had gone to prison because he had defended me, and how since he had gone I had been unable to make any money.

While I was talking, Arthur was playing with the dogs, but he was listening to what I said.

"Then how hungry you all must be!" he cried.

At this word, which the animals well knew, the dogs began to bark and Pretty-Heart rubbed his stomach vigorously.

"Oh, Mamma!" cried Arthur.

The lady said a few words in a strange language to a woman, whose head I could see through a half open door. Almost immediately the woman appeared with some food.

"Sit down, my child," said the lady.

I did so at once. Putting my harp aside I quickly sat down in the chair at the table; the dogs grouped themselves around me. Pretty-Heart jumped on my knee.

"Do your dogs eat bread?" asked Arthur.

"Do they eat bread!"

I gave them a piece which they devoured ravenously.

"And the monkey?" said Arthur.

But there was no occasion to worry about Pretty-Heart, for while I was serving the dogs he had taken a piece of crust from a meat pie and was almost choking himself underneath the table. I helped myself to the pie and, if I did not choke like Pretty-Heart, I gobbled it up no less gluttonously than he.

"Poor, poor child!" said the lady.

Arthur said nothing, but he looked at us with wide open eyes, certainly amazed at our appetites, for we were all as famished as one another, even Zerbino, who should have been somewhat appeased by the meat that he had stolen.

"What would you have eaten to-night if you had not met us?" asked Arthur.

"I don't think we should have eaten at all."

"And to-morrow?"

"Perhaps to-morrow we should have had the luck to meet some one like we have to-day."

Arthur then turned to his mother. For some minutes they spoke together in a foreign language. He seemed to be asking for something which at first she seemed not quite willing to grant. Then, suddenly, the boy turned his head. His body did not move.

"Would you like to stay with us?" he asked.

I looked at him without replying; I was so taken back by the question.

"My son wants to know if you would like to stay with us?" repeated the lady.

"On this boat?"

"Yes, my little boy is ill and he is obliged to be strapped to this board. So that the days will pass more pleasantly for him, I take him about in this boat. While your master is in prison, if you like, you may stay here with us. Your dogs and your monkey can give a performance every day, and Arthur and I will be the audience. You can play your harp for us. You will be doing us a service and we, on our side, may be useful to you."

To live on a boat! What a kind lady. I did not know what to say. I took her hand and kissed it.

"Poor little boy!" she said, almost tenderly.

She had said she would like me to play my harp: this simple pleasure I would give her at once. I wanted to show how grateful I was. I took my instrument and, going to the end of the boat, I commenced to play softly. The lady put a little silver whistle to her lips and blew it.

I stopped playing, wondering why she had whistled. Was it to tell me that I was playing badly, or to ask me to stop? Arthur, who saw everything that passed around him, noticed my uneasiness.

"My mamma blew the whistle for the horses to go on," he said.

That was so; the barge, towed by the horses, glided over the soft waters which lapped gently against the keel; on either side were trees and behind us fell the oblique rays from the setting sun.

"Will you play?" asked Arthur.

He beckoned to his mother. She sat down beside him. He took her hand and kept it in his, and I played to them all the pieces that my master had taught me.

CHAPTER XI. ANOTHER BOY'S MOTHER

Arthur's mother was English. Her name was Mrs. Milligan. She was a widow, and Arthur was her only son; at least, it was supposed that he was her only son living, for she had lost an elder child under mysterious conditions. When the child was six months old it had been kidnaped, and they had never been able to find any trace of him. It is true that, at the time he was taken, Mrs. Milligan had not been able to make the necessary searches. Her husband was dying, and she herself was dangerously ill and knew nothing of what was going on around her. When she regained consciousness her husband was dead and her baby had disappeared. Her brother-in-law, Mr. James Milligan, had searched everywhere for the child. There being no heir, he expected to inherit his brother's property. Yet, after all, Mr. James Milligan inherited nothing from his brother, for seven months after the death of her husband, Mrs. Milligan's second son, Arthur, was born.

But the doctors said that this frail, delicate child could not live. He might die at any moment. In the event of his death, Mr. James Milligan would succeed to the fortune. He waited and hoped, but the doctors' predictions were not fulfilled. Arthur lived. It was his mother's care that saved him. When he had to be strapped to a board, she could not bear the thought of her son being closed up in a house, so she had a beautiful barge built for him, and was now traveling through France on the various canals.

Naturally, it was not the first day that I learned all this about the English lady and her son. I learned these details little by little, while I was with her.

I was given a tiny cabin on the boat. What a wonderful little room it appeared to me! Everything was spotless. The only article of furniture that the cabin contained was a bureau, but what a bureau: bed, mattress, pillows, and covers combined. And attached to the bed were drawers containing brushes, combs, etc. There was no table or chairs, at least not in their usual shape, but against the wall was a plank, which when pulled down was found to be a little square table and chair. How pleased I was to get into that little bed. It was the first time in my life that I had felt soft sheets against my face. Mother Barberin's were very hard and they used to rub my cheeks, and Vitalis and I had more often slept without sheets, and those at the cheap lodging houses at which we stayed were just as rough as Mother Barberin's.

I woke early, for I wanted to know how my animals had passed the night. I found them all at the place where I had installed them the night before, and sleeping as though the beautiful barge had been their home for several months. The dogs jumped up as I approached, but Pretty-Heart, although he had one eye half open, did not move; instead he commenced to snore like a trombone.

I guessed at once what was the matter: Pretty-Heart was very sensitive; he got angry very quickly and sulked for a long time. In the present circumstances he was annoyed because I had not taken him into my cabin, and he showed his displeasure by pretending to be asleep.

I could not explain to him why I had been forced to leave him on deck, and as I felt that I had, at least in appearances, done him an injury, I took him in my arms and cuddled him, to show him that I was sorry. At first he continued to sulk, but soon, with his changeable temper, he thought of something else, and by his signs made me understand that if I would take him for a walk on land he would perhaps forgive me. The man who was cleaning the deck was willing to throw the plank across for us, and I went off into the fields with my troop.

The time passed, playing with the dogs and chasing Pretty-Heart; when we returned the horses were harnessed and the barge in readiness to start. As soon as we were all on the boat the horses began to trot along the towing path; we glided over the water without feeling a movement, and the only sound to be heard was the song of the birds, the swish of the water against the boat, and the tinkle of bells around the horses' necks.

Here and there the water seemed quite black, as though it was of great depth; in other parts it was as clear as crystal and we could see the shiny pebbles and velvety grass below.

I was gazing down into the water when I heard some one call my name. It was Arthur. He was being carried out on his board.

"Did you sleep well?" he asked, "better than in the field?"

I told him that I had, after I had politely spoken to Mrs. Milligan.

"And the dogs?" asked Arthur.

I called to them; they came running up with Pretty-Heart; the latter making grimaces as he usually did when he thought that we were going to give a performance.

Mrs. Milligan had placed her son in the shade and had taken a seat beside him.

"Now," she said to me, "you must take the dogs and the monkey away; we are going to work."

I went with the animals to the front of the boat.

What work could that poor little boy do?

I looked round and saw that his mother was making him repeat a lesson from a book she held in her hand. He seemed to be having great difficulty in mastering it, but his mother was very patient.

"No," she said at last, "Arthur, you don't know it, at all."

"I can't, Mamma, I just can't," he said, plaintively. "I'm sick."

"Your head is not sick. I can't allow you to grow up in utter ignorance because you're an invalid, Arthur."

That seemed very severe to me, yet she spoke in a sweet, kind way.

"Why do you make me so unhappy? You know how I feel when you won't learn."

"I cannot, Mamma; I cannot." And he began to cry.

But Mrs. Milligan did not let herself be won over by his tears, although she appeared touched and even more unhappy.

"I would have liked to have let you play this morning with Remi and the dogs," she said, "but you cannot play until you know your lessons perfectly." With that she gave the book to Arthur and walked away, leaving him alone.

From where I stood I could hear him crying. How could his mother, who appeared to love him so much, be so severe with the poor little fellow. A moment later she returned.

"Shall we try again?" she asked gently.

She sat down beside him and, taking the book, she began to read the fable called "The Wolf and the Sheep." She read it through three times, then gave the book back to Arthur and told him to learn it alone. She went inside the boat.

I could see Arthur's lips moving. He certainly was trying very hard. But soon he took his eyes off the book; his lips stopped moving. His look wandered everywhere, but not back to his book. Suddenly he caught my eye; I made a sign to him to go on with his lesson. He smiled, as though to thank me for reminding him, and again fixed his eyes on his book. But as before, he could not concentrate his thoughts; his eyes began to rove from first one side of the canal to the other. Just then a bird flew over the boat, swiftly as an arrow. Arthur raised his head to follow its flight. When it had passed he looked at me.

"I can't learn this," he said, "and yet I want to."

I went over to him.

"It is not very difficult," I said.

"Yes, it is, it's awfully difficult."

"It seems to me quite easy. I was listening while your mother read it, and I almost learned it myself."

He smiled as though he did not believe it.

"Do you want me to say it to you?"

"You can't."

"Shall I try? You take the book."

He took up the book again, and I began to recite the verse. I had it almost perfect.

"What! you know it?"

"Not quite, but next time I could say it without a mistake, I believe."

"How did you learn it?"

"I listened while your mother read it, but I listened attentively without looking about to see what was going on round about me."

He reddened, and turned away his eyes.

"I will try, like you," he said, "but tell me, what did you do to remember the words?"

I did not quite know how to explain, but I tried my best.

"What is the fable about?" I said. "Sheep. Well, first of all, I thought of sheep; the sheep were in a field. I could see them lying down and sleeping in the field; picturing them so, I did not forget."

"Yes, yes," he said, "I can see them, black and white ones! in a green field."

"What looks after the sheep usually?"

"Dogs."

"And?..."

"A shepherd."

"If they thought the sheep were quite safe, what did they do?"

"The dog slept while the shepherd played his flute in the distance with the other shepherds."

Little by little Arthur had the entire fable pictured in his mind's eye. I explained every detail, as well as I was able. When he was thoroughly interested we went over the lines together and at the end of half an hour he had mastered it.

"Oh, how pleased mamma will be!" he cried.

When his mother came out she seemed displeased that we were together. She thought that we had been playing, but Arthur did not give her time to say a word.

"I know it!" he cried. "Remi has taught it to me."

Mrs. Milligan looked at me in surprise, but before she could say a word Arthur had commenced to recite the fable. I looked at Mrs. Milligan: her beautiful face broke into a smile; then I thought I saw tears in her eyes, but she bent her head quickly over her son and put her arms about him. I was not sure if she was crying.

"The words mean nothing," said Arthur; "they are stupid, but the things that one sees! Remi made me see the shepherd with his flute, and the fields, and the dogs, and the sheep, then the wolves, and I could even hear the music that the shepherd was playing. Shall I sing the song to you, Mamma?"

And he sang a little sad song in English.

This time Mrs. Milligan did really cry, for when she got up from her seat, I saw that Arthur's cheeks were wet with her tears. Then she came to me and, taking my hand in hers, pressed it gently.

"You are a good boy," she said.

The evening before I had been a little tramp, who had come on the barge with his animals to amuse a sick child, but this lesson drew me apart from the dogs and the monkey. I was, from now, a companion, almost a friend, to the sick boy.

From that day there was a change in Mrs. Milligan's manner toward me, and between Arthur and myself there grew a strong friendship. I never once felt the difference in our positions; this may have been due to Mrs. Milligan's kindness, for she often spoke to me as though I were her child.

When the country was interesting we would go very slowly, but if the landscape was dreary, the horses would trot quickly along the towing path. When the sun went down the barge stopped; when the sun rose the barge started on again.

If the evenings were damp we went into the little cabin and sat round a bright fire, so that the sick boy should not feel chilly, and Mrs. Milligan would read to us and show us pictures and tell us beautiful stories.

Then, when the evenings were beautiful, I did my part. I would take my harp and when the boat had stopped I would get off and go at a short distance and sit behind a tree. Then, hidden by the branches, I played and sang my best. On calm nights Arthur liked to hear the music without being able to see who played. And when I played his favorite airs he would call out "Encore," and I would play the piece over again.

That was a beautiful life for the country boy, who had sat by Mother Barberin's fireside, and who had tramped the high roads with Signor Vitalis. What a difference between the dish of boiled potatoes that my poor foster mother had given me and the delicious tarts, jellies, and creams that Mrs. Milligan's cook made! What a contrast between the long tramps in the mud, the pouring rain, the scorching sun, trudging behind Vitalis, ... and this ride on the beautiful barge!

The pastry was delicious, and yes, it was fine, oh, so fine not to be hungry, nor tired, nor too hot, nor too cold, but in justice to myself, I must say that it was the kindness and love of this lady and this little boy that I felt the most. Twice I had been torn from those I loved, ... first from dear Mother Barberin, and then from Vitalis. I was left with only the dogs and the monkey, hungry and footsore, and then a beautiful lady, with a child of about my own age, had taken me in and treated me as though I were a brother.

Often, as I looked at Arthur strapped to his bench, pale and drawn, I envied him, I, so full of health and strength, envied the little sick boy. It was not the luxuries that surrounded him that I envied, not the boat. It was his mother. Oh, how I wanted a mother of my own! She kissed him, and he was able to put his arms around her whenever he wished,—this lady whose hand I scarcely dared touch when she held it out to me. And I thought sadly that I should never have a mother who would kiss me and whom I could kiss. Perhaps one day I should see Mother Barberin again, and that would make me very happy, but I could not call her mother now, for she was not my mother....

I was alone.... I should always be alone.... Nobody's boy.

I was old enough to know that one should not expect to have too much from this world, and I thought that, as I had no family, no father or mother, I should be thankful that I had friends. And I was happy, so happy on that barge. But, alas! it was not to last long. The day was drawing near for me to take up my old life again.

CHAPTER XII. THE MASTER'S CONSENT

It was all to end,—this beautiful trip that I had made on the barge. No nice bed, no nice pastry, no evenings listening to Mrs. Milligan. Ah! no Mrs. Milligan or Arthur!

One day I decided to ask Mrs. Milligan how long it would take me to get back to Toulouse. I wanted to be waiting at the prison door when my master came out. When Arthur heard me speak of going back, he began to cry.

"I don't want him to go! I don't want Remi to go," he sobbed.

I told him that I belonged to Vitalis, and that he had paid a sum of money for me, and that I must return to him the moment he wanted me. I had spoken of my foster parents, but had never said that they were not really my father and mother. I felt ashamed to admit that I was a foundling,—a child picked up in the streets! I knew how the children from the Foundlings' Hospital had been scorned. It seemed to me that it was the most abject thing in the world to be a foundling. I did not want Mrs. Milligan and Arthur to know. Would they not have turned from me in disdain!

"Mamma, we must keep Remi," continued Arthur.

"I should be very pleased to keep Remi with us," replied Mrs. Milligan; "we are so fond of him. But there are two things; first, Remi would have to want to stay...."

"Oh, he does! he does!" cried Arthur, "don't you, Remi? You don't want to go back to Toulouse?"

"The second is," continued Mrs. Milligan, "will his master give him up?"

"Remi comes first; he comes first," Arthur insisted.

Vitalis had been a good master, and I was very grateful for all he had taught me, but there was no comparison between my life with him and that which I should have with Arthur, and at the same time, there was also no comparison between the respect I had for Vitalis and the affection which I felt for Mrs. Milligan and her invalid boy. I felt that it was wrong for me to prefer these strangers to my master, but it was so. I loved Mrs. Milligan and Arthur.

"If Remi stays with us it will not be all pleasure," went on Mrs. Milligan; "he would have to do lessons the same as you; he would have to study a great deal; it would not be the free life that he would have in going tramping along the roads."

"Ah, you know what I would like,..." I began.

"There, there, you see, Mamma!" interrupted Arthur.

"All that we have to do now," continued Mrs. Milligan, "is to get his master's consent. I will write and ask him if he will come here, for we cannot return to Toulouse. I will send him his fare, and explain to him the reason why we cannot take the train. I'll invite him here, and I do hope he will accept.

"If he agrees to my proposition," added Mrs. Milligan, "I will then make arrangements with your parents, Remi, for of course they must be consulted."

Consult my parents! They will tell her what I have been trying to keep secret. That I am a foundling! Then neither Arthur nor Mrs. Milligan would want me!

A boy who did not know his own father or mother had been a companion to Arthur! I stared at Mrs. Milligan in affright. I did not know what to say. She looked at me in surprise. I did not dare reply to her question when she asked me what was the matter. Probably thinking that I was upset at the thought of my master coming, she did not insist.

Arthur looked at me curiously all the evening. I was glad when bedtime came, and I could close myself in my cabin. That was my first bad night on board the *Swan*. What could I do? What say?

Perhaps Vitalis would not give me up, then they would never know the truth. My shame and fear of them finding out the truth was so great that I began to hope that Vitalis would insist upon me staying with him.

Three days later Mrs. Milligan received a reply to the letter she had sent Vitalis. He said that he would be pleased to come and see her, and that he would arrive the following Saturday, by the two o'clock train. I asked permission to go to the station with the dogs and Pretty-Heart to meet him.

In the morning the dogs were restless as though they knew that something was going to happen. Pretty-Heart was indifferent. I was terribly excited. My fate was to be decided. If I had possessed the courage I would have implored Vitalis not to tell Mrs. Milligan that I was a foundling, but I felt that I could not utter the word, even to him.

I stood on a corner of the railway station, holding my dogs on a leash, with Pretty-Heart under my coat, and I waited. I saw little of what passed around me. It was the dogs who warned me that the train had arrived. They scented their master. Suddenly there was a tug at the leash. As I was not on my guard, they broke loose. With a bark they bounded forward. I saw them spring upon Vitalis. More sure, although less supple than the other two, Capi had jumped straight into his master's arms, while Zerbino and Dulcie jumped at his feet.

When Vitalis saw me, he put Capi down quickly, and threw his arms around me. For the first time he kissed me.

"God bless you, my boy," he said again, and again.

My master had never been hard with me, but neither had he ever been affectionate, and I was not used to these effusions. I was touched, and the tears came to my eyes, for I was in the mood when the heart is easily stirred. I looked at him. His stay in prison had aged him greatly. His back was bent, his face paler, and his lips bloodless.

"You find me changed, don't you, Remi?" he said; "I was none too happy in prison, but I'll be better now I'm out."

Then, changing the subject, he added:

"Tell me about this lady who wrote to me; how did you get to know her?"

I told him how I had met Mrs. Milligan and Arthur in their barge, the *Swan*, on the canal, and of what we had seen, and what we had done. I rambled along hardly knowing what I said. Now that I saw Vitalis, I felt that it would be impossible to tell him that I wanted to leave him and stay with Mrs. Milligan.

We reached the hotel where Mrs. Milligan was staying, before my story was ended. Vitalis had not mentioned what she had proposed to him in her letter, so I said nothing of her plan.

"Is this lady expecting me?" he asked, as we entered the hotel.

"Yes, I'll take you up to her apartment," I said.

"There's no occasion for that," he replied; "I'll go up alone; you wait here for me with Pretty-Heart and the dogs."

I had always obeyed him, but in this case I felt that it was only fair for me to go up with him to Mrs. Milligan's apartment. But with a sign he stopped the words on my lips, and I was forced to stay below with the dogs.

Why didn't he want me to be present when he spoke to Mrs. Milligan? I asked myself this question again and again. I was still pondering over it when he returned.

"Go and say good-by to the lady," he said, briefly. "I'll wait for you here. We shall go in ten minutes."

I was thunderstruck.

"Well," he said, "didn't you understand me? You stand there like a stupid! Hurry up!"

He had never spoken so roughly to me. Mechanically I got up to obey, not seeming to understand. "What did you say to her?" I asked, after I had gone a few steps.

"I said that I needed you and that you needed me, and consequently I was not going to give up my rights to you. Go; I give you ten minutes to say good-by."

I was so possessed by the fact that I was a foundling, that I thought that if I had to leave immediately it was because my master had told them about my birth.

Upon entering Mrs. Milligan's apartment I found Arthur in tears and his mother bending over him.

"You won't go, Remi! Oh, Remi, tell me you won't go," he sobbed.

I could not speak. Mrs. Milligan replied for me, telling Arthur that I had to do as I was told.

"Signor Vitalis would not consent to let us have you," said Mrs. Milligan in a voice so sad.

"He's a wicked man!" cried Arthur.

"No, he is not a wicked man," continued Mrs. Milligan; "he loves you ... and he needs you. He speaks like a man far above his position. He told me,—let me see, these were his words:

"'I love that child, and he loves me. The apprenticeship in the life that I give him is good for him, better, far better, than he would have with you. You would give him an education, that is true; you would form his mind, but not his character. It is the hardships of life that alone can do that. He cannot be your son; he will be mine. That is better than to be a plaything for your sick child, however sweet he may be. I also will teach the boy.'"

"But he isn't Remi's father," cried Arthur.

"That is true, but he is his master, and Remi belongs to him. For the time being, Remi must obey him. His parents rented him to Signor Vitalis, but I will write to them and see what I can do."

"Oh, no, no, don't do that," I cried.

"What do you mean?"

"Oh, no, please don't."

"But that is the only thing to do, my child."

"Oh, please, please don't."

If Mrs. Milligan had not spoken of my parents, I should have taken much more than the ten minutes to say good-by that my master had given me.

"They live in Chavanon, do they not?" asked Mrs. Milligan.

Without replying, I went up to Arthur and, putting my arms round him, clung to him for a moment then, freeing myself from his weak clasp, I turned and held out my hand to Mrs. Milligan.

"Poor child," she murmured, kissing me on the forehead.

I hurried to the door.

"Arthur, I will love you always," I said, choking back my sobs, "and I never, never will forget you, Mrs. Milligan."

"Remi! Remi!" cried Arthur.

I closed the door. One moment later I was with Vitalis.

"Off we go," he said.

And that was how I parted from my first boy friend.

CHAPTER XIII. WEARY DREARY DAYS

Again I had to tramp behind my master with the harp strapped to my shoulder, through the rain, the sun, the dust, and the mud. I had to play the fool and laugh and cry in order to please the "distinguished audience."

More than once in our long walks I lagged behind to think of Arthur, his mother, and the *Swan*. When I was in some dirty village how I would long for my pretty cabin on the barge. And how rough the sheets were now. It was terrible to think that I should never again play with Arthur, and never hear his mother's voice.

Fortunately in my sorrow, which was very deep, I had one consolation; Vitalis was much kinder, kinder than he had ever been before. His manner with me had quite changed. I felt that he was more to me than a master now. Often, if I dared, I would have embraced him, I so needed love. But I had not the courage, for Vitalis was not a man with whom one dared be familiar. At first it had been fear that kept me at a distance, but now it was something vague, which resembled a sentiment of respect.

When I left the village I had looked upon Vitalis the same as the other men of the poorer class. I was not able to make distinctions, but the two months that I had lived with Mrs. Milligan had opened my eyes and developed my intelligence. Looking at my master with more attention, it seemed to me that in manner and bearing he appeared to be very superior. His ways were like Mrs. Milligan's ways....

Weeks passed. On our tramps, now, my eyes were always turned in the direction of the water, not to the hills. I was always hoping that one day I should see the *Swan*. If I saw a boat in the distance I always thought that it might be the *Swan*. But it was not.

We passed several days at Lyons, and all my spare time I spent on the docks, looking up and down the river. I described the beautiful barge to the fishermen and asked them if they had seen it, but no one had seen it.

We had to leave Lyons at last and went on to Dijon; then I began to give up hope of ever seeing Mrs. Milligan again, for at Lyons I had studied all the maps of France, and I knew that the *Swan* could not go farther up the river to reach the Loire. It would branch off at Chalon. We arrived at Chalon, and we went on again without seeing it. It was the end of my dream.

To make things worse, the winter was now upon us, and we had to tramp along wearily in the blinding rain and slush. At night, when we arrived at a wretched inn, or in a barn, tired out, wet to the skin, I could not drop off to sleep with laughter on my lips. Sometimes we were frozen to the bone, and Pretty-Heart was as sad and mournful as myself.

My master's object was to get to Paris as quickly as possible, for it was only in Paris that we had a chance to give performances during the winter. We were making very little money now, so we could not afford to take the train.

After the cold sleet, the wind turned to the north. It had been very damp for several days. At first we did not mind the biting north wind in our faces, but soon the sky filled with great black clouds and the wintry sun disappeared altogether. We knew that a snowstorm was coming.

Vitalis was anxious to get to the next big town, where we could stay and give several performances, if very bad weather overtook us.

"Go to bed quickly," he said, when we got to an inn that night; "we are going to start at a very early hour to-morrow, because I don't want to be caught in a snowstorm."

He did not go to bed at once, but sat down by a corner of the kitchen fire to warm Pretty-Heart, who was suffering terribly from the cold. The monkey had not ceased moaning, although we had wrapped him up in plenty of coverlets.

The next morning I got up early as I had been told. It was not yet day, the sky was lowering and black, and there was not a star to be seen. When we opened the door a strong wind almost took us off our feet.

"If I were in your place," said the innkeeper to Vitalis, "I wouldn't venture out. We're going to have a terrible snowstorm."

"I'm in a hurry," replied Vitalis, "and I want to get to Troyes before it comes on."

"Thirty miles."

Nevertheless, we started.

Vitalis held Pretty-Heart tight against his body so as to give him some of his own warmth, and the dogs, pleased with the hard dry roads, raced before us. My master had bought a sheepskin for me at Dijon, and I wrapped myself up in it with the wool inside.

It was anything but agreeable when we opened our mouths, so we walked along in silence, hurrying as much to get warm as to get ahead. Although it was long past the hour of daybreak, the sky was still quite black. Although to the east a whitish band cut the clouds, yet the sun would not come out. Looking across the country, objects were now becoming more distinct. We could see the trees stripped of their leaves, and the shrubs and bushes with dry foliage rustling and cracking with the heavy gusts of wind. There was no one on the roads, nor in the fields, not a sound of cart wheels, nor the crack of a whip.

Suddenly, in the distance, we could see a pale streak which got larger and larger as it came towards us. Then we heard a sort of hissing murmur, the strange, harsh cry of the wild geese. The maddened flock flew over our heads; on they went, wildly fleeing from the north towards the south. Before they were out of sight, soft flakes were dropping gently from the skies and floating in the atmosphere.

The country through which we tramped was desolate and bleak, the mournful aspect seemed to add to the silence; only the shrill whistling of the north wind was heard. Snowflakes, like tiny butterflies, fluttered around us, whirling incessantly without touching the ground.

We made little headway. It seemed impossible that we could reach Troyes before the storm was fully upon us. But I did not worry; I thought that if the snow fell it would not be so cold.

I did not know what a snow storm could be. It was not long before I learned, and in a way that I shall never forget. The clouds were gathering from the northwest. The flakes no longer hovered in the air, but fell straight and swift, covering us from head to foot.

"We shall have to take shelter in the first house we come to," murmured Vitalis; "we cannot make Troyes."

I was pleased to hear him say that, but where could we find shelter? As far as the eye could reach there was not a house to be seen, nor anything to indicate that we were nearing a village.

Before us lay a forest with its dark depths, and on either side of us the hills. The snow came down faster and thicker.

We tramped in silence. My master lifted his sheepskin now and again for Pretty-Heart to breathe more easily. From time to time we had to turn our heads to one side, so that we also could breathe. The dogs no longer raced ahead; they walked at our heels asking for the shelter that we were unable to give them.

We went slowly and painfully on, blinded, wet and frozen, and, although we were now in the heart of the forest, the road through it was exposed to the full wind. Several times I saw my master glance to the left, as though he were looking for something, but he said nothing. What did he hope to find? I looked straight before me, down the long road. As far as my eye could reach, I could see nothing but woods on either side. I thought we should never come to the end of that forest.

I had seen the snow falling only through the window panes of a warm kitchen. How far off that warm kitchen seemed now! Our feet sunk into the white bed of snow, deeper and deeper. Then, suddenly, without saying a word, Vitalis pointed to the left. I looked and saw indistinctly a little hut made of branches.

We had to find the track that led to the hut. This was difficult, for the snow was already thick enough to efface all trace of a path. We scrambled through the bushes, and after crossing a ditch, we managed at last to reach the hut and get inside. The dogs, in ecstasy, rolled over and over on the dry ground, barking. Our satisfaction was no less keen than theirs.

"I thought there would be a wood-cutter's cabin somewhere in the forest," said Vitalis. "Now, it can snow!"

"Yes, let it snow," I said defiantly; "I don't care!"

I went to the door, or rather to the opening of the hut, for there was neither door nor window, and shook my coat and hat, so as not to wet the inside of our apartment.

Our quarters were very simply but strongly built. Its furniture consisted of a heap of dirt and some big stones for seats.

In a house like this it was not difficult to find fuel; we had only to take it down from the walls and the roof, dragging out a few faggots here and there. This was quickly done, and soon we had a bright flaming fire. It is true that the hut was soon filled with smoke, but what did that matter? There was a flame, and it was heat that we wanted. I lay down, supporting myself on my two hands, and blew the fire; the dogs sat around the grate gravely; with necks stretched out they presented their wet sides to the flames.

Pretty-Heart soon ventured to peep from under Vitalis' coat; prudently putting the end of his nose outside, he looked about to take in his surroundings. Evidently satisfied, he jumped quickly to the ground and taking the best place before the fire he held out his two little trembling hands to the flames.

That morning before I had risen, Vitalis had packed some provisions. There was some bread and a piece of cheese. We all expressed satisfaction at the sight of the food. Unfortunately, we were only able to have a very small piece, for not knowing how long we should have to stay in the hut, Vitalis thought it advisable to keep some for supper. I understood, but the dogs did not, and when they saw the bread put back in the bag before they had scarcely eaten, they held out their paws to their master, scratching his neck, and performing pantomime gestures to make him open the bag upon which their eyes were fixed. But Vitalis took no notice of them; the bag was not opened. The dogs settled themselves to go to sleep, Capi with his nose in the cinders. I thought that I would follow their example.

I do not know how long I slept; when I awoke the snow had stopped falling. I looked outside. It was very deep; if we ventured out it would come above our knees.

What time was it? I could not ask Vitalis. His big silver watch, by which Capi had told the hour, had been sold. He had spent all his money to pay his prison fine, and when he bought my sheepskin at Dijon he had parted with his big watch to pay for it. From the misty atmosphere it was impossible for me to tell what hour it might be.

There was not a sound to be heard; the snow seemed to have petrified every movement of life. I was standing in the opening of our cabin when I heard my master calling.

"Do you want to get on your way?" he asked.

"I don't know; I want to do what you wish."

"Well, I think we ought to stay here; we are at least sheltered and have warmth."

That was true, but I remembered that we had no food. However, I said nothing.

"I'm afraid it will snow again," continued Vitalis. "We don't want to spend the night outside. Better stay here."

Yes, we should have to stay in the hut and tighten our belts round our stomachs, that was all.

At supper Vitalis divided the remainder of the bread. Alas, there was but little, and it was quickly eaten; we gobbled up every crumb. When our frugal supper was over I thought that the dogs would begin making signs for more as they had done before, for they were ravenous. But they did nothing of the kind, and once again I realized how great was their intelligence.

When Vitalis thrust his knife into his trouser pocket, which indicated that the feast was over, Capi got up and smelled the bag in which the food was kept. He then placed his paw on the bag to feel it. This double investigation convinced him that there was nothing left to eat. Then, coming back to his place before the fire, he looked at Zerbino and Dulcie. The look clearly signified that they would get nothing more; then he stretched himself out his entire length with a sigh of resignation. "There is nothing more. It is useless to beg." He said this to them as plainly as though he had spoken aloud.

His companions, understanding this language, also stretched out before the fire sighing, but Zerbino's sigh in no wise betokened resignation, for added to a large appetite, Zerbino was very much of a gourmand, and this was a greater sacrifice for him than for the others.

The snow had commenced to fall again; it fell persistently. We could see the white carpet on the ground rise higher and higher until the small shrubs and bushes were hidden beneath it. When night came, big flakes were still falling from the black sky onto the shimmering earth.

As we had to sleep there, the best thing to do was to go to sleep as quickly as possible. I wrapped myself up in my sheepskin, which I had dried by the fire during the day, and I laid down beside the fire, my head on a flat stone which served for a pillow.

"You go to sleep," said Vitalis; "I'll wake you when it's my turn, for although we have nothing to fear from animals or people in this cabin, one of us must keep awake to see that the fire does not go out. We must be careful not to get cold, for it will be bitter when the snow stops."

I slept. In the small hours of the night my master woke me. The fire was still burning, and the snow had stopped falling.

"It's my turn to sleep now," said Vitalis; "as the fire goes down you throw on this wood that I've got already here."

He had piled up a heap of small wood by the grate. My master, who slept much lighter than I, did not wish me to wake him by pulling down the wood from the walls each time I needed it. So from this heap that he had prepared, I could take the wood and throw on the fire without making a noise. It was a wise thing to do, but alas, Vitalis did not know what the result would be.

He stretched out now before the fire with Pretty-Heart in his coverlet cuddled up against him, and soon, from his deep breathing, I knew that he had fallen asleep. Then I got up softly and went to the opening to see how it looked outside.

All the grass, the bushes, and the trees were buried in snow. Everywhere the eye rested was a dazzling white. The sky was dotted with twinkling stars, but although they were so bright it was the snow which shed the pale light over the earth. It was much colder now; it was freezing hard.

Oh! what should we have done in the depths of the forest in the snow and the cold if we had not found this shelter?

Although I had walked on tiptoe to the opening without scarcely making a sound, I had roused the dogs, and Zerbino had followed me. The splendor of the night was nothing to him; he looked on the scene for a moment, and then became bored and wanted to go outside. I ordered him to return to his place. Foolish dog, wasn't it better to stay by the warm fire in this terrible cold than to go prowling around. He obeyed me, but with a

86

very bad grace, and kept his eyes fixed on the entrance. I stayed there for a few minutes longer, looking at the white night. It was beautiful, but although I enjoyed it, somehow I felt a vague sadness. I could have gone inside and not looked, of course, but the white, mysterious scene held me fascinated.

At last I went back to the fire and having placed two or three long pieces of wood crossways upon one another, I sat down on the stone which had served me for a pillow. My master was sleeping calmly; the dogs and Pretty-Heart also slept, and the flames leaped from the fire and swirled upward to the roof, throwing out bright sparks. The spluttering flame was the only sound that broke the silence of the night. For a long time I watched the sparks, then little by little I began to get drowsy, without my being aware.

If I had been compelled to busy myself with getting the wood, I could have kept awake, but seated before the fire with nothing to do, I became so sleepy, and yet all the time I thought that I could manage to keep awake.

I sprang up suddenly, awakened by a violent barking! It was night. I probably had slept for a long time and the fire was almost out. No flames lit the hut now. Capi was barking loudly, furiously. But, strange! there was no sound from Zerbino or Dulcie.

"What's the matter?" cried Vitalis, waking up.

"I don't know."

"You've been to sleep, and the fire's gone out."

Capi had run to the opening, but had not ventured outside. He stood on the threshold barking.

"What has happened?" I asked in my turn.

In answer to Capi's barks came two or three mournful howls. I recognized Dulcie's voice. These howls came from behind our hut and at a very short distance.

I was going out. But Vitalis put his hand on my shoulder and stopped me.

"First," he said, in a tone of command, "put some wood on the fire."

While I obeyed, he took a sprig from the fire and blew it out until only the point remained burning. He held the torch in his hand.

"Come and see what is the matter," he said; "you walk behind me. Go ahead, Capi."

As we went out there was a frightful howl. Capi drew back, cowering behind us in terror.

"Wolves! Where are Zerbino and Dulcie?"

What could I say? The two dogs must have gone out while I slept. Zerbino had waited until I was asleep and had then crept out, and Dulcie had followed him. The wolves had got hold of them! There was fear in my master's voice when he asked for the dogs.

"Take a torch," he said, "we must go to their aid."

In our village I had heard them tell terrible stories of wolves, yet I could not hesitate. I ran back for a torch, then followed my master.

But outside we could see neither dogs nor wolves. On the snow we could see only the imprint of the two dogs' paws. We followed these traces around the hut, then at a certain distance we could see a space in the snow which looked as though some animals had been rolling in it.

"Go and look for them, Capi," said my master; at the same time he whistled to attract Zerbino and Dulcie.

But there was no barking in reply; no sound disturbed the mournful silence of the forest, and Capi, instead of running off as he was told, kept close to us, giving every sign of fear. Capi who was usually so obedient and brave!

There was not sufficient light for us to follow the imprints any distance. The snow around us was dazzling, but beyond seemed all vague and obscure.

Again Vitalis whistled and shouted for the missing dogs. There was no answering bark.

Oh, poor Zerbino; poor Dulcie!

"The wolves have got them," said Vitalis; "why did you let them go out?"

Yes? why? I had nothing to say.

"We must go and look for them," I said after a pause.

I went before him, but he stopped me.

"Where will you look for them?" he asked.

"I don't know; everywhere."

"We can't tell, in this dim light, where they have gone."

That was true, and the snow came up above our knees. Our two torches together could not penetrate the shadows.

88

"If they do not reply, it is because they are a long way off," he said. "We must not go on; the wolves might attack us also. We cannot defend ourselves."

It was dreadful to have to leave the poor dogs to their fate—our two friends; friends particularly to me. And the terrible part of it was that I knew that I was responsible. If I had not slept they would not have gone out.

My master had turned back to the hut. I followed, looking back at each step, stopping to listen. I heard nothing, and saw nothing but the snow.

When we reached the hut another surprise awaited us. The branches that I had thrown on the fire were aflame and lit up the darkest corners of the cabin, but Pretty-Heart was nowhere to be seen. His coverlets were there before the fire, but he was not in them. I called. Vitalis called, but he did not appear.

My master said that when he awoke the monkey was beside him, so it was while we were out that he had disappeared. With our burning torches held down to the snowy earth we started out to look for him. We found no trace of him.

We returned to the hut to see if he were hidden behind some faggots. We searched for a long time; ten times we looked in the same place, the same corners. I climbed up on Vitalis' shoulders to look amongst the branches of which the roof was made. We called again and again, but there was no answer.

Vitalis seemed angry. I was in despair. I asked my master if he thought that the wolves could have taken him also.

"No," he said, "the wolves would not dare come into the hut. I am afraid they got Zerbino and Dulcie when they went out, but they did not come in here. It is quite likely that Pretty-Heart was terrified and has hidden himself somewhere while we were outside; that is why I am so anxious. In this terrible weather he will catch cold, and cold is fatal for him."

"Well, let us keep on looking."

We went over the ground again, but all in vain.

"We must wait till day," said Vitalis.

"When will it be day?"

"In two or three hours, I think."

Vitalis sat down before the fire, with his head in his hands. I did not dare disturb him. I stood quite close to him, only moving occasionally to put some branches on the fire. Once or twice he got up and went to the door. He looked at the sky, listened attentively, then came back and sat down. I would rather that he had been angry with me, than that he should be so silent and sad.

The three hours passed slowly. It seemed that the night would never end. The stars were fading from the heavens, the sky was getting lighter. Day was breaking. But as morning came the cold grew more intense; the air which came through the door froze us to the bone.

If we did find Pretty-Heart, would he be alive?

The snow had quite stopped falling now and there was a pinkish light in the sky which foretold fine weather. As soon as it was quite light, Vitalis and I, armed with a stout stick, left the hut.

Capi did not appear so terrified as he had been the night before. With his eyes fixed on his master, he only waited for a sign from him to rush forward. As we were examining the ground for Pretty-Heart's footprints, Capi threw back his head and began to bark joyfully. He signified that we must look up, not on the ground.

In the great oak standing by the hut we found him.

Poor Pretty-Heart! Frightened by the howling of the dogs, he had jumped onto the roof of the cabin when we had gone out, and from there he had climbed to the top of an oak, where, feeling that he was in a safe place, he had remained crouching, without replying to our calls.

The poor little frail creature, he must be frozen!

My master called him gently. He did not move. We thought that he was already dead. For several minutes Vitalis continued to call him, but the monkey gave no sign of life. My heart ached with remorse. How severely I was being punished! I must atone.

"I'll go up and get him," I said.

"You'll break your neck."

"No, there is no danger. I can do it easily."

That was not true. There was danger. It was very difficult, for the large tree was covered with ice and snow.

When I was quite small I had learned to climb trees, and I was quite an adept in this art. I jumped and caught hold of the lowest branches. I held onto these, and, although blinded by the snow that fell in my eyes, I managed to climb up the trunk to the stronger branches. Once up there I had only to be careful not to lose my footing.

As I climbed I spoke softly to Pretty-Heart. He did not move, but looked at me with shining eyes. I had almost reached him and was about to stretch out my hand, when, with a spring, he had jumped to another branch. I followed him to this branch, but men, alas, and even youngsters are very inferior to monkeys when it comes to climbing trees. It is quite possible that I should never have caught him if the snow had not wet his feet. He did not like this and soon got tired of dodging me; then, letting himself drop from branch to branch, he jumped straight onto his master's shoulders and hid himself inside his coat.

It was a great thing to have found Pretty-Heart, but that was not all. Now we had to look for the dogs.

It was day now and easy for us to see what had happened. In the snow we read the death of our dogs. We followed their footprints for thirty yards. They had come out of the hut, one behind the other, Dulcie following Zerbino. Then we saw other footprints. On one side there were signs of a struggle where the wolves had sprung upon the dogs, and on the other sides were the footprints of the wolves where they trotted off, carrying their prey with them, to be devoured at their leisure. There was no trace of the dogs except a red trail of blood which here and there stained the snow.

The two poor dogs had gone to their death while I slept!

We had to get busy as quickly as possible with warming Pretty-Heart. We hurried back to the hut. While Vitalis held out the little creature's feet and hands to the fire, as one holds a tiny baby, I warmed his coverlets and we rolled him up in them. But he needed more than the coverlets; he needed a warm drink. My master and I sat by the fire, silent, watching the wood burn.

"Poor Zerbino; poor Dulcie!"

Each of us murmured these words; first he, then I.

The dogs had been our friends, our companions, in good and bad fortune, and to me in my loneliness they had meant so much. How deeply I reproached myself for not having kept watch. The wolves would not have come to attack us in our cabin; they would have stayed in the distance, frightened by the fire.

If only Vitalis would have scolded me! I wished that he would beat me. But he said nothing. He did not even look at me. He sat with his head bent over the fire; probably wondering what would become of us without the dogs.

CHAPTER XIV. THE DEATH OF PRETTY-HEART

The sun came out brightly. Its rays fell on the white snow, and the forest, which the night before had looked so bleak and livid, was now dazzling with a radiancy that blinded the eyes. Several times Vitalis passed his hand under the coverlet to feel Pretty-Heart, but the poor little monkey did not get warmer, and when I bent over him I could hear him shivering and shaking. The blood in his veins was frozen.

"We must get to a village or Pretty-Heart will die," said Vitalis. "Let us start at once."

His wrappings were well heated and the little creature was rolled in them. My master placed him under his vest, next his heart. We were ready.

"This was a shelter," said Vitalis, looking round the hut as we were going out, "that has made us pay dearly for its hospitality." His voice trembled.

He went out first, and I followed in his footsteps. When we had gone a few yards we had to call to Capi. Poor dog, he had remained standing outside the hut, his nose turned to the spot where his companions had been taken by the wolves.

Ten minutes later we reached the main road. We passed a cart; the driver told us that within an hour we should reach a village. This was encouraging, yet it was difficult, even painful, to walk. The snow came up to my waist. Many times I asked Vitalis after Pretty-Heart. Each time he told me that he was still shivering. At last we saw the white roofs of a fair sized village. We were not in the habit of putting up at the better class inns. We always chose a poor place, where we were sure we should not be driven away, and where they would not take all we had.

But this time Vitalis went into an inn where a beautiful sign hung outside the kitchen door. The door was open and we could see the great stove covered with shining copper saucepans, from which the steam was rising. Ah, how good that soup smelled to the famished wanderers!

My master, putting on his most "gentlemanly" airs, and with his hat on his head and his head thrown back, asked the landlady for a good bed and a fire. At first the landlady, who was a fine looking woman, had not condescended to notice us, but Vitalis' grand manner evidently impressed her. She spoke to a maid and told her to take us up to a room.

"Quick, get into bed," said Vitalis, while the servant was lighting the fire. I looked at him in astonishment. Why go to bed? I would rather sit down and eat something than go to bed.

"Quick, hurry up," repeated Vitalis.

There was nothing to do but to obey.

There was an eiderdown quilt on the bed. Vitalis pulled it right up to my chin.

"Try and get warm," he said; "the warmer you are the better."

It seemed to me that Pretty-Heart needed warming much more than I, because I was not very cold now. While I laid still under the eiderdown trying to get warm, Vitalis, to the servant's astonishment, turned little Pretty-Heart round and round before the fire as though he were going to roast him.

"Are you warm?" Vitalis asked me after a few minutes.

"I'm suffocating."

"That's right."

He came to the bed quickly. He put Pretty-Heart in, telling me to hold him close to my chest. The poor little animal, who always rebelled when he was made to do something that he did not want, seemed resigned to everything. He let me hold him close to my body without making a movement. But he was not cold now; his body was burning.

My master, who had gone down to the kitchen, soon returned, carrying a bowl of well sweetened wine. He tried to make Pretty-Heart drink a few spoonfuls, but the poor little creature could not unclench his teeth. With his brilliant eyes he looked at us imploringly as though to ask us not to torment him. Then he drew one arm from under the covers and held it out to us.

I wondered what he meant. I looked inquiringly at Vitalis, who explained: Before I had met them Pretty-Heart had had inflammation of the lungs and they had had to bleed him, taking the blood from his arm. Knowing that he was sick now he wanted us to bleed him so that he could get better as before.

Poor little monkey! Vitalis was touched to the heart, and this made him still more anxious. It was evident that Pretty-Heart was ill and he must be very ill indeed to refuse the sugared wine that he liked so much.

"Drink the wine, Remi, and stay in bed," said Vitalis. "I'll go for a doctor."

I must admit that I also liked sugared wine and besides I was very hungry. I did not let him tell me twice to drink it. After I had emptied the bowl I slid down under the eiderdown again, where the heat, aided by the wine, nearly suffocated me.

Vitalis was not gone long. He soon returned, bringing with him a gentleman wearing gold-rimmed spectacles—the doctor. Thinking that the doctor might not put himself out for a monkey, Vitalis had not told him who was his patient. When he saw me in bed, as red as a tomato, the doctor put his hand on my forehead and said at once: "Congestion."

He shook his head with an air which augured nothing good.

Anxious to undeceive him for fear he might bleed me, I cried: "Why, I'm not ill!"

"Not ill! Why, the child is delirious."

I lifted the quilt a bit and showed him Pretty-Heart, who had placed his little arm round my neck.

"He's the one that's ill," I said.

"A monkey!" he exclaimed, turning angrily to Vitalis. "You've brought me out in such weather to see a monkey!..."

Our master was a smart man who was not easily ruffled. Politely, and with his grand air, he stopped the doctor. Then he explained the situation, how he had been caught in a snowstorm, and how through fear of the wolves Pretty-Heart had jumped up in an oak tree, where he had been almost frozen to death. The patient might be only a monkey, but what a genius! and what a friend and companion to us! How could we confide such a wonderful, talented creature to the care of a simple veterinary surgeon? Every one knew that the village veterinary was an ass, while every one knew that doctors were scientific men, even in the smallest village. If one rings at a door which bears a doctor's name, one is sure to find a man of knowledge, and of generosity. Although the monkey is only an animal, according to naturalists they are so near like men that often an illness is treated the same for one as for the other. And was it not interesting, from a scientific point of view, to study how these illnesses differed. The doctor soon returned from the door where he had been standing.

Pretty-Heart, who had probably guessed that this person wearing the spectacles was a physician, again pushed out his arm.

"Look," cried Vitalis, "he wants you to bleed him."

That settled the doctor.

"Most interesting; a very interesting case," he murmured.

Alas! after examining him, the doctor told us that poor little Pretty-Heart again had inflammation of the lungs. The doctor took his arm and thrust a lancet into a vein without him making the slightest moan. Pretty-Heart knew that this ought to cure him.

After the bleeding he required a good deal of attention. I, of course, had not stayed in bed. I was the nurse, carrying out Vitalis' instructions.

Poor little Pretty-Heart! he liked me to nurse him. He looked at me and smiled sadly. His look was quite human. He, who was usually so quick and petulant, always playing tricks on one of us, was now quiet and obedient.

In the days that followed he tried to show us how friendly he felt towards us, even to Capi, who had so often been the victim of his tricks. As in the usual trend of inflammation of the lungs, he soon began to cough; the attacks tired him greatly, for his little body shook convulsively. All the money which I had, five sous, I spent on sugar sticks for him, but they made him worse instead of better. With his keen instinct, he soon noticed that every time he coughed I gave him a little piece of sugar stick. He took advantage of this and coughed every moment in order to get the remedy that he liked so much, and this remedy instead of curing him made him worse.

When I found out this trick I naturally stopped giving him the candy, but he was not discouraged. First he begged for it with an appealing look; then when he saw that I would not give it to him, he sat up in his seat and bent his little body with his hand on his stomach, and coughed with all his might. The veins in his forehead stood out, the tears ran from his eyes, and his pretense at choking, in the end, turned to a dreadful attack over which he had no control.

I had to stay at the inn with Pretty-Heart while my master went out alone. One morning upon his return he told me that the landlady had demanded the sum that we owed her. This was the first time that he had ever spoken to me about money. It was quite by chance that I had learned that he had sold his watch to buy my sheepskin. Now he told me that he had only fifty sous left. The only thing to do, he said, was to give a performance that same day. A performance without Zerbino, Dulcie or Pretty-Heart; why, that seemed to me impossible!

"We must get forty francs at once," he said. "Pretty-Heart must be looked after. We must have a fire in the room, and medicine, and the landlady must be paid. If we pay her what we owe her, she will give us another credit."

Forty francs in this village! in the cold, and with such poor resources at our command!

While I stayed at home with Pretty-Heart, Vitalis found a hall in the public market, for an out-of-door performance was out of the question. He wrote the announcements and stuck them up all over the village. With a few planks of wood he arranged a stage, and bravely spent his last fifty sous to buy some candles, which he cut in half so as to double the lights.

From the window of our room I saw him come and go, tramping back and forth in the snow. I wondered anxiously what program he could make. I was soon enlightened on this subject, for along came the town crier of the village, wearing a scarlet cap, and stopped before the inn. After a magnificent roll of his drum he read out our program.

Vitalis had made the most extravagant promises! There was to be present a world-renowned artist—that was Capi—and a young singer who was a marvel; the marvel was myself. But the most interesting part of the farce was that there was no fixed price for the entertainment. We relied upon the generosity of the audience, and the public need not pay until after it had seen, heard, and applauded.

That seemed to me extraordinarily bold. Who was going to applaud us? Capi certainly deserved to be celebrated, but I ... I was not at all convinced that I was a marvel.

Although Pretty-Heart was very ill at this moment, when he heard the drum, he tried to get up. From the noise and Capi's barks, he seemed to guess that it was to announce our performance.

I had to force him back on his bed; then he made signs to me to give him his general's uniform—the red coat and trousers with gold braid, and hat with the plume. He clasped his hands and went down on his knees to beg me. When he saw that he could get nothing from me by begging, he tried what anger would do, then finally melted into tears. It was evident that we should have a great deal of trouble to convince him that he must give up all idea of playing that night. I thought it would be better not to let him know when we started.

When Vitalis returned, he told me to get my harp ready and all the things we required for the entertainment. Pretty-Heart, who knew what this meant, turned to his master and commenced his entreaties again. He could not have better expressed his desires than by the sounds he uttered, the twisting of his face, and the turns of his body. There were real tears on his cheeks and they were real kisses that he imprinted on Vitalis' hand. "You want to play?" asked Vitalis, who had not been told what happened before.

"Yes, oh, yes!" Pretty-Heart's whole person seemed to cry out. He tried to jump to show that he was no longer sick. We know very well that if we took him out it would be his death.

It was time for us to start. Before going, I made up a good fire and wrapped Pretty-Heart up in his coverlets. He cried again and embraced me as much as he could, then we started.

As we tramped through the snow, my master told me what he expected of me. We could not, of course, give our usual repertoire, as our principal actors were missing, but Capi and I could vie with each other in doing our best. We had to collect forty francs! Forty francs! It was terrible! Impossible!

Vitalis had prepared everything. All we had to do now was to light the candles, but this was an extravagance that we could not indulge in until the room was filled, for our illuminations would not have to come to an end before our entertainment.

Whilst we took possession of our theater, the town crier, with his drum, came through the village streets for the last time. After I had dressed Capi and myself, I went outside and stood behind a pillar to watch the people arrive.

The roll of the drum became louder. It was approaching the market place and I could hear a babble of voices. Behind the drum came a score of youngsters, all keeping step. Without stopping the beating of his drum, the town crier took up his place between the two large lamps that were lit at the entrance of our theater. The public had only to walk in and take their seats for the performance to commence.

Alas! how long they were coming, and yet the drum at the door continued gayly its *rat ta ta ta*. All the boys in the village must have been there. But it was not the youngsters who were likely to give us forty francs. There would have to be some important people, open-handed and generous.

At last Vitalis decided that we ought to commence, although the hall was far from being full; but we could not wait longer, worried as we were by the terrible question of candles.

I had to appear first and sing a few songs, accompanying myself on the harp. I must confess the applause that I received was very weak. I had never thought very much of myself as an entertainer, but the marked coolness with which the audience received my efforts discouraged me. If I did not please them they would certainly not give us anything. It was not for the glory that I was singing; it was for poor Pretty-Heart. Ah, how I wanted to stir this public, to make them enthusiastic.... But I could see only too well that they did not consider me a marvel.

Capi was more successful. He received several encores. Thanks to Capi, the entertainment ended in a burst of applause. Not only did they clap their hands, but they stamped their feet.

The decisive moment had arrived. While Capi, with the cup in his jaws, ran through the audience, I danced a Spanish dance on the stage, with Vitalis playing an accompaniment. Would Capi collect forty francs? That was the question which made my heart beat while I smiled at the public in my pleasantest manner.

I was out of breath, but I still continued to dance, for I was not to stop until Capi had returned. He did not hurry himself; when he found that he did not receive a coin, he placed his paw against the person's pocket. At last I saw him about to return, and thought that I might stop, but Vitalis made me a sign to go on.

I continued to dance, and going a few steps nearer Capi, I saw that the cup was not full; far from it. Vitalis had also seen this. Bowing to the audience, he said:

"Ladies and gentlemen, I think that, without flattering ourselves, we have conscientiously carried out our program, yet as our candles are still burning, I will, if the public wishes, sing some songs myself. Our dog, Capi, will make another quest and those who have not yet given will perhaps give this time. Please have your money ready."

Although Vitalis had been my teacher, I had never really heard him sing, or at least not as he sung that evening. He selected two songs, an air from "Joseph" and one from "Richard the Lion Hearted."

Although I was only a little boy and was no judge as to whether one sang with technique or without, Vitalis' singing stirred me strangely. I went into a corner of the stage, for my eyes filled with tears as I listened to his beautiful notes.

Through a mist, I saw a young lady, who occupied the first row, clap her hands with all her might. I had already noticed that she was not a peasant like the rest of the people in the hall. She was a lady, young and beautiful, and from her handsome fur coat I took her to be the richest woman in the village. She had with her a little child who had applauded Capi heartily. It was probably her son for the likeness was striking.

After the first song, Capi went the round again. I saw with surprise that the lady had not put anything into his cup.

When my master had finished the air from the second opera, she beckoned me to her.

"I want to speak to that gentleman," she said.

I was surprised, I thought she would have done better to have dropped something into the cup. Capi returned. He had collected very little more on this second round.

"What does the lady want?" asked Vitalis.

"To speak to you."

"I have nothing to say."

"She did not give anything to Capi, perhaps she would like to give it now."

"Then it is for Capi to go to her, not for me."

However, he decided to go, and took the dog with him. I followed them. By now a servant had appeared, carrying a lantern and a rug. He stood beside the lady and the child. Vitalis bowed coldly to her.

"Forgive me for having disturbed you," she said, "but I wanted to congratulate you."

Vitalis bowed, without saying a word.

"I am a musician," continued the lady; "I am telling you this so that you will know how much I appreciate your superb talent."

Superb talent! My master! The dog trainer! I was amazed.

"An old man like me has no talent," he replied coldly.

"Do not think that I am inquisitive, but...." began the lady.

"I am quite willing to satisfy your curiosity, Madam," he said; "you are surprised that a dog trainer is able to sing a little. But I have not always been what I am now. When I was younger I was ... the servant of a great singer, and like a parrot I imitated him. I began to repeat some of the songs he practiced in my presence. That is all."

The lady did not reply. She looked hard at Vitalis. He seemed embarrassed.

"Good-by, sir," she said at last, laying a stress on the word "sir." "Good-by, and once more let me thank you for the exquisite delight you have given me this evening." And leaning towards Capi she dropped a gold piece in his cup.

I thought that Vitalis would escort her to the door, but he did nothing of the kind, and when she was out of hearing I heard him swear softly in Italian.

"She gave Capi a louis," I said.

I thought he was going to give me a blow, but he let his raised hand fall to his side.

"A louis," he said, as though he were coming out of a dream. "Ah, yes, poor Pretty-Heart. I had forgotten him. Let us go back to the little creature at once."

I climbed the stairs of the inn first and went into the room. The fire was not out, but there were no flames. I lit a candle quickly. I was surprised not to hear any sound from Pretty-Heart. I found him, lying under his coverlets, stretched out his full length, dressed in his general's uniform. He appeared to be asleep. I leaned over him and took his hand gently to wake him up. His hand was cold. Vitalis came into the room. I turned to him.

"Pretty-Heart is cold," I said.

My master came to my side and also leaned over the bed.

"He is dead," he said. "It was to be. Ah, Remi, boy, I did wrong to take you away from Mrs. Milligan. I am punished. Zerbino, Dulcie, and now Pretty-Heart and … this is not the end!"

CHAPTER XV. FAITHFUL FRIENDS

We were still a long way from Paris. We had to go by roads covered with snow, and walk from morning till night, the north wind blowing in our faces. How sad and weary were those long tramps.

Vitalis walked ahead, I at his heels, and Capi behind me. Thus in line we went onward without exchanging a word, for hours and hours, faces blue with cold, feet wet, stomachs empty. The people who passed us on the way turned round to gaze at us. Evidently they thought it strange.... Where was this old man leading his child and the dog?

The silence seemed terrible to me, and so sad. I would like to have talked just for company, but when I did venture to make a remark, Vitalis replied briefly, without even turning his head. Fortunately, Capi was more sociable, and as I trudged along I often felt his warm tongue on my hand. He licked me as much as to say, "Your friend, Capi, is here with you." Then I stroked him gently, without stopping. We understood each other; we loved each other.

On the slippery snow we went straight ahead, without stopping, sleeping at night in a stable or in a sheepfold, with a piece of bread, alas, very small, for our meal in the evening. This was our dinner and supper in one.

We did not tell the shepherds that we were dying of hunger, but Vitalis, with his usual cleverness, would say insinuatingly that "the little chap was very fond of sheep's milk, because, when he was a baby, he used to drink it." This story did not always take effect, but it was a good night for me when it did. Yes, I was very fond of sheep's milk and when they gave me some I felt much stronger the next day.

It seemed strange to me that, as we neared Paris, the country ceased to be beautiful. The snow was not white and dazzling now. I had heard what a wonderful place Paris was, and I expected something extraordinary. I did not know exactly what. I should not have been surprised to see trees of gold, streets of marble, palaces everywhere.

What were we poor things going to do when we reached Paris? I wanted to question Vitalis, but I did not dare, he seemed so gloomy. When we were in sight of the roofs and the church towers of the capital, he slackened his step to walk beside me.

"Remi," he said suddenly, "we are going to part when we get to Paris."

I looked at him. He looked at me. The sudden pallor of my face and the trembling of my lips told him what effect his words had on me. For a moment I could not speak.

"Going to part!" I murmured at last.

"Poor little chap, yes, we must part."

The tone in which he said this brought the tears to my eyes. It was so long since I had heard a kind word.

"Oh, you are so good," I cried.

"It is you who are good. You brave little heart. There comes a time in one's life when one feels these things. When all goes well, one goes along through life without thinking much who is with one, but when things go wrong, when one is on the wrong track, and above all when one is old, one wants to lean on somebody. You may be surprised that I have wanted to lean on you. And yet it is so. But only to see that your eyes are moist as you listen to me, comforts me, little Remi. I am very unhappy."

I did not know what to say. I just stroked his hand.

"And the misfortune is that we have to part just at the time when we are getting nearer to each other."

"But you're not going to leave me all alone in Paris?" I asked timidly.

"No, certainly not. What would you do in the big city, all by yourself, poor child. I have no right to leave you, remember that. The day when I would not let that good lady take you and bring you up as her son, that day I bound myself to do the best I could for you. I can do nothing at this moment, and that is why I think it is best to part. It is only for a time. We can do better if we separate during the last months of the bad season. What can we do in Paris with all gone but Capi?"

Hearing his name mentioned, dear Capi came beside us: he put his paw to his ear in military salute, then placed it on his heart, as though to tell us that we could count on his devotion. My master stopped to pass his hand affectionately over the dog's head.

"Yes, Capi, you're a good, faithful friend, but, alas! without the others we can't do much now."

"But my harp...."

"If I had two children like you it would be better. But an old man with just one little boy is bad business. I am not old enough. Now, if I were only blind or broken down! I am not in a pitiful state enough for people to stop and notice us. So, my boy, I have decided to give you to a *padrone*, until the end of the winter. He will take you with other children that he has, and you will play your harp...."

"And you?" I asked.

"I am known in Paris, I have stayed there several times. I will give violin lessons to the Italian children who play on the streets. I have only to say that I will give lessons to find all the pupils I want. And, in the meantime, I will train two dogs that will replace poor Zerbino and Dulcie. Then in the spring we will be together again, my little Remi. We are only passing through a bad time now; later, I will take you through Germany and England, then you will grow big and your mind will develop. I will teach you a lot of things and make a man of you. I promised this to Mrs. Milligan. I will keep my promise. That is the reason why I have already commenced to teach you English. You can speak French and Italian, that is something for a child of your age."

Perhaps it was all for the best as my master said, but I could only think of two things.

We were to be parted, and I was to have a *padrone*.

During our wanderings I had met several *padrones* who used to beat the children who worked for them. They were very cruel, and they swore, and usually they were drunk. Would I belong to one of those terrible men?

And then, even if fate gave me a kind master, it was another change. First, my foster mother, then Vitalis, then another.... Was it to be always so? Should I never find anyone that I could love and stay with always? Little by little I had grown attached to Vitalis. He seemed almost what I thought a father would be. Should I never have a father, have a family? Always alone in this great world! Nobody's boy!

Vitalis had asked me to be brave. I did not wish to add to his sorrows, but it was hard, so hard, to leave him.

As we walked down a dirty street, with heaps of snow on either side covered with cinders and rotten vegetables, I asked: "Where are we?"

"In Paris, my boy."

Where were my marble houses? And the trees of gold, and the finely dressed people. Was this Paris! Was I to spend the winter in a place like this, parted from Vitalis and Capi?

CHAPTER XVI. THE PADRONE

Although I knew later how beautiful was the city of Paris, the slums, being my first glimpse, created anything but a favorable impression.

Vitalis, who seemed to know his way, pushed through the groups of people who obstructed his passage along the narrow street we had just turned down.

"Mind, you don't lose me," cautioned Vitalis.

But his warning was not necessary, for I trod upon his heels, and to be more sure of him I held a corner of his coat in my hand.

We crossed a big courtyard to a dirty, dismal house where surely the sun had never penetrated. It was the worst looking place I had seen so far.

"Is Garofoli in?" asked Vitalis of a man who, by the light from a lantern, was hanging rags against the door.

"I don't know; go up and see for yourself," he growled; "the door's at the top of the stairs; it faces you."

"Garofoli is the *padrone*, Remi, I told you about," said Vitalis; "this is where he lives."

The street, the house, the staircase was not in the nature to reassure me. What would this new master be like?

Without knocking, Vitalis pushed open the door at the top of the stairs, on the top floor, and we found ourselves in a large attic. There was a great empty space in the middle of the room, and all around the walls were beds, a dozen in all. The walls and ceiling that had once been white were now filthy with smoke, dust, and dirt. On the walls was a drawing of a head in charcoal and some flowers and birds.

"Are you there, Garofoli?" asked Vitalis; "it is so dark I can't see any one. It's Vitalis."

A weak, drawling voice replied to Vitalis' question.

"Signor Garofoli has gone out; he will not be back for two hours."

A boy about twelve years of age came forward. I was struck by his strange looks. Even now, as I write, I can see him as I saw him then. He had no body, so to speak, for he seemed all legs and head. His great head was out of all proportion. Built so, he could not have been called handsome, yet there was something in his face which attracted one strangely, an expression of sadness and gentleness and, yes ... hopelessness. His large eyes held your own with sympathy.

"You are sure he will not be back for two hours?" asked Vitalis.

"Quite sure, Signor. That will be dinner time, and no one ever serves dinner but Signor Garofoli."

"Well, if he comes in before, tell him that Vitalis will be back in two hours."

"Very well, Signor."

I was about to follow Vitalis, when he stopped me.

"Stay here," he said; "you can rest.

"Oh, I'll come back," he added, reassuringly, noticing my look of anxiety.

"Are you Italian?" asked the boy, when Vitalis' heavy step could no longer be heard on the stairs.

"No," I replied in French, "I'm French."

"That's a good thing."

"What! you like the French better than the Italians?"

"Oh, no, I was thinking of you when I said 'that's a good thing,' because if you were Italian you would probably come here to work for Signor Garofoli, and I'd be sorry for you."

"Is he wicked, then?"

The boy did not reply, but the look he gave me spoke more than words. As though he did not wish to continue the conversation, he went over to the fireplace. On a shelf in the fireplace was an immense earthenware saucepan. I drew nearer to the fire to warm myself, and I noticed that the pot had something peculiar about it. The lid, through which a straight tube projected to allow the steam to escape, was fixed on the saucepan on one side with a hinge and on the other with a padlock.

"Why is that closed with a padlock?" I asked, inquisitively.

"So that I shan't take any of the soup. I have to look after it, but the boss doesn't trust me."

I could not help smiling.

"You laugh," he said sadly, "because you think that I'm a glutton. Perhaps, if you were in my place, you'd do the same as I've done. I'm not a pig, but I'm famished, and the smell of the soup as it comes out through the spout makes me still hungrier."

"Doesn't Signor Garofoli give you enough to eat?"

"He starves us...."

"Oh...."

"I'll tell you what I have done," went on the boy, "'cause if he's going to be your master, it will be a lesson for you. My name is Mattia. Garofoli is my uncle. My mother, who lives in Lucca in Italy, is very poor and has only enough for herself and my little sister, Christina. When Garofoli came to beautiful Lucca last year he brought me back with him. Oh, it was hard to leave my little sister.... Signor Garofoli has a lot of boys here, some of them are chimney sweeps, others rag pickers, and those who are not strong enough to work, sing in the streets or beg. Garofoli gave me two little white mice to show to the public and I had to bring him back thirty sous every night. As many sous as you are short a day, so many blows you get. It is hard to pick up thirty sous, but the blows are hard, too, especially when it's Garofoli who gives them. So I did everything that I could to get the money, but I was often short. Nearly all the other boys had their money when they returned at night, but I scarcely ever had mine and Garofoli was mad! There is another boy here, who also shows mice, and he's taxed forty sous, and he brings that sum back every night. Several times I went out with him to see how he made it...."

He paused.

"Well?" I asked.

"Oh, the ladies always said, 'Give it to the pretty little one, not the ugly boy.' The ugly one, of course, was I; so I did not go out with him any more. A blow hurts, but it hurts more to have things like that said, and before a lot of people! You don't know that because no one has ever told you that you are ugly. Well, when Garofoli saw that beating me didn't do any good, he tried another way. Each night he took away some of my supper. It's hard, but I can't say to the people in the streets, who are watching my mice: 'Give me something or I won't get any supper to-night!' They don't give for that reason."

"Why do they give?"

"Because you are pretty and nice, or because you remind them of a little boy they've lost, not because they think you're hungry. Oh, I know their ways. Say, ain't it cold to-day?"

"Awful cold."

"I didn't get fat on begging," went on the boy. "I got so pale and then, after a time, I often heard people say: 'That poor child is starving to death.'

A suffering look does what good looks can't do. But you have to be very starved for that. They used to give me food. That was a good time for me, because Garofoli had stopped giving me blows just then to see if it would hurt me more to go without supper, so when I got something to eat outside I didn't care. But one day Garofoli came along and saw me eating something, a bowl of soup that the fruiterer gave me, then he knew why I didn't mind going without supper at home. After that he made me stay at home and look after the soup here. Every morning before he goes out he puts the meat and the vegetables into the saucepan and locks the lid on, and all I have to do is to see that it boils. I smell the soup, but that's all. The smell of the soup doesn't feed you; it makes you more hungry. Am I very white? As I never go out now I don't hear people say so, and there's no mirror here."

"You don't seem any paler than others," I said.

"Ah, you say that because you don't want to frighten me, but I'm glad I'm sick. I want to be very ill."

I looked at him in amazement.

"You don't understand," he said, with a pitiful smile. "When one is very ill, they take care of you or they let you die. If they let me die it will be all over, I shan't be hungry any more, and there'll be no more beatings. And they do say that when we die we go up and live with God. Then, if I'm up there, I can look down on Mamma and Christina, and I can ask God not to let my little sister be unhappy. Also, if they send me to the Hospital, I shall be pleased."

The Hospital! No matter how sick I felt while tramping across the country, if I thought I might be sent to the hospital I always found strength to go on.

"I'm quite ill now, but not ill enough to be in Garofoli's way," he went on in his weak, drawling voice, "but I'm getting weaker. Garofoli, fortunately, hasn't given up beating me entirely. He beat me on the head eight days ago and, look, it's all swelled out now. You see here, this big bump? He told me yesterday it was a tumor, and the way that he spoke I believe that it's something serious. It hurts awful. I'm so giddy at night when I put my head on the pillow I moan and cry. So I think in two or three days he'll decide to send me to the hospital. I was in the hospital once, and the Sisters speak so kind to you. They say, 'Put out your tongue, little boy,' and 'There's a good boy,' every time you do anything they tell you to do. I think I am almost had enough now to be sent there."

He came and stood quite close to me, fixing his great eyes on me. Even though I had not the same reason for hiding the truth from him, I did not like to tell him how terrible he looked with his great glittering eyes, his hollow cheeks, and his bloodless lips.

"I should think you're ill enough to go to the hospital," I said.

"At last!"

With dragging limbs he went slowly over to the table and began to wipe it.

"Garofoli will be here shortly," he said; "we mustn't talk any more."

Wearily he went round the table, placing the plates and spoons. I counted twenty plates. So Garofoli had twenty boys. As I only saw twelve beds, they evidently slept, some of them, two in a bed. What beds! what sheets! the coverlets must have been brought from the stables when they were too old and not warm enough for the horses!

"Don't you come here," said the boy, "Try to get somewhere else."

"Where?"

"I don't know. No matter where, you'd be better than here."

The door opened and a child came into the room. He carried a violin under his arm and a big piece of wood in his hand.

"Give me that bit of wood," said Mattia, going up to the child.

But the little fellow held the piece of wood behind his back.

"No," he said.

"Give it me for the fire; the soup'll be better."

"Do you think I brought it for the soup? I've only made thirty-six sous to-day and I thought this bit of wood might save me a beating. It's to make up for the four sous I'm short."

"You'll have to pay. Each in his turn."

Mattia said this mechanically, as though the thought of the boy being punished gave him satisfaction. I was surprised to see a hard look come into his soft, sad eyes. I knew later that if you live with wicked people you get to be like them in time.

One by one the boys returned; each one as he came in hung his instrument on a nail above his bed. Those who were not musicians, but simply exhibitors of trained animals, put their mice and guinea pigs into a cage.

Then a heavy step sounded on the stairs and a little man wearing a gray overcoat came into the room. It was Garofoli. The moment he entered he fixed his eyes on me with a look that scared me. Mattia quickly and politely gave him Vitalis' message.

"Ah, so Vitalis is here," he said; "what does he want?"

"I don't know," replied Mattia.

"I'm not speaking to you, I'm speaking to this boy."

"He is coming back and he will tell you himself what he wants," I replied.

"Ah, here's a little fellow who knows the value of words. You're not Italian?"

"No, I'm French."

The moment Garofoli entered the room two small boys took their places, one on each side of him, and were waiting until he had finished speaking. Then one took his felt hat and placed it carefully on the bed, and the other brought forward a chair. They did this with the same gravity and respect that a choir boy waits upon a priest. When Garofoli was seated another little boy brought him a pipe stuffed with tobacco, and a fourth offered him a lighted match.

"It smells of sulphur, animal," he cried, throwing it in the grate.

The culprit hastened to repair his mistake; lighting another match he let it burn for a time before offering it to his master. But Garofoli would not accept it.

"No, you imbecile," he said, pushing the boy aside roughly. Then he turned to another child and said with an ingratiating smile:

"Ricardo, dearie, bring a match."

The "dearie" hastened to obey.

"Now," said Garofoli, when he was comfortably installed and his pipe burning; "now to business, my little angels. Bring the book, Mattia."

Garofoli made a sign to the boy who had lit the first match.

"You owe me a sou from yesterday; you promised to bring it to-day. How much have you brought?"

The child hesitated for a long time, his face showing distress, "I'm one sou short," he said at last.

"Ah, you're one sou short."

109

"It's not the sou for yesterday; it's a sou for to-day."

"That makes two sous! I've never seen the like of you!"

"It's not my fault."

"No excuses. You know the rules. Undo your coat; two blows for yesterday, two for to-day, and no supper, for your impudence. Ricardo, dearie, you're a good boy and you deserve some recreation. Take the strap."

Ricardo, the child who had lit the second match, took down from the wall a short-handled whip with two leather-knotted straps. Meanwhile, the boy who was short two sous was unfastening his coat. Then he dropped his shirt, baring his body to the waist.

"Wait a minute," said Garofoli, with an ugly smile; "you won't be the only one, perhaps; it's always pleasant to have a companion."

The children stood motionless before their master. At his cruel joke they all forced a laugh.

"The one who laughed most is the one who is short the most," said Garofoli; "I'm sure of that. Who laughed the loudest?"

All pointed to the boy who had come home first, bringing his piece of wood.

"How much are you short, you there?" demanded Garofoli.

"It's not my fault."

"And the one who says 'it's not my fault' will get an extra cut. How much is missing?"

"I brought back a big piece of wood, a beautiful piece of wood...."

"That's something. But go to the baker's and ask him to exchange your wood for bread, will he do it? How many sous are you missing? Speak out!"

"I've made thirty-six sous."

"You're four short, you rogue. And you can stand there before me like that! Down with your shirt! Ricardo, dearie, you're going to have a good time."

"But the bit of wood?" cried the boy.

"I'll give it to you for supper."

This cruel joke made all the children who were not to be punished laugh. All the other boys were then questioned as to how much they had brought home. Ricardo stood with whip in hand until five victims were placed in a row before him.

"You know, Ricardo," said Garofoli, "I don't like to look on, because a scene like this always makes me feel ill. But I can hear, and from the noise I am able to judge the strength of your blows. Go at it heartily, dearie; you are working for your bread."

He turned towards the fire, as though it were impossible for him to witness this chastisement.

I, in my corner, trembled with indignation and fear. This was the man who was going to be my master. If I did not bring him back the thirty or forty sous that he demanded of me, I should have to be whipped by Ricardo. Ah, I understood now how Mattia could speak of death so calmly.

The first lash of the whip, as it cut into the flesh, made the tears spring to my eyes. I thought that I was forgotten, but I made a mistake; Garofoli was looking at me out of the corner of his eye.

"There's a boy with a heart," he said, pointing to me; "he is not like you other rogues; you laugh when you see your comrades suffer. Take this little comrade for an example."

I trembled from head to foot. Their comrade!

At the second blow the victim uttered a wail, at the third a piercing shriek. Garofoli lifted his hand; Ricardo stopped with raised whip. I thought Garofoli was going to show mercy, but it was not so.

"You know how much it hurts me to hear you cry," said Garofoli, gently, addressing the victim. "You know that if the whip tears your skin, your cries pierce my heart. So then I warn you that for each cry you will receive another slash, and it will be your own fault. If you have any affection or gratitude you will keep silent. Go on, Ricardo."

Ricardo raised his arm and the strap curled on the backs of the victims.

"Oh, Mamma, Mamma," cried one.

Thank God, I saw no more of this frightful torture, for at this moment the door was thrown open and Vitalis entered.

In a glance, he understood all. He had heard the shrieks while climbing the stairs. Running to Ricardo, he snatched the whip from him, then, wheeling round upon Garofoli, he stood before him with folded arms.

It all happened so quickly that, for a moment, I was dumbfounded, but Garofoli quickly recovered himself and said gently:

"Isn't it terrible? That child has no heart."

"Shame! It's a shame!" cried Vitalis.

"That is just what I say," murmured Garofoli.

"Stop that," commanded Vitalis; "it's you, not the child! What a cowardly shame to torture these poor children who cannot defend themselves."

"Don't you meddle in what does not concern you, you old fool," cried Garofoli, changing his tone.

"It concerns the police," retorted Vitalis.

"You threaten me with the police, do you?" cried Garofoli.

"Yes, I do," replied my master, nowise intimidated by the bully's fury.

"Ah, Vitalis," he hissed, "so you'll talk? Well, I can talk also. Your affairs do not concern me, but there are others who are interested in you and if I tell, if I say one name.... Ah, who will have to hide his head in shame?"

My master was silent. Shame! His shame! I was amazed, but before I had time to think, he had taken me by the hand.

"Come, Remi," he said. And he drew me to the door.

"Oh," cried Garofoli, now laughing, "I thought you wanted to talk to me, old fellow."

"I have nothing to say to you."

Then, without another word, we went down the stairs, he still holding me tightly by the hand. With what relief I followed him! I had escaped from that tyrant! If I had dared I would have thrown my arms around Vitalis' neck.

CHAPTER XVII. POOR VITALIS

While we were in the street Vitalis said not a word, but soon we came to a narrow alley and he sat down on a mile-stone and passed his hand several times across his forehead.

"It may be fine to listen to the voice of generosity," he said, as though speaking to himself, "but now we're in the gutters of Paris, without a sou; not a bite to eat.... Are you hungry?" he asked, looking up at me.

"I haven't eaten anything since that little roll you gave me this morning."

"Poor, poor child, and you'll have to go to bed to-night without supper. And where are we going to sleep?"

"Did you count on sleeping at Garofoli's, then?"

"I counted upon you sleeping there, and as he would have given me twenty francs for you for the winter, I could have managed for the time being. But, seeing the way he treated those children, I could not give you to him."

"Oh, you are so good!"

"Perhaps in this old, hardened vagabond there is still a bit of the young man's heart left. This old vagabond calculated shrewdly, but the young man still in him upset all.... Now, where to go?" he murmured.

It was already late and the cold had increased. It was going to be a hard night. For a long time Vitalis sat on the stone. Capi and I stood silently before, waiting until he had come to some decision. Finally he rose.

"Where are we going?"

"To Gentilly, to try and find a race-course where I've slept sometimes. Are you tired?"

"I rested at Garofoli's."

"The pity is that I haven't rested, and I can't do much more. But we must get along. Forward! March! Children!"

This was his good humor signal for the dogs and myself when we were about to start, but this night he said it sadly.

Here we were, wandering in the streets of Paris; the night was dark and the gas jets, which flickered in the wind, lit the alleys but dimly. At each step we slipped on the ice-covered pavement. Vitalis held me by the hand, and Capi followed at our heels. From time to time, the poor dog stopped behind to look amongst a heap of garbage to see if he could find a bone or a crust, for he was oh, so hungry, but the garbage was covered with frozen snow and he searched in vain. With drooping ears he trotted on to catch up with us.

After the big streets, more alleys; after the alleys, more big streets; we walked on, and on; the few pedestrians that we met stared at us in astonishment. Was it our costumes? Was it the tired way we plodded along which arrested their attention? The policemen that we passed turned round and followed us with a glance.

Without saying a word, Vitalis tramped on, his back almost bent double, but despite the cold, his hand burned in mine. It seemed to me that he was trembling. Sometimes, when he stopped to lean for a minute against my shoulder, I felt all his body shaken with trembling. Ordinarily, I would not dare to have questioned him, but I felt I must to-night. Besides, I had a great wish to tell him how much I loved him or, at least, that I wanted to do something for him.

"You are ill?" I said, when he stopped again.

"I'm afraid so; anyway, I'm very tired. This cold is too severe for my old blood. I need a good bed and a supper before a fire. But that's a dream. Forward! March! Children."

Forward! March! We had left the city behind us; we were now in the suburbs. We saw no people or policemen or street lights, only a lighted window here and there, and over our heads the dark-blue sky dotted with a few stars. The wind, which blew more bitter and more violently, stuck our clothing to our bodies. Fortunately, it was at our backs, but as the sleeves of my coat were all torn near the shoulders, it blew in and slipped along my arms, chilling me to the bone.

Although it was dark and the streets continually crossed each other, Vitalis walked like a man who knows his way, and was perfectly sure of his road. So I followed, feeling sure that we should not lose ourselves. Suddenly, he stopped.

"Do you see a group of trees?" he asked.

"I don't see anything."

"You don't see a big black mass?"

I looked on all sides before answering. I saw no trees or houses. Space all around us. There was no other sound save the whistle of the wind.

"See, down there!" He stretched out his right hand before him, then, as I did not reply, for I was afraid to say that I saw nothing, he trudged on again.

Some minutes passed in silence; then he stopped once more and asked me if I did not see a group of trees. A vague fear made my voice tremble when I replied that I saw nothing.

"It is fear, my boy, that makes your eyes dance; look again."

"I tell you, I do not see any trees."

"Not on the big road?"

"I can't see anything."

"We've made a mistake."

I could say nothing, for I did not know where we were, nor where we were going.

"Let us walk for another five minutes and, if we do not see the trees, we will come back here. I might have made a mistake on the road."

Now that I knew that we had gone astray, I seemed to have no more strength left. Vitalis pulled me by the arm.

"Come, come."

"I can't walk any farther."

"Ah, and do you think I'm going to carry you?"

I followed him.

"Are there any deep ruts in the road?"

"No."

"Then we must turn back."

We turned. Now we faced the wind. It stung our faces like a lash. It seemed that my face was being scorched with a flame.

"We have to take a road leading from the cross-roads," said my master feebly; "tell me when you see it."

For a quarter of an hour we went on, struggling against the wind; in the doleful silence of the night the noise of our footsteps echoed on the dry, hard earth. Although scarcely able to put one foot before the other, it was I who dragged Vitalis. How anxiously I looked to the left! In the dark shadows I suddenly saw a little red light.

"See, there's a light," I said, pointing.

"Where?"

Vitalis looked; although the light was but a short distance off, he saw nothing. I knew then that his sight was going.

115

"What is that light to us?" he asked; "it is a lamp burning on the table of some worker, or it's near the bed of a dying person. We cannot go and knock at those doors. Away in the country, during the night, you can ask hospitality, but so near Paris ... we must not expect hospitality here. Come."

A few steps more and I thought I could make out the cross-roads and a black mass which must be the trees. I let go of my master's hand to go ahead quicker. There were deep ruts in the road.

"See, here are the ruts?" I cried.

"Give me your hand, we are saved," said Vitalis; "look, now you can see the group of trees."

I told him that I thought I could see the trees.

"In five minutes we shall be there," he murmured.

We trudged along, but the five minutes seemed an eternity.

"Where are the ruts?"

"They are still on the right."

"We must have passed the entrance to the race-course without seeing it. I think we'd better go back."

Once more we turned back.

"Do you see the trees?"

"Yes, there on the left."

"And the ruts?"

"There are not any."

"Am I blind?" asked Vitalis in a low voice, as he passed his hands across his eyes; "walk straight along by the trees, and give me your hand."

"Here is a wall."

"No, it's a heap of stones."

"No, I am sure it's a wall."

Vitalis took a step aside to see if it really was as I said. He stretched out his two hands and touched the wall.

"Yes, it's a wall," he murmured. "Where is the entrance. Look for the track."

I stooped down to the ground and felt all along to the end of the wall, but I found no entrance; then, turning back to where Vitalis stood, I

116

continued to feel along the wall on the other side. The result was the same; there was no opening, no gate.

"There is nothing," I said.

The situation was terrible. Without doubt my master was delirious. Perhaps there was no race-course here at all! Vitalis stood for a moment as though in a dream. Capi began to bark impatiently.

"Shall we look further?" I asked.

"No, the race-course is walled up."

"Walled up?"

"Yes, they have closed the opening, and it is impossible for us to get inside."

"Well, then?"

"What to do, eh? I don't know. Die here."

"Oh, Master! Master!"

"Yes, you don't want to die, you are so young. Life seems good to you. Let us walk on. Can you still walk a bit further, my child."

"Oh, but you?"

"When I can go no farther, I shall fall down like an old horse."

"Where shall we go?"

"Return to Paris. When we meet a policeman we will let him take us to the police station. I did not want that, but I cannot let you die of cold, boy. Come, little Remi, come. On, my children. Courage!"

We turned back the same way that we had come. What time was it? I had no idea. We had walked for hours, a long, long time, and so slowly. Perhaps it was midnight or one o'clock. The sky was still a somber blue, without moon, and with but few stars, and the few that had appeared seemed to me to be smaller than usual. The wind had increased; the snow beat in our faces; the houses that we passed were closed for the night. It seemed to me that if the people who slept there, warmly beneath the sheets, knew how cold we were outside, they would have opened their doors to us.

Vitalis walked slower and slower; when I spoke to him he made a sign to me to be silent. We were now nearing the city. Vitalis stopped. I knew that he had come to the end of his strength.

"Shall I knock at one of the doors?" I asked.

"No, they will not let us in. They are gardeners who live here. They supply the market. They would not get up at this hour to take us in. Let us go on."

But he had more will than strength. After a moment he stopped again.

"I must rest a little," he said, feebly; "I can't go on."

There was a gate leading to a big garden. The wind had blown a lot of straw, that covered a manure heap near the gate, into the street.

"I am going to sit here," said Vitalis.

"You said that if we sat down we should get too cold to get up again."

He made no reply, but signed for me to heap up the straw against the door; then he fell, rather than sat down upon it. His teeth chattered and all his body shook.

"Bring some more straw," he said; "with a lot of straw we can keep the wind from us."

The wind, yes, but not the cold. When I had gathered up all the straw that I could, I sat down beside Vitalis.

"Come quite close to me," he said, "and lift Capi on your lap. He will give you some warmth from his body."

Vitalis was ill. Did he know how ill? As I crept close up against him, he bent over and kissed me. That was the second time he had kissed me. Alas! it was the last.

Scarcely had I cuddled up against Vitalis than I felt my eyes close. I tried to keep them open, but I could not. I pinched my arms, but there was no feeling in my flesh. On my legs, which were drawn up to my chest, Capi slept already. The wind blew the wisps of straw upon us like dried leaves that fall from a tree. There was not a soul in the street, and around us was the silence of death.

This silence frightened me. Of what was I afraid? I did not know, but a vague fear came over me. It seemed to me that I was dying there. And then I felt very sad. I thought of Chavanon, of poor Mother Barberin. Must I die without seeing her again, and our little house, and my little garden! Then, I was no longer cold; it seemed that I was back in my little garden. The sun was shining and was so warm. The jonquils were opening their golden petals; the birds were singing in the trees and on the hedges. Yes, and Mother Barberin was hanging out the clothes that she had just washed in the brook, which rippled over the pebbles. Then I left Chavanon, and joined Arthur and Mrs. Milligan on the *Swan*. Then my eyes closed again, my heart seemed to grow heavy, and I remembered no more.

CHAPTER XVIII. NEW FRIENDS

When I awoke I was in a bed, and the flames from a big fire lit up the room in which I was lying. I had never seen this room before, nor the people who stood near the bed. There was a man in a gray smock and clogs, and three or four children. One, which I noticed particularly, was a little girl about six years old, with great big eyes that were so expressive they seemed as though they could speak.

I raised myself on my elbow. They all came closer.

"Vitalis?" I asked.

"He is asking for his father," said a girl, who seemed to be the eldest of the children.

"He is not my father; he is my master," I said; "where is he? where's Capi?"

If Vitalis had been my father they perhaps would have broken the news to me gently, but as he was only my master, they thought that they could tell me the truth at once.

They told me that my poor master was dead. The gardener, who lived on the grounds outside of which we had fallen exhausted, had found us early the next morning, when he and his son were starting off with their vegetables and flowers to the markets. They found us lying, huddled together in the snow, with a little covering of their straw over us. Vitalis was already dead, and I should have died but Capi had crept up to my chest and kept my heart warm. They had carried us into the house and I had been placed in one of the children's warm beds.

"And Capi?" I asked, when the gardener stopped talking.

"Capi?"

"Yes, the dog."

"I don't know, he's disappeared."

"He followed the body," said one of the children. "Didn't you see him, Benjamin?"

"Should say I did," answered another boy; "he walked behind the men who carried the stretcher. He kept his head down, and now and again he jumped up on the body, and when they made him get down he moaned and howled something terrible."

Poor Capi! how many times, as an actor, had he not followed Zerbino's funeral. Even the most serious children had been obliged to laugh at his display of grief. The more he moaned, the more they had laughed.

The gardener and his children left me alone. Not knowing quite what to do or what I was going to do, I got up and dressed. My harp had been placed at the foot of the bed upon which I was lying. I passed the strap over my shoulder and went into the room where the family were. I should have to go, but where? While in bed I had not felt very weak, but now I could scarcely stand; I was obliged to hold on to a chair to keep from falling. The odor of the soup was too much for me. I was reminded brutally that I had eaten nothing the night before. I felt faint, and staggering, I dropped into a chair by the fire.

"Don't you feel well, my boy?" asked the gardener.

I told him that I did not feel very well, and I asked him to let me sit by the fire for a little while.

But it was not the heat that I wanted; it was food. I felt weaker as I watched the family take their soup. If I had dared, I would have asked for a bowl, but Vitalis had taught me not to beg. I could not tell them I was hungry. Why? I don't know, quite, unless it was that I could not ask for anything that I was unable to return.

The little girl with the strange look in her eyes, and whose name was Lise, sat opposite to me. Suddenly, she got up from the table and, taking her bowl which was full of soup, she brought it over to me and placed it on my knees. Weakly, for I could no longer speak, I nodded my head to thank her. The father did not give me time to speak even if I had been able.

"Take it, my boy," he said. "What Lise gives is given with a kind heart. There is more if you want more."

If I want more! The bowl of soup was swallowed in a few seconds. When I put down the soup, Lise, who had remained standing before me, heaved a little sigh of content. Then she took my bowl and held it out to her father to have it refilled, and when it was full she brought it to me with such a sweet smile, that in spite of my hunger, I sat staring at her, without thinking to take it from her. The second bowlful disappeared promptly like the first. It was no longer a smile that curved Lise's pretty lips; she burst out laughing.

"Well, my boy," said her father, "you've got an appetite and no mistake."

I was much ashamed, but after a moment I thought it better to confess the truth than to be thought a glutton, so I told them that I had not had any supper the night before.

"And dinner?"

"No dinner, either."

"And your master?"

"He hadn't eaten, either."

"Then he died as much from starvation as from cold."

The hot soup had given me strength. I got up to go.

"Where are you going?" asked the father.

"I don't know."

"Got any friends or relations in Paris?"

"No."

"Where do you live?"

"We hadn't any home. We only got to the city yesterday."

"What are you going to do, then?"

"Play my harp and get a little money."

"In Paris? You had better return to your parents in the country. Where do they live?"

"I haven't any parents. My master bought me from my foster parents. You have been good to me and I thank you with all my heart and, if you like, I'll come back here on Sunday and play my harp while you dance."

While speaking I had walked towards the door, but I had only taken a few steps when Lise, who followed me, took my hand and pointed to my harp.

"You want me to play now?" I asked, smiling at her.

She nodded and clapped her hands.

Although I had no heart to play, I played my prettiest waltz for this little girl. At first she listened with her big, beautiful eyes fixed on me, then she began to keep time with her feet, and very soon was dancing gayly round the kitchen, while her brothers and sisters watched her. Her father was delighted. When the waltz was finished the child came and made me a pretty curtsy. I would have played for her all day, but the father thought she had danced enough so, instead, I sang the Neapolitan song that Vitalis had taught me. Lise stood opposite me, moving her lips as though repeating the words. Then, suddenly, she turned round and threw herself into her father's arms, crying.

"That's enough music," said the father.

"Isn't she a silly?" said the brother named Benjamin, scoffingly; "first she dances, and then she cries!"

"She's not so silly as you!" retorted the elder sister, leaning over the little one affectionately. "She understands...."

While Lise cried on her father's knee, I again strapped my harp to my shoulder, and made for the door.

"Where are you going?" asked the gardener. "Wouldn't you like to stay here and work? It won't be an easy life. You'll have to get up very early in the morning and work hard all day. But you may be sure that you won't have to go through what you did last night. You will have a bed and food and you will have the satisfaction of knowing that you have earned it. And, if you're a good boy, which I think you are, you will be one of the family."

Lise turned round and, through her tears, she looked at me and smiled. I could hardly believe what I heard. I just stared at the gardener. Then Lise jumped off her father's knee and came up and took my hand.

"Well, what do you say, boy?" asked the father.

A family! I should have a family. I should not be alone. The man I had lived with for several years, who had been almost a father to me, was dead, and dear, good Capi, my companion and friend, whom I loved so much, was lost. I had thought that all was over for me, and here was this good man offering to take me into his family. Life would begin again for me. He said he offered me food and lodging, but what meant more to me was this home life which would be mine also. These boys would be my brothers. This pretty little Lise would be my sister. I would no longer be nobody's boy. In my childish dreams I had more than once thought I might find my father and mother, but I had never thought that I should have brothers and sisters! And this was what was being offered to me. I quickly slipped the strap of my harp from off my shoulders.

"There's his reply," said the father, laughing. "I can see by your face how pleased you are; no need for you to say anything. Hang your harp up there on the wall and when you get tired of us you may take it down and go on your way again, but you must do like the swallows, choose your season to start on your flight. Don't go off in the depth of winter."

My new family consisted of the father, whose name was Pierre Acquin, two boys, Alexix and Benjamin, and two girls, Etiennette, the elder, and Lise, the youngest of the family.

Lise was dumb. She was not born dumb, but just before her fourth birthday, through an illness, she had lost the power of speech. This affliction, fortunately, had not impaired her intelligence; quite the contrary, her intelligence was developed to an extraordinary degree. She seemed to understand everything. And her sweet, pretty ways made her adored by the family.

Since the mother had died, Etiennette had been mother to the family. She had left school early to stay at home to cook and sew and clean the house for her father and brothers. They had quite forgotten that she was the daughter, the sister; they were so accustomed to seeing her doing the work of a servant, for she seldom went out and was never angry. Carrying Lise in her arms, dragging Benny by the hand, getting up at daybreak to get her father's breakfast, going to bed late after washing the dishes, she had not had time to be a child. At fourteen years her face was serious and sad. It was not the face of a little girl.

Five minutes after I had hung my harp on the wall, I was telling them all what had happened the night before, how we had hoped to sleep on the race-course, when I heard a scratching on the door which opened onto the garden; then there was a plaintive whine.

"Capi! Capi!" I cried, jumping up quickly.

But Lise was before me; she had already opened the door.

Capi sprang upon me. I took him in my arms; with little howls of joy, and his whole body trembling, he licked my face.

"And Capi?..." I asked.

My question was understood.

"Well, Capi will remain with you, of course," said the father.

As though he knew what we were saying, the dog jumped to the ground and putting his paw straight on his heart, he bowed. It made the children laugh, especially Lise, and to amuse them I wanted Capi to perform some of his tricks, but he had no wish to obey me; he jumped on my knee and commenced to lick my face; then he sprung down and began to drag me by the sleeve of my coat.

"He wants me to go out."

"To take you to your master."

The police, who had taken Vitalis away, had said that they wished to question me when I was better. It was very uncertain as to when they would come, and I was anxious to have news. Perhaps Vitalis was not dead as they had thought. Perhaps there was still a spark of life left in my master's body.

Upon seeing my anxiety, Monsieur Acquin offered to take me to the police station. When we arrived there I was questioned at length, but I would give no information until they had declared that poor Vitalis was really dead. Then I told them what I knew. It was very little. Of myself I was able to say that I had no parents and that Vitalis had hired me for a sum of money, which he had paid in advance to my foster mother's husband.

"And now?..." inquired the commissioner.

"We are going to take care of him," interrupted my new friend; "that is, if you will let us."

The commissioner was willing to confide me to his care and complimented him upon his kind act.

It is not easy for a child to hide much from a police officer who knows his business. They very soon trap persons into telling what they wish to hide. This was so in my case. The commissioner had quickly gleaned from me all about Garofoli.

"There is nothing to do but to take him to this chap, Garofoli," he said to one of his men. "Once in the street he mentions, he will soon recognize the house. You can go up with him and question the man."

The three of us started. As the officer had said, we found the street and the house. We went up to the fourth floor. I did not see Mattia. He had probably been taken off to the hospital. Upon seeing the officer and recognizing me, Garofoli paled and looked frightened, but he soon recovered himself when he learned that they had only come to question him about Vitalis.

"So the old fellow is dead?" he said.

"You know him? Well, tell us all you can about him."

"There is not much to tell. His name was not Vitalis. He was Carlo Balzini, and if you had lived thirty-five or forty years ago in Italy, that name alone would tell you all you want to know. Carlo Balzini was the greatest singer of the day. He sang in Naples, Rome, Milan, Venice, Florence, London and Paris. Then came the time when he lost his magnificent voice, and as he could not be the greatest of singers, he would not dim his fame by singing on cheaper stages unworthy of his great reputation. Instead he preferred to hide himself from the world and from all who had known him in his triumph. Yet he had to live. He tried several professions, but could not succeed, then finally he took to training dogs. But in his poverty he was still very proud and he would have died of shame if the public could have known that the brilliant Carlo Balzini had sunk to the depths he had. It was just a matter of chance that I learned his secret."

Poor Carlo Balzini; dear, dear Vitalis!

CHAPTER XIX. DISASTER

Vitalis had to be buried the next day, and M. Acquin promised to take me to the funeral. But the next day I could not rise from my bed, for in the night I was taken very ill. My chest seemed to burn like poor little Pretty-Heart's after he had spent the night in the tree. The doctor was called in. I had pneumonia. The doctor wanted me sent to the hospital, but the family would not hear of it. It was during this illness that I learned to appreciate Etiennette's goodness. She devoted herself to nursing me. How good and kind she was during that terrible sickness. When she was obliged to leave me to attend to her household duties, Lise took her place, and many times in my delirium I saw little Lise sitting at the foot of my bed with her big eyes fixed on me anxiously. In my delirium I thought that she was my guardian angel, and I would speak to her and tell her of all my hopes and desires. It was from this time that I began to consider her as something ideal, as a different being from the other people I met. It seemed surprising that she could live in our life; in my boyish imagination I could picture her flying away with big white wings to a more beautiful world.

I was ill for a very long time. At night, when I was almost suffocating, I had to have some one to sit up with me; then Alexix and Benny would take turns. At last I was convalescent, and then it was Lise who replaced Etiennette and walked with me down by the river. Of course during these walks she could not talk, but strange to say we had no need of words. We seemed to understand each other so well without talking. Then came the day when I was strong enough to work with the others in the garden. I had been impatient to commence, for I wanted to do something for my kind friends who had done so much for me.

As I was still weak, the task that was given to me was in proportion to my strength. Every morning after the frost had passed, I had to lift the glass frames and at night, before it got chilly, I had to close them again. During the day I had to shade the wall flowers with straw coverings to protect them from the sun. This was not difficult to do, but it took all my time, for I had several hundred glasses to move twice daily.

Days and months passed. I was very happy. Sometimes I thought that I was too happy, it could not last. M. Acquin was considered one of the cleverest florists round about Paris. After the wall flower season was over other flowers replaced them.

For many weeks we had been working very hard, as the season promised to be an especially good one. We had not even taken a rest on Sunday, but as all the flowers were now perfect and ready for the approaching season, it was decided that, for a reward, we were all to go and have dinner on Sunday, August 5th, with one of M. Acquin's friends, who was also a florist. Capi was to be one of the party. We were to work until four o'clock, and when all was finished we were to lock the gates and go to Arcueil. Supper was for six o'clock. After supper we were to come home at once, so as not to be late in getting to bed, as Monday morning we had to be up bright and early, ready for work. A few minutes before four we were all ready.

"Come on, all of you," cried M. Acquin gayly. "I'm going to lock the gates."

"Come, Capi."

Taking Lise by the hand, I began to run with her; Capi jumped around us, barking. We were all dressed up in our best, and looking forward to a good dinner. Some people turned round to watch us as we passed. I don't know what I looked like, but Lise in her blue dress and white shoes was the prettiest little girl that one could see. Time passed quickly.

We were having dinner out of doors when, just as we had finished, one of us remarked how dark it was getting. Clouds were gathering quickly in the sky.

"Children, we must go home," said M. Acquin, "there's going to be a storm."

"Go, already!" came the chorus.

"If the wind rises, all the glasses will be upset."

We all knew the value of those glass frames and what they mean to a florist. It would be terrible for us if the wind broke ours.

"I'll hurry ahead with Benny and Alexix," the father said. "Remi can come on with Etiennette and Lise."

They rushed off. Etiennette and I followed more slowly with Lise. No one laughed now. The sky grew darker. The storm was coming quickly. Clouds of dust swirled around us; we had to turn our backs and cover our eyes with our hands, for the dust blinded us. There was a streak of lightning across the sky, then came a heavy clap of thunder.

Etiennette and I had taken Lise by the hands; we were trying to drag her along faster, but she could scarcely keep up with us. Would the father, Benny and Alexix get home before the storm broke? If they were only in time to close the glass cases so that the wind could not get under them and upset them! The thunder increased; the clouds were so heavy that it seemed almost night. Then suddenly there was a downpour of hail, the stones struck us in the face, and we had to race to take shelter under a big gateway.

In a minute the road was covered with white, like in winter. The hailstones were as large as pigeon eggs; as they fell they made a deafening sound, and every now and again we could hear the crash of broken glass. With the hailstones, as they slid from the roofs to the street, fell all sorts of things, pieces of slate, chimney pots, tiles, etc.

"Oh, the glass frames!" cried Etiennette.

I had the same thought.

"Even if they get there before the hail, they will never have time to cover the glasses with straw. Everything will be ruined."

"They say that hail only falls in places," I said, trying to hope still.

"Oh, this is too near home for us to escape. If it falls on the garden the same as here, poor father will be ruined. And he counted so much on those flowers, he needs the money so badly."

I had heard that the glass frames cost as much as 1800 francs a hundred, and I knew what a disaster it would be if the hail broke our five or six hundred, without counting the plants and the conservatories. I would like to have questioned Etiennette, but we could scarcely hear each other speak, and she did not seem disposed to talk. She looked at the hail falling with a hopeless expression, like a person would look upon his house burning.

The hurricane lasted but a short while; it stopped as suddenly as it had commenced. It lasted perhaps six minutes. The clouds swept over Paris and we were able to leave our shelter. The hailstones were thick on the ground. Lise could not walk in them in her thin shoes, so I took her on my back and carried her. Her pretty face, which was so bright when going to the party, was now grief-stricken and the tears rolled down her cheeks.

Before long we reached the house. The big gates were open and we went quickly into the garden. What a sight met our eyes! All the glass frames were smashed to atoms. Flowers, pieces of glass and hailstones were all heaped together in our once beautiful garden. Everything was shattered!

Where was the father?

We searched for him. Last of all we found him in the big conservatory, of which every pane of glass was broken. He was seated on a wheelbarrow in the midst of the débris which covered the ground. Alexix and Benjamin stood beside him silently.

"My children, my poor little ones!" he cried, when we all were there.

He took Lise in his arms and began to sob. He said nothing more. What could he have said? It was a terrible catastrophe, but the consequences were still more terrible. I soon learned this from Etiennette.

Ten years ago their father had bought the garden and had built the house himself. The man who had sold him the ground had also lent him the money to buy the necessary materials required by a florist. The amount was payable in yearly payments for fifteen years. The man was only waiting for an occasion when the florist would be late in payment to take back the ground, house, material; keeping, of course, the ten-year payments that he had already received.

This was a speculation on the man's part, for he had hoped that before the fifteen years expired there would come a day when the florist would be unable to meet his notes. This day had come at last! Now what was going to happen?

We were not left long in doubt. The day after the notes fell due—this sum which was to have been paid from the sale of his season's flowers—a gentleman dressed all in black came to the house and handed us a stamped paper. It was the process server. He came often; so many times that he soon began to know us by name.

"How do you do, Mlle. Etiennette? Hello, Remi; hello, Alexix!"

And he handed us his stamped paper smilingly, as though we were friends. The father did not stay in the house. He was always out. He never told us where he went. Probably he went to call on business men, or he might have been at court.

What would the result be? A part of the winter passed. As we were unable to repair the conservatories and renew the glass frames, we cultivated vegetables and hardier flowers that did not demand shelter. They were not very productive, but at least it was something, and it was work for us. One evening the father returned home more depressed than usual.

"Children," he said, "it is all over."

I was about to leave the room, for I felt that he had something serious to say to his children. He signed to me to stop.

"You are one of the family, Remi," he said sadly, "and although you are not very old, you know what trouble is. Children, I am going to leave you."

There was a cry on all sides.

Lise flung her arms round her father's neck. He held her very tight.

"Ah, it's hard to leave you, dear children," he said, "but the courts have ordered me to pay, and as I have no money, everything here has to be sold, and as that is not enough, I have to go to prison for five years. As I am not able to pay with my money, I have to pay with my liberty."

We all began to cry.

"Yes, it's sad," he continued brokenly, "but a man can't do anything against the law. My attorney says that it used to be worse than it is."

There was a tearful silence.

"This is what I have decided is the best thing to do," continued the father. "Remi, who is the best scholar, will write to my sister Catherine and explain the matter to her and ask her to come to us. Aunt Catherine has plenty of common sense and she will be able to decide what should be done for the best."

It was the first time that I had written a letter, and this was a very painful one, but we still had a ray of hope. We were very ignorant children and the fact that Aunt Catherine was coming, and that she was practical, made us hope that everything could be made right. But she did not come as soon as we had hoped. A few days later the father had just left the house to call on one of his friends, when he met the police face to face coming for him. He returned to the house with them; he was very pale; he had come to say good-by to his children.

"Don't be so downcast, man," said one of them who had come to take him; "to be in prison for debt is not so dreadful as you seem to think. You'll find some very good fellows there."

I went to fetch the two boys, who were in the garden. Little Lise was sobbing; one of the men stooped down and whispered something in her ear, but I did not hear what he said.

The parting was over very quickly. M. Acquin caught Lise up in his arms and kissed her again and again, then he put her down, but she clung to his hand. Then he kissed Etiennette, Alexix and Benny and gave Lise into her sister's care. I stood a little apart, but he came to me and kissed me affectionately, just like the others, and then they took him away. We all stood in the middle of the kitchen crying; not one of us had a word to say.

Aunt Catherine arrived an hour later. We were still crying bitterly. For a country woman who had no education or money, the responsibility that had fallen upon her was heavy. A family of destitute children, the eldest not yet sixteen, the youngest a dumb girl. Aunt Catherine had been a nurse in a lawyer's family; she at once called upon this man to ask his advice, and it was he who decided our fate. When she returned from the lawyer's, she told us what had been arranged. Lise was to go and live with her. Alexix was to go to an uncle at Varses, Benny to another uncle, who was a florist at Saint-Quentin, and Etiennette to an aunt who lived at the seashore.

I listened to these plans, waiting until they came to me. When Aunt Catherine ceased speaking, and I had not been mentioned, I said, "And me?..."

"Why, you don't belong to the family."

"I'll work for you."

"You're not one of the family."

"Ask Alexix and Benny if I can't work, and I like work."

"And soup, also, eh?"

"But he's one of the family; yes, aunt, he's one of the family," came from all sides.

Lise came forwards and clasped her hands before her aunt with an expression that said more than words.

"Poor mite," said Aunt Catherine, "I know you'd like him to come and live with us, but we can't always get what we want. You're my niece, and if my man makes a face when I take you home, all I've to tell him is that you're a relation, and I'm going to have you with me. It will be like that with your other uncles and aunts. They will take a relation, but not strangers."

I felt there was nothing to say. What she said was only too true. I was not one of the family. I could claim nothing, ask nothing; that would be begging. And yet I loved them all and they all loved me. Aunt Catherine sent us to bed, after telling us that we were to be parted the next day.

Scarcely had we got upstairs than they all crowded round me. Lise clung to me, crying. Then I knew, that in spite of their grief at parting from one another, it was of me that they thought; they pitied me because I was alone. I felt, indeed, then that I was their brother. Suddenly an idea came to me.

"Listen," I said; "even if your aunts and uncles don't want me, I can see that you consider me one of the family."

"Yes, yes," they all cried.

Lise, who could not speak, just squeezed my hand and looked up at me with her big, beautiful eyes.

"Well, I'm a brother, and I'll prove it," I said stoutly.

"There's a job with Pernuit; shall I go over and speak to him to-morrow?" asked Etiennette.

"I don't want a job. If I take a job I shall have to stay in Paris, and I shan't see you again. I'm going to put on my sheepskin and take my harp, and go first to one place and then to another where you are all going to live. I shall see you all one after the other, and I'll carry the news from one to the other, so you'll all be in touch. I haven't forgotten my songs nor my dance music, and I'll get enough money to live."

Every face beamed. I was glad they were so pleased with my idea. For a long time we talked, then Etiennette made each one go to bed, but no one slept much that night, I least of all. The next day at daybreak Lise took me into the garden.

"You want to speak to me?" I asked.

She nodded her head.

"You are unhappy because we are going to be parted? You need not tell me; I can see it in your eyes, and I am unhappy, too."

She made a sign that it was something else she wanted to say.

"In fifteen days I shall be at Dreuzy, where you are going to live."

She shook her head.

"You don't want me to go to Dreuzy?"

In order for us to understand each other, I made more progress by questioning. She replied either with a nod or a shake of the head. She told me that she wanted to see me at Dreuzy, but pointing her finger in three directions, she made me understand that I must first go and see her brothers and sister.

"You want me first to go to Varses, then Esnandes and then Saint-Quentin?"

She smiled and nodded, pleased that I understood.

"Why?"

Then with her lips and hands, and above all with her eyes, she explained to me why she wished this. She wanted me to go and see her sister and brothers first, so that when I reached Dreuzy I could tell her news of them. They had to start at eight o'clock, and Aunt Catherine had ordered a cab to take them, first of all to the prison to say good-by to their father, and then each, with their baggage, to the different depots where they had to take their trains. At seven o'clock Etiennette, in her turn, took me in the garden.

"I want to give you a little keepsake, Remi," she said. "Take this little case; my godfather gave it to me. You'll find thread, needles and scissors in it; when you are tramping along the roads you'll need them, for I shan't be there to put a patch on your clothes, nor sew a button on. When you use my scissors, think of us all."

While Etiennette was speaking to me, Alexix loitered near; when she left me to return to the house, he came up.

"Say, Remi," he began, "I've got two five franc pieces. Take one; I'll be so pleased if you will."

Of the five of us, Alexix was the only one who cared very much for money. We always made fun of his greed; he saved up sou by sou, counting his hoard continually, he was always very proud when he had a brand new piece. His offer touched me to the heart; I wanted to refuse, but he insisted, and slipped a shiny silver piece into my hand. I knew that his friendship for me must be very strong if he were willing to share his treasure with me.

Benjamin, neither, had forgotten me; he also wanted to give me a present. He gave me his knife, and in exchange he exacted a sou, because he said "a knife cuts friendship."

The time passed quickly. The moment had come for us to part. As the cab was drawing up at the house, Lise again made a sign for me to follow her into the garden.

"Lise!" called her aunt.

She made no reply, but ran quickly down the path. She stopped at a big Bengal rose tree and cut off a branch, then, turning to me, she divided the stalk in two; there was a rose on either side. The language of the lips is a small thing compared with the language of the eyes; how cold and empty are words compared with looks!

"Lise! Lise!" cried her aunt.

The baggage was already in the cab. I took down my harp and called to Capi. At the sight of my old suit, he jumped and barked with joy. He loved his liberty on the high roads more than being closed up in the garden. They all got into the cab. I lifted Lise onto her aunt's lap. I stood there half dazed, then the aunt gently pushed me away and closed the door. They were off.

Through a mist I watched Lise as she leaned out of the window waving her hand to me, then the cab sharply turned the corner of the street and all I could see was a cloud of dust.

Leaning on my harp, with Capi sprawling at my feet, I stayed there looking absently down the street. A neighbor, who had been asked to lock up the house and keep the key, called to me:

"Are you going to stay there all day?"

"No, I'm off now."

"Where are you going?"

"Straight ahead."

"If you'd like to stay," he said, perhaps out of pity, "I'll keep you, but I can't pay you, because you're not very strong. Later I might give you something."

I thanked him, but said no.

"Well, as you like; I was only thinking for your own good. Good-by and good luck!"

He went away. The cab had gone, the house was locked up.

I turned away from the home where I had lived for two years, and where I had hoped always to live. The sky was clear, the weather warm, very different from the icy night when poor Vitalis and I had fallen exhausted by the wall.

So these two years had only been a halt. I must go on my way again. But the stay had done me good. It had given me strength and I had made dear friends. I was not now alone in the world, and I had an object in life, to be useful and give pleasure to those I loved.

CHAPTER XX. MATTIA

The world was before me; I could go where I liked, north, south, east or west. I was my own master. How many children there are who say to themselves, "If I could only do as I liked, ... if I were my own master!" And how impatiently they look forward to this day when they can do the things they have longed to do, ... often very foolish things. Between these children and myself there was a vast difference. When they do anything foolish there is a hand stretched out, and they are picked up if they fall. If I fell I should go down, down, down, and I might not be able to pick myself up again. I was afraid. I knew the dangers that beset me.

Before beginning my wanderings I wanted to see the man who had been so good to me. Aunt Catherine had not wished to take me with them when they had gone to say good-by, but I felt that, at least, I could go and see him now that I was alone.

I did not dare walk across Paris with Capi running at my heels. I was afraid that a policeman would stop and question me. My greatest fear was the police. I tied a string to Capi's collar. I was loath to do this, for I knew that it hurt his self-respect, but it had to be, and in this humiliating manner I dragged him along to the Clichy prison, where M. Acquin was serving his sentence. For some moments I looked in a sort of fear at the great prison doors, thinking that perhaps once they had closed on me I might not be able to get out again. I found it more difficult than I had thought to get into a prison, but I would not be discouraged. After much waiting and questioning, I was finally permitted to see M. Acquin.

"Ah, Remi, boy, I was expecting you," he said, as I entered the room where visitors were allowed to see the prisoners. "I scolded Aunt Catherine for not bringing you with the others."

I brightened up at these words.

"The children tell me that you are going on your wanderings again. Have you forgotten that you almost died of cold and hunger, my boy?"

"No, I've not forgotten that."

"You were not alone then; you had some one to look after you. At your age I don't think it is right to go tramping across the country alone."

"You don't want me to bring you news of your children, then?" I asked.

"They told me that you were going to see them all, one after the other," he replied, "but I am not thinking of us when I ask you to give up this wandering life."

"And if I do what you ask I should be thinking of myself and not of you ... of Lise."

This time he looked at me for several seconds, then he suddenly took both my hands.

"You have a heart, and I will not say another word, my boy. God will take care of you."

I threw my arms round his neck; the time had come for me to say good-by. For some moments he held me in silence, then suddenly he felt in his vest pocket and pulled out a large silver watch.

"Here, boy, take this," he said. "I want you to have it as a keepsake. It isn't of much value; if it had been I'd have sold it. It doesn't keep good time, either. When anything is wrong with it, just give it a thump. It is all I have."

I wanted to refuse such a beautiful present, but he forced it into my closed hands.

"Oh, I don't need to know the time," he said sadly; "the hours pass slowly enough. I should die counting them. Good-by, little Remi; always remember to be a good boy."

I was very unhappy. How good he had been to me! I lingered round the prison doors for a long time after I had left him. I might have stayed there perhaps until night if I had not suddenly touched a hard round object in my pocket. My watch!

All my grief was forgotten for the moment. My watch! My very own watch by which I could tell the time. I pulled it out to see the hour. Midday! It was a matter of small importance whether it was midday, ten o'clock or two o'clock. Yet, I was very pleased that it was midday. It would have been hard to say why, but such was the case. I knew that it was midday; my watch told me so. What an affair! It seemed to me that a watch was a sort of confidential friend of whom one could ask advice and to whom one could talk.

"Friend watch, what's the time?"

"Just twelve o'clock, my dear Remi."

"Really! Then it's time for me to do this or that. A good thing you reminded me; if you had not, I should have forgotten."

In my joy I had not noticed that Capi was almost as pleased as myself. He pulled me by the leg of my trousers and barked several times. As he continued to bark, I was forced to bestow some attention upon him.

"What do you want, Capi?" I asked.

He looked at me, but I failed to understand him. He waited some moments, then came and stood up against me, putting his paws on the pocket where I had placed my watch. He wanted to know the time to tell the "distinguished audience," like in the days when he had worked with Vitalis.

I showed the watch to him. He looked at it for some time, as though trying to remember, then, wagging his tail, he barked twelve times. He had not forgotten! We could earn money with my watch! That was something I had not counted upon.

Forward march, children!

I took one last look at the prison, behind the walls of which little Lise's father was shut, then went on my way.

The thing I needed most of all was a map of France. Knowing that in the book stalls on the quays I could procure one, I wended my way towards the river. At last I found one that was so yellow that the man let me have it for fifteen sous.

I was able to leave Paris now, and I decided to do so at once. I had a choice between two roads. I chose the road to Fontainebleau. As I went up the Rue Mouffetard, a host of memories rushed upon me. Garofoli! Mattia! Ricardo! the soup pot fastened with a padlock, the whip, and Vitalis, my poor, good master, who had died because he would not rent me to the *padrone*. As I passed the church I saw a little boy leaning against the wall, and I thought I recognized him. Surely it was Mattia, the boy with the big head, the great eyes and the soft, resigned look. But then he had not grown one inch! I went nearer to see better. Yes, it was Mattia. He recognised me. His pale face broke into a smile.

"Ah, it's you," he said. "You came to Garofoli's a long time ago with an old man with a white beard, just before I went to the hospital. Ah! how I used to suffer with my head then."

"Is Garofoli still your master?"

He glanced round before replying, then lowering his voice he said: "Garofoli is in prison. They took him because he beat Orlando to death."

I was shocked at this. I was pleased to hear that they had put Garofoli in prison, and for the first time I thought the prisons, which inspired me with so much horror, had their use.

"And the other boys?" I asked.

"Oh, I don't know. I was not there when Garofoli was arrested. When I came out of the hospital, Garofoli, seeing that it was no good to beat me 'cause I got ill, wanted to get rid of me, so he sold me for two years to the Gassot Circus. They paid him in advance. D'ye know the Gassot Circus? No? Well, it's not much of a circus, but it's a circus all the same. They wanted a child for dislocation, and Garofoli sold me to Mr. Gassot. I stayed with him until last Monday, when he sent me off because my head was too big to go into the box. After leaving the circus I went back to find Garofoli, but the place was all shut up, and a neighbor told me what had happened. Now that Garofoli's in prison I don't know where to go.

"And I haven't any money," he added, "and I haven't had a bite to eat since yesterday."

I was not rich, but I had enough to give something to poor Mattia. How I would have blessed one who would have given me a crust of bread when I was wandering round Toulouse, famished like Mattia now.

"Stay here until I come back," I said.

I ran to a bakery at the corner of the street and soon returned with a roll, which I offered him. He devoured it in a moment.

"Now," I said, "what do you want to do?"

"I don't know. I was trying to sell my violin when you spoke to me, and I would have sold it before, if I hadn't hated to part with it. My violin is all I have and when I'm sad, I find a spot where I can be alone and play to myself. Then I see all sorts of beautiful things in the sky, more beautiful than in a dream."

"Why don't you play your violin in the streets?"

"I did, but I didn't get anything."

How well I knew what it was to play and not get a coin.

"What are you doing?" he asked.

I don't know why, but on the spur of the moment, I put up a ridiculous bluff.

"I'm the boss of a company," I said proudly.

It was true, but the truth was very near a falsehood. My "company" only consisted of Capi.

"Oh, will you...." began Mattia.

"What?"

"Take me in your company?"

Not wishing to deceive him, I smiled and pointed to Capi.

"But that is all the company I have," I said.

"Well, what does that matter? I'll be another. Oh, please don't leave me; I shall die of hunger!"

Die of hunger! His words seemed to strike my very heart. I knew what it would be to die of hunger.

"I can play the violin, and I can dislocate," said Mattia breathlessly. "I can dance on the tight rope, I can sing, I'll do anything you like. I'll be your servant; I'll obey you. I don't ask for money; food only. And if I do badly, you can beat me, that is understood. All that I ask is, that you won't strike me on the head; that also must be understood, because my head is very sore since Garofoli beat me so much on it."

I felt like crying, to hear poor little Mattia speak so. How could I refuse to take him with me. Die of hunger! But with me there was also a chance that he might die of hunger. I told him so, but he would not listen to me.

"No, no," he said; "when there are two, one doesn't starve, because one helps the other. The one who has it gives to the one who hasn't."

I hesitated no longer. As I had some I must help him.

"Well, then, it's understood," I said.

Instantly he took my hand and actually kissed it in gratitude.

"Come with me," I said; "not as a servant, Mattia, but as my chum."

Shouldering my harp, I gave the signal:

"Forward, march!"

At the end of a quarter of an hour, we had left Paris behind.

I left Paris by this route because I wanted to see Mother Barberin. How many times I had wanted to write to her and tell her that I thought of her, and that I loved her with all my heart, but the horrible fear of Barberin restrained me. If Barberin found me by means of my letter, he might take me and sell me to another man. He probably had the right to do so. I preferred that Mother Barberin should think that I was an ungrateful boy rather than run the risk of falling into Barberin's power.

But though I dared not write, now that I was free, I could go and see her. Since I had taken Mattia into my "company" I had made up my mind to do so, for it seemed to me that it could easily be arranged. I would send him ahead and he could find out if she were alone, and then tell her that I was not far off, and was only waiting to know if it were safe for me to come and see her. Then, if Barberin were in the village, Mattia could ask her to come to some safe spot where I could meet her.

I tramped along in silence, working out this plan. Mattia trudged by my side; he also seemed to be thinking deeply. The idea came to me to show off my possessions to Mattia. Unfastening my bag, I proudly spread out my riches on the grass. I had three cotton shirts, three pairs of socks, five handkerchiefs, all in good condition, and one pair of shoes, slightly used.

Mattia was awestruck.

"And you, what have you got?" I asked.

"I've only got my violin."

"Well, we'll go shares, now we're chums; you'll have two shirts, two pairs of socks, and three handkerchiefs, but as it's only fair that we go shares in everything, you'll carry my bag for one hour and I'll carry it for another."

Mattia wanted to refuse the things, but as I had quickly fallen into the habit of commanding, which, I must say I found very pleasant, I told him to be silent. I had laid out Etiennette's needle case and also a little box in which I had placed Lise's rose. Mattia wanted to open this box, but I would not let him. I put it back in my bag without even lifting the lid.

"If you want to please me," I said, "you will never touch this box ... it's a present."

"I promise never to touch it," he said solemnly.

Since I had again donned my sheepskin and my harp there was one thing which caused me serious thought. That was my trousers. It seemed to me that an artist ought not to wear long trousers; to appear in public an artist should have short trousers with stockings coming over them, laced over and over with colored ribbons. Trousers were all right for a gardener, but now ... I was an artist! Yes, I must wear knickers. I quickly took the scissors from Etiennette's work-case.

"While I arrange my trousers," I said to Mattia, "you ought to show me how you play the violin."

"Oh, I'd like to."

He began to play, while I boldly stuck the points of my scissors into my trousers a little above the knee. I commenced to cut the cloth.

Yet, however, they were a beautiful pair of gray cloth trousers, with vest and coat to match, and I had been so proud of them when M. Acquin had given them to me, but I did not consider that I was spoiling them by shortening them, quite the contrary.

At first I scarcely listened to Mattia; I was too busy cutting my trousers, but soon I stopped manipulating the scissors and became all ears. Mattia played almost as well as Vitalis.

"Who taught you the violin?" I asked, clapping my hands.

"No one, I studied alone."

"Hasn't any one explained to you anything about music?"

"No, I play just what I hear."

"I'll teach you, I will."

"You know everything, then?"

"Well so I ought to, if I'm the director."

I wanted to show Mattia that I also was a musician. I took my harp and, wishing to impress him, I sang the famous canzonette. Then, as it should be between artists, he complimented me. He had great talent. We were worthy of each other.

I buckled my knapsack and Mattia, in turn, hoisted it on his shoulders.

We had to stop at the first village to give a performance. It was to be the "First appearance of Remi's Company."

"Teach me your song," said Mattia; "we'll sing it together, and I'll soon be able to accompany you on the violin. That'll be pretty."

Certainly, that would be pretty, and the "distinguished audience" would have a heart of stone if they were not generous in their offerings.

At the first village that we came to we had to pass before a large farm gate; looking in we saw a crowd of people dressed up in their best; some of them carried bouquets tied with satin streamers. It was a wedding. I thought that perhaps these people might like a little music and dance, so I went into the farmyard and suggested it to the first person that I met. This was a big, good-natured looking man with a red face; he wore a tall white collar and a Prince Albert coat. He did not reply to my question, but turning to the guests, he put his two fingers in his mouth and gave such a shrill whistle that it frightened Capi.

"Say, you all," he cried, "what about a little music; the musicians have arrived."

"Oh, music! music!" came the chorus.

"Take your places for the quadrilles!"

The dancers soon gathered in the middle of the yard. Mattia and I took our places up in a wagon.

"Can you play the quadrilles?" I whispered anxiously.

"Yes."

He struck a few notes on his violin. By luck I knew the air. We were saved. Although Mattia and I had never played together, we did not do badly. It is true the people had not much ear for music.

"Can one of you play the cornet?" asked the big man with the red face.

"I can," said Mattia, "but I haven't the instrument with me."

"I'll go and find one; the violin's pretty, but it's squeaky."

I found that day that Mattia could play everything. We played until night, without stopping. It did not matter for me, but poor Mattia was very weak. From time to time I saw him turn pale as though he felt ill, yet he continued to play, blowing with all his might. Fortunately, I was not the only one who saw that he was ill; the bride remarked it also.

"That's enough," she said; "that little chap is tired out. Now all hands to your pockets for the musicians!"

I threw my cap to Capi, who caught it in his jaws.

"Give your offerings to our secretary, if you please," I said.

They applauded, and were delighted at the manner in which Capi bowed. They gave generously; the husband was the last, and he dropped a five franc piece in the cap. The cap was full of silver coins. What a fortune!

We were invited to supper, and they gave us a place to sleep in the hay loft. The next day when we left this hospitable farm we had a capital of twenty-eight francs!

"I owe this to you, Mattia," I said, after we had counted it; "I could not have made an orchestra all alone."

With twenty-eight francs in our pockets we were rich. When we reached Corbeil I could very well afford to buy a few things that I considered indispensable: first, a cornet, which would cost three francs at a second-hand shop, then some red ribbons for our stockings and, lastly, another knapsack. It would be easier to carry a small bag all the time than a heavy one in turns.

"A boss like you, who doesn't beat one, is too good," said Mattia, laughing happily from time to time.

Our prosperous state of affairs made me decide to set out for Mother Barberin's as soon as possible. I could take her a present. I was rich now. There was something that, more than anything else, would make her happy, not only now, but in her old age—a cow that would replace poor Rousette. How happy she would be if I gave her a cow, and how proud I should be. Before arriving at Chavanon I would buy a cow and Mattia would lead it by a rope, right into Mother Barberin's yard.

Mattia would say to her: "Here is a cow I've brought you."

"A cow!" she would say; "you've made a mistake, my boy," and she would sigh.

"No, I haven't," Mattia would answer; "you're Mother Barberin of Chevanon, aren't you? Well, the prince (like in fairy tales) has sent you this as a present."

"What prince?"

Then I would appear and take her in my arms, and after we had hugged each other we would make some pancakes and apple fritters which would be eaten by the three of us and not by Barberin, as on that Shrove Tuesday when he had returned to upset our frying pan and put our butter in his onion soup. What a beautiful dream! But to realize it we must first buy the cow!

How much would a cow cost? I had not the slightest idea; a great deal probably, but still.... I did not want a very big cow. Because the fatter the cow the higher the price, and then the bigger the cow the more nourishment it would require, and I did not want my present to be a source of inconvenience to Mother Barberin. The essential, for the moment, was to find out the price of cows or, rather, of a cow of the kind that I wanted. Fortunately, that was not difficult for we often met many farmers and cattle dealers at the different villages where we stopped. I put the question to the first I met at the inn that day.

He burst out laughing and gave a bang on the table. Then he called the landlady.

"This little musician wants to know how much a cow costs, not a very large one, but a very healthy one that'll give plenty of milk!"

Every one laughed. I didn't care, though.

"Yes, she must give good milk and not eat too much," I said.

"And she mustn't mind being led along the lanes by a halter."

When he had had his laugh, he was quite willing to enter a discussion with me, and to take the matter seriously. He had just the very thing, a nice cow which gave delicious milk—real cream!—and she hardly ate anything. If I would put down fifty écus, the cow was mine. Although I had had trouble in making him talk at first, once he commenced it was difficult to stop him. Finally, we were able to retire for the night, and I dreamed of all I had learned from him.

Fifty écus; that was one hundred and fifty francs! I had nothing like that great sum. Perhaps if our luck still continued I could, if I saved sou by sou, get together the hundred and fifty francs. But it would take time. In that case we should have to go, first of all, to Varses and see Benny and give all the performances that we could on our way. And then on our return we would have the money and we would go to Chavanon and act the fairy tale, "The Prince's Cow."

I told Mattia of my plan and he raised no objections.

CHAPTER XXI. MEETING OLD FRIENDS

It took us nearly three months to do this journey, but when at last we reached the outskirts of Varses we found that we had indeed employed our time well. In my leather purse I now had one hundred and twenty-eight francs. We were only short of twenty-two francs to buy Mother Barberin's cow.

Mattia was almost as pleased as I, and he was very proud that he had contributed his part to such a sum. His part was great, for I am sure that without him, Capi and I could not have collected anything like the sum of one hundred and twenty-eight francs! From Varses to Chavanon we could easily gain the twenty-two francs that we were short.

It was three o'clock in the afternoon when we arrived at Varses and a radiant sun shone in the clear sky, but the nearer we got to the town the darker became the atmosphere. Between the sky and the earth hung a cloud of smoke.

I knew that Alexix's uncle was a miner at Varses, but I did not know whether he lived in the town itself or outside. I simply knew that he worked in a mine called the "Truyère."

Upon entering the town I asked where this mine was situated, and I was directed to the left bank of the river Divonne, in a little dale, traversed by a ravine, after which the mine had been named. This dale is as unattractive as the town.

At the office they told us where Uncle Gaspard, Alexix's uncle, lived. It was in a winding street, which led from the hill to the river, at a little distance from the mine.

When we reached the house, a woman who was leaning up against the door talking to two or three neighbors told me that Gaspard, the miner, would not be back until six o'clock.

"What do you want of him?" she asked.

"I want to see Alexix, his nephew."

"Oh? you're Remi?" she said. "Alexix has spoken of you. He's been expecting you. Who's that boy?" She pointed to Mattia.

"He's my friend."

This woman was Alexix's aunt. I thought she would ask us to go in and rest, for we were very dusty and tired, but she simply repeated that if I would return at six o'clock I could see Alexix, who was then at the mine. I had not the heart to ask for what was not offered. I thanked her and went into the town to find a baker, to get something to eat. I was ashamed of this reception, for I felt that Mattia would wonder what it meant. Why should we have tramped so many miles for this.

It seemed to me that Mattia would have a poor idea of my friends, and that when I should speak to him of Lise he would not listen to me with the same interest. And I wanted him very much to like Lise. The cold welcome that the aunt had given us did not encourage me to return to the house, so at a little before six o'clock, Mattia, Capi, and I went to the entrance of the mine to wait for Alexix.

We had been told by which gallery the miners would come out, and a little after six we began to see in the dark shadows of the gallery some tiny lights which gradually became larger. The miners, with lamp in hand, were coming up into the day, their work finished. They came on slowly, with heavy gait, as though they suffered in the knees. I understood how this was later, when I myself had gone over the staircases and ladders which led to the last level. Their faces were as black as chimney sweeps; their clothes and hats covered with coal dust. Each man entered the lamplighter's cabin and hung up his lamp on a nail.

Although keeping a careful lookout, I did not see Alexix until he had rushed up to me. I should have let him pass without recognizing him. It was hard to recognize in this boy, black from head to foot, the chum who had raced with me down the garden paths in his clean shirt, turned up to the elbows, and his collar thrown open, showing his White skin.

"It's Remi," he cried, turning to a man of about forty years, who walked near him, and who had a kind, frank face like M. Acquin. This was not surprising, considering that they were brothers. I knew that this was Uncle Gaspard.

"We've been expecting you a long time," he said, smiling.

"The road is long from Paris to Varses," I said, smiling back.

"And your legs are short," he retorted, laughing.

Capi, happy at seeing Alexix, expressed his joy by tugging at the leg of his trousers with all his might. During this time I explained to Uncle Gaspard that Mattia was my friend and partner, and that he played the cornet better than any one.

"And there's Monsieur Capi," said Uncle Gaspard; "you'll be rested tomorrow, so you can entertain us, for it's Sunday. Alexix says that that dog is cleverer than a schoolmaster and a comedian combined."

As much as I felt ill at ease with the aunt, so I felt at ease with Uncle Gaspard.

"Now, you two boys talk together," he said cheerily, "I am sure that you have a lot to say to each other. I'm going to have a chat with this young man who plays the cornet so well."

Alexix wanted to know about my journey, and I wanted to know about his work; we were so busy questioning each other that neither of us waited for a reply.

When we arrived at the house, Uncle Gaspard invited us to supper; never did an invitation give me such pleasure, for I had wondered as we walked along if we should have to part at the door, the aunt's welcome not having given us much hope.

"Here's Remi and his friend," said the father, entering the house.

We sat down to supper. The meal did not last long, for the aunt, who was a gossiper, was only serving delicatessen that evening. The hardworking miner ate his delicatessen supper without a word of complaint. He was an easy going man who, above all, liked peace: He never complained;

if he had a remark to pass it was said in a quiet, gentle way. The supper was soon over.

Uncle Gaspard told me that I could sleep with Alexix that night, and told Mattia that if he would go with him into the bakehouse he would make him up a bed there.

That evening and the greater part of the night Alexix and I spent talking.

Everything that Alexix told me excited me strangely. I had always wanted to go down in a mine, but when I spoke of it the next day to Uncle Gaspard he told me that he could not possibly take me down as only those who worked in the colliery were permitted to enter.

"If you want to be a miner," he said, "it will be easy. It's not worse than any other job. It's better than being a singer on the streets. You can stay here with Alexix. We'll get a job for Mattia also, but not in playing the cornet, oh no."

I had no intention of staying at Varses; there was something else I had set myself to do. I was about to leave the town without my curiosity being satisfied when circumstances came about in which I learned, in all their horror, the dangers to which the miners are exposed.

On the day that I was to leave Varses a large block of coal fell on Alexix's hand and almost crushed his finger. For several days he was obliged to give the hand complete rest. Uncle Gaspard was in despair, for now he had no one to push his car and he was afraid that he also would be obliged to stay at home, and he could ill afford to do this.

"Why can't I take his place?" I asked, when he returned home after hunting in vain for a boy.

"I was afraid the car would be too heavy for you, my boy," he said, "but if you'd be willing to try, you'd help me a mighty lot. It is hard to find a boy for a few days only."

"And while you are down in the mine I'll go off with Capi and earn the rest of the money for the cow," cried Mattia.

The three months that we had lived together in the open air had completely changed Mattia. He was no longer the poor, pale boy whom I had found leaning up against the church; much less was he the monster whom I had seen for the first time in Garofoli's attic, looking after the soup, and from time to time clasping his hands over his poor aching head. Mattia never had a headache now. He was never unhappy, neither was he thin or sad. The beautiful sun and the fresh air had given him health and spirits.

On our tramps he was always laughing and in a good humor, seeing the best side of everything, amused at anything, happy at nothing. How lonely I would have been without him!

We were so utterly different in character, perhaps that was why we got on so well together. He had a sweet, sunny disposition, a little careless, and with a delightful way of overcoming difficulties. We might well have quarreled when I was teaching him to read and giving his lessons in music, for I had not the patience of a schoolmaster. I was often unjust to him, but never once did he show signs of anger.

It was understood that while I was down in the mine Mattia and Capi were to go off into the suburbs and give "musical and dramatic performances" and thereby increase our fortune. Capi, to whom I explained this arrangement, appeared to understand and accordingly barked approval.

The next day, following close in Uncle Gaspard's footsteps, I went down into the deep, dark mine. He bade me be very cautious, but there was no need for his warning. It is not without a certain fear and anxiety that one leaves the light of day to enter into the bowels of the earth. When far down the gallery I instinctively looked back, but the daylight at the end of the long black tube looked like a white globe,—like the moon in a dark, starless sky. Soon the big, black pit yawned before us. Down below I could see the swaying lamps of other miners as they descended the ladder. We reached the stall where Uncle Gaspard worked on the second level. All those employed in pushing the cars were young boys, with the exception of one whom they called Professor. He was an old man who, in his younger days had worked as a carpenter in the mine but through an accident, which had crushed his fingers, had been obliged to give up his trade. I was soon to learn what it meant to be a miner.

CHAPTER XXII. IMPRISONED IN A MINE

A few days later, while pushing my car along the rails, I heard a terrible roaring. The noise came from all sides. My first feeling was one of terror and I thought only of saving myself, but I had so often been laughed at for my fears that shame made me stay. I wondered if it could be an explosion. Suddenly, hundreds of rats raced past me, fleeing like a regiment of cavalry. Then I heard a strange sound against the earth and the walls of the gallery, and the noise of running water. I raced back to Uncle Gaspard.

"Water's coming into the mine!" I cried.

"Don't be silly."

"Oh, listen!"

There was something in my manner that forced Uncle Gaspard to stop his work and listen. The noise was now louder and more sinister.

"Race for your life. The mine's flooded!" he shouted.

"Professor! Professor!" I screamed.

We rushed down the gallery. The old man joined us. The water was rising rapidly.

"You go first," said the old man when we reached the ladder.

We were not in a position to show politeness. Uncle Gaspard went first, I followed, then came the professor. Before we had reached the top of the ladder a rush of water fell, extinguishing our lamps.

"Hold on," cried Uncle Gaspard.

We clung to the rungs. But some men who were below us were thrown off. The fall of water had turned into a veritable avalanche.

We were on the first landing. Water was here also. We had no lights, for our lamps had been put out.

"I'm afraid we are lost," said the professor quietly; "say your prayers, my boy."

At this moment seven or eight miners with lamps came running in our direction, trying to reach the ladder. The water was now rushing through the mine in a regular torrent, dragging in its mad course pieces of wood, whirling them round like feathers.

"We must make for an airshaft, boys," said the professor. "That is the only place where we might find refuge. Give me a lamp."

Usually no one took any notice of the old man when he spoke, unless it was to make fun of him, but the strongest man there had lost his nerve and it was the voice of the old man, whom they had mocked so often, that they were now ready to obey. A lamp was handed to him. He seized it and dragged me along with him, taking the lead. He, more than any man, knew every nook and corner of the mine. The water was up to my waist. The professor led us to the nearest airshaft. Two miners refused to enter, saying that we were throwing ourselves into a blind alley. They continued along the gallery and we never saw them again.

Then came a deafening noise. A rush of water, a splintering of wood, explosions of compressed air, a dreadful roaring which terrified us.

"It's the deluge," shrieked one.

"The end of the world!"

"Oh, God, have mercy on us."

Hearing the men shrieking their cries of despair, the professor said calmly, but in a voice to which all listened.

"Courage, boys, now as we are going to stay here for a while we must get to work. We can't stay long, huddled together like this. Let us scoop out a hollow in the shale so as to have a place to rest upon."

His words calmed the men. With hands and lamphooks they began to dig into the soil. The task was difficult, for the airshaft in which we had taken refuge was on a considerable slope and very slippery. And we knew that it meant death if we made a false step. A resting place was made, and we were able to stop and take note of each other. We were seven: the professor, Uncle Gaspard, three miners, Pages, Comperou and Bergounhoux, and a car pusher named Carrory, and myself.

The noise in the mine continued with the same violence; there are no words with which to describe the horrible uproar. It seemed to us that our last hour had come. Mad with fear, we gazed at one another, questioningly.

"The evil genius of the mine's taking his revenge," cried one.

"It's a hole broke through from the river above," I ventured to say.

The professor said nothing. He merely shrugged his shoulder, as though he could have argued out the matter in full day, under the shade of a mulberry tree, eating an onion.

"It's all folly about the genius of the mine," he said at last, "The mine is flooded, that's a sure thing. But what has caused the flood, we down here can't tell...."

"Well, if you don't know what it is, shut up," cried the men.

Now that we were dry and the water was not touching us, no one wanted to listen to the old man. The authority which his coolness in danger had gained for him was already lost.

"We shan't die from drowning," he said at last, quietly; "look at the flame in your lamps, how short it is now."

"Don't be a wizard, what do you mean? Speak out."

"I am not trying to be a wizard, but we shan't be drowned. We are in a bell of air, and it is this compressed air which stops the water from rising. This airshaft, without an outlet, is doing for us what the diving bell does for the diver. The air has accumulated in the shaft and now resists the water, which ebbs back."

"It is the foul air that we have to fear.... The water is not rising a foot now; the mine must be full...."

"Where's Marius?" cried Pages, thinking of his only son, who worked on the third level.

"Oh, Marius! Marius," he shrieked.

There was no reply, not even an echo. His voice did not go beyond our "bell."

Was Marius saved? One hundred and fifty men drowned! That would be too horrible. One hundred and fifty men, at least, had gone down into the mine, how many had been able to get out by the shafts, or had found a refuge like ourselves?

There was now utter silence in the mine. At our feet the water was quite still, not a ripple, not a gurgle. The mine was full. This heavy silence, impenetrable and deathly, was more stupefying than the frightful uproar that we had heard when the water first rushed in. We were in a tomb, buried alive, more than a hundred feet under ground. We all seemed to feel the awfulness of our situation. Even the professor seemed crushed down. Suddenly, I felt some warm drops fall on my hand. It was Carrory.... He was crying, silently. Then came a voice, shrieking:

"Marius! my boy, Marius!"

The air was heavy to breathe; I felt suffocated; there was a buzzing in my ears. I was afraid, afraid of the water, the darkness, and death. The silence oppressed me, the uneven, jagged walls of our place of refuge seemed as though they would fall and crush me beneath their weight. Should I never see Lise again, and Arthur, and Mrs. Milligan, and dear old Mattia. Would they be able to make little Lise understand that I was dead, and that I could not bring her news from her brothers and sister! And Mother Barberin, poor Mother Barberin!...

"In my opinion, they are not trying to rescue us," said Uncle Gaspard, breaking the silence at last. "We can't hear a sound."

"How can you think that of your comrades?" cried the professor hotly. "You know well enough that in every mine accident the miners have never deserted one another, and that twenty men, one hundred men, would sooner be killed than leave a comrade without assistance. You know that well enough."

"That is true," murmured Uncle Gaspard.

150

"Make no error, they are trying their hardest to reach us. They have two ways, ... one is to bore a tunnel to us down here, the other is to drain off the water."

The men began a vague discussion as to how long it would take to accomplish this task. All realized that we should have to remain at least eight days in our tomb. Eight days! I had heard of miners being imprisoned for twenty-four days, but that was in a story and this was reality. When I was able to fully grasp what this meant, I paid no heed to the talk around me. I was stunned.

Again there was silence. All were plunged in thought. How long we remained so I cannot tell, but suddenly there was a cry;

"The pumps are at work!"

This was said with one voice, for the sounds that had just reached our ears had seemed to touch us by an electric current and we all rose up. We should be saved!

Carrory took my hand and squeezed it.

"You're a good boy," he said.

"No, you are," I replied.

But he insisted energetically that I was a good boy. His manner was as though he were intoxicated. And so he was; he was intoxicated with hope. But before we were to see the beautiful sun again and hear the birds in the trees, we were to pass through long, cruel days of agony, and wonder in anguish if we should ever see the light of day again.

We were all very thirsty. Pages wanted to go down and get some water, but the professor advised him to stay where he was. He feared that the débris which we had piled up would give way beneath his weight and that he would fall into the water.

"Remi is lighter, give him a boot, and he can go down and get water for us all," he said.

Carrory's boot was handed to me, and I prepared to slip down the bank.

"Wait a minute," said the professor; "let me give you a hand."

"Oh, but it's all right, professor," I replied; "if I fall in I can swim."

"Do as I tell you," he insisted; "take my hand."

In his effort to help me he either miscalculated his step, or the coal gave way beneath him, for he slid over the inclined plane and fell head first into the black waters. The lamp, which he held to light me, rolled after him and disappeared also. Instantly we were plunged in darkness, for we were burning only one light,—there was a simultaneous cry from every man. Fortunately, I was already in position to get to the water. Letting myself slide down on my back, I slipped into the water after the old man.

In my wanderings with Vitalis I had learned to swim and to dive. I was as much at ease in the water as on land, but how could I direct my course in this black hole? I had not thought of that when I let myself slip; I only thought that the old man would be drowned. Where should I look? On which side should I swim? I was wondering, when I felt a firm hand seize my shoulder. I was dragged beneath the water. Kicking out my foot sharply, I rose to the surface. The hand was still grasping my shoulder.

"Hold on, professor," I cried; "keep your head up and we're saved!"

Saved! neither one nor the other was saved. For I did not know which way to swim.

"Speak out, you fellows!" I cried.

"Remi, where are you?"

It was Uncle Gaspard's voice; it came from the left.

"Light the lamp!"

There was instantly a light. I had only to stretch out my hand to touch the bank. With one hand I clutched at a block of coal and drew up the old man. It was high time, for he had already swallowed a great deal of water and was partly unconscious. I kept his head well above water and he soon came round. Our companions took hold of him and pulled him up while I hoisted him from behind. I clambered up in my turn.

After this disagreeable accident which, for the moment, had caused us some distraction, we again fell into fits of depression and despair, and with them came thoughts of approaching death. I became very drowsy; the place was not favorable for sleep; I could easily have rolled into the water. Then the professor, seeing the danger I ran, took my head upon his chest and put his arm around my body. He did not hold me very tight, but enough to keep me from falling, and I laid there like a child on his mother's knee. When I moved, half awake, he merely changed the position of his arm that had grown stiff, then sat motionless again.

"Sleep, little chap," he whispered, leaning over me; "don't be afraid. I've got you, Remi."

And I slept without fear, for I knew very well he would not let go of me.

We had no idea of time. We did not know if we had been there two days or six days. Opinions differed. We spoke no more of our deliverance. Death was in our hearts.

"Say what you like, professor," cried Bergounhoux; "you have calculated how long it will take them to pump out the water, but they'll never be in time to save us. We shall die of hunger or suffocation...."

"Have patience," answered the professor. "I know how long we can live without food and I have made my calculations. They will do it in time."

At this moment big Comperou burnt into sobs.

"The good Lord is punishing me," he cried, "and I repent! I repent! If I get out of here I swear to atone for the wrong I have done, and if I don't get out you boys will make amends for me. You know Rouquette, who was sentenced for five years for stealing a watch from Mother Vidal?... I was the thief! I took it! It's under my bed now.... Oh...."

"Throw him in the water," cried both Pages and Bergounhoux.

"Do you want to appear, then, before the Lord with a crime on your conscience?" cried the professor; "let him repent!"

"I repent! I repent," wailed Comperou, more feebly than a child, in spite of his great strength.

"To the water! To the water!" cried Pages and Bergounhoux, trying to get at the sinner, who was crouching behind the professor.

"If you want to throw him in the water, you'll throw me with him!"

"No! No!"

Finally, they said they would not push him in the water, but upon one condition; he was to be left in a corner and no one was to speak to him or to pay any attention to him.

"Yes, that's what he deserves," said the professor. "That's only fair."

After the professor's words, which seemed like a judgment condemning Comperou, we all huddled together and got as far away from him as possible, leaving a space between us and the unfortunate man. For several hours, I should think, he sat there, grief stricken, his lips moving every now and again, to say:

"I repent! I repent!"

And then Pages and Bergounhoux would cry out:

"It's too late! It's too late! You repent because you're afraid now; you should have repented six months ago, a year ago."

He gasped painfully, but still repeated:

"I repent! I repent!"

He was in a high fever; all his body shook and his teeth were chattering.

"I'm thirsty," he said; "give me the boot." There was no more water in the boot. I got up to go and fetch some, but Pages, who had seen me, called to me to stop, and at the same moment Uncle Gaspard pulled me by the arm.

"We swore we would pay no attention to him," he said.

For some minutes Comperou repeated that he was thirsty; seeing that we would not give him anything to drink, he rose up to go to the water himself.

"He'll drag down the rubbish!" cried Pages.

"Let him at least have his freedom," said the professor.

He had seen me go down by letting myself slide on my back. He wanted to do the same, but I was light, whilst he was heavy. Scarcely was he on his back than the coal gave way beneath him and, with his legs stretched out and his arms striking into space, he slipped into the black hole. The water splashed up to where we were. I leaned forward ready to go down, but Uncle Gaspard and the professor each grasped me by the arm.

Half dead, and trembling with horror, I drew myself back.

Time passed. The professor was the only one who could speak with courage. But our depression finally made his spirits droop. Our hunger had become so great that we ate the rotten wood about us. Carrory, who was like an animal, was the most famished of all; he had cut up his other boot and was continually chewing the pieces of leather. Seeing what hunger had led us to, I must confess that I began to have terrible fears. Vitalis had often told me tales of men who had been shipwrecked. In one story, a crew who had been shipwrecked on a desert island where there was nothing to eat, had eaten the ship's boy. Seeing my companions in such a famished state I wondered if that fate was to be mine. I knew that the professor and Uncle Gaspard would never eat me, but of Pages, Bergounhoux, and Carrory, especially Carrory with his great white teeth which he dug into the leather of his boot, I was not quite so sure.

Once, when I was half asleep, I had been surprised to hear the professor speak in almost a whisper, as though he was dreaming. He was talking of the clouds, the wind, and the sun. Then Pages and Bergounhoux began to chatter with him in a foolish manner. Neither waited for the other to reply. Uncle Gaspard seemed hardly to notice how foolish they were. Were they all gone mad? What was to be done?

Suddenly, I thought I would light a lamp. To economize we had decided only to have a light when it was absolutely necessary. When they saw the light they apparently regained their senses. I went to get some water for them. The waters were going down!

After a time they began to talk strangely again. My own thoughts were vague and wild, and for long hours and perhaps days we laid there chattering to one another foolishly. After a time we became quieter and Bergounhoux said that before dying we should put down our last wishes. We lit a lamp and Bergounhoux wrote for us all, and we each signed the paper. I gave my dog and harp to Mattia and I expressed a wish for Alexix to go to Lise and kiss her for me, and give her the dried rose that was in my vest pocket. Dear little Lise....

After some time, I slipped down the bank again, and saw that the waters were lowering considerably. I hurried back to my companions and told them that now I could swim to the ladders and tell our rescuers in what part of the mine we had taken refuge. The professor forbade me to go, but I insisted.

"Go on, Remi, and I'll give you my watch," cried Uncle Gaspard.

The professor thought for a moment, then took my hand.

"Do as you think, boy," he said; "you have a heart. I think that you are attempting the impossible, but it is not the first time that what was thought impossible has been successful. Kiss us, boy."

I kissed the professor and Uncle Gaspard and then, having thrown off my clothes, I went into the water.

"You keep shouting all the while," I said, before taking the plunge; "your voices will guide me."

I wondered if the space under the roof of the gallery was big enough for me to move freely. That was the question. After some strokes I found that I could swim if I went gently. I knew that there was a meeting of galleries not far away, but I had to be cautious, for if I made a mistake in the course I should lose my way. The roof and the walls of the gallery were not enough to guide me; on the ground there was a surer guide, the rails. If I followed them I should be sure to find the ladders. From time to time I let my feet go down and, having touched the iron rails, I rose up again, gently. With the voices of my companions behind me and the rails under my feet, I was not lost. As the voices became less distinct, the noise of the pumps increased. I was advancing. Thank God, I should soon see the light of day!

Going straight down the middle of the gallery, I had only to turn to the right to touch the rail. I went on a little farther, then dived again to touch the rail. It was not there! I went from side to side of the gallery, but there was no rail!

I had made a mistake.

The voices of my companions only reached me in the faintest murmur. I took in a deep breath, then plunged again but with no more success. There were no rails!

I had taken the wrong level; without knowing, I must have turned back. But how was it the others were not shouting. If they were I could not hear them. I was distracted, for I did not know which way to turn in this cold, black water.

Then, suddenly, I heard the sounds of voices again and I knew which way to turn. After having taken a dozen strokes back, I turned to the right, then to the left, but only found the walls. Where were the rails? I was sure now that I was in the right level, then I suddenly realized that the railroad had been carried away by the rush of waters, and that I had no guide. Under these circumstances it was impossible for me to carry out my plan, and I was forced to turn back.

I swam back quickly to our place of refuge, the voices guiding me. As I approached, it seemed to me that my companions' voices were more assured as though they felt stronger. I was soon at the entrance of the shaft! I hallooed to them.

"Come back; come back," shouted the professor.

"I could not find the way," I called out.

"Never mind, the tunnel is nearly finished: they hear our cries and we can hear theirs. We shall soon speak."

I climbed quickly up to our landing and listened. We could hear the blows from the picks and the cries of those who worked for our freedom came to us feebly, but yet very distinct. After the first rush of joy, I realized that I was frozen. As there were no warm clothes to give me, they buried me up to the neck in coal dust and Uncle Gaspard and the professor huddled up against me to keep me warm.

We knew now that our rescuers would soon reach us through the tunnel and by the water, but these last hours of our imprisonment were the hardest to bear. The blows from the picks continued, and the pumping had not stopped for one moment. Strange, the nearer we reached the hour of our deliverance, the weaker we grew. I was lying in the coal dust trembling, but I was not cold. We were unable to speak.

Suddenly, there was a noise in the waters of the gallery and, turning my head, I saw a great light coming towards us. The engineer was at the head of several men. He was the first to climb up to us. He had me in his arms before I could say a word.

It was time, for my heart was failing me, yet I was conscious that I was being carried away, and I was wrapped up in a blanket after our rescuers had waded through the water in the gallery. I closed my eyes; when I opened them again it was daylight! We were in the open air! At the same time something jumped on me. It was Capi. With a bound he had sprung upon me as I laid in the engineer's arms. He licked my face again and again. Then my hand was taken; I felt a kiss and heard a weak voice murmuring: "Remi! oh, Remi!"

It was Mattia. I smiled at him, then I glanced round.

A mass of people were crowded together in two straight rows, leaving a passage down the center. It was a silent crowd, for they had been requested not to excite us by their cries, but their looks spoke for their lips. In the first row I seemed to see some white surplices and gilt ornaments which shone in the sun. They were the priests, who had come to the entrance of the mine to offer prayers for our deliverance. When we were brought out, they went down on their knees in the dust.

Twenty arms were stretched out to take me, but the engineer would not give me up. He carried me to the offices, where beds had been prepared to receive us.

Two days later I was walking down the village street followed by Mattia, Alexix, and Capi. There were some who came and shook me by the hands with tears in their eyes, and there were others who turned away their heads. These were in mourning, and they asked themselves bitterly why this orphan child had been saved when their fathers and sons were still in the mine, ghastly corpses, drifting hither and thither in the dark waters.

CHAPTER XXIII. ONCE MORE UPON THE WAY

I had made some friends in the mine. Such terrible experiences, born in common, unites one. Uncle Gaspard and the professor, in particular, had grown very fond of me and, although the engineer had not shared our captivity, he had become attached to me like one is to a child that one has snatched from death. He invited me to his house. I had to tell his daughter all that had happened to us in the mine.

Every one wanted to keep me at Varses. The engineer told me that if I wished he would find me a position in the offices; Uncle Gaspard said he would get me a permanent job in the mine; he seemed to think it quite natural that I should return to the colliery; he himself was soon going down again with that indifference that men show who are accustomed to brave danger each day. I had no wish to go back. A mine was very interesting, and I was very pleased that I had seen one, but I had not the slightest desire to return. I preferred to have the sky over my head, even a sky full of snow. The open-air life suited me better, and so I told them. Every one was surprised, especially the professor. Carrory, when he met me, called me a "chicken."

During the time that they were all trying to persuade me to stay at Varses, Mattia became very preoccupied and thoughtful. I questioned him, but he always answered that nothing was the matter. It was not until I told him that we were starting off on our tramps in three days' time, that he admitted the cause of his sadness.

"Oh, I thought that you would stay and that you would leave me," he said.

I gave him a good slap, so as to teach him not to doubt me.

Mattia was quite able to look after himself now. While I was down in the mine he had earned eighteen francs. He was very proud when he handed me this large sum, for with the hundred and twenty-eight that we already had, this made a total of one hundred and forty-six francs. We only wanted four francs more to be able to buy the Prince's cow.

"Forward! March! Children!" With baggage strapped on our back we set forth on the road, with Capi barking and rolling in the dust for joy.

Mattia suggested that we get a little more money before buying the cow; the more money we had, the better the cow, and the better the cow, the more pleased Mother Barberin would be.

While tramping from Paris to Varses I had begun to give Mattia reading lessons and elementary music lessons. I continued, these lessons now. Either I was not a good teacher, which was quite possible, or Mattia was not a good pupil, which also was quite possible; the lessons were not a success. Often I got angry and, shutting the book with a bang, told him that he was a thickhead.

"That's true," he said, smiling; "my head is only soft when it's banged. Garofoli found out that!"

How could one keep angry at this reply. I laughed and we went on with the lessons. But with music, from the beginning, he made astonishing progress. In the end, he so confused me with his questions, that I was obliged to confess that I could not teach him any more. This confession mortified me exceedingly. I had been a very proud professor, and it was humiliating for me not to be able to answer my pupil's questions. And he did not spare me, oh, no!

"I'd like to go and take one lesson from a real master," he said, "only just one, and I'll ask him all the questions that I want answered."

"Why didn't you take this lesson from a real master while I was in the mine?"

"Because I didn't want to take what he would charge out of your money."

I was hurt when Mattia had spoken thus of a *real* master, but my absurd vanity could not hold out against his last words.

"You're a good boy," I said; "my money is your money; you earn it also, and more than I, very often. You can take as many lessons as you like, and I'll take them with you."

The master, the *real* master that we required, was not a villager, but an *artiste*, a great *artiste*, such as might be found only in important towns. Consulting our map we found that the next big town was Mendes.

It was already night when we reached Mendes and, as we were tired out, we decided that we could not take a lesson that evening. We asked the landlady of the inn where we could find a good music master. She said that she was very surprised that we asked such a question; surely, we knew Monsieur Espinassous!

"We've come from a distance," I said.

"You must have come from a very great distance, then?"

"From Italy," replied Mattia.

Then she was no longer astonished, and she admitted that, coming from so far then, we might not have heard of M. Espinassous.

"Is this professor very busy?" I asked, fearing that such a celebrated musician might not care to give just one lesson to two little urchins like ourselves.

"Oh, yes, I should say he is busy; how couldn't he be?"

"Do you think that he would receive us to-morrow morning?"

"Sure! He receives every one, when they have money in their pockets ... naturally."

We understood that, of course.

Before going to sleep, we discussed all the questions that we intended asking the celebrated professor the next day. Mattia was quite elated at our luck in finding just the kind of musician we wanted.

Next morning we took our instruments, Mattia his violin and I my harp, and set out to find M. Espinassous. We did not take Capi, because we thought that it would not do to call on such a celebrated person with a dog. We tied him up in the inn stables. When we reached the house which our landlady indicated was the professor's, we thought that we must have made a mistake, for before the house two little brass plaques were swinging, which was certainly not the sign of a music professor. The place bore every appearance of a barber's shop. Turning to a man, who was passing, we asked him if he could direct us to M. Espinassous' house.

"There it is," he said, pointing to the barber's shop.

After all, why should not a professor live with a barber? We entered. The shop was partitioned off into two equal parts. On the right were brushes, combs, jars of cream, and barbers' chairs. On the left, hanging on the walls and on the shelves, were various instruments, violins, cornets, trombones, etc.

"Monsieur Espinassous?" inquired Mattia.

Fluttering like a bird, the dapper little man, who was in the act of shaving a man, replied: "I am Monsieur Espinassous."

I glanced at Mattia as much as to say that the barber musician was not the man we were looking for, that it would be wasting good money to consult him, but Mattia, instead of understanding my look, sat down in a chair with a deliberate air.

"Will you cut my hair after you have shaved that gentleman?" he asked.

"Certainly, young man, and I'll give you a shave also, if you like."

"Thanks," replied Mattia.

I was abashed at his assurance. He looked at me out of the corner of his eye, to ask me to wait before getting annoyed.

When the man was shaved, M. Espinassous, with towel over his arm, prepared to cut Mattia's hair.

"Monsieur," said Mattia, while the barber tied the sheet round his neck, "my friend and I had an argument, and as we know that you are a celebrated musician, we thought that you would give us your advice and settle the matter for us."

"What is it, young man?"

Now I knew what Mattia was driving at! First of all, he wanted to see if this barber-musician was capable of replying to our questions; if so, he intended to get a music lesson at the price of a haircut.

All the while Mattia was having his hair cut, he asked questions. The barber-musician was highly amused, but answered each question put to him quickly and with pleasure. When we were ready to leave he asked Mattia to play something on his violin. Mattia played a piece.

"And you don't know a note of music!" cried the barber, clapping his hands, and looking affectionately at Mattia as though he had known and loved him all his life. "It is wonderful!"

Mattia took a clarionette from amongst the instruments and played on it; then a cornet.

"Why, the youngster's a prodigy!" cried M. Espinassous in rapture; "if you will stay here with me I'll make you a great musician. In the mornings you shall learn to shave my customers and the rest of the day you shall study music. Don't think, because I'm a barber, I don't know music. One has to live!"

I looked at Mattia. What was he going to reply? Was I to lose my friend, my chum, my brother?

"Think for your own good, Mattia," I said, but my voice shook.

"Leave my friend?" he cried, linking his arm in mine; "that I never could, but thank you all the same, Monsieur."

M. Espinassous insisted, and told Mattia that later they would find the means to send him to the Conservatoire in Paris, because he would surely be a great musician!

"Leave Remi? never!"

"Well, then," replied the barber, sorrowfully, "let me give you a book and you can learn what you do not know from that." He took a book out of one of the drawers, entitled, "The Theory of Music." It was old and torn, but what did that matter? Taking a pen, he sat down and wrote on the first page:

"To a child who, when he becomes celebrated, will remember the barber of Mendes."

I don't know if there were any other professors of music at Mendes, but that was the only one we knew, and we never forgot him.

CHAPTER XXIV. FRIENDSHIP THAT IS TRUE

I loved Mattia when we arrived at Mendes, but when we left the town I loved him even more. I could not tell him before the barber how I felt when he cried out: "Leave my friend!"

I took his hand and squeezed it as we tramped along.

"It's till death doth us part now, Mattia," I said.

"I knew that long ago," he replied, smiling at me with his great, dark eyes.

We heard that there was going to be an important cattle fair at Ussel, so we decided to go there and buy the cow. It was on our way to Chavanon. We played in every town and village on the road, and by the time we had reached Ussel we had collected two hundred and forty francs. We had to economize in every possible manner to save this sum, but Mattia was just as interested and eager to buy the animal as I. He wanted it to be white; I wanted brown in memory of poor Rousette. We both agreed, however, that she must be very gentle and give plenty of milk.

As neither of us knew by what signs one could tell a good cow, we decided to employ the services of a veterinarian. We had heard many stories of late how people had been deceived when buying a cow, and we did not want to run any risk. It would be an expense to employ a veterinarian, but that could not be helped. We had heard of one man who had bought an animal for a very low price and when he had got her home he found that she had a false tail; another man, so we were told, had bought a cow which seemed to be in a very healthy state, and had every appearance of giving plenty of milk, but she only gave two glasses of milk in twenty-four hours. By a little trick, practiced by the cattle dealer, the animal was made to look as though she had plenty of milk.

Mattia said that as far as the false tail went we had nothing to fear, for he would hang onto the tail of every cow with all his might, before we entered into any discussion with the seller. When I told him that if it were a real tail he would probably get a kick in the stomach or on his head, his imagination cooled somewhat.

It was several years since I had arrived at Ussel with Vitalis, where he had bought me my first pair of shoes with nails. Alas! out of the six of us who started, Capi and I were the only ones left. As soon as we got to the town, after having left our baggage at the same inn where I had stayed before with Vitalis and the dogs, we began to look about for a veterinarian. We found one and he seemed very amused when we described to him the kind of a cow we wanted, and asked if he would come and buy it for us.

"But what in the world do you two boys want with a cow, and have you got the money?" he demanded.

We told him how much money we had, and how we got it, and that we were going to give a present, a surprise, to Mother Barberin of Chavanon, who had looked after me when I was a baby. He showed a very kindly interest then, and promised to meet us the next morning at the fair at seven o'clock. When we asked him his charges he refused flatly to accept anything. He sent us off laughing and told us to be at the fair on time.

The next day at daybreak the town was full of excitement. From our room at the inn we could hear the carts and wagons rolling over the cobblestones in the street below, and the cows bellowing, the sheep bleating, the farmers shouting at their animals and joking with each other. We jumped into our clothes and arrived at the fair at six o'clock, for we wanted to make a selection before the veterinarian arrived.

What beautiful cows they were, ... all colors, and all sizes, some fat, some thin, and some with their calves; there were also horses and great fat pigs, scooping holes in the ground, and little plump sucking pigs, squealing as though they were being skinned alive. But we had eyes for nothing but the cows; they stood very quiet, placidly chewing. They permitted us to make a thorough examination, merely blinking their eyelids. After one hour's inspection, we had found seventeen that pleased us, this for one quality, that for another, a third because she was red, two because they were white, which, of course, brought up a discussion between Mattia and myself. The veterinarian arrived. We showed him the cows we liked.

"I think this one ought to be a good one," Mattia said, pointing to a white animal.

"I think that is a better one," I said, indicating a red one.

The veterinarian stopped the argument we had begun by ignoring both and passing on to a third one. This one had slim legs, red coat with brown ears and cheeks, eyes bordered with black, and a whitish circle around her muzzle.

"This is just the one you want," said the veterinarian.

It was a beauty! Mattia and I now saw that this was the best. The veterinarian asked a heavy looking peasant, who held the cow by a rope, how much he wanted for it.

"Three hundred francs," he replied.

Our mouths dropped. Three hundred francs! I made a sign to the veterinarian that we must pass on to another; he made another sign that he would drive a bargain. Then a lively discussion commenced between the veterinarian and the peasant. Our bidder went up to 170, the peasant came down to 280. When they reached this sum, the veterinarian began to examine the cow more critically. She had weak legs, her neck was too short, her horns too long, she hadn't any lungs and her teats were not well formed. No, she certainly would not give much milk.

The peasant said that as we knew so much about cows, he would let us have her for 250 francs, because he felt sure she would be in good hands. Thereupon we began to get scared, for both Mattia and I thought that it must be a poor cow then.

"Let us go and see some others," I suggested, touching the veterinarian's arm.

Hearing this, the man came down ten francs. Then, little by little, he came down to 210 francs, but he stopped there. The veterinarian had nudged me and given me to understand that he was not serious in saying what he did about the cow, that it was an excellent animal, but then 210 francs was a large sum for us.

During this time Mattia had gone behind her and pulled a long wisp of hair from her tail and the animal had given him a kick. That decided me.

"All right, 210 francs," I said, thinking the matter was settled. I held out my hand to take the rope.

"Have you brought a halter?" asked the man. "I'm selling my cow, not the halter."

He said that, as we were friends, he would let me have the halter for sixty sous. We needed a halter, so I parted with the sixty sous, calculating that we should now have but twenty sous left. I counted out the two hundred and thirteen francs, then again I stretched out my hand.

"Have you got a rope?" inquired the man. "I've sold you the halter, but I haven't sold you the rope."

The rope cost us our last twenty sous.

The cow was finally handed over to us, but we had not a sou left to buy food for the animal, nor for ourselves. After warmly thanking the veterinarian for his kindness, we shook hands and said good-by to him, and went back to the inn, where we tied our cow up in the stable. As it was a very busy day in the town on account of the fair, and people from all parts had come in, Mattia and I thought that it would be better for each to go his own way and see what we could make. In the evening Mattia brought back four francs and I three francs fifty centimes.

With seven francs fifty we felt that we were again rich. We persuaded the kitchen maid to milk our cow and we had the milk for supper. Never had we tasted anything so good! We were so enthusiastic about the quality of the milk that we went into the stable as soon as we had finished to embrace our treasure. The cow evidently appreciated this caress, for she licked our faces to show her appreciation.

To understand the pleasure that we felt at kissing our cow and to be kissed by her, it must be remembered that neither Mattia nor I had been overburdened with caresses; our fate had not been that of the petted and pampered children who are obliged to defend themselves against too many kisses.

The next morning we rose with the sun and started for Chavanon. How grateful I was to Mattia for the help he had given me; without him I never could have collected such a big sum. I wanted to give him the pleasure of leading the cow, and he was very proud indeed to pull her by the rope while I walked behind. She looked very fine; she walked along slowly, swaying a little, holding herself like an animal that is aware of her value. I did not want to tire her out, so I decided not to get to Chavanon that evening late; better, I thought, get there early in the morning. That is what we intended to do; this is what happened:

I intended to stay the night in the village where I had spent my first night with Vitalis, when Capi, seeing me so unhappy, came to me and lay down beside me. Before reaching this village we came to a nice green spot, and, throwing down our baggage, we decided to rest. We made our cow go down into a ditch. At first I wanted to hold her by the rope, but she seemed very docile, and quite accustomed to grazing, so after a time I twisted the rope around her horns and sat down near her to eat my supper. Naturally we had finished eating long before she had, so after having admired her for some time and not knowing what to do next, we began to play a little game with each other. When we had finished our game, she was still eating. As I went to her, she pulled at the grass sharply, as much as to say that she was still hungry.

"Wait a little," said Mattia.

"Don't you know that a cow can eat all day long?" I replied.

"Well, wait a little."

We got our baggage and instruments together, but still she would not stop eating.

"I'll play her a piece on the cornet," said Mattia, who found it difficult to keep still. "There was a cow at Gassot's Circus and she liked music."

He commenced to play a lively march.

At the first note the cow lifted up her head; then suddenly, before I could throw myself at her horns to catch hold of the rope, she had gone off at a gallop. We raced after her as fast as we could, calling to her to stop. I shouted to Capi to stop her. Now one cannot be endowed with every talent. A cattle driver's dog would have jumped at her nose, but Capi was a genius, so he jumped at her legs. Naturally, this made her run faster. She raced back to the last village we had passed through. As the road was straight, we could see her in the distance, and we saw several people blocking her way and trying to catch hold of her. We slackened our speed, for we knew now that we should not lose her. All we should have to do would be to claim her from the good people who had stopped her going farther. There was quite a crowd gathered round her when we arrived on the scene, and instead of giving her up to us at once, as we expected they would, they asked us *how* we got the animal and *where* we got her. They insisted that we had stolen her and that she was running back to her owner. They declared that we ought to go to prison until the truth could be discovered. At the very mention of the word "prison" I turned pale and began to stammer. I was breathless from my race and could not utter a word. At this moment a policeman arrived, and, in a few words, the whole affair was explained to him. As it did not seem at all clear, he decided to take possession of the cow and have us locked up until we could prove that it belonged to us. The whole village seemed to be in the procession which ran behind us up to the town hall, which was also the station house. The mob pushed us and sneered at us and called us the most horrible names, and I do believe that if the officer had not defended us they would have lynched us as though we were criminals of the deepest dye. The man who had charge of the town hall, and who was also jailer and sheriff, did not want to admit us. I thought what a kind man! However, the policeman insisted that we be locked up, and the jailer finally turned the big key in a double-locked door and pushed us into the prison. Then I saw why he had made some difficulty about receiving us. He had put his provision of onions to dry in this prison and they were strewn out on every bench. He heaped them all together in a corner. We were searched, our money, matches and knives taken from us. Then we were locked up for the night.

"I wish you'd give me a good slap," said Mattia miserably, when we were alone; "box my ears or do something to me."

"I was as big a fool as you to let you play the cornet to a cow," I replied.

"Oh, I feel so bad about it," he said brokenly; "our poor cow, the Prince's cow!" He began to cry.

Then I tried to console him by telling him that our situation was not very serious. We would prove that we bought the cow; we would send to Ussel for the veterinarian ... he would be a witness.

"But if they say we stole the money to buy it," he said, "we can't prove that we earned it, and when one is unfortunate they always think you're guilty." That was true.

"And who'll feed her?" went on Mattia dismally.

Oh, dear, I did hope that they would feed our poor cow.

"And what are we going to say when they question us in the morning?" asked Mattia.

"Tell them the truth."

"And then they'll hand you over to Barberin, or if Mother Barberin is alone at her place and they question her to see if we are lying, we can't give her a surprise."

"Oh, dear!"

"You've been away from Mother Barberin for a long time; how do you know if she isn't dead?"

This terrible thought had never occurred to me, and yet poor Vitalis had died, ... how was it I had not thought that I might lose her....

"Why didn't you say that before?" I demanded.

"Because when I'm happy I don't have those ideas. I have been so happy at the thought of offering your cow to Mother Barberin and thinking how pleased she'd be, I never thought before that she might be dead."

It must have been the influence of this dismal room, for we could only see the darkest side of everything.

"And, oh," cried Mattia, starting up and throwing out his arms, "if Mother Barberin is dead and that awful Barberin is alive and we go there, he'll take our cow and keep it himself."

It was late in the afternoon when the door was thrown open and an old gentleman with white hair came into our prison.

"Now, you rogues, answer this gentleman," said the jailer, who accompanied him.

"That's all right, that's all right," said the gentleman, who was the public prosecutor, "I'll question this one." With his finger he indicated me. "You take charge of the other; I'll question him later."

I was alone with the prosecutor. Fixing me with his eye, he told me that I was accused of having stolen a cow. I told him that we bought the animal at the fair at Ussel, and I named the veterinarian who had assisted us in the purchase.

"That will be verified," he replied. "And now what made you buy that cow?"

I told him that I was offering it as a token of affection to my foster mother.

"Her name?" he demanded.

"Madame Barberin of Chavanon," I replied.

"The wife of a mason who met with a serious accident in Paris a few years ago. I know her. That also will be verified."

"Oh!..."

I became very confused. Seeing my embarrassment, the prosecutor pressed me with questions, and I had to tell him that if he made inquiries of Madame Barberin our cow would not be a surprise after all, and to make it a surprise had been our chief object. But in the midst of my confusion I felt a great satisfaction to know that Mother Barberin was still alive, and in the course of the questions that were put to me I learned that Barberin had gone back to Paris some time ago. This delighted me.

Then came the question that Mattia had feared.

"But how did you get all the money to buy the cow?"

I explained that from Paris to Varses and from Varses to Ussel we had collected this sum, sou by sou.

"But what were you doing in Varses?" he asked.

Then I was forced to tell him that I had been in a mine accident.

"Which of you two is Remi?" he asked, in a softened voice.

"I am, sir," I replied.

"To prove that, you tell me how the catastrophe occurred. I read the whole account of it in the papers. You cannot deceive me. I can tell if you really are Remi. Now, be careful."

I could see that he was feeling very lenient towards us. I told him my experience in the mine, and when I had finished my story, I thought from his manner, which was almost affectionate, that he would give us our freedom at once, but instead he went out of the room, leaving me alone, a prey to my thoughts. After some time he returned with Mattia.

"I am going to have your story investigated at Ussel," he said. "If it is true, as I hope it is, you will be free to-morrow."

"And our cow?" asked Mattia anxiously.

"Will be given back to you."

"I didn't mean that," replied Mattia; "but who'll feed her, who'll milk her?"

"Don't worry, youngster," said the prosecutor.

Mattia smiled contentedly.

"Ah, then if they milk our cow," he asked, "may we have some milk for supper?"

"You certainly shall!"

As soon as we were alone I told Mattia the great news that had almost made me forget that we were locked up.

"Mother Barberin is alive, and Barberin has gone to Paris!" I said.

"Ah, then the Prince's cow will make a triumphal entry."

He commenced to dance and sing with joy. Carried away by his gayety, I caught him by the hands, and Capi, who until then had been lying in a corner, quiet and thoughtful, jumped up and took his place between us, standing up on his hind paws. We then threw ourselves into such a wild dance that the jailer rushed in to see what was the matter, probably afraid for his onions. He told us to stop, but he spoke very differently to what he had before. By that, I felt that we were not in a very serious plight. I had further proof of this when a moment later he came in carrying a big bowl of milk, our cow's milk. And that was not all. He brought a large piece of white bread and some cold veal, which he said the prosecutor had sent us. Decidedly, prisons were not so bad after all; dinner and lodging for nothing!

Early the next morning the prosecutor came in with our friend the veterinarian, who had wanted to come himself to see that we got our freedom. Before we left, the prosecutor handed us an official stamped paper.

"See, I'm giving you this," he said; "you are two silly boys to go tramping through the country without any papers. I have asked the mayor to make out this passport for you. This is all you will need to protect you in the future. Good luck, boys."

He shook hands with us, and so did the veterinarian.

We had entered the village miserably, but we left in triumph. Leading our cow by the rope and walking with heads held high, we glanced over our shoulders at the villagers, who were standing on their doorsteps staring at us.

I did not want to tire our cow, but I was in a hurry to get to Chavanon that same day, so we set out briskly. By evening we had almost reached my old home. Mattia had never tasted pancakes, and I had promised him some as soon as we arrived. On the way I bought one pound of butter, two pounds of flour and a dozen eggs. We had now reached the spot where I had asked Vitalis to let me rest, so that I could look down on Mother Barberin's house, as I thought for the last time.

"Take the rope," I said to Mattia.

With a spring I was on the parapet. Nothing had been changed in our valley; it looked just the same; the smoke was even coming out of the chimney. As it came towards us it seemed to me I could smell oak leaves. I jumped down from the parapet and hugged Mattia, Capi sprang up on me, and I squeezed them both tight.

"Come, let's get there as quickly as possible now," I cried.

"What a pity," sighed Mattia. "If this brute only loved music, what a triumphal entry we could make."

As we arrived at one of the turns in the road, we saw Mother Barberin come out of her cottage and go off in the direction of the village. What was to be done? We had intended to spring a surprise upon her. We should have to think of something else.

Knowing that the door was always on the latch, I decided to go straight into the house, after tying our cow up in the cowshed. We found the shed full of wood now, so we heaped it up in a corner, and put our cow in poor Rousette's place.

When we got into the house, I said to Mattia: "Now, I'll take this seat by the fire so that she'll find me here. When she opens the gate, you'll hear it creak; then you hide yourself with Capi."

I sat down in the very spot where I had always sat on a winter night. I crouched down, making myself look as small as possible, so as to look as near like Mother Barberin's little Remi as I could. From where I sat I could watch the gate. I looked round the kitchen. Nothing was changed, everything was in the same place; a pane of glass that I had broken still had the bit of paper pasted over it, black with smoke and age. Suddenly I saw a white bonnet. The gate creaked.

"Hide yourself quickly," I said to Mattia.

I made myself smaller and smaller. The door opened and Mother Barberin came in. She stared at me.

"Who is there?" she asked.

I looked at her without answering; she stared back at me. Suddenly she began to tremble.

"Oh, Lord, is it my Remi!" she murmured.

I jumped up and caught her in my arms.

"Mamma!"

"My boy! my boy!" was all that she could say, as she laid her head on my shoulder.

Some minutes passed before we had controlled our emotion. I wiped away her tears.

"Why, how you've grown, my boy," she cried, holding me at arms' length, "you're so big and so strong! Oh, my Remi!"

A stifled snort reminded me that Mattia was under the bed. I called him. He crept out.

"This is Mattia," I said, "my brother."

"Oh, then you've found your parents?" she cried.

"No, he's my chum, but just like a brother. And this is Capi," I added, after she had greeted Mattia. "Come and salute your master's mother, Capitano."

Capi got on his hind paws and bowed gravely to Mother Barberin. She laughed heartily. Her tears had quite vanished. Mattia made me a sign to spring our surprise.

"Let's go and see how the garden looks," I said.

"I have kept your bit just as you arranged it," she said, "for I knew that some day you would come back."

"Did you get my Jerusalem artichokes?"

"Ah, you planted them to surprise me! You always liked to give surprises, my boy."

The moment had come.

"Is the cowshed just the same since poor Rousette went?" I asked.

"Oh, no; I keep my wood there now."

We had reached the shed by this time. I pushed open the door and at once our cow, who was hungry, began to bellow.

"A cow! A cow in my cowshed!" cried Mother Barberin.

Mattia and I burst out laughing.

"It's a surprise," I cried, "and a better one than the Jerusalem artichokes."

She looked at me in a dazed, astonished manner.

"Yes, it's a present for you. I did not come back with empty hands to the mamma who was so good to the little lost boy. This is to replace Rousette. Mattia and I bought it for you with the money we earned."

"Oh, the dear boys!" she cried, kissing us both.

She now went inside the shed to examine her present. At each discovery she gave a shriek of delight.

"What a beautiful cow," she exclaimed.

Then she turned round suddenly.

"Say, you must be very rich now?"

"I should say so," laughed Mattia; "we've got fifty-eight sous left."

I ran to the house to fetch the milk pail, and while in the house I arranged the butter, eggs, and flour in a display on the table, then ran back to the shed. How delighted she was when she had a pail three-quarters full of beautiful frothy milk.

There was another burst of delight when she saw the things on the table ready for pancakes, which I told her we were dying to have.

"You must have known that Barberin was in Paris, then?" she said. I explained to her how I had learned so.

"I will tell you why he has gone," she said, looking at me significantly.

"Let's have the pancakes first," I said; "don't let's talk about him. I have not forgotten how he sold me for forty francs, and it was my fear of him, the fear that he would sell me again, that kept me from writing to tell you news of myself."

"Oh, boy, I thought that was why," she said, "but you mustn't speak unkindly of Barberin."

"Well, let's have the pancakes now," I said, hugging her.

We all set briskly to prepare the ingredients and before long Mattia and I were cramming pancakes down our throats. Mattia declared that he had never tasted anything so fine. As soon as we had finished one we held out our plates for another, and Capi came in for his share. Mother Barberin was scandalized that we should give a dog pancakes, but we explained to her that he was the chief actor in our company and a genius, and that he was treated by us with every consideration. Later, while Mattia was out getting some wood ready for the next morning, she told me why Barberin had gone to Paris.

"Your family is looking for you," she said, almost in a whisper. "That's what Barberin has gone up to Paris about. He's looking for you."

"My family," I exclaimed. "Oh, have I a family of my own? Speak, tell all, Mother Barberin, dear Mother Barberin!"

Then I got frightened. I did not believe that my family was looking for me. Barberin was trying to find me so that he could sell me again. I would not be sold! I told my fears to Mother Barberin, but she said no, my family was looking for me. Then she told me that a gentleman came to the house who spoke with a foreign accent, and he asked Barberin what had become of the little baby that he had found many years ago in Paris. Barberin asked him what business that was of his. This answer was just like Barberin would give.

"You know from the bakehouse one can hear everything that is said in the kitchen," said Mother Barberin, "and when I knew that they were talking about you, I naturally listened. I got nearer and then I trod on a twig of wood that broke."

"'Oh, we're not alone,' said the gentleman to Barberin.

"'Yes, we are; that's only my wife,' he replied. The gentleman then said it was very warm in the kitchen and that they could talk better outside. They went out and it was three hours later when Barberin came back alone. I tried to make him tell me everything, but the only thing he would say was that this man was looking for you, but that he was not your father, and that he had given him one hundred francs. Probably he's had more since. From this, and the fine clothes you wore when he found you, we think your parents must be rich.

"Then Jerome said he had to go off to Paris," she continued, "to find the musician who hired you. This musician said that a letter sent to Rue Mouffetard to a man named Garofoli would reach him."

"And haven't you heard from Barberin since he went?" I asked, surprised that he had sent no news.

"Not a word," she said. "I don't even know where he is living in the city."

Mattia came in just then. I told him excitedly that I had a family, and that my parents were looking for me. He said he was pleased for me, but he did not seem to share my joy and enthusiasm. I slept little that night. Mother Barberin had told me to start off to Paris and find Barberin at once and not delay my parent's joy at finding me. I had hoped that I could spend several days with her, and yet I felt that she was right. I would have to see Lise before going. That could be managed, for we could go to Paris by way of the canal. As Lise's uncle kept the locks and lived in a cottage on the banks, we could stop and see her.

I spent that day with Mother Barberin, and in the evening we discussed what I would do for her when I was rich. She was to have all the things she wanted. There was not a wish of hers that should not be gratified when I had money.

"The cow that you have given me in your poor days will be more to me than anything you can give me when you're rich, Remi," she said fondly.

The next day, after bidding dear Mother Barberin a loving farewell, we started to walk along the banks of the canal. Mattia was very thoughtful. I knew what was the matter. He was sorry that I had rich parents. As though that would make any difference in our friendship! I told him that he should go to college and that he should study music with the very best masters, but he shook his head sadly. I told him that he should live with me as my brother, and that my parents would love him just the same because he was my friend. But still he shook his head.

In the meantime, as I had not my rich parents' money to spend, we had to play in all the villages through which we passed to get money for our food. And I also wanted to make some money to buy a present for Lise. Mother Barberin had said that she valued the cow more than anything I could give her when I became rich, and perhaps, I thought, Lise would feel the same about a gift. I wanted to give her a doll. Fortunately a doll would not cost so much as a cow. The next town we came to I bought her a lovely doll with fair hair and blue eyes.

Walking along the banks of the canal I often thought of Mrs. Milligan and Arthur and their beautiful barge, and wondered if we should meet it on the canal. But we never saw it.

One evening we could see in the distance the house where Lise lived. It stood amongst the trees and seemed to be in an atmosphere of mist. We could see the window lit up by the flames from a big fire inside. The reddish light fell across our path as we drew nearer. My heart beat quickly. I could see them inside having supper. The door and the window were shut, but there were no curtains to the window, and I looked in and saw Lise sitting beside her aunt. I signed to Mattia and Capi to be silent, and then taking my harp from my shoulder, I put it on the ground.

"Oh, yes," whispered Mattia, "a serenade. What a fine idea!"

"No, not you; I'll play alone."

I struck the first notes of my Neapolitan song. I did not sing, for I did not want my voice to betray me. As I played, I looked at Lise. She raised her head quickly and her eyes sparkled. Then I commenced to sing. She jumped from her chair and ran to the door. In a moment she was in my arms. Aunt Catherine then came out and invited us in to supper. Lise quickly placed two plates on the table.

"If you don't mind," I said, "will you put a third; we have a little friend with us." And I pulled out the doll from my bag and placed her in the chair next to Lise. The look that she gave me I shall never forget!

CHAPTER XXV. MOTHER, BROTHERS AND SISTERS

If I had not been in a hurry to get to Paris I should have stayed a long time with Lise. We had so much to say to each other and could say so little in the language that we used. She told me with signs how good her uncle and aunt had been to her and what beautiful rides she had in the barges, and I told her how I had nearly perished in the mine where Alexix worked and that my family were looking for me. That was the reason that I was hurrying to Paris and that was why it had been impossible for me to go and see Etiennette.

Naturally most of the talk was about my family, my rich family and all I would do when I had money. I would make her father, brothers, sisters, and above all herself, happy. Lise, unlike Mattia, was delighted. She quite believed that if one had money one ought to be very happy, because, would not her father have been happy if he had only had the money to pay his debts? We took long walks, all three of us, Lise, Mattia and I, accompanied by the doll and Capi. I was very happy those few days. In the evening we sat in front of the house when it was not too damp and before the fireplace when the mist was thick. I played the harp and Mattia played his violin or cornet. Lise preferred the harp, which made me very proud. When the time came and we had to separate and go to bed, I played and sang her my Neapolitan song.

Yet we had to part and go on our way. I told her that I would come back for her soon. My last words to her were: "I'll come and fetch you in a carriage drawn by four horses."

And she quite believed me and she made a motion as though she were cracking a whip to urge on the horses. She also, the same as I, could see my riches and my horses and carriages.

I was so eager to get to Paris now that if it had not been for Mattia I would have stopped only to collect what was absolutely necessary for our food. We had no cow to buy now, nor doll. It was not for me to take money to my rich parents.

"Let us get all we can," said Mattia, forcing me to take my harp, "for we don't know if we shall find Barberin at once. One would think that you had forgotten that night when you were dying of hunger."

"Oh, I haven't," I said lightly, "but we're sure to find him at once. You wait."

"Yes, but I have not forgotten how I leaned up against the church that day when you found me. Ah, I don't want to be hungry in Paris."

"We'll dine all the better when we get to my parents'," I replied.

"Well, let's work just as though we are buying another cow," urged Mattia.

This was very wise advice but I must admit that I did not sing with the same spirit. To get the money to buy a cow for Mother Barberin or a doll for Lise was quite a different matter.

"How lazy you'll be when you're rich," said Mattia. The nearer we got to Paris the gayer I became; and the more melancholy grew Mattia. As I had assured him that we should not be parted I wondered why he should be sad now. Finally, when we reached the gates of Paris, he told me how great was his fear of Garofoli, and that if he saw him he knew that he would take him again.

"You know how afraid you are of Barberin, so you can imagine how I fear Garofoli. If he's out of prison he'll be sure to catch me. Oh, my poor head; how he used to bang it! And then he will part us; of course he'd like to have you as one of his pupils, but he could not force you to stay, but he has a right to me. He's my uncle."

I had not thought of Garofoli. I arranged with Mattia that I should go to the various places that Mother Barberin had mentioned as to where I might find Barberin. Then I would go to the Rue Mouffetard and after that he should meet me at seven o'clock outside the Notre Dame Cathedral.

We parted as though we were never going to meet again. Mattia went in one direction, I in another. I had written down on paper the names of the places where Barberin had lived before. I went first to one place, then to another. At one lodging house they told me that he had lived there four years ago but that he had not been there since. The landlord told me that he'd like to catch the rogue, for he owed him one week's rent. I grew very despondent. There was only one place left for me to inquire; that was at a restaurant. The man who kept the place said that he had not seen him for a very long time, but one of the customers sitting eating at a table called out that he had been living at the Hotel du Cantal of late.

Before going to the Hotel du Cantal I went to Garofoli's place to see if I could find out something about him so that I could take back some news to poor Mattia. When I reached the yard I saw, as on my first visit, the same old man hanging up dirty rags outside the door.

"Has Garofoli returned?" I asked.

The old man looked at me without replying, then began to cough. I could see that he would not tell me anything unless I let him know that *I* knew all about Garofoli.

"You don't mean to say he is still in prison?" I exclaimed. "Why, I thought he'd got out long ago."

"No, he's got another three months yet."

Garofoli three more months in prison! Mattia could breathe. I left the horrible yard as quickly as possible and hurried off to the Hotel du Cantal. I was full of hope and joy and quite disposed to think kindly of Barberin; if it had not been for Barberin, I might have died of cold and hunger when I was a baby. It was true he had taken me from Mother Barberin to sell me to a stranger, but then he had no liking for me and perhaps he was forced to do it for the money. After all it was through him that I was finding my parents. So now I ought not to harbor any bitterness against him.

I soon reached the Hotel du Cantal which was only a hotel in name, being nothing better than a miserable lodging house.

"I want to see a man named Barberin; he comes from Chavanon," I said to a dirty old woman who sat at a desk. She was very deaf and asked me to repeat what I had said.

"Do you know a man named Barberin?" I shouted.

Then she threw up her hands to heaven so abruptly that the cat sleeping on her knees sprang down in terror.

"Alas! Alas!" she cried, then she added: "Are you the boy he was looking for?"

"Oh, you know?" I cried excitedly. "Well, where's Barberin?"

"Dead," she replied, laconically.

I leaned on my harp.

"Dead!" I cried loud enough for her to hear. I was dazed. How should I find my parents now?

"You're the boy they're looking for; I'm sure you are," said the old woman again.

"Yes, yes, I'm the boy. Where's my family? Can you tell me?"

"I don't know any more than just what I've told you, my boy; I should say my young gentleman."

"What did Barberin say about my parents? Oh, do tell me," I said imploringly.

She threw her arms up towards heaven.

"Ah, if that isn't a story!"

"Well, tell it me. What is it?"

At this moment a woman who looked like a servant came forward. The mistress of the Hotel du Cantal turned to her: "If this isn't an affair! This boy here, this young gentleman, is the man Barberin talked so much about."

"But didn't Barberin speak to you about my family?" I asked.

"I should say so—more than a hundred times. A very rich family it is, that you've got, my boy, my young gentleman."

"And where do they live and what is their name?"

"Barberin wouldn't tell us anything. He was that mysterious. He wanted to get all the reward for himself."

"Didn't he leave any papers?"

"No, nothing except one that said he came from Chavanon. If we hadn't found that, we couldn't have let his wife know he's dead."

"Oh, you did let her know?"

"Sure, why not?"

I could learn nothing from the old woman. I turned slowly towards the door.

"Where are you going?" she asked.

"Back to my friend."

"Ah, you have a friend! Does he live in Paris?"

"We got to Paris only this morning."

"Well, if you haven't a place to lodge in, why don't you come here? You will be well taken care of and it's an honest house. If your family get tired of waiting to hear from Barberin they may come here and then they'll find you. What I say is for your own interest. What age is your friend?"

"He is a little younger than I."

"Just think! two boys on the streets of Paris! You could get into such a bad place; now this is real respectable on account of the locality."

The Hotel du Cantal was one of the dirtiest lodging houses that I had ever seen and I had seen some pretty dirty ones! But what the old woman said was worth considering, besides we could not be particular. I had not found my family in their beautiful Paris mansion yet. Mattia had been right to want to get all the money we could on our way to the city. What should we have done if we had not our seventeen francs in our pockets?

"How much will you charge for a room for my friend and myself?" I asked.

"Ten cents a day. That's not much."

"Well, we'll come back to-night."

"Come back early; Paris is a bad place at night for boys," she called after me.

Night was falling. The street lamps were lit. I had a long way to walk to the Cathedral, where I was to meet Mattia. All my high spirits had vanished. I was very tired and all around me seemed gloomy. In this great Paris full of light and noise I felt so utterly alone. Would I ever find my own people? Was I ever to see my real mother and my real father? When I reached the Cathedral I had still twenty minutes to wait for Mattia. I felt this night that I needed his friendship more than ever. What a comfort it was to think that I was going to see him so gay, so kind, such a friend!

A little before seven I heard a quirk hark, then out of the shadows jumped Capi! He sprang onto my knees and licked me with his soft wet tongue. I hugged him in my arms and kissed his cold nose. It was not long before Mattia appeared. In a few words I told him that Barberin was dead and that there was now little hope that I could ever find my family. Then he gave me all the sympathy of which I was in need. He tried to console me and told me not to despair. He wished as sincerely as I that we could find my parents.

We returned to the Hotel du Cantal. The next morning I wrote to Mother Barberin to express my grief for her loss and to ask her if she had had any news from her husband before he died. By return mail she sent me word that her husband had written to her from the hospital, where they had taken him, and said that if he did not get better she was to write to Greth and Galley's, Lincoln Square, London, for they were the lawyers who were looking for me. He told her that she was not to take any steps until she was sure that he was dead.

"We must go to London," said Mattia, when I had finished reading the letter that the priest had written for her. "If the lawyers are English, that shows that your parents are English."

"Oh, I'd rather be the same as Lise and the others. But," I added, "if I'm English I'll be the same as Mrs. Milligan and Arthur."

"I'd rather you were Italian," said Mattia.

In a few minutes our baggage was ready and we were off. It took us eight days to hike from Paris to Bologne, stopping at the principal towns en route. When we reached Bologne we had thirty-two francs in our purse. We took passage on a cargo boat that was going the next day to London. What a rough journey we had! Poor Mattia declared that he would never go on the sea again. When at last we were steaming up the Thames I begged him to get up and see the wonderful sights, but he implored me to let him alone. At last the engine stopped and the ropes were thrown to the ground, and we landed in London.

I knew very little English, but Mattia had picked up quite a great deal from an Englishman who had worked with him at the Gassot Circus. When we landed he at once asked a policeman to direct us to Lincoln Square. It seemed to be a very long way. Many times we thought that we had lost ourselves but again upon making inquiries we found that we were going in the right direction. Finally we reached Temple Bar and a few steps further we came to Green Square.

My heart heat so quickly when we stood before the door of Greth and Galley's office that I had to ask Mattia to wait a moment until I had recovered myself. After Mattia had stated to the clerk my name and my business, we were shown at once into the private office of the head of the firm, Mr. Greth. Fortunately this gentleman spoke French, so I was able to speak to him myself. He questioned me upon every detail of my life. My answers evidently convinced him that I was the boy he was looking for, for he told me that I had a family living in London and that he would send me to them at once.

"One moment, sir. Have I a father?" I asked, scarcely able to say the word "father."

"Yes, not only a father, but a mother, brothers and sisters," he replied.

"Oh...."

He touched a bell and a clerk appeared whom he told to take charge of us.

"Oh, I had forgotten," said Mr. Greth, "your name is Driscoll; your father's name is Mr. John Driscoll."

In spite of Mr. Greth's ugly face I think I could have jumped at him and hugged him if he had given me time, but with his hand he indicated the door and we followed the clerk.

CHAPTER XXVI. BITTER DISAPPOINTMENT

When we got to the street the clerk hailed a cab and told us to jump in. The strange looking vehicle, with the coachman sitting on a box at the back of a hood that covered us, I learned later was a hansom cab. Mattia and I were huddled in a corner with Capi between our legs. The clerk took up the rest of the seat. Mattia had heard him tell the coachman to drive us to Bethnal-Green. The driver seemed none too anxious to take us there. Mattia and I thought it was probably on account of the distance. We both knew what "Green" meant in English, and Bethnal-Green undoubtedly was the name of the park where my people lived. For a long time the cab rolled through the busy streets of London. It was such a long way that I thought perhaps their estate was situated on the outskirts of the city. The word "green" made us think that it might be in the country. But nothing around us announced the country. We were in a very thickly populated quarter; the black mud splashed our cab as we drove along; then we turned into a much poorer part of the city and every now and again the cabman pulled up as though he did not know his way. At last he stopped altogether and through the little window of the hansom a discussion took place between Greth & Galley's clerk and the bewildered cabman. From what Mattia could learn the man said that it was no use, he could not find his way, and he asked the clerk which direction he should take. The clerk replied that he did not know for he had never been in that thieves' locality before. We both caught the word "thieves." Then the clerk gave some money to the coachman and told us to get out of the cab. The man grumbled at his fare and then turned round and drove off. We were standing now in a muddy street before what the English call a gin palace. Our guide looked about him in disgust, then entered the swing-doors of the gin palace. We followed. Although we were in a miserable part of the city I had never seen anything more luxurious. There were gilt framed mirrors everywhere, glass chandeliers and a magnificent counter that shone like silver. Yet the people who filled this place were filthy and in rags. Our guide gulped down a drink standing before the beautiful counter, then asked the man who had served him if he could direct him to the place he wanted to find. Evidently he got the information he required for he hurried out again through the swing-doors, we following close on his heels. The streets through which we walked now were even narrower and from one house across to another were swung wash lines from which dirty rags were hanging. The women who sat in their doorways were pale and their matted fair hair hung loose over their shoulders. The children were almost naked and the few clothes that they did wear were but rags. In the alley were some pigs wallowing in the stagnant water from which a fetid odor arose. Our guide stopped. Evidently he had lost his way. But at this moment a policeman appeared. The clerk spoke to him and the officer told him he would show him the way.... We followed the policeman down more narrow streets. At last we stopped at a yard in the middle of which was a little pond.

"This is Red Lion Court," said the officer.

Why were we stopping there? Could it be possible that my parents lived in this place? The policeman knocked at the door of a wooden hut and our guide thanked him. So we had arrived. Mattia took my hand and gently pressed it. I pressed his. We understood one another. I was as in a dream when the door was opened and we found ourselves in a room with a big fire burning in the grate.

Before the fire in a large cane chair sat an old man with a white beard, and his head covered with a black skull cap. At a table sat a man of about forty and a woman about six years his junior. She must have been very pretty once but now her eyes had a glassy stare and her manners were listless. Then there were four children—two boys and two girls—all very fair like their mother. The eldest boy was about eleven, the youngest girl, scarcely three. I did not know what the clerk was saying to the man, I only caught the name "Driscoll," my name, so the lawyer had said. All eyes were turned on Mattia and me, only the baby girl paid attention to Capi.

"Which one is Remi?" asked the man in French.

"I am," I said, taking a step forward.

"Then come and kiss your father, my boy."

When I had thought of this moment I had imagined that I should be overwhelmed with happiness and spring into my father's arms, but I felt nothing of the kind. I went up and kissed my father.

"Now," he said, "there's your grandfather, your mother, your brothers and sisters."

I went up to my mother first and put my arms about her. She let me kiss her but she did not return my caress; she only said two or three words which I did not understand.

"Shake hands with your grandfather," said my father, "and go gently; he's paralyzed."

I also shook hands with my brothers and my eldest sister. I wanted to take the little one in my arms but she was too occupied with Capi and pushed me away. As I went from one to the other I was angry with myself. Why could I not feel any pleasure at having found my family at last. I had a father, a mother, brothers, sisters and a grandfather. I had longed for this moment, I had been mad with joy in thinking that I, like other boys, would have a family that I could call my own to love me and whom I could love.... And now I was staring at my family curiously, finding nothing in my heart to say to them, not a word of affection. Was I a monster? If I had found my parents in a palace instead of in a hovel should I have had more affection for them? I felt ashamed at this thought. Going over again to my mother I put my arms round her and kissed her full on the lips. Evidently she did not understand what made me do this, for instead of returning my kisses she looked at me in a listless manner, then turning to her husband, my father, she shrugged her shoulders and said something that I could not understand but which made him laugh. Her indifference and my father's laugh went right to my heart. It did not seem to me that my affection should have been received in such a way.

"Who is he?" asked my father, pointing to Mattia. I told him that Mattia was my dearest friend and how much I owed him.

"Good," said my father; "would he like to stay and see the country?" I was about to answer for Mattia, but he spoke first.

"That's just what I want," he exclaimed.

My father then asked why Barberin had not come with me. I told him that he was dead. He seemed pleased to hear this. He repeated it to my mother, who also seemed pleased. Why were they both pleased that Barberin was dead?

"You must be rather surprised that we have not searched for you for thirteen years," said my father, "and then suddenly to go off and look up this man who found you when you were a baby."

I told him that I was very surprised, and that I'd like to know about it.

"Come near the fire then and I'll tell you all about it."

I flung the bag from my shoulders and took the chair that he offered me. As I stretched out my legs, wet, and covered with mud, to the fire my grandfather spat on one side, like an old cat that is annoyed.

"Don't pay any attention to him," said my father; "the old chap doesn't like any one to sit before his fire, but you needn't mind him, if you're cold."

I was surprised to hear any one speak like this of an old man. I kept my legs under my chair, for I thought that attention should be paid to him.

"You are my eldest son now," said my father; "you were born a year after my marriage with your mother. When I married there was a young girl who thought that I was going to marry her, and out of revenge she stole you from us when you were six months old. We searched everywhere for you but we did not go so far as Paris. We thought that you were dead until three months ago when this woman was dying she confessed the truth. I went over to France at once and the police in that locality where you had been left, told me that you had been adopted by a mason named Barberin who lived at Chavanon. I found him and he told me that he had loaned you to a musician named Vitalis and that you were tramping through France. I could not stay over there any longer, but I left Barberin some money and told him to search for you, and when he had news to write to Greth and Galley. I did not give him my address here, because we are only in London during the winter; the rest of the year we travel through England and Scotland. We are peddlers by trade, and I have my own caravans. There, boy, that is how it is you have come back to us after thirteen years. You may feel a little timid at first because you can't understand us, but you'll soon pick up English and be able to talk to your brothers and sisters. It won't be long before you're used to us."

Yes, of course I should get used to them; were they not my own people? The fine baby linen, the beautiful clothes had not spoken the truth. But what did that matter! Affection was worth more than riches. It was not money that I pined for, but to have affection, a family and a home. While my father was talking to me they had set the table for supper. A large joint of roast beef with potatoes round it was placed in the middle of the table.

"Are you hungry, boys?" asked my father, addressing Mattia and myself. Mattia showed his white teeth.

"Well, sit down to table."

But before sitting down he pushed my grandfather's cane rocker up to the table. Then taking his own place with his back to the fire, he commenced to cut the roast beef and gave each one a fine big slice and some potatoes.

Although I had not been brought up exactly on the principle of good breeding, I noticed that my brothers and sister's behaved very badly at table; they ate more often with their fingers, sticking them into the gravy and licking them without my father and mother seeming to notice them. As to my grandfather, he gave his whole attention to what was before him, and the one hand that he was able to use went continually from his plate to his mouth. When he let a piece fall from his shaking fingers my brothers and sisters laughed.

I thought that we should spend the evening together round the fire, but my father said that he was expecting friends, and told us to go to bed. Beckoning to Mattia and me he took a candle and went out to a stable that led from the room where we had been eating. In this stable were two big caravans. He opened the door of one and we saw two small beds, one above the other.

"There you are, boys, there are your beds," he said. "Sleep well."

Such was the welcome into my family.

CHAPTER XXVII. A DISTRESSING DISCOVERY

My father left the candle with us, but locked the caravan on the outside. We got into bed as quickly as possible, without chatting, as was our habit. Mattia did not seem to want to talk any more than I and I was pleased that he was silent. We blew the candle out, but I found it impossible to go to sleep. I thought over all that had passed, turning over and over in my narrow bed. I could hear Mattia, who occupied the berth above mine, turn over restlessly also. He could not sleep any more than I.

Hours passed. As it grew later a vague fear oppressed me. I felt uneasy, but I could not understand why it was that I felt so. Of what was I afraid? Not of sleeping in a caravan even in this vile part of London! How many times in my vagabond life had I spent the night less protected than I was at this moment! I knew that I was sheltered from all danger and yet I was oppressed with a fear that amounted almost to terror.

The hours passed one after the other; suddenly I heard a noise at the stable door which opened onto another street. Then came several regular knocks at intervals. Then a light penetrated our caravan. I glanced hastily round in surprise and Capi, who slept beside my bed, woke up with a growl. I then saw that this light came in through a little window of the caravan against which our berths were placed, and which I had not noticed when going to bed because there was a curtain hanging over it. The upper part of this window touched Mattia's bed and the lower part touched mine. Afraid that Capi might wake up all the house, I put my hand over his mouth, then looked outside.

My father had entered the stable and quietly opened the door on the other side, then he closed it again in the same cautious manner after admitting two men heavily laden with bundles which they carried on their shoulders. Then he placed his finger on his lip, and with the other hand which held the lantern, he pointed to the caravan in which we were sleeping. I was about to call out that they need not mind us, but I was afraid I should wake up Mattia, who now, I thought, was sleeping quietly, so I kept still. My father helped the two men unload their bundles, then he disappeared, but soon he returned with my mother. During his absence the men had opened their baggage. There were hats, underclothes, stockings, gloves, etc. Evidently these men were merchants who had come to sell their goods to my parents. My father took each object and examined it by the light of the lantern and passed it on to my mother, who with a little pair of scissors cut off the tickets and put them in her pocket. This appeared strange to me, as also the hour that they had chosen for this sale.

While my mother was examining the goods my father spoke to the men in a whisper. If I had known English a little better I should perhaps have caught what he said, but all I could hear was the word "police," that was said several times and for that reason caught my ear.

When all the goods had been carefully noted, my parents and the two men went into the house, and again our caravan was in darkness. They had evidently gone inside to settle the bill. I wanted to convince myself that what I had seen was quite natural, yet despite my desire I could not believe so. Why had not these men who had come to see my parents entered by the other door? Why did they talk of the police in whispers as though they were afraid of being heard outside? Why had my mother cut off the tickets after she had bought the goods? I could not drive these thoughts from my mind. After a time a light again filled our caravan. I looked out this time in spite of myself. I told myself that I ought not to look, and yet ... I looked. I told myself that it was better that I should not know, and yet I wanted to see.

My father and mother were alone. While my mother quickly made a bundle of the goods, my father swept a corner of the stable. Under the dry sand that he heaped up there was a trap door. He lifted it. By then my mother had finished tying up the bundles and my father took them and lowered them through the trap to a cellar below, my mother holding the lantern to light him. Then he shut the trap door and swept the sand over it again. Over the sand they both strewed wisps of straw as on the rest of the stable floor. Then they went out.

At the moment when they softly closed the door it seemed to me that Mattia moved in his bed and that he lay back on his pillow. Had he seen? I did not dare ask him. From head to foot I was in a cold perspiration. I remained in this state all night long. A cock crowed at daybreak; then only did I drop off to sleep.

The noise of the key being turned in the door of our caravan the next morning woke me. Thinking that it was my father who had come to tell us that it was time to get up, I closed my eyes so as not to see him.

"It was your brother," said Mattia; "he has unlocked the door and he's gone now."

We dressed. Mattia did not ask me if I had slept well, neither did I put the question to him. Once I caught him looking at me and I turned my eyes away.

We had to go to the kitchen, but neither my father nor mother were there. My grandfather was seated before the fire in his big chair as though he had not moved since the night before, and my eldest sister, whose name was Annie, was wiping the table. Allen, my eldest brother, was sweeping the room. I went over to them to wish them good morning, but they continued with their work without taking any notice of me. I went towards my grandfather, but he would not let me get near him, and like the evening before, he spat at my side, which stopped me short.

"Ask them," I said to Mattia, "what time I shall see my mother and father?"

Mattia did as I told him, and my grandfather, upon hearing one of us speak English, seemed to feel more amiable.

"What does he say?"

"He says that your father has gone out for the day and that your mother is asleep, and that if we like we may go out."

"Did he only say that?" I asked, finding this translation very short.

Mattia seemed confused.

"I don't know if I understood the rest," he said.

"Tell me what you think you understood."

"It seemed to me that he said that if we found some bargains in the city we were not to miss them. He said that we lived at the expense of fools."

My grandfather must have guessed that Mattia was explaining what he had said to me, for with the hand that was not paralyzed, he made a motion as though he were slipping something into his pocket, then he winked his eye.

"Let us go out," I said quickly.

For two or three hours we walked about, not daring to go far for fear we might become lost. Bethnal-Green was even more horrible in the daytime than it had been at night. Mattia and I hardly spoke a word. Now and again he pressed my hand.

When we returned to the house my mother had not left her room. Through the open door I could see that she was leaning her head on the table. Thinking that she was sick I ran to her to kiss her, as I was unable to speak to her. She lifted up her head, which swayed. She looked at me but did not see me. I smelled the odor of gin on her hot breath. I drew back. Her head fell again on her arms resting on the table.

"Gin," said my grandfather, grinning.

I remained motionless. I felt turned to stone. I don't know how long I stood so. Suddenly I turned to Mattia. He was looking at me with eyes full of tears. I signed to him and again we left the house. For a long time we walked about, side by side, holding each other's hands, saying nothing, going straight before us without knowing where we were going.

"Where do you want to go, Remi?" he asked at last, anxiously.

"I don't know. Somewhere so we can talk. I want to speak to you, Mattia. We can't talk in this crowd."

We had by this time come to a much wider street at the end of which was a public garden. We hurried to this spot and sat down on a bench.

"You know how much I love you, Mattia boy," I began, "and you know that it was through friendship for you that I asked you to come with me to see my people. You won't doubt my friendship, no matter what I ask of you?"

"Don't be such a silly," he said, forcing a smile.

"You want to laugh so that I won't break down," I replied. "If I can't cry when I'm with you, when can I cry? But.... Oh ... oh, Mattia, Mattia!"

Throwing my arms around dear old Mattia's neck, I burst into tears. Never had I felt so miserable. When I had been alone in this great world, never had I felt so unhappy as I did at this moment. After my burst of sobs

I forced myself to be calm. It was not because I wanted Mattia's pity that I had brought him to this garden, it was not for myself; it was for him.

"Mattia," I said resolutely, "you must go back to France."

"Leave you? Never!"

"I knew beforehand what you would reply and I am pleased, oh, so pleased that you wish to be with me, but, Mattia, you *must* go back to France at once!"

"Why? Tell me that."

"Because.... Tell me, Mattia. Don't be afraid. Did you sleep last night? Did you see?"

"I did not sleep," he answered.

"And you saw...?"

"All."

"And you understood?"

"That those goods had not been paid for. Your father was angry with the men because they knocked at the stable door and not at the house door. They told him that the police were watching them."

"You see very well, then, that you must go," I said.

"If I must go, you must go also; it is no better for one than for the other."

"If you had met Garofoli in Paris and he had forced you to go back to him, I am sure you would not have wanted me to stay with you. I am simply doing what you would do yourself."

He did not reply.

"You must go back to France," I insisted; "go to Lise and tell her that I cannot do for her father what I promised. I told her that the first thing I did would be to pay off his debts. You must tell her how it is, and go to Mother Barberin also. Simply say that my people are not rich as I had thought; there is no disgrace in not having money. *But don't tell them anything more.*"

"It is not because they are poor that you want me to go, so I shan't go," Mattia replied obstinately. "I know what it is, after what we saw last night; you are afraid for me."

"Mattia, don't say that!"

"You are afraid one day that I shall cut the tickets off goods that have not been paid for."

"Mattia, Mattia, don't!"

190

"Well, if you are afraid for me, I am afraid for you. Let us both go."

"It's impossible; my parents are nothing to you, but this is my father and mother, and I must stay with them. It is my family."

"Your family! That man who steals, your father! That drunken woman your mother!"

"Don't you dare say so, Mattia," I cried, springing up from my seat; "you are speaking of my father and mother and I must respect them and love them."

"Yes, so you should if they are your people, but ... are they?"

"You forget their many proofs."

"You don't resemble your father or your mother. Their children are all fair, while you are dark. And then how is it they could spend so much money to find a child? Put all these things together and in my opinion you are not a Driscoll. You might write to Mother Barberin and ask her to tell you just what the clothes were like that you wore when you were found. Then ask that man you call your father to describe the clothes his baby had on when it was stolen. Until then I shan't move."

"But suppose one day Mattia gets a bang on his poor head?"

"That would not be so hard if he received the blow for a friend," he said, smiling.

We did not return to the Red Lion Court until night. My father and mother passed no remark upon our absence. After supper my father drew two chairs to the fireside, which brought a growl from my grandfather, and then asked us to tell him how we had made enough money to live on in France. I told the story.

"Not only did we earn enough to live on, but we got enough to buy a cow," said Mattia with assurance. In his turn he told how we came by the cow.

"You must be clever kids," said my father; "show us what you can do."

I took my harp and played a piece, but not my Neapolitan song. Mattia played a piece on his violin and a piece on his cornet. It was the cornet solo that brought the greatest applause from the children who had gathered round us in a circle.

"And Capi, can he do anything?" asked my father. "He ought to be able to earn his food."

I was very proud of Capi's talents. I put him through all his tricks and as usual he scored a great success.

"Why, that dog is worth a fortune," exclaimed my father.

I was very pleased at this praise and assured him that Capi could learn anything that one wished to teach him. My father translated what I said into English, and it seemed to me that he added something more which made everybody laugh, for the old grandfather winked his eye several times and said, "Fine dog!"

"This is what I suggest," said my father, "that is if Mattia would like to live with us?"

"I want to stay with Remi," replied Mattia.

"Well, this is what I propose," continued my father. "We're not rich and we all work. In the summer we travel through the country and the children go and sell the goods to those who won't take the trouble to come to us, but in the winter we haven't much to do. Now you and Remi can go and play music in the streets. You'll make quite a little money as Christmas draws near, but Ned and Allen must take Capi with them and he'll make the people laugh with his tricks; in that way the talent will be distributed."

"Capi won't work well with any one but me," I said quickly. I could not bear to be parted from my dog.

"He'll learn to work with Allen and Ned easy," said my father; "we'll get more money this way."

"Oh, but we'll get ever so much more with Capi," I insisted.

"That's enough," replied my father briefly; "when I say a thing I mean it. No arguments."

I said nothing more. As I laid down in my bed that night Mattia whispered in my ear: "Now to-morrow you write to Mother Barberin." Then he jumped into bed.

But the next morning I had to give Capi his lesson, I took him in my arms and while I gently kissed him on his cold nose, I explained to him what he had to do; poor doggy! how he looked at me, how he listened! I then put his leash in Allen's hand and he followed the two boys obediently, but with a forlorn air.

My father took Mattia and me across London where there were beautiful houses, splendid streets with wide pavements, and carriages that shone like glass, drawn by magnificent horses and driven by big fat coachmen with powdered wigs. It was late when we got back to Red Lion Court, for the distance from the West End to Bethnal-Green is great. How pleased I was to see Capi again. He was covered with mud, but in a good humor. I was so pleased to see him, that after I had rubbed him well down with dry straw, I wrapped him in my sheepskin and made him sleep in my bed.

Things went on this way for several days. Mattia and I went one way and Capi, Ned, and Allen another. Then one evening my father told me that we could take Capi the next day with us, as he wanted the two boys to do something in the house. Mattia and I were very pleased and we intended to do our utmost to bring back a good sum of money so that he would let us have the dog always. We had to get Capi back and we would not spare ourselves, neither one of us. We made Capi undergo a severe washing and combing early in the morning, then we went off.

Unfortunately for our plan a heavy fog had been hanging over London for two entire days. It was so dense that we could only see a few steps before us, and those who listened to us playing behind these fog curtains could not see Capi. It was a most annoying state of affairs for our "takings." Little did we think how indebted we should be to the fog a few minutes later. We were walking through one of the most popular streets when suddenly I discovered that Capi was not with us. This was extraordinary, for he always kept close at our heels. I waited for him to catch up with us. I stood at the entrance of a dark alley and whistled softly, for we could see but a short distance. I was beginning to fear that he had been stolen from us when he came up on the run, holding a pair of woolen stockings between his teeth. Placing his fore paws against me he presented them to me with a bark. He seemed as proud as when he had accomplished one of his most difficult tricks and wanted my approval. It was all done in a few seconds. I stood dumbfounded. Then Mattia seized the stockings with one hand and pulled me down the alley with the other.

"Walk quick, but don't run," he whispered.

He told me a moment later that a man who had hurried past him on the pavement was saying, "Where's that thief? I'll get him!" We went out by the other end of the alley.

"If it had not been for the fog we should have been arrested as thieves," said Mattia.

For a moment I stood almost choking. They had made a thief of my good honest Capi!

"Hold him tight," I said, "and come back to the house."

We walked quickly.

The father and mother were seated at the table folding up material. I threw the pair of stockings down. Allen and Ned laughed.

"Here's a pair of stockings," I said; "you've made a thief of my dog. I thought you took him out to amuse people."

I was trembling so I could scarcely speak, and yet I never felt more determined.

"And if it was not for amusement," demanded my father, "what would you do, I'd like to know?"

"I'd tie a cord round Capi's neck, and although I love him dearly, I'd drown him. I don't want Capi to become a thief any more than I want to be one myself, and if I thought that I ever should become a thief, I'd drown myself at once with my dog."

My father looked me full in the face. I thought he was going to strike me. His eyes gleamed. I did not flinch.

"Oh, very well, then," said he, recovering himself; "so that it shall not happen again, you may take Capi out with you in the future."

I showed my fist to the two boys. I could not speak to them, but they saw by my manner that if they dared have anything more to do with my dog, they would have me to reckon with. I was willing to fight them both to protect Capi.

From that day every one in my family openly showed their dislike for me. My grandfather continued to spit angrily when I approached him. The boys and my eldest sister played every trick they possibly could upon me. My father and mother ignored me, only demanding of me my money every evening. Out of the whole family, for whom I had felt so much affection when I had landed in England, there was only baby Kate who would let me fondle her, and she turned from me coldly if I had not candy or an orange in my pocket for her.

Although I would not listen to what Mattia had said at first, gradually, little by little, I began to wonder if I did really belong to this family. I had done nothing for them to be so unkind to me. Mattia, seeing me so greatly worried, would say as though to himself: "I am just wondering what kind of clothes Mother Barberin will tell us you wore...."

At last the letter came. The priest had written it for her. It read:

"My little Remi: I was surprised and sorry to learn the contents of your letter. From what Barberin told me and also from the clothes you had on when you were found, I thought that you belonged to a very rich family. I can easily tell you what you wore, for I have kept everything. You were not wound up in wrappings like a French baby; you wore long robes and underskirts like little English babies. You had on a white flannel robe and over that a very fine linen robe, then a big white cashmere pelisse lined with white silk and trimmed with beautiful white embroidery, and you had a lovely lace bonnet, and then white woolen socks with little silk rosettes. None of these things were marked, but the little flannel jacket you had next to your skin and the flannel robe had both been marked, but the marks had been carefully cut out. There, Remi, boy, that is all I can tell you. Don't worry, dear child, that you can't give us all the fine presents that you promised. Your cow that you bought with your savings is worth all the presents in the world to me. I am pleased to tell you that she's in good health and gives the same fine quantity of milk, so I am very comfortably off now, and I never look at her without thinking of you and your little friend Mattia. Let me have news of you sometimes, dear boy, you are so tender and affectionate, and I hope, now you have found your family, they will all love you as you deserve to be loved. I kiss you lovingly.

"Your foster mother,

"WIDOW BARBERIN."

Dear Mother Barberin! she imagined that everybody must love me because she did!

"She's a fine woman," said Mattia; "very fine, she thought of me! Now let's see what Mr. Driscoll has to say."

"He might have forgotten the things."

"Does one forget the clothes that their child wears when it was kidnaped? Why, it's only through its clothes that they can find it."

"Wait until we hear what he says before we think anything."

It was not an easy thing for me to ask my father how I was dressed on the day that I was stolen. If I had put the question casually without any underthought, it would have been simple enough. As it was I was timid. Then one day when the cold sleet had driven me home earlier than usual, I took my courage in both hands, and broached the subject that was causing me so much anxiety. At my question my father looked me full in the face. But I looked back at him far more boldly than I imagined that I could at this moment. Then he smiled. There was something hard and cruel in the smile but still it was a smile.

"On the day that you were stolen from us," he said slowly, "you wore a flannel robe, a linen robe, a lace bonnet, white woolen shoes, and a white embroidered cashmere pelisse. Two of your garments were marked F.D., Francis Driscoll, your real name, but this mark was cut out by the woman who stole you, for she hoped that in this way you would never be found. I'll show you your baptismal certificates which, of course, I still have."

He searched in a drawer and soon brought forth a big paper which he handed to me.

"If you don't mind," I said with a last effort, "Mattia will translate it for me."

"Certainly."

Mattia translated it as well as he could. It appeared that I was born on Thursday, August the 2nd, and that I was the son of John Driscoll and Margaret Grange, his wife.

What further proofs could I ask?

"That's all very fine," said Mattia that night, when we were in our caravan, "but how comes it that peddlers were rich enough to give their children lace bonnets and embroidered pelisses? Peddlers are not so rich as that!"

"It is because they were peddlers that they could get those things cheaper."

Mattia whistled, but he shook his head, then again he whispered: "You're not that Driscoll's baby, but you're the baby that Driscoll stole!"

I was about to reply but he had already climbed up into his bed.

CHAPTER XXVIII. A MYSTERIOUS STRANGER

If I had been in Mattia's place, I should perhaps have had as much imagination as he, but I felt in my position that it was wrong for me to have such thoughts. It had been proved beyond a doubt that Mr. Driscoll was my father. I could not look at the matter from the same point of view as Mattia. He might doubt ... but I must not. When he tried to make me believe as he did, I told him to be silent. But he was pig-headed and I was not always able to get the better of his obstinacy.

"Why are you dark and all the rest of the family fair?" he would ask repeatedly.

"How was it that poor people could dress their baby in fine laces and embroidery?" was another often repeated question. And I could only reply by putting a question myself.

"Why did they search for me if I was not their child? Why had they given money to Barberin and to Greth and Galley?"

Mattia could find no answer to my question and yet he would not be convinced.

"I think we should both go back to France," he urged.

"That's impossible."

"Because it's your duty to keep with your family, eh? But is it your family?"

These discussions only had one result, they made me more unhappy than I had ever been. How terrible it is to doubt. Yet, in spite of my wish not to doubt, I doubted. Who would have thought when I was crying so sadly because I thought I had no family that I should be in such despair now that I had one. How could I know the truth? In the meantime I had to sing and dance and laugh and make grimaces when my heart was full.

One Sunday my father told me to stay in the house because he wanted me. He sent Mattia off alone. All the others had gone out; my grandfather alone was upstairs. I had been with my father for about an hour when there was a knock at the door. A gentleman, who was unlike any of the men who usually called on my father, came in. He was about fifty years old and dressed in the height of fashion. He had white pointed teeth like a dog and when he smiled he drew his lips back over them as though he was going to bite. He spoke to my father in English, turning continually to look at me.

Then he began to talk French; he spoke this language with scarcely an accent.

"This is the young boy that you spoke to me about?" he said. "He appears very well."

"Answer the gentleman," said my father to me.

"Yes, I am quite well," I replied, surprised.

"You have never been ill?"

"I had pneumonia once."

"Ah, when was that?"

"Three years ago. I slept out in the cold all night. My master, who was with me, was frozen to death, and I got pneumonia."

"Haven't you felt any effects of this illness since?"

"No."

"No fatigue, no perspiration at night?"

"No. When I'm tired it's because I have walked a lot, but I don't get ill."

He came over to me and felt my arms, then put his head on my heart, then at my back and on my chest, telling me to take deep breaths. He also told me to cough. That done he looked at me for a long time. It was then that I thought he wanted to bite me, his teeth gleamed in such a terrible smile. A few moments later he left the house with my father.

What did it mean? Did he want to take me in his employ? I should have to leave Mattia and Capi. No, I wouldn't be a servant to anybody, much less this man whom I disliked already.

My father returned and told me I could go out if I wished. I went into the caravan. What was my surprise to find Mattia there. He put his finger to his lips.

"Go and open the stable door," he whispered, "I'll go out softly behind you. They mustn't know that I was here."

I was mystified but I did as he asked.

"Do you know who that man was who was with your father?" he asked excitedly when we were in the street. "It was Mr. James Milligan, your friend's uncle."

I stood staring at him in the middle of the pavement. He took me by the arm and dragged me on.

"I was not going out all alone," he continued, "so I went in there to sleep, but I didn't sleep. Your father and a gentleman came into the stable and I heard all they said; at first I didn't try to listen but afterward I did.

"'Solid as a rock,' said the gentleman; 'nine out of ten would have died, but he pulled through with pneumonia.'

"'How is your nephew?' asked your father.

"'Better. Three months ago the doctors again gave him up, but his mother saved him once more. Oh, she's a marvelous mother, is Mrs. Milligan.'

"You can imagine when I heard this name if I did not glue my ears to the window.

"'Then if your nephew is better,' continued your father, 'all you've done is useless.'

"'For the moment, perhaps,' replied the other, 'but I don't say that Arthur is going to live; it would be a miracle if he did, and I am not afraid of miracles. The day he dies the only heir to that estate will be myself.'

"'Don't worry; I'll see to that,' said Driscoll.

"'Yes, I count on you,' replied Mr. Milligan."

My first thought was to question my father, but it was not wise to let them know that they had been overheard. As Mr. Milligan had business with my father he would probably come to the house again, and the next time, Mattia, whom he did not know, could follow him.

A few days later Mattia met a friend of his, Bob, the Englishman, whom he had known at the Gassot Circus. I could see by the way he greeted Mattia that he was very fond of him. He at once took a liking to Capi and myself. From that day we had a strong friend, who, by his experience and advice, was of great help to us in time of trouble.

CHAPTER XXIX. IN PRISON

Spring came slowly, but at last the day arrived for the family to leave London. The caravans had been repainted and were loaded with merchandise. There were materials, hats, shawls, handkerchiefs, sweaters, underwear, ear-rings, razors, soap, powders, cream, everything that one could imagine.

The caravans were full. The horses bought. Where, and how? I did not know but we saw them come and everything was then ready for the departure. We did not know if we were to stay with the old grandfather or go with the family, but my father, finding that we made good money playing, told us the night before that we should go on the road with him and play our music.

"Let us go back to France," urged Mattia; "here's a good chance now."

"Why not travel through England?"

"Because I tell you something's going to happen if we stay here, and besides we might find Mrs. Milligan and Arthur in France. If he has been ill she will be sure to take him on their barge, now the summer is coming."

I told him that I must stay.

The same day we started. I saw in the afternoon how they sold the things that cost so little. We arrived at a large village and the caravans were drawn up on the public square. One of the sides was lowered and the goods displayed temptingly for the purchasers to inspect.

"Look at the price! Look at the price!" cried my father. "You couldn't find anything like this elsewhere for the price! I don't sell 'em; I'm giving 'em away. Look at this!"

"He must have stolen them," I heard the people say when they saw the prices. If they had glanced at my shamed looks, they would have known that they were right in their suppositions.

If they did not notice me, Mattia did. "How much longer can you bear this?" he asked.

I was silent.

"Let us go back to France," he urged again. "I feel that something is going to happen, and going to happen soon. Don't you think sooner or later the police will get on to Driscoll, seeing how cheap he's selling the things? Then what'll happen?"

"Oh, Mattia...."

"If you will keep your eyes shut I must keep mine open. We shall both be arrested and we haven't done anything, but how can we prove that? Aren't we eating the food that is paid for by the money that he gets for these things?"

I had never thought of that; it struck me now like a blow in the face.

"But we earn our food," I stammered, trying to defend ourselves.

"That's true, but we're living with thieves," replied Mattia, speaking more frankly than he had ever done before, "and then if we're sent to prison, we can't look for your family. And I'm anxious to see Mrs. Milligan to warn her against that James Milligan. You don't know what he might not do to Arthur. Let us go while we can."

"Let me have a few more days to think it over, Mattia," I said.

"Hurry up, then. Jack the Giant Killer smelled flesh—I smell danger."

Circumstances did for me what I was afraid to do. Several weeks had passed since we left London. My father had set up his caravans in a town where the races were about to be held. As Mattia and I had nothing to do with selling the goods, we went to see the race-course, which was at some distance from the town. Outside the English race-courses there is usually a fair going on. Mountebanks of all descriptions, musicians, and stall holders gather there two or three days in advance.

We were passing by a camp fire over which a kettle was hanging when we recognized our friend Bob, who had been with Mattia in the circus. He was delighted to see us again. He had come to the races with two friends and was going to give an exhibition of strength. He had engaged some musicians but they had failed him at the last moment and he was afraid that the performance the next day would be a failure. He had to have musicians to attract a crowd. Would we help him out? The profits would be divided between the five of us that made up the company. There would even be something for Capi, for he would like to have Capi perform his tricks in the intervals. We agreed and promised to be there the next day at the time he mentioned.

When I told of this arrangement to my father he said that he wanted Capi and that we could not have him. I wondered if they were going to make my dog do some dirty trick. From my look my father guessed my thoughts.

"Oh, it's all right," he said; "Capi's a good watch dog; he must stand by the caravans. In a crowd like we shall have we might easily be robbed. You two go alone and play with your friend Bob, and if you are not finished until late, which will be quite likely, you can join us at the Old Oak Tavern. We shall go on our way again to-morrow."

We had spent the night before at the Old Oak Tavern, which was a mile out on a lonely road. The place was kept by a couple whose appearance did not inspire one with confidence. It was quite easy to find this place. It was on a straight road. The only annoying thing was that it was a long walk for us after a tiring day.

But when my father said a thing I had to obey. I promised to be at the Tavern. The next day, after tying Capi to the caravan, where he was to be on guard, I hurried off to the race-course with Mattia.

We began to play as soon as we arrived and kept it up until night. My fingers ached as though they had been pricked with a thousand pins and poor Mattia had blown his cornet so long that he could scarcely breathe. It was past midnight. Just as they were doing their last turn a big bar of iron which they were using in their feats fell on Mattia's foot. I thought that his foot was broken. Fortunately it was only severely bruised. No bones were broken, but still he could not walk.

It was decided that he should stay there that night with Bob and that I should go on alone to the Old Oak Tavern, for I had to know where the Driscoll family was going the next day. All was dark when I reached the tavern. I looked round for the caravans. They were nowhere to be seen. All I could see, beside one or two miserable wagons, was a big cage from which, as I drew near, came the cry of a wild beast. The beautiful gaudy colored caravans belonging to the Driscoll family were gone.

I knocked at the tavern door. The landlord opened it and turned the light from his lantern full on my face. He recognised me, but instead of letting me go in he told me to hurry after my parents, who had gone to Lewes, and said that I'd better not lose any time joining them. Then he shut the door in my face.

Since I had been in England I had learned to speak English fairly well. I understood clearly what he said, but I had not the slightest idea where Lewes was situated, and besides I could not go, even if I found out the direction, and leave Mattia behind. I began my weary tramp back to the race-course; an hour later I was sleeping beside Mattia in Bob's wagon.

The next morning Bob told me how to get to Lewes and I was ready to start. I was watching him boil the water for breakfast when I looked up from the fire and saw Capi being led towards us by a policeman. What did it mean? The moment Capi recognized me he gave a tug at his leash and escaping from the officer bounded toward me and jumped into my arms.

"Is that your dog?" asked the policeman.

"Yes."

"Then come with me, you're under arrest."

He seized me by the collar.

"What do you mean by arresting him?" cried Bob, jumping up from the fire.

"Are you his brother?"

"No, his friend."

"Well, a man and a boy robbed St. George's Church last night. They got up a ladder and went through the window. This dog was there to give the alarm. They were surprised in the act and in their hurry to get out by the window, the dog was left in the church. I knew that with the dog I'd be sure to find the thieves; here's one, now where's his father?"

I could not utter a word. Mattia, who had heard the talk, came out of the caravan and limped over to me. Bob was telling the policeman that I could not be guilty because I had stayed with him until one o'clock, then I went to the Old Oak Tavern and spoke to the landlord there, and came back here at once.

"It was a quarter after one that the church was entered," said the officer, "and this boy left here at one o'clock so he could have met the other and got to the church."

"It takes more than a quarter of an hour to go from here to the town," said Bob.

"On the run, no," replied the policeman, "and what proves that he left here at one o'clock?"

"I can prove it; I swear it," cried Bob.

The policeman shrugged his shoulders. "This boy can explain to the magistrate," he said.

As I was being led away, Mattia threw his arms about my neck, as though it was because he wanted to embrace me, but Mattia had another object.

"Keep up your courage," he whispered, "we won't forsake you."

"Take care of Capi," I said in French, but the officer understood.

"Oh, no," he said; "I'll keep that dog. He helped me to find you; he may help me to find the other."

Handcuffed to the policeman I had to pass under the gaze of a crowd of people, but they did not jeer me like the peasants in France had done at my first arrest; these people, almost all of them, were antagonistic to the police; they were gypsies, tramps, in fact, the Bohemian vagabond.

There were no onions strewn over this prison where I was now locked up. This was a real jail with iron bars at the windows, the sight of which put all thought of escape from my mind. In the cell there was only a bench and a hammock. I dropped onto the bench and remained for a long time with my head buried in my hands. Mattia and Bob, even with the help of other friends, could never get me away from here. I got up and went over to the window; the bars were strong and close together. The walls were three feet thick. The ground beneath was paved with large stones. The door was covered with a plate of sheet iron.... No, I could not escape.

I began to wonder if it would be possible for me to prove my innocence, despite Capi's presence in the church. Mattia and Bob could help me by proving an alibi. If they could prove this I was saved in spite of the mute testimony that my poor dog had carried against me. I asked the jailer when he brought in some food if it would be long before I should appear before the magistrate. I did not know then that in England you are taken into court the day after arrest. The jailer, who seemed a kindly sort of man, told me that it would certainly be the next day.

I had heard tales of prisoners finding messages from their friends in the food that was brought in to them. I could not touch my food, but I at once began to crumble my bread. I found nothing inside. There were some potatoes also; I mashed them to a pulp, but I found not the tiniest note. I did not sleep that night.

The next morning the jailer came into my cell carrying a jug of water and a basin. He told me to wash myself if I wished to, for I was to appear before the judge, and a good appearance never went against one. When the jailer returned he told me to follow him. We went down several passages, then came to a small door which he opened.

"Pass in," he said.

The room I entered was very close. I heard a confused murmur of voices. Although my temples were throbbing and I could scarcely stand, I was able to take in my surroundings. The room was of fair size with large windows and high ceiling. The judge was seated on a raised platform. Beneath him in front sat three other court officials. Near where I stood was a gentleman wearing a robe and wig. I was surprised to find that this was my lawyer. How was it I had an attorney? Where did he come from?

Amongst the witnesses, I saw Bob and his two friends, the landlord of the Old Oak Tavern, and some men whom I did not know. Then on another stand opposite, amongst several other persons, I saw the policeman who had arrested me. The public prosecutor in a few words stated the crime. A robbery had been committed in St. George's Church. The thieves, a man and a child, had climbed up a ladder and broken a window to get in. They had with them a dog to give the alarm. At a quarter after one, a late pedestrian had seen a light in the church and had at once aroused the sexton. Several men ran to the church; the dog barked and the thieves escaped through the window, leaving the dog behind them. The dog's intelligence was remarkable. The next morning the animal had led the policeman to the race-course where he had recognized his master, who was none other than the accused now standing in the prisoner's dock. As to the second thief, they were on his trail, and they hoped to arrest him shortly.

There was little to be said for me; my friends tried to prove an alibi, but the prosecutor said that I had ample time to meet my accomplice at the church and then run to the Old Oak Tavern after. I was asked then how I could account for my dog being in the church at quarter after one. I replied that I could not say, for the dog had not been with me all day. But I declared that I was innocent. My attorney tried to prove that my dog had wandered into the church during the day and had been locked in when the sexton closed the door. He did his best for me, but the defense was weak. Then the judge said that I should be taken to the county jail to wait for the Grand Jury to decide if I should, or should not, be held for the assizes.

The assizes!

I fell back on my bench. Oh, why had I not listened to Mattia.

CHAPTER XXX. ESCAPE

I had not been acquitted because the judge was expecting the arrest of the man who had entered the church with the child. They would then know if I was this man's accomplice. They were on the trail, the prosecutor had said, so I should have the shame and sorrow of appearing in the prisoner's dock at the Assizes beside *him*.

That evening, just before dusk, I heard the clear notes of a cornet. Mattia was there! Dear old Mattia! he wanted to tell me that he was near and thinking of me. He was evidently in the street on the other side of the wall opposite my window. I heard footsteps and the murmur of a crowd. Mattia and Bob were probably giving a performance.

Suddenly I heard a clear voice call out in French, "To-morrow at daybreak!" Then at once Mattia played his loudest on the cornet.

It did not need any degree of intelligence to understand that Mattia had not addressed these French words to an English public. I was not sure what they meant, but evidently I had to be on the alert at daybreak the next morning. As soon as it was dark I got into my hammock, but it was some time before I could go to sleep, although I was very tired. At last I dropped off to sleep. When I awoke it was night. The stars shone in the dark sky and silence reigned everywhere. A clock struck three. I counted the hours and the quarter hours. Leaning against the wall I kept my eyes fixed on the window. I watched the stars go out one by one. In the distance I could hear the cocks crowing. It was daybreak.

I opened the window very softly. What did I expect? There were still the iron bars and the high wall opposite. I could not get out, and yet foolish though the thought was, I expected my freedom. The morning air chilled me but I stayed by my window, looking out without knowing at what, listening without knowing to what. A big white cloud came up in the sky. It was daybreak. My heart throbbed wildly. Then I seemed to hear a scratching on the wall, but I had heard no sound of footsteps. I listened. The scratching continued. I saw a head appear above the wall. In the dim light I recognized Bob.

He saw me with my face pressed against the bars.

"Silence!" he said softly.

He made a sign for me to move away from the window. Wondering, I obeyed. He put a peashooter to his mouth and blew. A tiny ball came through the air and fell at my feet. Bob's head disappeared.

I pounced on the ball. It was tissue paper made into a tiny ball like a pea. The light was too dim for me to see what was written on it; I had to wait till day. I closed my window cautiously and lay down again in my hammock with the tiny bit of paper in my hand. How slowly the light came! At last I was able to read what was written on the paper. I read:

"To-morrow you will be taken in the train to the county jail. A policeman will be in the compartment with you. Keep near the same door by which you enter. At the end of forty minutes (count them carefully), the train will slacken speed as it nears a junction; then open the door and jump out. Climb the small hill on the left. We'll be there. Keep your courage up; above all, jump well forward and fall on your feet."

Saved! I should not appear before the Assizes! Good Mattia, dear old Bob! How good of Bob to help Mattia, for Mattia, poor little fellow, could not have done this alone.

I re-read the note. Forty minutes after the train starts.... Hill to the left.... It was a risky thing to do to jump from a train, but even if I killed myself in doing so, I would better do it. Better die than be condemned as a thief.

Would they think of Capi?

After I had again read my note, I chewed it into a pulp.

The next day, in the afternoon, a policeman came into my cell and told me to follow him. He was a man over fifty and I thought with satisfaction that he did not appear to be very nimble.

Things turned out just as Bob had said. The train rolled off. I took my place near the door where I had entered. The policeman sat opposite me; we were alone in the compartment.

"Do you speak English?" asked the policeman.

"I understand if you don't talk too rapidly," I replied.

"Well, then, I want to give you a little advice, my boy," he said; "don't try and fool the law. Just tell me how it all happened, and I'll give you five shillings. It'll be easier for you if you have a little money in jail."

I was about to say that I had nothing to confess, but I felt that might annoy the man, so I said nothing.

"Just think it over," he continued, "and when you're in jail don't go and tell the first comer, but send for me. It is better to have one who is interested in you, and I'm very willing to help you."

I nodded my head.

"Ask for Dolphin; you'll remember my name?"

"Yes, sir."

I was leaning against the door. The window was down and the air blew in. The policeman found that there was too much air so he moved into the middle of the seat. My left hand stole softly outside and turned the handle; with my right hand I held the door.

The minutes passed; the engine whistled and slackened its speed. The moment had come. I pushed open the door quickly and sprang out as far as I could. Fortunately, my hands, which I held out before me, touched the grass, yet the shock was so great that I rolled on the ground unconscious. When I came to my senses I thought that I was still in the train for I felt myself being carried along. Looking round I saw that I was lying at the bottom of a cart. Strange! My cheeks were wet. A soft warm tongue was licking me. I turned slightly. An ugly yellow dog was leaning over me. Mattia was kneeling beside me.

"You're saved," he said, pushing aside the dog.

"Where am I?"

"You are in a cart. Bob's driving."

"How goes it?" cried Bob from his seat. "Can you move your arms and legs?"

I stretched out and did what he asked.

"Good," said Mattia; "nothing broken."

"What happened?"

"You jumped from the train as we told you, but the shock stunned you, and you rolled into a ditch. When you didn't come, Bob left the cart, crept down the hill, and carried you back in his arms. We thought you were dead. Oh, Remi, I was afraid."

I stroked his hand. "And the policeman?" I asked.

"The train went on; it didn't stop."

My eyes again fell on the ugly yellow dog that was looking at me with eyes that resembled Capi's. But Capi was white....

"What dog is that?" I asked.

Before Mattia could reply the ugly little animal had jumped on me, licking me furiously and whining.

"It's Capi; we dyed him!" cried Mattia, laughing.

"Dyed him? Why?"

"So that he wouldn't be recognized. Now Bob wants to make you more comfortable."

While Bob and Mattia were making me comfortable I asked them where we were going.

"To Little Hampton," said Mattia, "where Bob's brother has a boat that goes over to France to fetch butter and eggs from Normandy. We owe everything to Bob. What could a poor little wretch like me have done alone? It was Bob's idea that you jump from the train."

"And Capi? Who's idea was it to get him?"

"Mine. But it was Bob's to paint him yellow so that he wouldn't be recognized after we stole him from Policeman Jerry. The judge called Jerry 'intelligent'; he wasn't so very intelligent to let us get Capi away. True, Capi smelled me and almost got off alone. Bob knows the tricks of dog thieves."

"And your foot?"

"Better, or almost better. I haven't had time to think of it."

Night was falling. We had still a long distance to go.

"Are you afraid?" asked Mattia, as I lay there in silence.

"No, not afraid," I answered, "for I don't think that I shall be caught. But it seems to me that in running away I admit my guilt. That worries me."

"Better anything, Bob and I thought, than that you should appear at the Assizes. Even if you got off it's a bad thing to have gone through."

Convinced that after the train stopped the policeman would lose no time looking for me, we went ahead as quickly as possible. The villages through which we drove were very quiet; lights were seen in only a few of the windows. Mattia and I got under a cover. For some time a cold wind had been blowing and when we passed our tongues over our lips we tasted salt. We were nearing the sea. Soon we saw a light flashing every now and again. It was a lighthouse. Suddenly Bob stopped his horse, and jumping down from the cart, told us to wait there. He was going to see his brother to ask him if it would be safe for him to take us on his boat.

Bob seemed to be away a very long time. We did not speak. We could hear the waves breaking on the shore at a short distance. Mattia was trembling and I also.

"It is cold," he whispered.

Was it the cold that made us shake? When a cow or a sheep in the field at the side touched against the fence we trembled still more. There were footsteps on the road. Bob was returning. My fate had been decided. A rough-looking sailor wearing a sou'wester and an oilskin hat was with Bob.

"This is my brother," said Bob; "he'll take you on his boat. So we'll have to part now; no one need know that I brought you here."

I wanted to thank Bob but he cut me short. I grasped his hand.

"Don't speak of it," he said lightly, "you two boys helped me out the other night. One good turn deserves another. And I'm pleased to have been able to help a friend of Mattia's."

We followed Bob's brother down some winding quiet streets till we came to the docks. He pointed to a boat, without saying a word. In a few moments we were on board. He told us to go down below into a little cabin.

"I start in two hours' time," he said; "stay there and don't make a sound."

But we were not trembling now. We sat in the dark side by side.

CHAPTER XXXI. HUNTING FOR THE SWAN

For some time after Bob's brother left we heard only the noise of the wind and the sea dashing against the keel, then footsteps were heard on the deck above and the grinding of pulleys. A sail was hoisted, then suddenly the boat leaned to one side and began to rock. In a few moments it was pitching heavily on the rough sea.

"Poor Mattia," I said, taking his hand.

"I don't care, we're saved," he said; "what if I am seasick?"

The next day I passed my time between the cabin and deck. Mattia wanted to be left alone. When at last the skipper pointed out Harfleur I hurried down to the cabin to tell him the good news. As it was late in the afternoon when we arrived at Harfleur, Bob's brother told us that we could sleep on the boat that night if we wished.

"When you want to go back to England," he said the next morning, as we wished him good-by, and thanked him for what he had done for us, "just remember that the *Eclipse* sails from here every Tuesday."

It was a kind invitation, but Mattia and I each of us had our reason for not wishing to cross the sea again ... yet awhile.

Fortunately we had our profits from Bob's performance. In all we had twenty-seven francs and fifty centimes. Mattia wanted to give Bob the twenty-seven francs in payment for the expenses he had been put to for my flight, but he would not accept a penny.

"Well, which way shall we go?" I asked when we landed in France.

"By the canal," replied Mattia promptly, "because I have an idea. I believe the *Swan* is on the canal this summer, now that Arthur's been so ill, and I think we ought to find it," he added.

"But what about Lise and the others?" I asked.

"We'll see them while we're looking for Mrs. Milligan. As we go up the canal, we can stop and see Lise."

With a map that we bought, we searched for the nearest river: it was the Seine.

"We'll go up the Seine and ask all the fishermen along the banks if they've seen the *Swan*. It isn't like any other boat from what you say, and if they've seen it they'll remember."

Before beginning the long journey that was probably ahead of us I bought some soft soap to clean Capi. To me, Capi yellow—was not Capi. We washed him thoroughly, each one taking it in turns until he was tired out. But Bob's dye was an excellent quality and when we had finished he was still yellow, but a shade paler. It would require many shampoos before we could get him back to his original color. Fortunately Normandy is a country of brooks and each day we gave him a bath.

We reached the top of a hill one morning and Mattia spied the Seine away ahead of us, winding in a large curve. From then on, we began to question the people. Had they seen the *Swan*, a beautiful barge with a veranda? No one had seen it. It must have passed in the night. We went on to Rouen, where again we commenced our questions, but with no better result. We would not be discouraged but went forward questioning every one. We had to stop to get money for our food as we went along, so it took us five weeks to reach the suburbs of Paris.

Fortunately, upon arriving at Charenton, we soon knew which direction we had to take. When we put the important question, we received for the first time the answer for which we had longed. A boat which resembled the *Swan*, a large pleasure boat, had passed that way; turning to the left, it had continued up the Seine.

We were by the docks. Mattia was so overjoyed that he commenced to dance amongst the fishermen. Stopping suddenly he took his violin and frantically played a triumphal march. While he played I questioned the man who had seen the barge. Without a doubt it was the *Swan*. It had passed through Charenton about two months ago.

Two months! What a lead it had! But what did that matter! We had our legs and they had the legs of two good horses and we should join them some day. The question of time did not count. The great thing, the wonderful thing was that the *Swan* was found!

"Who was right?" cried Mattia.

If I had dared I would have admitted to Mattia that I had very great hopes, but I felt that I could not analyze my thoughts, not even to myself. We had no need to stop now and question the people. The *Swan* was ahead of us. We had only to follow the Seine. We went on our way, getting nearer to where Lise lived. I wondered if she had seen the barge as it passed through the locks by her home. At night we never complained of weariness and we were always ready the next morning to set out at an early hour.

"Wake me up," said Mattia, who was fond of sleeping. And when I woke him he was never long in jumping to his feet.

To economize we ate hard-boiled eggs, which we bought from the grocers, and bread. Yet Mattia was very fond of good things.

"I hope Mrs. Milligan has that cook still who made those tarts," he said; "apricot tarts must be fine!"

"Haven't you ever tasted them?"

"I've tasted apple puffs, but I've never tasted apricot tarts. I've seen them. What are those little white things they stick all over the fruit?"

"Almonds."

"Oh...." And Mattia opened his mouth as though he were swallowing a whole tart.

At each lock we had news of the *Swan;* every one had seen the beautiful barge and they spoke of the kind English lady and the little boy lying on a sofa under the veranda.

We drew nearer to Lise's home, two more days, then one, then only a few hours. We came in sight of the house. We were not walking now, we were running. Capi, who seemed to know where we were going, started ahead at a gallop. He was going to let Lise know that we were coming. She would come to meet us. But when we got to the house there was a woman standing at the door whom we did not know.

"Where's Madame Suriot?" we inquired.

For a moment she stared at us as though we were asking a foolish question.

"She doesn't live here now," she said at last; "she's in Egypt."

"In Egypt!"

Mattia and I looked at one another in amazement. Egypt! We did not know just where Egypt was situated, but we thought, vaguely, it was far away, very far, somewhere beyond the seas.

"And Lise? Do you know Lise?"

"The little dumb girl? Yes, I know her! She went off with an English lady on a barge."

Lise on the *Swan!* Were we dreaming? Mattia and I stared at one another.

"Are you Remi?" then asked the woman.

"Yes."

"Well, Suriot was drowned...."

"Drowned!"

"Yes, he fell into the lock and got caught below on a nail. And his poor wife didn't know what to do, and then a lady that she lived with before she married was going to Egypt, and she told her she would take her as nurse to look after the children. She didn't know what to do with little Lise and while she was wondering an English lady and her little sick son came along the canal in a barge. They talked. And the English lady, who was looking for some one to play with her son, for he was tired of being always alone, said she would take Lise along and she would educate the little girl. The lady said she would have doctors who would cure her and she would be able to speak some day. Before they went, Lise wanted her aunt to explain to me what I was to say to you if you came to see her. That's all."

I was so amazed that I could find no words. But Mattia never lost his head like me.

"Where did the English lady go?" he asked.

"To Switzerland. Lise was to have written to me so that I could give you her address, but I haven't received the letter yet."

CHAPTER XXXII. FINDING A REAL MOTHER

"Forward! March! Children!" cried Mattia after we had thanked the woman. "It is not only Arthur and Mrs. Milligan now that we are going after, but Lise. What luck! Who knows what's in store for us!"

We went on our way in search of the *Swan*, only stopping just to sleep and to earn a few sous.

"From Switzerland one goes to Italy," said Mattia softly. "If, while running after Mrs. Milligan, we get to Lucca, how happy my little Christina will be."

Poor dear Mattia! He was helping me to seek those I loved and I had done nothing to help him see his little sister.

At Lyons we gained on the *Swan*. It was now only six weeks ahead of us. I doubted if we could catch up with it before it reached Switzerland. And then I did not know that the river Rhone was not navigable up to the Lake of Geneva. We had thought that Mrs. Milligan would go right to Switzerland on her boat. What was my surprise when arriving at the next town to see the *Swan* in the distance. We began to run along the banks of the river. What was the matter? Everything was closed up on the barge.

There were no flowers on the veranda. What had happened to Arthur? We stopped, looking at each other both with the same sorrowful thoughts.

A man who had charge of the boat told us that the English lady had gone to Switzerland with a sick boy and a little dumb girl. They had gone in a carriage with a maid; the other servants had followed with the baggage. We breathed again.

"Where is the lady?" asked Mattia.

"She has taken a villa at Vevy, but I cannot say where; she is going to spend the summer there."

We started for Vevy. Now they were not traveling away from us. They had stopped and we should be sure to find them at Vevy if we searched. We arrived there with three sous in our pockets and the soles off our boots. But Vevy is not a little village; it is a town, and as for asking for Mrs. Milligan, or even an English lady with a sick son and a dumb girl, we knew that that would be absurd. There are so many English in Vevy; the place is almost like an English pleasure resort. The best way, we thought, was to go to all the houses where they might be likely to live. That would not be difficult; we had only to play our music in every street. We tried everywhere, but yet we could see no signs of Mrs. Milligan.

We went from the lake to the mountains, from the mountains to the lake, looking to the right and to the left, questioning from time to time people who, from their expression, we thought would be disposed to listen and reply. Some one sent us to a chalet built way up on the mountain; another assured us that she lived down by the lake. They were indeed English ladies who lived up in the chalet on the mountain and the villa down by the lake; but not our Mrs. Milligan.

One afternoon we were playing in the middle of the road. The house before us had a large iron gate; the house behind stood way back in a garden. In the front of it there was a stone wall. I was singing my loudest. I sung the first verse of my Neapolitan song and was about to commence the second when we heard a weak strange voice singing. Who could it be? What a strange voice!

"Arthur?" inquired Mattia.

"No, no, it is not Arthur. I have never heard that voice before."

But Capi commenced to whine and gave every sign of intense joy while jumping against the wall.

"Who is singing?" I cried, unable to contain myself.

"Remi!" called a weak voice.

My name instead of an answer! Mattia and I looked at one another, thunderstruck. As we stood looking stupidly into each other's faces, I saw a handkerchief being waved at the end of the wall. We ran to the spot. It was not until we got to the hedge which surrounded the other side of the garden that we saw the one who was waving.

Lise! At last we had found her and not far away were Mrs. Milligan and Arthur!

But who had sung? That was the question that Mattia and I asked as soon as we found words.

"I," answered Lise.

Lise was singing! Lise was talking!

The doctors had said that one day Lise would recover her speech, and very probably, under the shock of a violent emotion, but I did not think that it could be possible. And yet the miracle had happened, and it was upon knowing that I had come to her and hearing me sing the Neapolitan song I used to sing to her, that she had felt this intense emotion, and was restored to her voice. I was so overcome at this thought that I had to stretch out my hand to steady myself.

"Where is Mrs. Milligan?" I asked, "and Arthur?"

Lise moved her lips, but she could only utter inarticulate sounds, then impatiently she used the language of her hands, for her tongue was still clumsy in forming words. She pointed down the garden and we saw Arthur lying in an invalid's chair. On one side of him was his mother, and on the other ... Mr. James Milligan. In fear, in fact almost terror, I stooped down behind the hedge. Lise must have wondered why I did so. Then I made a sign to her to go.

"Go, Lise, or you'll betray me," I said. "Come to-morrow here at nine o'clock and be alone, then I can talk to you."

She hesitated for a moment, then went up the garden.

"We ought not to wait till to-morrow to speak to Mrs. Milligan," said Mattia. "In the meantime that uncle might kill Arthur. He has never seen me and I'm going to see Mrs. Milligan at once and tell her."

There was some reason in what Mattia proposed, so I let him go off, telling him that I would wait for him at a short distance under a big chestnut tree. I waited a long time for Mattia. More than a dozen times I wondered if I had not made a mistake in letting him go. At last I saw him coming back, accompanied by Mrs. Milligan. I ran to her, and, seizing the hand that she held out to me, I bent over it. But she put her arms round me and, stooping down, kissed me tenderly on the forehead.

"Poor, dear child," she murmured.

With her beautiful white fingers she pushed the hair back from my forehead and looked at me for a long time.

"Yes, yes," she whispered softly.

I was too happy to say a word.

"Mattia and I have had a long talk," she said, "but I want you to tell me yourself how you came to enter the Driscoll family."

I told her what she asked and she only interrupted me to tell me to be exact on certain points. Never had I been listened to with such attention. Her eyes did not leave mine.

When I had finished she was silent for some time, still looking at me. At last she said: "This is a very serious matter and we must act prudently. But from this moment you must consider yourself as the friend," she hesitated a little, "as the brother of Arthur. In two hours' time go to the Hotel des Alpes; for the time being you will stay there. I will send some one to the hotel to meet you. I am obliged to leave you now."

Again she kissed me and after having shaken hands with Mattia she walked away quickly.

"What did you tell Mrs. Milligan?" I demanded of Mattia.

"All that I have said to you and a lot more things," he replied. "Ah, she is a kind lady, a beautiful lady!"

"Did you see Arthur?"

"Only from a distance, but near enough to see that he looked a nice sort of boy."

I continued to question Mattia, but he answered me vaguely.

Although we were in our ragged street suits, we were received at the hotel by a servant in a black suit and a white tie. He took us to our apartment. How beautiful we thought our bedroom. There were two white beds side by side. The windows opened onto a balcony overlooking the lake. The servant asked us what we would like for dinner, which he would serve us on the balcony if we wished.

"Have you any tarts?" asked Mattia.

"Yes, rhubarb tarts, strawberry tarts, and gooseberry tarts."

"Good. Then you can serve these tarts."

"All three?"

"Certainly."

"And what entrée? What meat? Vegetables?"

At each offer Mattia opened his eyes, but he would not allow himself to be disconcerted.

"Anything, just what you like," he replied coolly.

The butler left the room gravely.

The next day Mrs. Milligan came to see us; she was accompanied by a tailor and a shirt maker who took our measures for some suits and shirts. Mrs. Milligan told us that Lise was still trying to talk and that the doctor had declared that she would soon be cured, then after having spent an hour with us she left us, again kissing me tenderly and shaking hands warmly with Mattia.

For four days she came, each time she was more affectionate and loving to me, yet still with a certain restraint. The fifth day the maid, whom I had known on the *Swan*, came in her place. She told us that Mrs. Milligan was expecting us and that a carriage was at the hotel doors to take us to her. Mattia took his seat in the brougham as though he had been used to riding in a carriage all his life. Capi also jumped in without any embarrassment and sat down on the velvet cushions.

The drive was short, it seemed to me very short, for I was like one in a dream, my head filled with foolish ideas, or at least what I thought might be foolish. We were shown into a drawing-room. Mrs. Milligan, Arthur, and Lise were there. Arthur held out his arms. I rushed over to him, then I kissed Lise. Mrs. Milligan kissed me.

"At last," she said, "the day has come when you can take the place that belongs to you."

I looked to her to ask her to explain. She went over to a door and opened it. Then came the grand surprise! Mother Barberin entered. In her arms she carried some baby's clothes, a white cashmere pelisse, a lace bonnet, some woolen shoes. She had only time to put these things on the table before I was hugging her. While I fondled her, Mrs. Milligan gave an order to the servant. I heard only the name of Milligan, but I looked up quickly. I know that I turned pale.

"You have nothing to fear," said Mrs. Milligan gently; "come over here and place your hand in mine."

James Milligan came into the room, smiling and showing his white pointed teeth. When he saw me, the smile turned to a horrible grimace. Mrs. Milligan did not give him time to speak.

"I asked for you to come here," she said, her voice shaking, "to introduce you to my eldest son, whom I have at last found"; she pressed my hand. "But you have met him already; you saw him at the home of the man who stole him, when you went there to inquire after his health."

"What does this mean?" demanded Milligan.

"That the man who is serving a sentence for robbing a church has made a full confession. He has stated how he stole my baby and took it to Paris and left it there. Here are the clothes that my child wore. It was this good woman who brought up my son. Do you wish to read this confession. Do you wish to examine these clothes?"

James Milligan looked at us as though he would like to have strangled us, then he turned on his heels. At the threshold he turned round and said: "We'll see what the courts will think of this boy's story."

My mother, I may call her so now, replied quietly: "*You* may take the matter to the courts; I have not done so because you are my husband's brother."

The door closed. Then, for the first time in my life, I kissed my mother as she kissed me.

"Will you tell your mother that I kept the secret?" said Mattia, coming up to us.

"You knew all, then?"

"I told Mattia not to speak of all this to you," said my mother, "for though I did believe that you were my son, I had to have certain proofs, and get Madame Barberin here with the clothes. How unhappy we should have been if, after all, we had made a mistake. We have these proofs and we shall never be parted again. You will live with your mother and brother?" Then, pointing to Mattia and Lise, "and," she added, "with those whom you loved when you were poor."

CHAPTER XXXIII. THE DREAM COME TRUE

Years have passed. I now live in the home of my ancestors, Milligan Park. The miserable little wanderer who slept so often in a stable was heir

218

to an old historical castle. It is a beautiful old place about twenty miles west of the spot where I jumped from the train to escape from the police. I live here with my mother, my brother and my wife.

We are going to baptize our first child, little Mattia. To-night all those who were my friends in my poorer days will meet under my roof to celebrate the event and I am going to offer to each one as a little token a copy of my "Memoirs," which for the last six months I have been writing and which to-day I have received from the bookbinder.

This reunion of all our friends is a surprise for my wife; she will see her father, her sister, her brothers, her aunt. Only my mother and brother are in the secret. One will be missing from this feast. Alas! poor master! poor Vitalis! I could not do much for you in life, but at my request, my mother has had erected a marble tomb and placed your bust, the bust of Carlo Balzini, upon the tomb. A copy of this bust is before me now as I write, and often while penning my "Memoirs," I have looked up and my eyes have caught yours. I have not forgotten you; I shall never forget you, dear master, dear Vitalis.

Here comes my mother leaning on my brother's arm, for it is now the son who supports the mother, for Arthur has grown big and strong. A few steps behind my mother comes an old woman dressed like a French peasant and carrying in her arms a little baby robed in a white pelisse. It is dear Mother Barberin, the little baby is my son Mattia.

Arthur brings me a copy of the *Times* and points to a correspondence from Vienna which states that Mattia, the great musician, has completed his series of concerts, and that, in spite of his tremendous success in Vienna, he is returning to England to keep an engagement which cannot be broken. I did not need to read the article for, although all the world now calls Mattia the Chopin of the violin, I have watched him develop and grow. When we were all three working together under the direction of our tutors, Mattia made little progress in Latin and Greek, but quickly outstripped his professors in music. Espinassous, the barber-musician of Mendes, had been right.

A footman brings me a telegram:

"Sea very rough! Alas! Have been very ill, but managed to stop on my way at Paris for Christina. Shall be with you at 4 o'clock. Send carriage to meet us. MATTIA."

Mentioning Christina, I glanced at Arthur, but he turned away his eyes. I knew that Arthur loved Mattia's little sister, and I knew that in time, although not just yet, my mother would become reconciled to the match. Birth was not everything. She had not opposed my marriage, and later, when she saw that it was for Arthur's happiness, she would not oppose his.

Lise comes down the gallery, my beautiful wife. She passes her arm round my mother's neck.

"Mother dear," she said, "there is some secret afoot and I believe that you are in the plot. I know if it is a surprise and you are in it, it is something for our happiness, but I am none the less curious."

"Come, Lise, you shall have the surprise now," I said, as I heard the sound of carriage wheels on the gravel outside.

One by one our guests arrive and Lise and I stand in the hall to welcome them. There is Mr. Acquin, Aunt Catherine and Etiennette, and a bronze young man who has just returned from a botanical expedition and is now the famous botanist—Benjamin Acquin. Then comes a young man and an old man. This journey is doubly interesting to them for when they leave us they are going to Wales to visit the mines. The young one is to make observations which he will carry back to his own country to strengthen the high position which he now holds in the Truyère mine, and the other to add to the fine collection of minerals which the town of Varses has honored him by accepting. It is the old professor and Alexix. Lise and I greet our guests, the landau dashes up from the opposite direction with Arthur, Christina and Mattia. Following in its wake is a dog cart driven by a smart looking man, beside whom is seated a rugged sailor. The gentleman holding the reins is Bob, now very prosperous, and the man by his side is his brother, who helped me to escape from England.

When the baptismal feast is over, Mattia draws me aside to the window.

"We have often playful to indifferent people," he said; "let us now, on this memorable occasion, play for those we love?"

"To you there is no pleasure without music, eh, Mattia, old boy," I said, laughing; "do you remember how you scared our cow?"

Mattia grinned.

From a beautiful box, lined with velvet, he drew out an old violin which would not have brought two francs if he had wished to sell it. I took from its coverings a harp, the wood of which had been washed so often by the rain, that it was now restored to its original color.

"Will you sing your Neapolitan song?" asked Mattia.

"Yes, for it was that which gave Lise back her speech," I said, smiling at my wife who stood beside me.

Our guests drew round us in a circle. A dog suddenly came forward. Good old Capi, he is very old and deaf but he still has good eyesight. From the cushion which he occupies he has recognized the harp and up he comes, limping, for "the Performance." In his jaws he holds a saucer; he wants to make the rounds of the "distinguished audience." He tries to walk on his two hind paws, but strength fails him, so he sits down gravely and with his paw on his heart he bows to the society.

Our song ended, Capi gets up as best he can and "makes the round." Each one drops something into the saucer and Capi delightedly brings it to me. It is the best collection he has ever made. There are only gold and silver coins—170 francs.

I kiss him on his cold nose as in other days, and the thought of the miseries of my childhood gives me an idea. I tell my guests that this sum shall be the first subscription to found a Home for little street musicians. My mother and I will donate the rest.

"Dear Madam," said Mattia, bending over my mother's hand, "let me have a little share in this good work. The proceeds of my first concert in London will be added to Capi's collection."

And Capi barked approval. THE END

BOOK TWO.
NOBODY'S GIRL

("EN FAMILLE")

INTRODUCTION

"NOBODY'S GIRL," published in France under the title "En Famille", follows "Nobody's Boy" as a companion juvenile story, and takes place with it as one of the supreme juvenile stories of the world. Like "Nobody's Boy" it was also crowned by the Academy, and that literary judgment has also been verified by the test of time.

"Nobody's Girl" is not a human document, such as is "Nobody's Boy", because it has more story plot, and the adventure is in a more restricted field, but it discloses no less the nobility of a right-minded child, and how loyalty wins the way to noble deeds and life. This is another beautiful literary creation of Hector Malot which every one can recommend as an ennobling book, of interest not only to childhood, page by page to the thrilling conclusion, but to every person who loves romance and character.

Only details, irrelevant for readers in America, have been eliminated. Little Perrine's loyal ideals, with their inspiring sentiments, are preserved by her through the most discouraging conditions, and are described with the simplicity for which Hector Malot is famous. The building up of a little girl's life is made a fine example for every child. Every reader of this story leaves it inspired for the better way.

THE PUBLISHERS.

CHAPTER I. **PERRINE AND PALIKARE**

IT WAS Saturday afternoon about 3 o'clock. There was the usual scene; outside the Gates of Bercy there was a crowd of people, and on the quays, four rows deep, carts and wagons were massed together. Coal carts, carts heaped with hay and straw, all were waiting in the clear, warm June sunshine for the examination from the custom official. All had been hurrying to reach Paris before Sunday.

Amongst the wagons, but at some little distance from the Gates, stood an odd looking cart, a sort of caravan. Over a light frame work which was erected on four wheels was stretched a heavy canvas; this was fastened to the light roof which covered the wagon. Once upon a time the canvas might have been blue, but it was so faded, so dirty and worn, that one could only guess what its original color had been. Neither was it possible to make out the inscriptions which were painted on the four sides. Most of the words were effaced. On one side there was a Greek word, the next side bore part of a German word, on the third side were the letters F I A, which was evidently Italian, and on the last a newly painted French word stood out boldly. This was *PHOTOGRAPHIE*, and was evidently the translation of all the others, indicating the different countries through which the miserable wagon had come before it had entered France and finally arrived at the Gates of Paris.

Was it possible that the donkey that was harnessed to it had brought the cart all this distance? At first glance it seemed impossible, but although the animal was tired out, one could see upon a closer view that it was very robust and much bigger than the donkeys that one sees in Europe. Its coat was a beautiful dark grey, the beauty of which could be seen despite the dust which covered it. Its slender legs were marked with jet black lines, and worn out though the poor beast was, it still held its head high. The harness, worthy of the caravan, was fastened together with various colored strings, short pieces, long pieces, just what was at hand at the moment; the strings had been carefully hidden under the flowers and branches which had been gathered along the roads and used to protect the animal from the sun and the flies.

Close by, seated on the edge of the curb, watching the donkey, was a little girl of about thirteen years of age. Her type was very unusual, but it was quite apparent that there was a mixture of race. The pale blond of her hair contrasted strangely with the deep, rich coloring of her cheeks, and the sweet expression of her face was accentuated by the dark, serious eyes.

Her mouth also was very serious. Her figure, slim and full of grace, was garbed in an old, faded check dress, but the shabby old frock could not take away the child's distinguished air.

As the donkey had stopped just behind a large cart of straw, it would not have required much watching, but every now and again he pulled out the straw, in a cautious manner, like a very intelligent animal that knows quite well that it is doing wrong.

"Palikare! stop that!" said the girl for the third time.

The donkey again dropped his head in a guilty fashion, but as soon as he had eaten his wisps of straw he began to blink his eyes and agitate his ears, then again discreetly, but eagerly, tugged at what was ahead of him; this in a manner that testified to the poor beast's hunger.

While the little girl was scolding him, a voice from within the caravan called out:

"Perrine!"

Jumping to her feet, the child lifted up the canvas and passed inside, where a pale, thin woman was lying on a mattress.

"Do you need me, mama?"

"What is Palikare doing, dear?" asked the woman.

"He is eating the straw off the cart that's ahead of us."

"You must stop him."

"He's so hungry."

"Hunger is not an excuse for taking what does not belong to us. What will you say to the driver of that cart if he's angry?"

"I'll go and see that Palikare doesn't do it again," said the little girl.

"Shall we soon be in Paris?"

"Yes, we are waiting for the customs."

"Have we much longer to wait?"

"No, but are you in more pain, mother?"

"Don't worry, darling; it's because I'm closed in here," replied the woman, gasping. Then she smiled wanly, hoping to reassure her daughter.

The woman was in a pitiable plight. All her strength had gone and she could scarcely breathe. Although she was only about twenty-nine years of age, her life was ebbing away. There still remained traces of remarkable beauty: Her head and hair were lovely, and her eyes were soft and dark like her daughter's.

"Shall I give you something?" asked Perrine.

"What?"

"There are some shops near by. I can buy a lemon. I'll come back at once."

"No, keep the money. We have so little. Go back to Palikare and stop him from eating the straw."

"That's not easy," answered the little girl.

She went back to the donkey and pushed him on his haunches until he was out of reach of the straw in front of him.

At first the donkey was obstinate and tried to push forward again, but she spoke to him gently and stroked him, and kissed him on his nose; then he dropped his long ears with evident satisfaction and stood quite still.

There was no occasion to worry about him now, so she amused herself with watching what was going on around her.

A little boy about her own age, dressed up like a clown, and who evidently belonged to the circus caravans standing in the rear, had been strolling round her for ten long minutes, without being able to attract her attention. At last he decided to speak to her.

"That's a fine donkey," he remarked.

She did not reply.

"It don't belong to this country. If it does, I'm astonished."

She was looking at him, and thinking that after all he looked rather like a nice boy, she thought she would reply.

"He comes from Greece," she said.

"Greece!" he echoed.

"That's why he's called Palikare."

"Ah! that's why."

But in spite of his broad grin he was not at all sure why a donkey that came from Greece should be called Palikare.

"Is it far ... Greece?"

"Very far."

"Farther than ... China?"

"No, but it's a long way off."

"Then yer come from Greece, then?"

"No, farther than that."

"From China?"

"No, but Palikare's the only one that comes from Greece."

"Are you going to the Fair?"

"No."

"Where yer goin'?"

"Into Paris."

"I know that, but where yer goin' to put up that there cart?"

"We've been told that there are some free places round the fortifications."

The little clown slapped his thighs with his two hands.

"The fortifications: *Oh la la!*"

"Isn't there any place?"

"Yes."

"Well, then?"

"It ain't the place for you ... round the fortifications! Have yer got any men with yer? Big strong men who are not afraid of a stab from a dagger. One who can give a jab as well as take one."

"There is only my mother and me, and mother is ill."

"Do you think much of that donkey?" he asked quickly.

"I should say so!"

"Well, the first thing he'll be stolen. He'll be gone tomorrow. Then the rest'll come after, and it's Fatty as tells yer so."

"Really?"

"Should say so! You've never been to Paris before?"

"No, never."

"That's easy to see. Some fools told you where to put your cart up, but you can't put it there. Why don't you go to Grain-of-Salt?"

"I don't know Grain-of-Salt."

"Why, he owns the Guillot Fields. You needn't be afraid of him, and he'd shoot anybody who tried to get in his place."

"Will it cost much to go there?"

"It costs a lot in winter, when everybody comes to Paris, but at this time I'm sure he won't make you pay more than forty sous a week. And your donkey can find its food in the field. Does he like thistles?"

"I should say he does like them!"

"Well, then, this is just the place for him, and Grain-of-Salt isn't a bad chap," said the little clown with a satisfied air.

"Is that his name ... Grain-of-Salt?"

"They call him that 'cause he's always thirsty. He's only got one arm."

"Is his place far from here?"

"No, at Charonne; but I bet yer don't even know where Charonne is?"

"I've never been to Paris before."

"Well, then, it's over there." He waved his arms vaguely in a northerly direction.

"Once you have passed through the Gates, you turn straight to the right," he explained, "and you follow the road all along the fortifications for half an hour, then go down a wide avenue, then turn to your left, and then ask where the Guillot Field is. Everybody knows it."

"Thank you. I'll go and tell mama. If you'll stand beside Palikare for a minute, I'll go and tell her at once."

"Sure, I'll mind him for yer. I'll ask him to teach me Greek."

"And please don't let him eat that straw."

Perrine went inside the caravan and told her mother what the little clown had said.

"If that is so," said the sick woman, "we must not hesitate; we must go to Charonne. But can you find the way?"

"Yes, it's easy enough. Oh, mother," she added, as she was going out, "there are such a lot of wagons outside; they have printed on them 'Maraucourt Factories,' and beneath that the name, 'Vulfran Paindavoine.' There are all kinds of barrels and things in the carts. Such a number!"

"There is nothing remarkable in that, my child," said the woman.

"Yes, but it's strange to see so many wagons with the same name on them," replied the girl as she left the caravan.

Perrine found the donkey with his nose buried in the straw, which he was eating calmly.

"Why, you're letting him eat it!" she cried to the boy.

"Well, why not?" he retorted.

"And if the man is angry?"

"He'd better not be with me," said the small boy, putting himself in a position to fight and throwing his head back.

227

But his prowess was not to be brought into action, for at this moment the custom officer began to search the cart of straw, and then gave permission for it to pass on through the Gates of Paris.

"Now it's your turn," said the boy, "and I'll have to leave you. Goodbye, Mademoiselle. If you ever want news of me ask for Double Fat. Everybody knows me."

The employés who guard the entrances of Paris are accustomed to strange sights, yet the man who went into Perrine's caravan looked surprised when he found a young woman lying on a mattress, and even more surprised when his hasty glance revealed to him the extreme poverty of her surroundings.

"Have you anything to declare?" he asked, continuing his investigations.

"Nothing."

"No wine, no provisions?"

"Nothing."

This was only too true; apart from the mattress, the two cane chairs, a little table, a tiny stove, a camera and a few photographic supplies, there was nothing in this wagon; no trunks, no baskets, no clothes....

"All right; you can pass," said the man.

Once through the Gates, Perrine, holding Palikare by the bridle, followed the stretch of grass along the embankment. In the brown, dirty grass she saw rough looking men lying on their backs or on their stomachs. She saw now the class of people who frequent this spot. From the very air of these men, with their bestial, criminal faces, she understood why it would be unsafe for them to be there at night. She could well believe that their knives would be in ready use.

Looking towards the city, she saw nothing but dirty streets and filthy houses. So this was Paris, the beautiful Paris of which her father had so often spoken. With one word she made her donkey go faster, then turning to the left she inquired for the Guillot Field.

If everyone knew where it was situated, no two were of the same opinion as to which road she should take to get there, and several times, in trying to follow the various directions which were given to her, she lost her way.

At last she found the place for which she was looking. This must be it! Inside the field there was an old omnibus without wheels, and a railway car, also without wheels, was on the ground. In addition, she saw a dozen little round pups rolling about. Yes, this was the place!

Leaving Palikare in the street, she went into the field. The pups at once scrambled at her feet, barked, and snapped at her shoes.

"Who's there?" called a voice.

She looked around and saw a long, low building, which might have been a house, but which might serve for anything else. The walls were made of bits of stone, wood and plaster. Even tin boxes were used in its construction. The roof was made of tarred canvas and cardboard, and most of the window panes were of paper, although in one or two instances there was some glass. The man who designed it was another Robinson Crusoe, and his workman a man Friday.

A one-armed man with a shaggy beard was sorting out rags and throwing them into the baskets around him.

"Don't step on my dogs," he cried; "come nearer."

She did as she was told.

"Are you the owner of the Guillot Field?" she asked.

"That's me!" replied the man.

In a few words she told him what she wanted. So as not to waste his time while listening, he poured some red wine out of a bottle that stood on the ground and drank it down at a gulp.

"It can be arranged if you pay in advance," he said, sizing her up.

"How much?" she asked.

"Forty sous a week for the wagon and twenty for the donkey," he replied.

"That's a lot of money," she said, hesitatingly.

"That's my price."

"Your summer price?"

"Yes, my summer price."

"Can my donkey eat the thistles?"

"Yes, and the grass also if his teeth are strong enough."

"We can't pay for the whole week because we are only going to stay one day. We are going through Paris on our way to Amiens, and we want to rest."

"Well, that's all right; six sous a day for the cart and three for the donkey."

One by one she pulled out nine sous from the pocket in her skirt.

"That's for the first day," she said, handing them to the man.

"You can tell your people they can all come in," he said, "How many are there? If it's a whole company it's two sous extra for each person."

"I have only my mother."

"All right; but why didn't your mother come and settle this?"

"She is in the wagon, ill."

"Ill! Well, this isn't a hospital."

Perrine was afraid that he would not let her sick mother come in.

"I mean she's a little bit tired. We've come a long way."

"I never ask people where they come from," replied the man gruffly. He pointed to a corner of the field, and added: "You can put your wagon over there and tie up the donkey. And if it squashes one of my pups you'll pay me five francs, one hundred sous ... understand?"

As she was going he called out:

"Will you take a glass of wine?"

"No, thanks," she replied; "I never take wine."

"Good," he said; "I'll drink it for you."

He drained another glass, then returned to his collection of rags.

As soon as she had installed Palikare in the place that the man had pointed out to her, which was accomplished not without some jolts, despite the care which she took, Perrine climbed up into the wagon.

"We've arrived at last, poor mama," she said, bending over the woman.

"No more shaking, no more rolling about," said the woman weakly.

"There, there; I'll make you some dinner," said Perrine cheerfully. "What would you like?"

"First, dear, unharness Palikare; he is very tired also; and give him something to eat and drink."

Perrine did as her mother told her, then returned to the wagon and took out the small stove, some pieces of coal and an old saucepan and some sticks. Outside, she went down on her knees and made a fire; at last, after blowing with all her might, she had the satisfaction of seeing that it had taken.

"You'd like some rice, wouldn't you?" she asked, leaning over her mother.

"I am not hungry."

"Is there anything else you would fancy? I'll go and fetch anything you want. What would you like, mama, dearie?"

"I think I prefer rice," said her mother.

Little Perrine threw a handful of rice into the saucepan that she had put on the fire and waited for the water to boil; then she stirred the rice with two white sticks that she had stripped of their bark. She only left her cooking once, to run over to Palikare to say a few loving words to him. The donkey was eating the thistles with a satisfaction, the intensity of which was shown by the way his long ears stood up.

When the rice was cooked to perfection, Perrine filled a bowl and placed it at her mother's bedside, also two glasses, two plates and two forks. Sitting down on the floor, with her legs tucked under her and her skirts spread out, she said, like a little girl who is playing with her doll: "Now we'll have a little din-din, mammy, dear, and I'll wait on you."

In spite of her gay tone, there was an anxious look in the child's eyes as she looked at her mother lying on the mattress, covered with an old shawl that had once been beautiful and costly, but was now only a faded rag.

The sick woman tried to swallow a mouthful of rice, then she looked at her daughter with a wan smile.

"It doesn't go down very well," she murmured.

"You must force yourself," said Perrine; "the second will go down better, and the third better still."

"I cannot; no, I cannot, dear!"

"Oh, mama!"

The mother sank back on her mattress, gasping. But weak though she was, she thought of her little girl and smiled.

"The rice is delicious, dear," she said; "you eat it. As you do the work you must feed well. You must be very strong to be able to nurse me, so eat, darling, eat."

Keeping back her tears, Perrine made an effort to eat her dinner. Her mother continued to talk to her. Little by little she stopped crying and all the rice disappeared.

"Why don't you try to eat, mother?" she asked. "I forced myself."

"But I'm ill, dear."

"I think I ought to go and fetch a doctor. We are in Paris now and there are good doctors here."

"Good doctors will not put themselves out unless they are paid."

"We'll pay."

"With what, my child?"

"With our money. You have seven francs in your pocket and a florin which we could change here. I've got 17 sous. Feel in your pocket."

The black dress, as worn as Perrine's skirt but not so dusty, for it had been brushed, was lying on the bed, and served for a cover. They found the seven francs and an Austrian coin.

"How much does that make in all?" asked Perrine; "I don't understand French money."

"I know very little more than you," replied her mother.

Counting the florin at two francs, they found they had nine francs and eighty-five centimes.

"You see we have more than what is needed for a doctor," insisted Perrine.

"He won't cure me with words; we shall have to buy medicine."

"I have an idea. You can imagine that all the time I was walking beside Palikare I did not waste my time just talking to him, although he likes that. I was also thinking of both of us, but mostly of you, mama, because you are sick. And I was thinking of our arrival at Maraucourt. Everybody has laughed at our wagon as we came along, and I am afraid if we go to Maraucourt with it we shall not get much of a welcome. If our relations are very proud, they'll be humiliated.

"So I thought," she added, wisely, "that as we don't need the wagon any more, we could sell it. Now that you are ill, no one will let me take their pictures, and even if they would we have not the money to buy the things for developing that we need. We must sell it."

"And how much can we get for it?"

"We can get something; then there is the camera and the mattress."

"Everything," said the sick woman.

"But you don't mind, do you, mother, dear?..."

"We have lived in this wagon for more than a year," said her mother; "your father died here, and although it's a poor thing, it makes me sad to part with it.... It is all that remains of him ... there is not one of these old things here that does not remind us of him...."

She stopped, gasping; the tears were rolling down her cheeks.

"Oh, forgive me, mother, for speaking about it," cried Perrine.

"My darling, you are right. You are only a child, but you have thought of the things that I should have. I shall not be better tomorrow nor the next day, and we must sell these things, and we must decide to sell...."

The mother hesitated. There was a painful silence.

"Palikare," said Perrine at last.

"You have thought that also?" asked the mother.

"Yes," said Perrine, "and I have been so unhappy about it, and sometimes I did not dare look at him for fear he would guess that we were going to part with him instead of taking him to Maraucourt with us. He would have been so happy there after such a long journey."

"If we were only sure of a welcome, but they may turn us away. If they do, all we can do then is to lie down by the roadside and die, but no matter what it costs, we must get to Maraucourt, and we must present ourselves as well as we can so that they will not shut their doors upon us...."

"Would that be possible, mama?... The memory of papa ... he was so good. Could they be angry with him now he is dead?"

"I am speaking as your father would have spoken, dear ... so we will sell Palikare. With the money that we get for him we will have a doctor, so that I can get stronger; then, when I am well enough, we will buy a nice dress for you and one for me, and then we'll start. We will take the train as far as we can and walk the rest of the way."

"That boy who spoke to me at the Gates told me that Palikare was a fine donkey, and he knows, for he is in a circus. It was because he thought Palikare was so beautiful that he spoke to me."

"I don't know how much an Eastern donkey would bring in Paris, but we'll see as soon as we can," said the sick woman.

Leaving her mother to rest, Perrine got together their soiled clothing and decided to do some washing. Adding her own waist to a bundle consisting of three handkerchiefs, two pairs of stockings and two combinations, she put them all into a basin, and with her washboard and a piece of soap she went outside. She had ready some boiling water which she had put on the fire after cooking the rice; this she poured over the things. Kneeling on the grass, she soaped and rubbed until all were clean; then she rinsed them and hung them on a line to dry.

While she worked, Palikare, who was tied up at a short distance from her, had glanced her way several times. When he saw that she had finished her task he stretched his neck towards her and sent forth five or six brays ... an imperative call.

"Did you think I had forgotten you?" she called out. She went to him, changed his place, gave him some water to drink from her saucepan, which she had carefully rinsed, for if he was satisfied with all the food that they gave him, he was very particular about what he drank. He would only drink pure water from a clean vessel, or red wine ... this he liked better than anything.

She stroked him and talked to him lovingly, like a kind nurse would to a little child, and the donkey, who had thrown himself down on the grass the moment he was free, placed his head against her shoulder. He loved his young mistress, and every now and again he looked up at her and shook his long ears in sign of utter content.

All was quiet in the field and the streets close by were now deserted. From the distance came the dim roar of the great city, deep, powerful, mysterious; the breath and life of Paris, active and incessant, seemed like the roar of a mighty ocean going on and on, in spite of the night that falls.

Then, in the softness of the coming night, little Perrine seemed to feel more impressed with the talk that she had had with her mother, and leaning her head against her donkey's, she let the tears, which she had kept back so long, flow silently, and Palikare, in mute sympathy, bent his head and licked her hands.

CHAPTER II. GRAIN-OF-SALT IS KIND

MANY times that night Perrine, lying beside her mother, had jumped up and run to the well for water so as to have it fresh. In spite of her desire to fetch the doctor as early as possible the next morning, she had to wait until Grain-of-Salt had risen, for she did not know what doctor to call in. She asked him.

Certainly he knew of a good doctor! and a famous one, too! who made his rounds in a carriage, not on foot, like doctors of no account. Dr. Cendrier, rue Rublet, near the Church; he was the man! To find the street she had only to follow the railway tracks as far as the station.

When he spoke of such a great doctor who made his rounds in a carriage, Perrine was afraid that she would not have enough money to pay him, and timidly she questioned Grain-of-Salt, not daring to ask outright what she wanted to know. Finally he understood.

"What you'd have to pay?" he asked. "It's a lot, but it won't be more than forty sous, and so as to make sure, you'll have to pay him in advance."

Following the directions that Grain-of-Salt gave her, she easily found the house, but the doctor had not yet risen, so she had to wait. She sat down on a bench in the street, outside a stable door, behind which a coachman was harnessing a horse to a carriage. She thought if she waited there she would be sure to catch the doctor as he left the house, and if she gave him her forty sous he would consent to come. She was quite sure that he would not if she had simply asked him to visit a patient who was staying in the Guillot Field.

She waited a long time; her suspense increased at the thought that her mother would be wondering what kept her away so long.

At last an old-fashioned carriage and a clumsy horse came out of the stables and stood before the doctor's house. Almost immediately the doctor appeared, big, fat, with a grey beard.

Before he could step into his carriage Perrine was beside him. She put her question tremblingly.

"The Guillot Field?" he said. "Has there been a fight?"

"No, sir; it's my mother who is ill."

"Who is your mother?"

"We are photographers."

He put his foot on the step. She offered him her forty sous quickly.

"We can pay you," she hastened to say.

"Then it's sixty sous," said he.

She added twenty sous more. He took the money and slipped it into his waistcoat pocket.

"I'll be with your mother in about fifteen minutes," he said.

She ran all the way back, happy, to take the good news.

"He'll cure you, mama; he's a real, real doctor!" she said, breathlessly.

She quickly busied herself with her mother, washing her hands and face and arranging her hair, which was beautiful, black and silky; then she tidied up the "room," which only had the result of making it look emptier and poorer still.

She had not long to wait. Hearing the carriage in the road, she ran out to meet the doctor. As he was walking towards the house she pointed to the wagon.

"We live there in our wagon," she said.

He did not seem surprised; he was accustomed to the extreme poverty of his patients; but Perrine, who was looking at him, noticed that he frowned when he saw the sick woman lying on the mattress in the miserable cart.

"Put out your tongue and give me your hand," he said.

Those who pay forty or a hundred francs for a visit from a doctor have no idea of the brevity with which the poor people's cases are diagnosed. In less than a minute his examination was made.

"A case for the hospital," he said.

Simultaneously, little Perrine and her mother uttered a cry.

"Now, child, leave me alone with your mother," he said in a tone of command.

For a moment Perrine hesitated, but at a sign from her mother she left the wagon and stood just outside.

"I am going to die," said the woman in a low voice.

"Who says that? What you need is nursing, and you can't get that here."

"Could I have my daughter at the hospital?"

"She can see you Thursdays and Sundays."

"What will become of her without me," murmured the mother, "alone in Paris? If I have to die I want to go holding her hand in mine."

"Well, anyway, you can't be left in this cart. The cold nights would be fatal for you. You must take a room. Can you?"

"If it is not for long, perhaps."

"Grain-of-Salt can rent you one, and won't charge much; but the room is not all. You must have medicine and good food and care, all of which you would get at the hospital."

"Doctor, that is impossible," said the sick woman. "I cannot leave my little girl. What would become of her?"

"Well, it's as you like; it's your own affair. I have told you what I think."

"You can come in, little girl, now," he called out. Then taking a leaf from his note pad, he wrote out a prescription.

"Take that to the druggist, near the Church," he said, handing it to Perrine. "No other, mind you. The packet marked *No. 1* give to your mother. Then give her the potion every hour. Give her the Quinquina wine

236

when she eats, for she must eat anything she wants, especially eggs. I'll drop in again this evening."

She ran out after him.

"Is my mama very ill?" she asked.

"Well ... try and get her to go to the hospital."

"Can't you cure her?"

"I hope so, but I can't give her what she'll get at the hospital. It is foolish for her not to go. She won't go because she has to leave you. Nothing will happen to you, for you look like a girl who can take care of yourself."

Striding on, he reached his carriage. Perrine wanted him to say more, but he jumped in quickly and was driven off. She returned to the wagon.

"Go quickly to the druggist; then get some eggs. Take all the money; I must get well," said the mother.

"The doctor said he could cure you," said Perrine. "I'll go quickly for the things."

But all the money she took was not enough. When the druggist had read the prescription he looked at Perrine.

"Have you the money to pay for this?" he asked.

She opened her hand.

"This will come to seven francs, fifty," said the man who had already made his calculation.

She counted what she had in her hand and found that she had six francs eighty-five centimes, in counting the Austrian florin as two francs. She needed thirteen sous more.

"I have only six francs eighty-five centimes. Would you take this florin? I have counted that," she said.

"Oh, no; I should say not!" replied the man.

What was to be done? She stood in the middle of the store with her hand open. She was in despair.

"If you'll take the florin there will be only thirteen sous lacking," she said at last, "and I'll bring them this afternoon."

But the druggist would not agree to this arrangement. He would neither give her credit for thirteen sous nor accept the florin.

"As there is no hurry for the wine," he said, "you can come and fetch it this afternoon. I'll prepare the other things at once and they'll only cost you three francs fifty."

With the money that remained she bought some eggs, a little Vienna loaf which she thought might tempt her mother's appetite, and then she returned to the Field, running as fast as she could all the way.

"The eggs are fresh," she said. "I held them up to the light. And look at the bread! Isn't it a beautiful loaf, mama? You'll eat it, won't you?"

"Yes, darling."

Both were full of hope. Perrine had absolute faith in the doctor, and was certain that he would perform the miracle. Why should he deceive them? When one asks the doctor to tell the truth, doesn't he do so?

Hope had given the sick woman an appetite. She had eaten nothing for two days; now she ate a half of the roll.

"You see," said Perrine, gleefully.

"Everything will be all right soon," answered her mother with a smile.

Perrine went to the house to inquire of Grain-of-Salt what steps she should take to sell the wagon and dear Palikare.

As for the wagon, nothing was easier. Grain-of-Salt would buy it himself; he bought everything, furniture, clothes, tools, musical instruments ... but a donkey! That was another thing. He did not buy animals, except pups, and his advice was that they should wait for a day and sell it at the Horse Market. That would be on Wednesday.

Wednesday seemed a long way off, for in her excitement, and filled with hope, Perrine had thought that by Wednesday her mother would be strong enough to start for Maraucourt. But to have to wait like this! There was one thing, though: With what she got for the wagon she could buy the two dresses and the railway tickets, and if Grain-of-Salt paid them enough, then they need not sell Palikare. He could stay at the Guillot Field and she could send for him after they arrived at Maraucourt. Dear Palikare! How contented he would be to have a beautiful stable to live in and go out every day in the green fields.

But alas! Grain-of-Salt would not give one sou over fifteen francs for the wagon.

"Only fifteen francs!" she murmured.

"Yes, and I am only doing that to oblige you. What do you think I can do with it?" he said. He struck the wheels and the shafts with an iron bar; then shrugged his shoulders in disgust.

After a great deal of bargaining all she could get was two francs fifty on the price he had offered, and the promise that he would not take it until after they had gone, so that they could stay in it all day, which she thought would be much better for her mother than closed up in the house.

After she had looked at the room that Grain-of-Salt was willing to rent, she realized how much the wagon meant to them, for in spite of the pride in which he spoke of his "Apartments," and the contempt in which he spoke of the wagon, Perrine was heartbroken at the thought that she must bring her dear mother to this dirty smelling house.

As she hesitated, wondering if her mother would not be poisoned from the odor which came from the heaps of things outside, Grain-of-Salt said impatiently:

"Hurry up! The rag pickers will be here in a moment and I'll have to get busy."

"Does the doctor know what these rooms are like?" she asked.

"Sure! He came to this one lots of times to see the Baroness."

That decided her. If the doctor had seen the rooms he knew what he was doing in advising them to take one, and then if a Baroness lived in one, her mother could very well live in the other.

"You'll have to pay one week in advance," said the landlord, "and three sous for the donkey and six for the wagon."

"But you've bought the wagon," she said in surprise.

"Yes, but as you're using it, it's only fair that you should pay."

She had no reply to make to this. It was not the first time that she had been cheated. It had happened so often on their long journey.

"Very well," said the poor little girl.

She employed the greater part of the day in cleaning their room, washing the floor, wiping down the walls, the ceiling, the windows. Such a scrubbing had never been seen in that house since the place had been built!

During the numerous trips that she made from the house to the pump she saw that not only did grass and thistles grow in the Field, but there were flowers. Evidently some neighbors had thrown some plants over the fence and the seeds had sprung up here and there. Scattered about she saw a few roots of wall-flowers, pinks and even some violets!

What a lovely idea! She would pick some and put them in their room. They would drive away the bad odor, and at the same time make the place look gay.

It seemed that the flowers belonged to no one, for Palikare was allowed to eat them if he wished, yet she was afraid to pick the tiniest one without first asking Grain-of-Salt.

"Do you want to sell them?" he asked.

"No, just to put a few in our room," she replied.

"Oh, if that's it you may take as many as you like, but if you are going to sell them, I might do that myself. As it's for your room, help yourself, little one. You like the smell of flowers. I like the smell of wine. That's the only thing I can smell."

She picked the flowers, and searching amongst the heap of broken glass she found an old vase and some tumblers.

The miserable room was soon filled with the sweet perfume of wallflowers, pinks and violets, which kept out the bad odors of the rest of the house, and at the same time the fresh, bright colors lent a beauty to the dark walls.

While working, she had made the acquaintance of her neighbors. On one side of their room lived an old woman whose gray head was adorned with a bonnet decorated with the tri-color ribbon of the French flag. On the other side lived a big man, almost bent double. He wore a leather apron, so long and so large that it seemed to be his only garment. The woman with the tri-color ribbons was a street singer, so the big man told her, and no less a person than the Baroness of whom Grain-of-Salt had spoken. Every day she left the Guillot Field with a great red umbrella and a big stick which she stuck in the ground at the crossroads or at the end of a bridge. She would shelter herself from the sun or the rain under her red umbrella and sing, and then sell to the passersby copies of the songs she sang.

As to the big man with the apron, he was a cobbler, so she learned from the Baroness, and he worked from morning to night. He was always silent, like a fish, and for this reason everybody called him Father Carp. But although he did little talking he made enough noise with his hammer.

At sunset Perrine's room was ready. Her mother, as she was helped in, looked at the flowers with surprise and pleasure.

"How good you are to your mama, darling," she murmured as she clung to Perrine's arm.

"How good I am to myself," Perrine cried gayly, "because if I do anything that pleases you, I am so happy."

At night they had to put the flowers outside. Then the odors of the old house rose up terribly strong, but the sick woman did not dare complain.

What would be the use, for she could not leave the Guillot Field to go elsewhere?

Her sleep was restless, and when the doctor came the next morning he found her worse, which made him change the treatment, and Perrine was obliged to go again to the druggist. This time he asked five francs to fill out the prescription. She did not flinch, but paid bravely, although she could scarcely breathe when she got outside the store. If the expenses continued to increase at this rate poor Palikare would have to be sold on Wednesday. He would have to go now anyway. And if the doctor prescribed something else the next day, costing five francs or more, where would she find the money?

When, with her mother and father, she had tramped over the mountains, they had often been hungry, and more than once since they had left Greece on their way to France they had been without food. But hunger in the mountains and in the country was another thing—there was always the chance that they would find some wild fruit or vegetables. But in Paris there was no hope for those who had no money in their pockets.

What would become of them? And the terrible thing was that she must take the responsibility. Her mother was too ill now to think or plan, and Perrine, although only a child, realized that she must now be the mother.

On Tuesday morning her fears were realized. After a brief examination, the doctor took from his pocket that terrible notebook that Perrine dreaded to see and began to write. She had the courage to stop him.

"Doctor, if the medicines which you are ordering are not all of the same importance," she said, "will you please write out those which are needed the most?"

"What do you mean?" he asked angrily.

She trembled but continued bravely:

"I mean that we have not much money today, and we shall not get any perhaps until tomorrow ... so...."

He looked at her, then glanced round the room, as though for the first time remarking their poverty; then he put his notebook back in his pocket.

"We won't change the treatment until tomorrow, then," he said. "There is no hurry for this. Continue the same today."

"No hurry!" Perrine repeated the words to herself. There was no hurry then ... her mother was not so ill as she had feared; they had just to wait and hope....

Wednesday was the day for which she was waiting, yet at the same time how she dreaded it. Dear, dear Palikare.... Whenever her mother did not need her she would run out into the field and kiss his nose and talk to him, and as he had no work to do, and all the thistles to eat that he wanted and his little mistress' love, he was the happiest donkey in the world.

"Ah, if you only knew," murmured Perrine, as she caressed him.

But he did not know. All he knew was that she loved him and that the thistles were good. So, as she kissed and kissed, he brayed in contentment and shook his long ears as he looked at her from the corner of his eyes.

Besides, he had made friends with Grain-of-Salt and had received a proof of his friendship in a way that flattered his greed. On Monday, having broken loose, he had trotted up to Grain-of-Salt, who was occupied in sorting out the rags and bones that had just arrived, and he stood beside him. The man was about to pour out a drink from the bottle that was always beside him when he saw Palikare, his eyes fixed on him, his neck stretched out.

"What are you doing here?" he asked. As the words were not said in anger, the donkey knew, and he did not move.

"Want a drink ... a glass of wine?" he asked mockingly. The glass that he was about to put to his lips he offered in a joke to the donkey. Palikare, taking the offer seriously, came a step nearer and pushing out his lips to make them as thin and as long as possible, drank a good half of the glass which had been filled to the brim.

"*Oh la la! la la!*" cried Grain-of-Salt, bursting with laughter. "Baroness! Carp! Come here!"

At his calls, the Baroness and Carp, also a rag picker who came into the field at that moment and a man with a push-cart who sold red and yellow and blue sugar sticks, ran up.

"What's the matter?" demanded the Baroness.

He filled the glass again and held it out to the donkey, who, as before, absorbed half of the contents amidst the laughter and shouts of those who looked on.

"I heard that donkeys liked wine, but I never believed it," said the candy man.

"You ought to buy him; he'd be a good companion for you," said the Baroness.

"A fine pair," said another.

But Grain-of-Salt did not buy him, although he took a great liking to him, and told Perrine that he would go with her on Wednesday to the Horse Market. This was a great relief for Perrine, for she had wondered how she would ever be able to find the place; neither did she know how to discuss prices, and she was very much afraid that she would be robbed. She had heard so many stories about Paris thieves, and what could she have done to protect herself?...

Wednesday morning came. At an early hour she busied herself with brushing Palikare and making his beautiful coat shine so that he would look his best. How she kissed him! How she stroked him while her tears fell!

When Palikare saw that instead of being hitched to the wagon, a rope was put round his neck, his surprise was great; and still more surprised was he when Grain-of-Salt, who did not want to walk all the way from Charonne to the Horse Market, climbed up on a chair and from the chair onto his back. But as Perrine held him and spoke to him, he offered no resistance. Besides, was not Grain-of-Salt his friend?

They started thus. Palikare, still surprised, walked gravely along, led by Perrine. On through the streets they went. At first they met but few vehicles, and soon they arrived at a bridge which jutted into a large garden.

"That's the Zoo," said Grain-of-Salt, "and I'm sure that they haven't got a donkey there like yours."

"Then perhaps we can sell him to the Zoo," exclaimed Perrine, thinking that in a zoological garden all the animals have to do is to walk about and be looked at. That would be very nice for dear Palikare!

"An affair with the Government," said Grain-of-Salt; "better not, 'cause the Government...."

From his expression it was evident that Grain-of-Salt had no faith in the Government.

From now on the traffic was intense. Perrine needed all her wits and eyes about her. After what seemed a long time they arrived at the Market and Grain-of-Salt jumped off the donkey. But while he was getting down Palikare had time to gaze about him, and when Perrine tried to make him go through the iron gate at the entrance he refused to budge.

He seemed to know by instinct that this was a market where horses and donkeys were sold. He was afraid. Perrine coaxed him, commanded him, begged him, but he still refused to move. Grain-of-Salt thought that if he pushed him from behind he would go forward, but Palikare, who would not permit such familiarity, backed and reared, dragging Perrine with him.

There was already a small circle of onlookers around them. In the first row, as usual, there were messenger boys and errand boys, each giving his word of advice as to what means to use to force the donkey through the gate.

"That there donkey is going to give some trouble to the fool who buys him," cried one.

These were dangerous words that might affect the sale, so Grain-of-Salt thought he ought to say something.

"He's the cleverest donkey that ever was!" he cried. "He knows he's going to be sold, and he's doin' this 'cause he loves us and don't want to leave us!"

"Are you so sure of that, Grain-of-Salt?" called out a voice in the crowd.

"Zooks! who knows my name here?" cried the one addressed.

"Don't you recognize La Rouquerie?"

"My faith, that's so," he cried, as the speaker came forward. They shook hands.

"That donkey yours?"

"No; it belongs to this little gal."

"Do you know anything about it?"

"We've had more than one glass together, and if you want a good donkey I'll speak for him."

"I need one and yet I don't need one," said La Rouquerie.

"Well, come and take a drink. 'Tain't worthwhile to pay for a place in the Market...."

"Especially if he won't budge!"

"I told you he was a smart one; he's that intelligent."

"If I buy him it's not for his tricks nor 'cause he can take a drink with one, but he must work."

"He can work, sure! He's come all the way from Greece without stopping."

"From Greece!"

Grain-of-Salt made a sign to Perrine to follow him, and Palikare, now that he knew that he was not going into the market, trotted beside her docilely. She did not even have to pull his rope.

Who was this prospective buyer? A man? A woman? From the general appearance and the hairless face it might be a woman of about fifty, but from the clothes, which consisted of a workingman's blouse and trousers and a tall leather hat like a coachman wears, and from the short, black pipe which the individual was smoking, it surely was a man. But whatever it was, Perrine decided that the person looked kind. The expression was not hard or wicked.

Grain-of-Salt and the stranger turned down a narrow street and stopped at a wine shop. They sat down at one of the tables outside on the pavement and ordered a bottle of wine and two glasses. Perrine remained by the curb, still holding her donkey.

"You'll see if he isn't cunning," said Grain-of-Salt, holding out his full glass.

Palikare stretched out his neck, thinned his lips and quickly drank the half glass of wine.

But this feat did not give La Rouquerie any particular satisfaction.

"I don't want him to drink my wine, but to drag my cart with the rabbit skins," she said.

"Didn't I just tell you that he came from Greece, draggin' a wagon the whole way?"

"Ah, that's another thing!"

The strange looking woman carefully examined the animal; then she gave the greatest attention to every detail; then asked Perrine how much she wanted for him. The price which Perrine had arranged with her landlord beforehand was one hundred francs. This was the sum that she asked.

La Rouquerie gave a cry of amazement. One hundred francs! Sell a donkey without any guarantee for that sum! Were they crazy? Then she began to find all kind of faults with the unfortunate Palikare.

"Oh, very well," said Grain-of-Salt, after a lengthy discussion; "we'll take him to the Market."

Perrine breathed. The thought of only getting twenty francs had stunned her. In their terrible distress what would twenty francs be? A hundred francs even was not sufficient for their pressing needs.

"Let's see if he'll go in any more now than he did then," cried La Rouquerie.

Palikare followed Perrine up to the Market gates obediently, but once there he stopped short. She insisted, and talked, and pulled at the rope, but it was no use. Finally he sat down in the middle of the street.

"Palikare, do come! Do come, dear Palikare," Perrine said, imploringly.

But he sat there as though he did not understand a word of what she was saying. A crowd gathered round and began to jeer.

"Set fire to his tail," cried one.

Grain-of-Salt was furious, Perrine in despair.

"You see he won't go in," cried La Rouquerie. "I'll give thirty francs, that's ten more'n I said, 'cause his cunning shows that this donkey is a good boy, but hurry up and take the money or I'll buy another."

Grain-of-Salt consulted Perrine with a glance; he made her a sign that she ought to accept the offer. But she seemed stunned at such a fraud. She was standing there undecided when a policeman told her roughly that she was blocking up the street and that she must move on.

"Go forward, or go back, but don't stand there," he ordered.

She could not go forward, for Palikare had no intention of doing so. As soon as he understood that she had given up all hope of getting him into the Market, he got up and followed her docilely, agitating his long ears with satisfaction.

"Now," said La Rouquerie, after she had put thirty francs into poor Perrine's hand, "you must take him to my place, for I'm beginning to know him and he's quite capable of refusing to come with me. I don't live far from here."

But Grain-of-Salt would not consent to do this; he declared that the distance was too far for him.

"You go with the lady alone," he said to Perrine, "and don't be too cut up about your donkey. He'll be all right with her. She's a good woman."

"But how shall I find my way back to Charonne?" asked Perrine, bewildered. She dreaded to be lost in the great city.

"You follow the fortifications ... nothing easier."

As it happened, the street where La Rouquerie lived was not far from the Horse Market, and it did not take them long to get there. There were heaps of garbage before her place, just like in Guillot Field.

The moment of parting had come. As she tied Palikare up in a little stable, her tears fell on his head.

"Don't take on so," said the woman; "I'll take care of him, I promise you."

"We loved him so much," said little Perrine. Then she went on her way.

CHAPTER III. "POOR LITTLE GIRL"

WHAT was she to do with thirty francs when she had calculated that they must at least have one hundred? She turned this question over in her mind sadly as she walked along by the fortifications. She found her way back easily. She put the money into her mother's hand, for she did not know how to spend it. It was her mother who decided what to do.

"We must go at once to Maraucourt," she said.

"But are you strong enough?" Perrine asked doubtfully.

"I must be. We have waited too long in the hope that I should get better. And while we wait our money is going. What poor Palikare has brought us will go also. I did not want to go in this miserable state...."

"When must we go? Today?" asked Perrine.

"No; it's too late today. We must go tomorrow morning. You go and find out the hours of the train and the price of the tickets. It is the Gare du Nord station, and the place where we get out is Picquigny."

Perrine anxiously sought Grain-of-Salt. He told her it was better for her to consult a time table than to go to the station, which was a long way off. From the time table they learned that there were two trains in the morning, one at six o'clock and one at ten, and that the fare to Picquigny, third class, was nine francs twenty-five centimes.

"We'll take the ten o'clock train," said her mother, "and we will take a cab, for I certainly cannot walk to the station."

And yet when nine o'clock the next day came she could not even get to the cab that Perrine had waiting for her. She attempted the few steps from her room to the cab, but would have fallen to the ground had not Perrine held her.

"I must go back," she said weakly. "Don't be anxious ... it will pass."

But it did not pass, and the Baroness, who was watching them depart, had to bring a chair. The moment she dropped into the seat she fainted.

"She must go back and lie down," said the Baroness, rubbing her cold hands. "It is nothing, girl; don't look so scared ... just go and find Carp. The two of us can carry her to her room. You can't go ... not just now."

The Baroness soon had the sick woman in her bed, where she regained consciousness.

"Now you must just stay there in your bed," said the Baroness, kindly. "You can go just as well tomorrow. I'll get Carp to give you a nice cup of bouillon. He loves soup as much as the landlord loves wine; winter and summer he gets up at five o'clock and makes his soup; good stuff it is, too. Few can make better."

Without waiting for a reply, she went to Carp, who was again at his work.

"Will you give me a cup of your bouillon for our patient?" she asked.

He replied with a smile only, but he quickly took the lid from a saucepan and filled a cup with the savory soup.

The Baroness returned with it, carrying it carefully, so as not to spill a drop.

"Take that, my dear lady," she said, kneeling down beside the bed. "Don't move, but just open your lips."

A spoonful was put to the sick woman's lips, but she could not swallow it. Again she fainted, and this time she remained unconscious for a longer time. The Baroness saw that the soup was not needed, and so as not to waste it, she made Perrine take it.

A day passed. The doctor came, but there was nothing he could do.

Perrine was in despair. She wondered how long the thirty francs that La Rouquerie had given her would last. Although their expenses were not great, there was first one thing, then another, that was needed. When the last sous were spent, where would they go? What would become of them if they could get no more money?

She was seated beside her mother's bedside, her beautiful little face white and drawn with anxiety. Suddenly she felt her mother's hand, which she held in hers, clasp her fingers more tightly.

"You want something?" she asked quickly, bending her head.

"I want to speak to you ... the hour has come for my last words to you, darling," said her mother.

"Oh, mama! mama!" cried Perrine.

"Don't interrupt, darling, and let us both try to control ourselves. I did not want to frighten you, and that is the reason why, until now, I have said nothing that would add to your grief. But what I have to say must be said, although it hurts us both. We are going to part...."

In spite of her efforts, Perrine could not keep back her sobs.

"Yes, it is terrible, dear child, and yet I am wondering if, after all, it is not for the best ... that you will be an orphan. It may be better for you to go alone than to be taken to them by a mother whom they have scorned. Well, God's will is that you should be left alone ... in a few hours ... tomorrow, perhaps...."

For a moment she stopped, overcome with emotion.

"When I ... am gone ... there will be things for you to do. In my pocket you will find a large envelope which contains my marriage certificate. The certificate bears my name and your father's. You will be asked to show it, but make them give it back to you. You might need it later on to prove your parentage. Take great care of it, dear. However, you might lose it, so I want you to learn it by heart, so that you will never forget it. Then, when a day comes and you need it, you must get another copy. You understand? Remember all that I tell you."

"Yes, mama; yes."

"You will be very unhappy, but you must not give way to despair. When you have nothing more to do in Paris ... when you are left alone ... then you must go off at once to Maraucourt ... by train if you have enough money ... on foot, if you have not. Better to sleep by the roadside and have nothing to eat than to stay in Paris. You promise to leave Paris at once, Perrine?"

"I promise, mama," sobbed the little girl.

The sick woman made a sign that she wanted to say more, but that she must rest for a moment. Little Perrine waited, her eyes fixed on her mother's face.

"You will go to Maraucourt?" said the dying woman after a few moments had passed. "You have no right to claim anything ... what you get must be for yourself alone ... be good, and make yourself loved. All is there ... for you. I have hope ... you will be loved for yourself ... they cannot help loving you ... and then your troubles will be over, my darling."

She clasped her hands in prayer. Then a look of heavenly rapture came over her face.

"I see," she cried; "I see ... my darling will be loved! She will be happy ... she will be cared for. I can die in peace now with this thought ... Perrine, my Perrine, keep a place in your heart for me always, child...."

These words, which seemed like an exaltation to Heaven, had exhausted her; she sank back on the mattress and sighed. Perrine waited ... waited. Her mother did not speak. She was dead. Then the child left the bedside and went out of the house. In the field she threw herself down on the grass and broke into sobs. It seemed as though her little heart would break.

It was a long time before she could calm herself. Then her breath came in hiccoughs. Vaguely she thought that she ought not to leave her mother alone. Someone should watch over her.

The field was now filled with shadows; the night was falling. She wandered about, not knowing where she went, still sobbing.

She passed the wagon for the tenth time. The candy man, who had watched her come out of the house, went towards her with two sugar sticks in his hand.

"Poor little girl," he said, pityingly.

"Oh!..." she sobbed.

"There, there! Take these," he said, offering her the candy. "Sweetness is good for sorrow."

CHAPTER IV. A HARD ROAD TO TRAVEL

THE last prayers had been uttered. Perrine still stood before the grave. The Baroness, who had not left her, gently took her arm.

"Come," she said; "you must come away," she added more firmly as Perrine attempted to resist her.

Holding her tightly by the arm, she drew her away. They walked on for some moments, Perrine not knowing what was passing around her, nor understanding where they were leading her. Her thoughts, her spirit, her heart, were with her mother.

At last they stopped in one of the side paths; then she saw standing round her the Baroness, who had now let go of her arm, Grain-of-Salt and the candy man, but she saw them only vaguely. The Baroness had black ribbons on her bonnet; Grain-of-Salt was dressed like a gentleman and wore a high silk hat; Carp had replaced his leather apron by a black Prince Albert which came down to his feet, and the candy man had cast aside his white blouse for a cloth coat. For, like the real Parisian who practises the cult of the dead, they had dressed themselves up in their best to pay respect to the one they had just buried.

"I want to tell you, little one," commenced Grain-of-Salt, who thought that he should speak first, being the most important person present; "I want to tell you that you can stay as long as you like in Guillot Fields without paying."

"If you'd like to sing with me," said the Baroness, "you can earn enough to live on. It's a nice profession."

"If you'd like to go into the candy business, I'll teach you; that's a real trade and a nice one," said the candy man.

Carp said nothing, but with a smile and a gesture he let her understand that she could always find a bowl of soup at his place ... and good soup, too!

Perrine's eyes filled with fresh tears, soft tears which washed away the bitterness of the burning ones which for two days had flowed from her eyes.

"How good you all are to me," she murmured.

"One does what one can," said Grain-of-Salt.

"One should not leave an honest little girl like you on the streets of Paris," said the Baroness.

"I must not stay in Paris," replied Perrine; "I must go at once to my relations."

"You have relations?" exclaimed Grain-of-Salt, looking at the others with an air which said that he did not think that those relations could be worth much. "Where are your relations?"

"Near Amiens."

"And how can you go to Amiens? Have you got money?"

"Not enough to take the train, but I'm going to walk there."

"Do you know the way?"

"I have a map in my pocket...."

"Yes, but does that tell you which road you have to take from here, here in Paris?"

"No, but if you will tell me...."

They all were eager to give her this information, but it was all so confused and contradictory that Grain-of-Salt cut the talk short.

"If you want to lose yourself in Paris, just listen to what they are saying," he said. "Now, this is the way you must go," and he explained to her which road she should take. "Now, when do you want to go?"

"At once; I promised my mother," said Perrine.

"You must obey her," said the Baroness, solemnly, "but not before I've kissed you; you're a good girl."

The men shook hands with her.

251

She knew she must leave the cemetery, yet she hesitated and turned once more towards the grave that she had just left, but the Baroness stopped her.

"As you are obliged to go, go at once; it is best," she said.

"Yes, go," said Grain-of-Salt.

When she had climbed into the car on the belt line she took an old map of France from her pocket which she had consulted many times alone since they left Italy. From Paris to Amiens the road was easy; she had only to take the Calais road; this was indicated on her map by a little black line. From Amiens she would go to Boulogne, and as she had learned also to calculate distances, she thought that to Maraucourt it ought to be about one hundred and fifty-eight miles.

But could she do all those miles, regularly ... go on day after day? She knew that to walk four or five miles by chance on one day was a very different matter to taking a long, continuous journey like she was contemplating. There would be bad days ... rainy days ... and how long would her money last? She had only five francs thirty-five centimes left. The train pulled up at the station at which she had to get out. Now she had to turn to the right, and as the sun would not go down for two or three hours she hoped to be far away from Paris by night, and find a place in the open country where she could sleep.

Yet as far as her eyes could see there was nothing but houses and factories, factories with great tall chimneys sending forth clouds of thick, black smoke, and all along the road wagons, tramways and carts. Again she saw a lot of trucks bearing the name that she had noticed while waiting to pass through the Gates: "Maraucourt Factories, Vulfran Paindavoine."

Would Paris ever end? Would she ever get out of this great city? She was not afraid of the lonely fields, nor the silence of the country at night, nor the mysterious shadows, but of Paris, the crowd, the lights. She was now on the outskirts of the city. Before leaving it (although she had no appetite), she thought she would buy a piece of bread so that she would have something to eat before going to sleep. She went into a baker shop.

"I want some bread, please," she said.

"Have you any money?" demanded the woman, who did not seem to put much confidence in Perrine's appearance.

"Yes, and I want one pound, please. Here is five francs. Will you give me the change?"

Before cutting the bread the woman took up the five franc piece and examined it.

"What! that!" she exclaimed, making it ring on the marble slab.

"It's a five franc piece," said Perrine.

"Who told you to try and pass that off on me?" asked the woman, angrily.

"No one, and I am asking you for a pound of bread for my supper."

"Well, then, you won't get any bread, and you'd better get out of here as quickly as you can before I have you arrested."

"Arrested! Why?" she stammered in surprise.

"Because you're a thief!"

"Oh!..."

"You want to pass counterfeit money on me. You vagabond ... you thief! Be off! No, wait; I'll get a policeman."

Perrine knew that she was not a thief, whether the money was real or false, but vagabond she was. She had no home, no parents. What would she answer the policeman? They would arrest her for being a vagabond.

She put this question to herself very quickly, but although her fear was great, she thought of her money.

"If you don't wish to sell me the bread, at least you can give me back my money," she said, holding out her hand.

"So that you can pass it on someone else, eh? I'll keep your money. If you want it, go and fetch the police," cried the woman, furiously. "Be off, you thief."

The woman's loud cries could be heard in the street, and several people by now had gathered round the door.

"What's the matter?" someone cried.

"Why, this girl here is trying to rob my till," shouted the woman. "There never is a cop when one wants one."

Terrified, Perrine wondered how she could get out, but they let her pass as she made for the door, hissing her and calling her names as she ran. She ran on and on, too afraid to turn round to see if anyone was following her.

After a few minutes, which to her seemed hours, she found herself in the country, and was able to stop and breathe. No one was calling after her; no one following her.

After her fears had calmed down she realized that she had nothing to eat and no money. What should she do? Instinctively she glanced at the fields by the wayside. She saw beets, onions, cabbages, but there was nothing there ready to eat, and besides, even if there had been ripe melons and trees laden with fruit, what good would they have been to her; she could not stretch out her hand to pick the fruit any more than she could stretch it out to beg of the passersby. No, little Perrine was not a thief, nor a beggar, nor a vagabond.

She felt very depressed. It was eventide, and in the quietness of the twilight she realized how utterly alone she was; but she knew that she must not give way; she felt that while there was still light she must walk on, and by the time night fell perhaps she would have found a spot where she could sleep in safety.

She had not gone far before she found what she thought would be the very place. As she came to a field of artichokes she saw a man and woman picking artichoke heads and packing them in baskets, which they piled up in a cart that stood by the roadside. She stopped to look at them at their work. A moment later another cart driven by a girl came up.

"So you're getting yours all in?" called out the girl.

"Should say so, and it's none too soon," replied the man. "It's no fun sleeping here all night to watch for those rogues. I at least shall sleep in my bed tonight."

"And what about Monneau's lot?" grinned the girl.

"Oh, Monneau's a sly dog," answered the man; "he counts on us others watching out for his. He's not going to be here tonight. Serve him right if he finds all his gone!"

All three laughed heartily. They were not over-anxious that Monneau should prosper. Didn't he profit by their watch to take his own slumbers in peace?

"That'll be a joke, eh?"

"Wait for me," said the girl. "I won't be a jiffy; then we'll go together."

The man and the woman waited, and in a few minutes the girl had finished her task and the two carts, laden with artichokes, went towards the village. Perrine stood in the deserted road looking at the two fields, which presented such a difference in appearance. One was completely stripped of its vegetables; the other was filled with a splendid crop. At the end of the field was a little hut made of branches where the man who watched the field had slept. Perrine decided that she would stay there for the night, now that she knew it would not be occupied by the watch. She did not fear that she would be disturbed, yet she dared not take possession of the place until it was quite dark. She sat down by a ditch and waited, thankful that she had found what she wanted. Then at last, when it was quite dark and all was quiet, she picked her way carefully over the beds of artichokes and slipped into the hut. It was better inside than she had hoped, for the ground was covered with straw and there was a wooden box that would serve her for a pillow.

Ever since she had run from the baker's shop it had seemed to her that she was like a tracked animal, and more than once she had looked behind her with fear, half expecting to see the police on her heels.

She felt now in the hut that she was safe. Her nerves relaxed. After a few minutes she realized that she had another cause for anxiety. She was hungry, very hungry. While she was tramping along the roads, overwhelmed by her great loss, it had seemed to her that she would never want to eat or drink again. She felt the pangs of hunger now and she had only one sou left. How could she live on one sou for five or six days? This was a very serious question. But then, had she not found shelter for the night; perhaps she would find food for the morrow.

She closed her eyes, her long black lashes heavy with tears. The last thing at night she had always thought of her dead father; now it was the spirits of both her father and her mother that seemed to hover around her. Again and again she stretched out her arms in the darkness to them, and then, worn out with fatigue, with a sob she dropped off to sleep.

But although she was tired out, her slumbers were broken. She turned and tossed on the straw. Every now and again the rumbling of a cart on the road would wake her, and sometimes some mysterious noise, which in the silence of the night made her heart beat quickly. Then it seemed to her that she heard a cart stop near the hut on the road. She raised herself on her elbow to listen.

She had not made a mistake; she heard some whispering. She sprang to her feet and looked through the cracks of the hut. A cart had stopped at the end of the field, and by the pale light from the stars she could dimly see the form of a man or woman throwing out baskets to two others, who carried them into the field. This was Monneau's lot. What did it mean at such an hour? Had Monneau come so late to cut his artichokes?

Then she understood! These were the thieves! They had come to strip Monneau's field! They quickly cut the artichoke heads and heaped them up in the baskets. The woman had taken the cart away; evidently they did not want it to stay on the road while they worked for fear of attracting the attention of anyone passing by.

What would happen to her if the thieves saw her? She had heard that thieves sometimes killed a person who caught them at their work. There was the chance that they would not discover her. For they certainly knew that the hut would not be occupied on this night that they had planned to strip the field. But if they caught her? And then ... if they were arrested, she would be taken with them!

At this thought cold beads of perspiration broke out on her forehead. Thieves work quickly; they would soon have finished!

But presently they were disturbed. From the distance could be heard the noise of a cart on the paved road. As it drew nearer they hid themselves, lying down flat between the artichoke beds.

The cart passed. Then they went on with their work even more quickly. In spite of their feverish haste it seemed to little Perrine that they would never be finished. Every moment she feared that someone would come and catch them and she be arrested with them.

If she could only get away. She looked about her to see if it were possible for her to leave the hut. This could easily be done, but then they would be sure to see her once she was on the road. It would be better to remain where she was.

She lay down again and pretended to sleep. As it was impossible for her to go out without being seen, it was wiser to pretend that she had not seen anything if they should come into the hut.

For some time they went on cutting the artichokes. Then there was another noise on the road. It was their cart coming back. It stopped at the end of the field. In a few minutes the baskets were all stowed in the cart and the thieves jumped in and drove off hurriedly in the direction of Paris.

If she had known the hour she could have slept until dawn, but not knowing how long she had been there, she thought that it would be better if she went on her way. In the country people are about at an early hour. If, when day broke, the laborers going to work saw her coming out of the hut, or even if they saw her round about the field, they might suspect her of having been with the thieves and arrest her.

So she slipped out of the hut, ears on the alert for the slightest noise, eyes glancing in every direction.

She reached the main road, then hurried off. The stars in the skies above were disappearing, and from the east a faint streak of light lit the shadows of the night and announced the approach of day.

CHAPTER V. STORMS AND FEARS

SHE had not walked far before she saw in the distance a black mass silhouetted against the dawning light to the grey sky. Chimneys, houses and steeples rose up in the coming dawn, leaving the rest of the landscape obscure in the shadows.

She reached the first straggling cottages of the village. Instinctively she trod more softly on the paved road. This was a useless precaution, for with the exception of the cats which ran about the streets, everyone slept, and her little footsteps only awoke a few dogs who barked at her behind closed gates.

She was famished; she was weak and faint with hunger.

What would become of her if she dropped unconscious? She was afraid she might soon. So that this would not happen, she thought it better to rest a minute, and as she was now passing before a barn full of hay, she went in quietly and threw herself down on the soft bed. The rest, the warmth, and also the sweet smell of the hay, soothed her and soon she slept.

When she awoke the sun was already high in the heavens and was casting its rays over the fields where men and women were busily at work.

The pangs of hunger were now more acute than ever. Her head whirled; she was so giddy that she could scarcely see where she went as she staggered on. She had just reached the top of a hill, and before her, close by, was the village with its shops. She would spend her last sou for a piece of bread! She had heard of people finding money on the road; perhaps she would find a coin tomorrow; anyhow, she must have a piece of bread now.

She looked carefully at the last sou she possessed. Poor little girl, she did not know the difference between real money and false, and although she thought this sou looked real, she was very nervous when she entered the first baker shop that she came across.

"Will you cut me a sou's worth of bread?" she asked, timidly.

The man behind the counter took from the basket a little penny roll and handed it to her. Instead of stretching out her hand, she hesitated.

"If you'll cut a piece for me," she said, "it doesn't matter if it is not today's bread."

The baker gave her a large piece of bread that had been on the counter for two or three days.

What did that matter? The great thing was that it was larger than the little penny roll. It was worth two rolls.

As soon as it was in her hand her mouth filled with water. But she would not eat it until she had got out of the village. This she did very quickly. As soon as she had passed the last house, she took her little knife from her pocket and made a cross on the piece of bread so as to be able to cut it into four equal parts. She took one piece, keeping the three others for the three following days, hoping that it might last her until she reached Amiens.

She had calculated this as she had hurried through the village, and it had seemed such an easy matter. But scarcely had she swallowed a mouthful of her little piece of bread than she felt that the strongest arguments had no power against hunger. She was famished! She must eat! The second piece followed the first, the third followed the second. Never had her will power been so weak. She was hungry; she must have it ... all ... all. Her only excuse was that the pieces were so tiny. When all four were put together, the whole only weighed a half a pound. And a whole pound would not have been enough for her in her ravenous condition. The day before she had only had a little cup of soup that Carp had given her. She devoured the fourth piece.

She went on her way. Although she had only just eaten her piece of bread, a terrible thought obsessed her. Where would she next get a mouthful? She now knew what torture she would have to go through ... the pangs of hunger were terrible to endure. Where should she get her next meal? She walked through two more villages. She was getting thirsty now, very thirsty. Her tongue was dry, her lips parched. She came to the last house in the village, but she did not dare ask for a glass of water. She had noticed that the people looked at her curiously, and even the dogs seemed to show their teeth at the ragged picture she presented.

She must walk on. The sun was very hot now, and her thirst became more intense as she tramped along the white road. There was not a tree along the road, and little clouds of dust rose around her every instant, making her lips more parched. Oh, for a drink of water! The palate of her mouth seemed hard, like a corn.

The fact that she was thirsty had not worried her at first. One did not have to go into a shop to buy water. Anybody could have it. When she saw a brook or a river she had only to make a cup of her hands and drink all she wanted. But she had walked miles in the dust and could see no sign of water. At last she picked up some little round stones and put them in her mouth. Her tongue seemed to be moister while she kept them there. She changed them from time to time, hoping that she would soon come to a brook.

Then suddenly the atmosphere changed, and although the heat was still suffocating, the sun was hidden. Thick black clouds filled the sky. A storm was coming on, there would be rain, and she would be able to hold her mouth up to it, or she could stoop down to the puddles that it made and drink!

The wind came up. A terrific swirl, carrying clouds of dust and leaves, swept over the country and battered down the crops, uprooting plants and shrubs in its mad fracas. Perrine could not withstand this whirlwind. As she was lifted off her feet, a deafening crash of thunder shook the earth. Throwing herself down in the ditch, she laid flat on her stomach, covering her mouth and her eyes with her two small hands. The thunder rolled heavily on.

A moment ago she had been mad with thirst and had prayed that the storm would break quickly; now she realized that the storm would not only bring thunder and rain, but lightning—terrible flashes of lightning that almost blinded her.

And there would be torrents of rain and hail! Where could she go? Her dress would be soaked, and how could she dry it?

She clambered out of the ditch. In the distance she saw a wood. She thought that she might find a nook there where she could take shelter.

She had no time to lose. It was very dark. The claps of thunder became more frequent and louder, and the vivid lightning played fantastically on the black sky.

Would she be able to reach the wood before the storm broke? She ran as quickly as her panting breath would allow, now and again casting a look behind her at the black clouds which seemed to be sweeping down upon her.

She had seen terrible storms in the mountains when travelling with her father and mother, but they were with her then; now she was alone. Not a soul near her in this desolate country. Fortunately the wind was behind her; it blew her along, at times carrying her off her feet. If she could only keep up this pace; the storm had not caught up with her yet.

Holding her elbows against her little body and bending forward, she ran on ... but the storm also made greater strides.

At this moment came a crash, louder and heavier. The storm was just over her now and the ground around her was cleaved with blue flames. It was better to stop running now; far better be drenched than struck down by lightning.

Soon a few drops of rain fell. Fortunately she was nearing the wood, and now she could distinguish clearly the great trees. A little more courage. Many times her father had told her that if one kept one's courage in times of danger one stood a better chance of being saved. She kept on.

When at last she entered the forest it was all so black and dark she could scarcely make out anything. Then suddenly a flash of lightning dazzled her, and in the vivid glare she thought she saw a little cabin not far away to which led a bad road hollowed with deep ruts. Again the lightning flashed across the darkness, and she saw that she had not made a mistake. About fifty steps farther on there was a little hut made of faggots, that the woodcutters had built.

She made a final dash; then, at the end of her strength, worn out and breathless, she sank down on the underbrush that covered the floor.

She had not regained her breath when a terrible noise filled the forest. The crash, mingled with the splintering of wood, was so terrific that she thought her end had come. The trees bent their trunks, twisting and writhing, and the dead branches fell everywhere with a dull, crackling sound.

Could her hut withstand this fury? She crawled to the opening. She had no time to think—a blue flame, followed by a frightful crash, threw her over, blinded and dazed. When she came to herself, astonished to find that she was still alive, she looked out and saw that a giant oak that stood near the hut had been struck by lightning. In falling its length the trunk had been stripped of its bark from top to bottom, and two of the biggest branches were twisted round its roots.

She crept back, trembling, terrified at the thought that Death had been so near her, so near that its terrible breath had laid her low. As she stood there, pale and shaking, she heard an extraordinary rolling sound, more powerful than that of an express train. It was the rain and the hail which was beating down on the forest. The cabin cracked from top to bottom; the roof bent under the fury of the tempest, but it did not fall in. No house, however solid, could be to her what this little hut was at this moment, and she was mistress of it.

She grew calm; she would wait here until the storm had passed. A sense of well-being stole over her, and although the thunder continued to rumble and the rain came down in a deluge, and the wind whistled through the trees, and the unchained tempest went on its mad way through the air and on the earth, she felt safe in her little hut. Then she made a pillow for her head from the underbrush, and stretching herself out, she fell asleep.

When she awoke the thunder had stopped, but the rain was still falling in a fine drizzle. The forest, with its solitude and silence, did not terrify her. She was refreshed from her long sleep and she liked her little cabin so much that she thought she would spend the night there. She at least had a roof over her head and a dry bed.

She did not know how long she had slept, but that did not matter; she would know when night came.

She had not washed herself since she had left Paris, and the dust which had covered her from head to foot made her skin smart. Now she was alone, and there was plenty of water in the ditch outside and she would profit by it.

In her pocket she had, beside her map and her mother's certificate, a few little things tied up in a rag. There was a piece of soap, a small comb, a thimble, and a spool of thread, in which she had stuck two needles. She undid her packet; then taking off her vest, her shoes, and her stockings, she leaned over the ditch, in which the water flowed clear, and soaped her face, shoulders and feet. For a towel she had only the rag she had used to tie up her belongings, and it was neither big nor thick, but it was better than nothing.

This *toilette* did her almost as much good as her sleep. She combed her golden hair in two big braids and let them hang over her shoulders. If it were not for the little pain in her stomach, and the few torn places in her shoes, which had been the cause of her sore feet, she would have been quite at ease in mind and body.

She was hungry, but there was nothing she could do. She could not find a bit of nourishment in this cabin, and as it was still raining, she felt that she ought not to leave this shelter until the next day.

Then when night came her hunger became more intense, till finally she began to cut some twigs and nibble on them, but they were hard and bitter, and after chewing on them for a few minutes she threw them away. She tried the leaves; they went down easier.

While she ate her meal and darned her stockings, night came on. Soon all was dark and silent. She could hear no other sound than that of the raindrops falling from the branches.

Although she had made up her mind to spend the night there, she experienced a feeling of fright at being all alone in this black forest. True, she had spent a part of the day in the same place, running no other danger than that of being struck, but the woods in the daytime are not like the woods at night, with the solemn silence and the mysterious shadows, which make one conjure up the vision of so many weird things.

What was in the woods? she wondered. Wolves, perhaps!

At this thought she became wide awake, and jumping up, she found a big stick, which she cut to a point with her knife; then she strewed branches and fagots all around her, piling them high. She could at least defend herself behind her rampart.

Reassured, she laid down again, and it was not long before she was asleep.

The song of a bird awoke her. She recognized at once the sweet, shrill notes of a blackbird. Day was breaking. She began to shake, for she was chilled to the bone. The dampness of the night had made her clothes as wet as though she had been through a shower.

She jumped to her feet and shook herself violently like a dog. She felt that she ought to move about, but she did not want to go on her way yet, for it was not yet light enough for her to study the sky to see if it were going to rain again. To pass the time, and still more with the wish to be on the move, she arranged the fagots which she had disturbed the night before. Then she combed her hair and washed herself in the ditch, which was full of water.

When she had finished the sun had risen, and the sky gleamed blue through the branches of the trees. There was not the slightest cloud to be seen. She must go.

Although she had darned her stockings well which had worn away through the holes in her shoes, the continual tramp, tramp, tramp, made her little feet ache. After a time, however, she stepped out with a regular step on the road, which had been softened by the rain, and the rays from the beautiful sun fell upon her back and warmed her.

Never had she seen such a lovely morning. The storm, which had washed the roads and the fields, had given new life to the plants. Surely this was a good omen. She was full of hope.

Her imagination began to soar on wings. She hoped that somebody had had a hole in their pockets and had lost some money, and that she could find it on the road. She hoped she might find something, not a purse full, because she would have to try to find the owner, but just a little coin, one penny, or perhaps ten cents. She even thought that she might find some work to do, something that could bring her in a few cents.

She needed so little to be able to live for three or four days.

She trudged along with her eyes fixed on the ground, but neither a copper nor a silver coin did she see, and neither did she meet anybody who could give her work.

Oh, for something to eat! She was famished. Again and again she had to sit down by the wayside, she was so weak from lack of food.

She wondered if she found nothing would she have to sit down by the road and die.

Finally she came to a field and saw four young girls picking peas. A peasant woman seemed to be in charge.

Gathering courage, she crossed over the road and walked towards the woman. But the woman stopped her before she could reach her.

"What cher want?" she shouted.

"I want to know if I can help, too," answered Perrine.

"We don't want no one!"

"You can give me just what you wish."

"Where d'ye come from?"

"From Paris."

One of the girls raised her head and cast her an angry look.

"The galavanter!" she cried, "she comes from Paris to try to get our job."

"I told yer we don't want nobody," said the woman again.

There was nothing to do but to go on her way, which she did with a heavy heart.

"Look out! A cop's comin'!" cried one of the girls.

Perrine turned her head quickly, and they all burst out laughing, amused at the joke.

She had not gone far before she had to stop. She could not see the road for the tears which filled her eyes. What had she done to those girls that they should be so mean to her?

Evidently it was as difficult for tramps to get work as it was for them to find pennies. She did not dare ask again for a job. She dragged her feet along, only hurrying when she was passing through the villages so that she could escape the stares.

She was almost prostrated when she reached a wood. It was mid-day and the sun was scorching; there was not a breath of air. She was exhausted and dripping with perspiration. Then her heart seemed to stop and she fell to the ground, unable to move or think.

A wagon coming up behind her passed by.

"This heat'll kill one," shouted the driver.

In a half conscious state she caught his words. They came to her like in a dream; it was as though sentence had been passed upon her.

So she was to die? She had thought so herself, but now a messenger of Death was saying so.

Well, she would die. She could keep up no longer. Her father was dead, and her mother was dead, now she was going to die. A cruel thought flitted through her dull brain. She wondered why she could not have died with them rather than in a ditch like a poor animal.

She tried to make a last effort to get to the wood where she could find a spot to lie down for her last sleep, somewhere away from the road. She managed to drag herself into the wood, and there she found a little grassy spot where violets were growing. She laid down under a large tree, her head on her arm, just as she did at night when she went to sleep.

CHAPTER VI. THE RESCUE

SOMETHING warm passing over her face made her open her eyes. Dimly she saw a large velvety head bending over her. In terror she tried to throw herself on one side, but a big tongue licked her cheek and held her to the grass. So quickly had this happened that she had not had time to recognize the big velvety head which belonged to a donkey, but while the great tongue continued to lick her face and hands she was able to look up at it.

Palikare! It was dear, dear Palikare! She threw her arms around her donkey's neck and burst into tears.

"My darling, dear, darling Palikare," she murmured.

When he heard his name he stopped licking her and lifting his head he sent forth five or six triumphant brays of happiness. Then, as though that was not enough to express his contentment, he let out five or six more, but not quite so loud.

Perrine then noticed that he was without a harness or a rope.

While she stroked him with her hand and he bent his long ears down to her, she heard a hoarse voice calling:

"What yer found, old chap? I'll be there in a minute. I'm comin', old boy."

There was a quick step on the road, and Perrine saw what appeared to be a man dressed in a smock and wearing a leather hat and with a pipe in his mouth.

"Hi, kid, what yer doin' with my donkey?" he cried, without taking the pipe from his lip.

Then Perrine saw that it was the rag woman to whom she had sold Palikare at the Horse Market. The woman did not recognize her at first. She stared hard at her for a moment.

"Sure I've seen yer somewhere," she said at last.

"It was I who sold you Palikare," said Perrine.

"Why, sure it's you, little one, but what in Heaven's name are you doin' here?"

Perrine could not reply. She was so giddy her head whirled. She had been sitting up, but now she was obliged to lie down again, and her pallor and tears spoke for her.

"What's the matter? Are you sick?" demanded La Rouquerie.

Although Perrine moved her lips as though to speak, no sound came. Again she was sinking into unconsciousness, partly from emotion, partly from weakness.

But La Rouquerie was a woman of experience; she had seen all miseries.

"The kid's dying of hunger," she muttered to herself.

She hurried over the road to a little truck over the sides of which were spread out some dried rabbit skins. The woman quickly opened a box and took out a slice of bread, a piece of cheese and a bottle. She carried it back on the run.

Perrine was still in the same condition.

"One little minute, girlie; one little minute," she said encouragingly.

Kneeling down beside little Perrine, she put the bottle to her lips.

"Take a good drink; that'll keep you up," she said.

True, the good drink brought the blood back to her cheeks.

"Are you hungry?"

"Yes," murmured Perrine.

"Well, now you must eat, but gently; wait a minute."

She broke off a piece of bread and cheese and offered it to her.

"Eat it slowly," she said, advisedly, for already Perrine had devoured the half of what was handed to her. "I'll eat with you, then you won't eat so fast."

Palikare had been standing quietly looking on with his big soft eyes. When he saw La Rouquerie sit down on the grass beside Perrine, he also knelt down beside them.

"The old rogue, he wants a bite, too," said the woman.

"May I give him a piece?" asked Perrine.

"Yes, you can give him a piece or two. When we've eaten this there is more in the cart. Give him some; he is so pleased to see you again, good old boy. You know he *is* a good boy."

"Yes, isn't he a dear?" said Perrine, softly.

"Now when you've eaten that you can tell me how you come to be in these woods pretty near starved to death. Sure it'd be a pity for you to kick the bucket yet awhile."

After she had eaten as much as was good for her, Perrine told her story, commencing with the death of her mother. When she came to the scene she had had with the baker woman at St. Denis, the woman took her pipe from her mouth and called the baker woman some very bad names.

"She's a thief, a thief!" she cried. "I've never given bad money to no one, 'cause I never take any from nobody. Be easy! She'll give that back to me next time I pass by her shop, or I'll put the whole neighborhood against her. I've friends at St. Denis, and we'll set her store on fire if she don't give it up!"

Perrine finished her story.

"You was just about goin' to die," said La Rouquerie; "what was the feelin' like?"

"At first I felt very sad," said Perrine, "and I think I must have cried like one cries in the night when one is suffocating; then I dreamed of Heaven and of the good food I should have there. Mama, who was waiting for me, had made me some milk chocolate; I could smell it."

"It's funny that this heat wave, which was going to kill you, really was the cause of yer bein' saved. If it hadn't been for this darned heat I never should have stopped to let that donkey rest in this wood, and then he wouldn't have found yer. What cher goin' to do now?"

"Go on my way."

"And tomorrow? What yer got to eat? One's got to be young like you to take such a trip as this."

"But what could I do?"

La Rouquerie gravely took two or three puffs at her pipe. She was thoughtful for a moment; then she said:

"See here, I'm goin' as far as Creil, no farther. I'm buyin' odds and ends in the villages as I go along. It's on the way to Chantilly, so you come along with me. Now yell out a bit if you've got the strength: 'Rabbit skins! Rags and bones to sell!'"

Perrine straightened herself and cried out as she was told.

"That's fine! You've got a good, clear voice. As I've got a sore throat, you can do the calling out for me, so like that you'll earn your grub. When we get to Creil I know a farmer there who goes as far as Amiens to get eggs and things. I'll ask him to take you in his cart. When you get to Amiens you can take the train to where yer relations hang out."

"But what with? How can I take a train?"

"I'll advance you the five francs that I'm goin' to get back from that baker. I'll get it! So I'll give yer five francs for your fare."

CHAPTER VII. MARAUCOURT AT LAST

THINGS came to pass as La Rouquerie had arranged. For eight days Perrine ran through the streets of the villages and towns crying out: "Rabbit skins! Rags! Bones!"

"You've got a voice that would make yer famous for this here business," said La Rouquerie admiringly, as Perrine's clear treble was heard in the streets. "If yer'd stay with me you'd be doin' me a service and yer wouldn't be unhappy. You'd make a livin'. Is it a go?"

"Oh, thank you, but it's not possible," replied Perrine.

Finding that the reasons she advanced were not sufficient to induce Perrine to stay with her, La Rouquerie put forth another:

"And yer wouldn't have to leave Palikare."

This was a great grief, but Perrine had made up her mind.

"I must go to my relations; I really must," she said.

267

"Did your relatives save yer life, like that there donkey?" insisted La Rouquerie.

"But I promised my mother."

"Go, then, but you see one fine day you'll be sorry yer didn't take what I offered yer p'raps."

"You are very kind and I shall always remember you."

When they reached Creil, La Rouquerie hunted up her friend, the farmer, and asked him to give Perrine a lift in his cart as far as Amiens. He was quite willing, and for one whole day Perrine enjoyed the comfort of lying stretched out on the straw, behind two good trotting horses. At Essentaux she slept in a barn.

The next day was Sunday, and she was up bright and early and quickly made her way to the railway station. Handing her five francs to the ticket seller she asked for a ticket to Picquigny. This time she had the satisfaction of seeing that her five francs was accepted. She received her ticket and seventy-five cents in change.

It was 12 o'clock when the train pulled in at the station at Picquigny. It was a beautiful, sunny morning, the air was soft and warm, far different from the scorching heat which had prostrated her in the woods, and she ... how unlike she was from that miserable little girl who had fallen by the wayside. And she was clean, too. During the days she had spent with La Rouquerie she had been able to mend her waist and her skirt, and had washed her linen and shined her shoes. Her past experience was a lesson: she must never give up hope at the darkest moment; she must always remember that there was a silver cloud, if she would only persevere.

She had a long walk after she got out of the train at Picquigny. But she walked along lightly past the meadows bordered with poplars and limes, past the river where the villagers in their Sunday clothes were fishing, past the windmills which, despite the fact that the day was calm, were slowly moving round, blown by the breeze from the sea which could be felt even there.

She walked through the pretty village of St. Pipoy, with its red roofs and quaint church, and over the railway tracks which unites the towns wherein Vulfran Paindavoine has his factories, and which joins the main line to Boulogne.

As Perrine passed the pretty church the people were coming out from mass. Listening to them as they talked in groups she heard again the sing-song manner of talking that her father had often imitated so as to amuse her.

On the country road she saw a young girl walking slowly ahead of her carrying a very heavy basket on her arm.

"Is this the way to Maraucourt?" Perrine asked.

"Yes, this road ... quite straight."

"Quite straight," said Perrine laughing, "it isn't so very straight after all."

"If you are going to Maraucourt, I'm going there too, and we could go together," suggested the girl.

"I will if you'll let me help you carry your basket," said Perrine with a smile.

"I won't say no to that, for it's sure heavy!"

The girl put her basket on the ground and breathed a sigh of relief.

"You don't belong to Maraucourt, do you?" asked the girl.

"No, do you?"

"Sure I do."

"Do you work in the factories?"

"Should say so, everybody does here."

"How much do they pay?"

"Ten sous."

"And is it hard work?"

"Not very; but you have to have a sharp eye and not waste time. Do you want to get in there?"

"Yes, if they'd have me."

"Should say they would have you; they take anybody. If they didn't how do you think they'd get the seven thousand hands they've got. Just be there tomorrow morning at 6 o'clock at the gate. We must hurry now or I'll be late. Come on."

She took the handle of the basket on one side and Perrine took it on the other side and they set out on the road, keeping in step down the middle.

Here was an opportunity for Perrine to learn what held interest for her. It was too good for her not to seize it. But she was afraid to question this girl openly. She must put the questions she wanted answered in a way that would not arouse her suspicions.

"Were you born at Maraucourt?" she began.

"Sure, I'm a native and my mother was too, my father came from Picquigny."

"Have you lost them?"

"Yes, I live with my grandmother who keeps a grocery store and restaurant. She's Madame Françoise."

"Ah! Madame Françoise."

"What! do you know her?"

"No, I just said, 'Ah, Madame Françoise.'"

"She's known everywhere for her 'eats' and 'cause she was nurse to Monsieur Edmond Paindavoine. Whenever the men want to ask the boss, Monsieur Vulfran Paindavoine, for anything, they get my grandmother to ask for them."

"Does she always get what they want?"

"Sometimes yes, sometimes no; Monsieur Vulfran ain't always obliging."

"If your grandmother was nurse to Monsieur Edmond why doesn't she ask him?"

"M. Edmond? he's the boss' son, and he went away from here before I was born, no one's seen him since. He had a quarrel with his father, and his father sent him to India to buy jute. The boss has made his fortune out of jute. He's rich, as rich as...."

She could not think how rich M. Vulfran was so she said abruptly: "Now shall we change arms?"

"If you like. What is your name?"

"Rosalie. What's yours?"

Perrine did not want to give her real name, so she chanced on one.

"Aurelie," she said.

They rested for a while, then went on again at their regular step.

"You say that the son had a quarrel with his father," said Perrine, "then went away?"

"Yes, and the old gentleman got madder still with him 'cause he married a Hindu girl, and a marriage like that doesn't count. His father wanted him to marry a young lady who came of a very fine family, the best in Picardy. It was because he wanted his son to marry this other girl that he built the beautiful mansion he's got. It cost millions and millions of francs. But M. Edmond wouldn't part with the wife he's got over there to take up with the young lady here, so the quarrel got worse and worse, and now they don't even know if the son is dead or alive. They haven't had news of him for years, so they say. Monsieur Vulfran doesn't speak to anyone about it, neither do the two nephews."

"Oh, he has nephews?"

"Yes, Monsieur Theodore Paindavoine, his brother's son, and Monsieur Casimir Bretoneux, his sister's son, who help him in the business. If M. Edmond doesn't come back the fortune and all the factories will go to his two nephews."

"Oh, really!"

"Yes, and that'll be a sad thing, sad for the whole town. Them nephews ain't no good for the business ... and so many people have to get their living from it. Sure, it'll be a sad day when they get it, and they will if poor M. Edmond doesn't come back. On Sundays, when I serve the meals, I hear all sorts of things."

"About his nephews?"

"Yes, about them two and others also. But it's none of our business; let's talk of something else."

"Yes, why not?"

As Perrine did not want to appear too inquisitive, she walked on silently, but Rosalie's tongue could not be still for very long.

"Did you come along with your parents to Maraucourt?" she asked.

"I have no parents."

"No father, no mother!"

"No."

"You're like me, but I've got a grandmother who's very good, and she'd be still better if it wasn't for my uncles and aunts; she has to please them. If it wasn't for them I should not have to work in the factories; I should stay at home and help in the store, but grandmother can't do as she wants always. So you're all alone?"

"Yes, all alone."

"Was it your own idea to leave Paris and come to Maraucourt?"

"I was told that I might find work at Maraucourt, so instead of going further on to some relations, I stopped here. If you don't know your relations, and they don't know you, you're not sure if you're going to get a welcome."

"That's true. If there are kind ones, there are some mighty unkind ones in this world."

"Yes, that is so," Perrine said, nodding her pretty head.

"Well, don't worry; you'll find work in the factories. Ten sous a day is not much, but it's something, and you can get as much as twenty-two sous. I'm going to ask you a question; you can answer or not, as you like. Have you got any money?"

"A little."

"Well, if you'd like to lodge at my grandmother's, that'll cost you twenty-eight sous a week, pay in advance."

"I can pay twenty-eight sous."

"Now, I don't promise you a fine room all to yourself at that price; there'll be six in the same room, but you'll have a bed, some sheets and a coverlet. Everybody ain't got that."

"I'd like it and thank you very much."

"My grandmother don't only take in lodgers who can only pay twenty-eight sous. We've got some very fine rooms in our house. Our boarders are employed at the factories. There's Monsieur Fabry, the engineer of the building; Monsieur Mombleux, the head clerk, and Mr. Bendit, who has charge of the foreign correspondence. If you ever speak to him always call him Mr. Benndite. He's an Englishman, and he gets mad if you pronounce his name 'Bendit.' He thinks that one wants to insult him, just as though one was calling him 'Thief'!"

"I won't forget; besides, I know English."

"You know English! You!"

"My mother was English."

"So, so! Well, that'll be fine for Mr. Bendit, but he'd be more pleased if you knew every language. His great stunt on Sunday is to read prayers that are printed in twenty-five languages. When he's gone through them once, he goes over them again and again. Every Sunday he does the same thing. All the same, he's a very fine man."

CHAPTER VIII. GRANDFATHER VULFRAN

THROUGH the great trees which framed the road on either side, Perrine could see beyond the hill the tops of some high chimneys and buildings.

"We're coming to Maraucourt," said Rosalie; "you'll see Monsieur Paindavoine's mansion soon, then the factories. We shan't see the village until we get down the other side of the hill. Over by the river there's the church and cemetery."

Then, as they neared the spot where the poplars were swaying, there came into view a beautiful chateau towering grandly above the trees, with its façade of stone gabled roofs and chimneys standing out magnificently in a park planted with trees and shrubs which stretched out as far as the meadows.

Perrine stopped short in amazement, whilst Rosalie continue to step out. This made them jolt the basket, whereupon Rosalie plumped it down on the ground and stretched herself.

"Ah, you think that fine, don't you?" said Rosalie, following Perrine's glance.

"Why, it's beautiful," said Perrine, softly.

"Well, old Monsieur Vulfran lives there all alone. He's got a dozen servants to wait on him, without counting the gardeners and stablemen who live in those quarters over there at the end of the park. That place over there is the electric power house for lighting up the chateau. Fine, ain't it? And you should see the inside! There's gold everywhere, and velvets, and such carpets! Them nephews want to live there with him, but he won't have 'em. He even eats his meals all alone."

They took up the basket and went on again. Soon they saw a general view of the works. But to Perrine's eyes there seemed only a confusion of buildings, some old, some new, just a great gray mass with big, tall chimneys everywhere. Then they came to the first houses of the village, with apple trees and pear trees growing in the gardens. Here was the village of which her father had spoken so often.

What struck her most was the number of people she saw. Groups of men, women and children dressed up in their Sunday clothes stood chatting before the houses or sat in the low rooms, the windows of which were thrown wide open. A mass of people, people everywhere. In the low-ceiling rooms, where those from outside could see all that was passing within, some were drinking bright colored drinks, others had jugs of cider, while others had on the tables before them black coffee or whisky. And what a tapping of glasses and voices raised in angry dispute!

"What a lot of people there seem to be drinking," said Perrine.

"That's because it's Sunday. They got two weeks' pay yesterday. They can't always drink like this; you'll see."

What was characteristic of most of the houses was that nearly all, although old and badly built of brick or wood, affected an air of coquetry, at least in the painting that embellished the doors and windows. This attracted the eye like a sign. And in truth it was a sign, for in default of other preparations, the bright paint gave a promise of cleanliness which a glance at the inside of the place belied at once.

"We've arrived," said Rosalie, pointing with her free hand to a small red brick house which stood a little way from the road, behind a ragged hedge. Adjoining the house was a store where general provisions were sold, and also liquor. The floors above were rented to the best lodgers, and behind the house was a building which was rented out to the factory hands. A little gate in the hedge led to a small garden planted with apple trees and to a gravel walk leading to the house.

As soon as Rosalie and Perrine entered the yard, a woman, still young, called out from the doorway: "Hurry up, you slow coach! Say, you take a time to go to Picquigny, don't you?"

"That's my Aunt Zenobie," whispered Rosalie; "she's none too nice."

"What yer whispering there?" yelled the disagreeable woman.

"I said that if somebody hadn't been there to help carry this basket I wouldn't be here by now," retorted Rosalie.

"You'd better hold your tongue!"

These words were uttered in such a shrill tone that they brought a tall old woman to the door.

"Who are you going on at now, Zenobie?" she asked, calmly.

"She's mad 'cause I'm late, grandmother; but the basket's awful heavy," said Rosalie.

"There, there!" said the grandmother, placidly; "put it down and go and get your supper; you'll find it kept warm on the stove."

"You wait for me here in the yard," said Rosalie to Perrine; "I'll be out in a minute and we'll have supper together. You go and buy your bread. You'll find the baker in the third house on the left. Hurry up."

When Perrine returned she found Rosalie seated at a table under a big apple tree. On the table were two plates full of meat stew and potatoes.

"Sit down and share my stew," said Rosalie.

"But ..." hesitated Perrine.

"You don't like to take it; you can. I asked my grandmother, and it's all right."

In that case Perrine thought that she should accept this hospitality, so she sat down at the table opposite her new friend.

"And it's all arranged about your lodging here," said Rosalie, with her mouth full of stew. "You've only to give your twenty-eight sous to grandmother. That's where you'll be."

Rosalie pointed to a house a part of which could be seen at the end of the yard; the rest of it was hidden by the brick house. It looked such a dilapidated old place that one wondered how it still held together.

"My grandmother lived there before she built this house," explained Rosalie. "She did it with the money that she got when she was nurse for Monsieur Edmond. You won't be comfortable down there as you would in this house, but factory hands can't live like rich people, can they?"

Perrine agreed that they could not.

At another table, standing a little distance from theirs, a man about forty years of age, grave, stiff, wearing a coat buttoned up and a high hat, was reading a small book with great attention.

"That's Mr. Bendit; he's reading his Bible," whispered Rosalie.

Then suddenly, with no respect for the gentleman's occupation, she said: "Monsieur Bendit, here's a girl who speaks English."

"Ah!" he said, without raising his eyes from his Bible.

Two minutes elapsed before he lifted his eyes and turned them to Perrine.

"Are you an English girl?" he asked in English.

"No, but my mother was," replied Perrine in the same language.

Without another word he went on with his reading.

They were just finishing their supper when a carriage coming along the road stopped at the gate.

"Why, it's Monsieur Vulfran in his carriage!" cried Rosalie, getting up from her seat and running to the gate.

Perrine did not dare leave her place, but she looked towards the road.

Two people were in the buggy. A young man was driving for an old man with white hair, who, although seated, seemed to be very tall. It was M. Paindavoine.

Rosalie went up to the buggy.

"Here is someone," said the young man, who was about to get out.

"Who is it?" demanded M. Paindavoine.

It was Rosalie who replied to this question.

"It's Rosalie, monsieur," she said.

"Tell your grandmother to come and speak to me," said the gentleman.

Rosalie ran to the house and came hurrying back with her grandmother.

"Good day, Monsieur Vulfran," said the old woman.

"Good day, Françoise."

"What can I do for you, sir; I'm at your service."

"I've come about your brother Omer. I've just come from his place. His drunken wife was the only person there and she could not understand anything."

"Omer's gone to Amiens; he comes back tonight."

"Tell him that I have heard that he has rented his hall to some rascals to hold a public meeting and ... I don't wish that meeting to take place."

"But if they've rented it, sir?"

"He can compromise. If he doesn't, the very next day I'll put him out. That's one of the conditions that I made. I'll do what I say. I don't want any meeting of that sort here."

"There have been some at Flexelles."

"Flexelles is not Maraucourt. I do not want the people of my village to become like those at Flexelles. It's my duty to guard against that. You understand? Tell Omer what I say. Good day, Françoise."

"Good day, Monsieur Vulfran."

He fumbled in his vest pocket.

"Where is Rosalie?"

"Here I am, Monsieur Vulfran."

He held out a ten cent piece.

"This is for you," he said.

"Oh, thank you, Monsieur Vulfran," said Rosalie, taking the money with a smile.

The buggy went off.

Perrine had not lost a word of what had been said, but what impressed her more than the actual words was the tone of authority in which they had been spoken. "I don't wish that meeting to take place." She had never heard anyone speak like that before. The tone alone bespoke how firm was the will, but the old gentleman's uncertain, hesitating gestures did not seem to accord with his words.

Rosalie returned to her seat, delighted.

"Monsieur Paindavoine gave me ten cents," she said.

"Yes, I saw him," replied Perrine.

"Let's hope Aunt Zenobie won't know, or she'll take it to keep it for me."

"Monsieur Paindavoine did not seem as though he knew you," said Perrine.

"Not know me? Why, he's my godfather!" exclaimed Rosalie.

"But he said 'Where is Rosalie?' when you were standing quite near him."

"That's because he's blind," answered Rosalie, placidly.

"Blind!" cried Perrine.

She repeated the word quite softly to herself two or three times.

"Has he been blind long?" she asked, in the same awed voice.

"For a long time his sight was failing," replied Rosalie, "but no one paid any attention; they thought that he was fretting over his son being away. Then he got pneumonia, and that left him with a bad cough, and then one day he couldn't see to read, then he went quite blind. Think what it would have meant to the town if he had been obliged to give up his factories! But no; he wasn't going to give them up; not he! He goes to business just the same as though he had his sight. Those who counted on being the master there, 'cause he fell ill have been put in their places." She lowered her voice. "His nephews and Talouel; they're the ones I mean."

Aunt Zenobie came to the door.

"Say, Rosalie, have you finished, you young loafer?" she called.

"I've only just this minute got through," answered Rosalie, defiantly.

"Well, there are some customers to wait on ... come on."

"I'll have to go," said Rosalie, regretfully. "Sorry I can't stay with you."

"Oh, don't mind me," said little Perrine, politely.

"See you tonight."

With a slow, reluctant step Rosalie got up and dragged herself to the house.

CHAPTER IX. ONE SLEEPLESS NIGHT

AFTER her new friend had left, Perrine would like to have still sat at the table as though she were in her own place, but it was precisely because she was not in the place where she belonged that she felt she could not. She had learned that the little garden was reserved for the boarders and that the factory hands were not privileged to sit there. She could not see any seats near the old tumble-down house where she was to lodge, so she left the table and sauntered down the village street.

Although she went at a slow step, she had soon walked down all the streets, and as everyone stared at her, being a stranger, this had prevented her from stopping when she had wanted to.

On the top of the hill opposite the factories she had noticed a wood. Perhaps she would be alone there and could sit down without anyone paying attention to her.

She climbed the hill, then stretched herself out on the grass and looked down over the village ... her father's birthplace, which he had described so often to her mother and herself.

She had arrived at Maraucourt! This name, which she had repeated so often since she had trod on French soil, the name she had seen on the big vans standing outside the Gates of Paris. This was not a country of dreams. She was in Maraucourt; before her she could see the vast works which belonged to her grandfather. He had made his fortune here, bit by bit, sou by sou, until now he was worth millions.

Her eyes wandered from the great chimneys to the railway tracks, where all was quiet on this Sabbath day, to the winding streets and the quaint houses with their tiled or thatched roofs. Amongst the very old houses there was one which seemed more pretentious than the others. It stood in a large garden in which there were great trees and a terrace, and at the remote corner of the garden a wash-house.

That house had been described to her so many times, she recognized it. It was the one in which her grandfather had lived before he had built the beautiful chateau. How many hours her father, when a boy, had spent in that wash-house on washing days, listening to the washerwomen's chatter and to the stories they told, quaint old legends. He had remembered them all those years, and later on had told them to his little daughter. There was the "Fairy of the Cascade", "The Whirling Dwarf", and lots of others. She remembered them all, and her dead father had listened to the old women telling them at that very spot down there by the river.

The sun was in her eyes now, so she changed her place. She found another grassy nook and sat down again, very thoughtful. She was thinking of her future, poor little girl.

She was sure of getting work now, and bread and a place in which to sleep, but that was not all. How would she ever be able to realize her dead mother's hopes? She trembled; it all seemed so difficult; but at least she had accomplished one great thing in having reached Maraucourt.

She must never despair, never give up hope, and now that she had a roof over her head and ten sous a day, although not much, it was far better now for her than a few days ago, when she had been penniless, famished, and had had no place where to lay her head.

She thought it would be wise, as she was beginning a new life on the morrow, that she should make a plan of what she should and what she should not say. But she was so ignorant of everything, and she soon realized that this was a task beyond her. If her mother had reached Maraucourt she would have known just what to have done. But she, poor little girl, had had no experience; she had not the wisdom nor the intelligence of a grown-up person; she was but a child, and alone.

This thought and the memory of her mother brought tears to her eyes. She began to cry unrestrainedly.

"Mother, dear mother," she sobbed.

Then her mother's last words came to her: "I see ... I know that you will be happy!"

Her mother's words might come true. Those who are at Death's door, their souls hovering between Heaven and earth, may have sometimes a divine knowledge of things which are not revealed to the living.

This burst of emotion, instead of making her more despondent, did her good. After she had wiped her tears away she was more hopeful, and it seemed to her that the light evening breeze which fanned her cheek from time to time brought her a kiss from her mother, touching her wet cheeks and whispering to her her last words: "I see ... I know you will be happy."

And why should it not be so? Why should her mother not be near her, leaning over her at this moment like a guardian angel? For a long time she sat deep in thought. Her beautiful little face was very grave. She wondered, would everything come out all right for her in the end?

Then mechanically her eye fell on a large cluster of marguerites. She got up quickly and picked a few, closing her eyes so as not to choose.

She came back to her place and, taking up one with a hand that shook, she commenced to pick off the petals, one at a time, saying: "I shall succeed; a little; a lot; completely; not at all." She repeated this very carefully until there were only a few petals left on the last flower.

How many, she did not want to count, for their number would have told her the answer. So, with a heart beating rapidly, she quickly pulled off the last petals.

"I shall succeed; a little; a lot; completely...."

At the same moment a warm breeze passed over her hair, over her lips. It was surely her mother's reply in a kiss, the tenderest that she had ever given her.

The night fell. She decided to go. Already down the straight road as far as the river white vapors were rising, floating lightly around the great trees. Here and there little lights from behind the windows of the houses pierced the gathering darkness, and vague sounds broke the silence of the peaceful Sabbath evening.

There was no need for her to stay out late now, for she had a roof to cover her and a bed to sleep in; besides, as she was to get up early the next day to go to work, it would be better to go to bed early.

As she walked through the village she recognized that the noises that she had heard came from the cabarets. They were full. Men and women were seated at the tables drinking. From the open door the odor of coffee, hot alcohol and tobacco filled the street as though it were a vast sink.

She passed one cabaret after another. There were so many that to every three houses there was at least one in which liquor was sold. On her tramps along the high roads and through the various towns she had seen many drinking places, but nowhere had she heard such words, so clear and shrill, as those which came confusedly from the low rooms.

When she reached Mother Françoise's garden she saw Mr. Bendit still reading. Before him was a lighted candle, a piece of newspaper protecting the light, around which the moths and mosquitoes flew. But he paid no attention to them, so absorbed was he in his reading.

Yet, as she was passing him, he raised his head and recognized her. For the pleasure of speaking in his own language, he spoke to her in English.

"I hope you'll have a good night's rest," he said.

"Thank you," she replied. "Good night, sir."

"Where have you been?" he continued in English.

"I took a walk as far as the woods," she replied in the same language.

"All alone?"

"Yes; I do not know anyone here."

"Then why don't you stay in and read. There is nothing better to do on Sunday than read."

"I have no books."

"Oh! Well, I'll lend you. Good night."

"Good night, sir."

Rosalie was seated in the doorway taking the fresh air.

"Do you want to go to bed now?" she asked.

"Yes, I'd like to," replied Perrine.

"I'll take you up there then, but first you'll have to arrange with grandmother. Go to the café; she's there."

The matter, having been arranged by Rosalie and her grandmother beforehand, was quickly settled. Perrine laid her twenty-eight sous on the table and two sous extra for lighting for the week.

"So you are going to stay in our village, little one?" asked Mother Françoise, with a kindly, placid air.

"Yes, if it is possible."

"You can do it if you'll work."

"That is all I ask," replied Perrine.

"Well, that's all right. You won't stop at ten sous; you'll soon get a franc or perhaps two, then later on you'll marry a good workingman who'll earn three. Between you, that'll be five francs a day. With that you're rich ... if you don't drink; but one mustn't drink. It's a good thing that M. Vulfran can give employment to the whole county. There is the land, to be sure, but tilling ground can't provide a living to all who have to be fed."

Whilst the old nurse babbled this advice with the importance and the authority of a woman accustomed to having her word respected, Rosalie was getting some linen from a closet, and Perrine, who, while listening, had been looking at her, saw that the sheets were made of a thick yellow canvas. It was so long since she had slept in sheets that she ought to think herself fortunate to get even these, hard though they were. La Rouquerie on her tramps had never spent money for a bed, and a long time ago the sheets they had in the wagon, with the exception of those kept for her mother, had been sold or worn to rags.

She went with Rosalie across the yard where about twenty men, women and children were seated on a clump of wood or standing about, talking and smoking, waiting for the hour to retire. How could all these people live in the old house, which seemed far from large?

At the sight of the attic, after Rosalie had lit a candle stuck behind a wire trellis, Perrine understood. In a space of six yards long and a little more than three wide, six beds were placed along the length of the walls, and the passage between the beds was only one yard wide. Six people, then, had to spend the night in a place where there was scarcely room for two. Although a little window opened on the yard opposite the door, there was a rank, sharp odor which made Perrine gasp. But she said nothing.

"Well," said Rosalie, "you think it's a bit small, eh?"

"Yes, it is, rather," was all she said.

"Four sous a night is not one hundred sous, you know," remarked Rosalie.

"That is true," answered Perrine, with a smothered sigh.

After all, it was better for her to have a place in this tiny room than be out in the woods and fields. If she had been able to endure the odor in Grain-of-Salt's shack, she would probably be able to bear it here.

"There's your bed," said Rosalie, pointing to one placed near the window.

What she called a bed was a straw mattress placed on four feet and held together by two boards. Instead of a pillow there was a sack.

"You know," said Rosalie, "this is fresh straw; they never give old straw to anyone to sleep on. In the hotels they do that sort of thing, but we don't here."

Although there were too many beds in the little room, there was not one chair.

"There are some nails on the walls," said Rosalie, in reply to Perrine's questioning look; "you can hang your clothes up there."

There were also some boxes and baskets under the bed. If the lodgers had any underwear they could make use of these, but as Perrine had only what she was wearing, the nail at the head of the bed was sufficient.

"They're all honest here," remarked Rosalie, "and if La Noyelle talks in the night it's 'cause she's been drinking; she's a chatterbox. Tomorrow you get up with the others. I'll tell you where you have to go to wash. Good night."

"Good night, and thank you," replied Perrine.

She hurriedly undressed, thankful that she was alone and would not have to submit to the inquisitive regards of the other occupants of the room. But when she was between the sheets she did not feel so comfortable as she had hoped, for they were very rough and hard. But then the ground had seemed very hard the first time she had slept on it, and she had quickly grown accustomed to it.

It was not long before the door was opened and a young girl about fifteen came in and commenced to get undressed. From time to time she glanced at Perrine, but without saying a word. As she was in her Sunday clothes, her disrobing took longer than usual, for she had to put away her best dress in a small box and hang her working clothes on the nail for the next day.

A second girl came in, then a third, then a fourth. There was a babble of tongues, all talking at the same time, each relating what had happened during the day. In the narrow space between the beds they pulled out and pushed back their boxes or baskets, and with each effort came an outburst of impatience and furious upbraidings against the landlady.

"What a hole!"

"She'll be putting another bed in here soon."

"Sure! But I won't stay!"

"Where would yer go? It ain't no better nowhere else."

The complaining, mixed with a desultory chatter, continued. At length, however, when the two who had first arrived were in bed, a little order was established. Soon all the beds were occupied but one.

But even then the conversation did not cease. They had discussed the doings of the day just passed, so now they went on to the next day, to the work at the factories, the quarrels, the doings of the heads of the concern—M. Vulfran Paindavoine and his nephews, whom they called "the kids," and the foreman, Talouel. They spoke of this man by name only once, but the names they called him bespoke better than words what they thought of him.

Perrine experienced a strange contradictory feeling which surprised her. She wanted to hear everything, for this information might be of great importance to her, yet on the other hand she felt embarrassed, almost ashamed, to listen to such talk.

Most of the talk was rather vague to Perrine, not knowing the persons to whom it applied, but she soon gathered that "Skinny", "Judas", and

"Sneak" were all one and the same man, and that man was Talouel, the foreman. The factory hands evidently considered him a bully; they all hated him, yet feared him.

"Let's go to sleep," at last said one.

"Yes, why not?"

"La Noyelle hasn't come in yet."

"I saw her outside when I came in."

"How was she?"

"Full. She couldn't stand up."

"Ugh! d'ye think she can get upstairs?"

"Not sure about that."

"Suppose we lock the door?"

"Yes, and what a row she'd make!"

"Like last Sunday; maybe worse."

They groaned. At this moment the sound of heavy shambling footsteps was heard on the stairs.

"Here she is."

The steps stopped, then there was a fall, followed by a moan.

"She's fallen down!"

"Suppose she can't get up?"

"She'd sleep as well on the stairs as here."

"And we'd sleep better."

The moaning continued, interrupted by calls for help.

"Come, Laide," called out a thick voice; "give us a hand, my child."

But Laide did not move. After a time the calls ceased.

"She's gone to sleep. That's luck."

But the drunken girl had not gone to sleep at all; on the contrary, she was using every effort to get up the stairs again.

"Laide, come and give me a hand, child. Laide, Laide," she cried.

She evidently made no progress, for the calls still came from the bottom of the stairs, and became more and more persistent. Finally she began to cry.

"Little Laide, little Laide, come to me," she wailed. "Oh! oh! the stairs are slipping; where am I?"

A burst of laughter came from each bed.

"It's cause yer ain't come in yet, Laide; that's why yer don't come. I'll go and find yer."

"Now she's gone and we'll have some peace," said one.

"No, she'll go to look for Laide and won't find her, and it'll all begin over again. We'll never get to sleep."

"Go and give her a hand, Laide," advised one.

"Go yerself," retorted Laide.

"But she wants you."

Laide decided to go, and slipping on her skirt, she went down the stairs.

"Oh, my child, my child," cried La Noyelle, brokenly, when she caught sight of her.

The joy of seeing Laide drove all thoughts of getting upstairs safely away.

"Come with me, little one, and I'll treat you to a glass; come on," urged the drunken creature.

But Laide would not be tempted.

"No, come on to bed," she said.

The woman continued to insist.

They argued for a long time, La Noyelle repeating the words, "a little glass."

"I want to go to sleep," said one of the girls in bed. "How long is this going to keep up? And we got to be up early tomorrow."

"Oh, Lord! and it's like this every Sunday," sighed another.

And little Perrine had thought that if she only had a roof over her head she would be able to sleep in peace! The open fields, with their dark shadows and the chances of bad weather, was far better than this crowded room, reeking with odors that were almost suffocating her. She wondered if she would be able to pass the night in this dreadful room.

The argument was still going on at the foot of the stairs. La Noyelle's voice could be heard repeating "a little glass."

"I'm goin' to help Laide," said one, "or this'll last till tomorrow." The woman got up and went down the narrow stairs. Then came the sound of angry voices, heavy footsteps and blows. The people on the ground floor came out to see what was the matter, and finally everyone in the house was awake.

At last La Noyelle was dragged into the room, crying out in despair.

"What have I done to you that you should be so unkind to me?"

Ignoring her complaints, they undressed her and put her into bed, but even then she did not sleep, but continued to moan and cry.

"What have I done to you girls that you should treat me so badly. I'm very unhappy, and I'm thirsty."

She continued to complain until everyone was so exasperated that they one and all shouted out in anger.

However, she went on all the same. She carried on a conversation with an imaginary person till the occupants of the room were driven to distraction. Now and again her voice dropped as though she were going off to sleep, then suddenly she cried out in a shriller voice, and those who had dropped off into a slumber awoke with a start and frightened her badly, but despite their anger she would not stop.

Perrine wondered if it really was to be like that every Sunday. How could they put up with her? Was there no place in Maraucourt where one could sleep peacefully?

It was not alone the noise that disturbed her, but the air was now so stifling that she could scarcely breathe.

At last La Noyelle was quiet, or rather it was only a prolonged snore that came from her lips.

But although all was silent Perrine could not sleep. She was oppressed. It seemed as though a hammer was beating on her forehead, and she was perspiring from head to foot.

It was not to be wondered at. She was suffocating for want of air; and if the other girls in the room were not stifled like her, it was because they were accustomed to this atmosphere, which to one who was in the habit of sleeping in the open air was unbearable.

But she thought that if they could endure it she should. But unfortunately one does not breathe as one wishes, nor when one wishes. If she closed her mouth she could not get enough air into her lungs.

What was going to happen to her? She struggled up in bed, tearing at the paper which replaced the window pane against which her bed was placed. She tore away the paper, doing so as quietly as possible so as not to wake the girls beside her. Then putting her mouth to the opening she leaned her tired little head on the window sill. Finally in sheer weariness she fell asleep.

CHAPTER X. THE HUT ON THE ISLAND

WHEN she awoke a pale streak of light fell across the window, but it was so feeble that it did not lighten the room. Outside the cocks were crowing. Day was breaking.

A chill, damp air was penetrating through the opening she had made in the window, but in spite of that the bad odor in the room still remained. It was dreadful!

Yet all the girls slept a deep slumber, only broken now and again with a stifled moan.

Very quietly she got up and dressed. Then taking her shoes in her hands she crept down the stairs to the door. She put on her shoes and went out.

Oh! the fresh, delicious air! Never had she taken a breath with such thankfulness. She went through the little yard with her mouth wide open, her nostrils quivering, her head thrown back. The sound of her footsteps awoke a dog, which commenced to bark; then several other dogs joined in.

But what did that matter? She was no longer a little tramp at whom dogs were at liberty to bark. If she wished to leave her bed she had a perfect right to do so; she had paid out money for it.

The yard was too small for her present mood; she felt she must move about. She went out onto the road and walked straight ahead without knowing where.

The shades of night still filled the roads, but above her head she saw the dawn already whitening the tops of the trees and the roofs of the houses. In a few minutes it would be day. At this moment the clang of a bell broke the deep silence. It was the factory clock striking three. She still had three more hours before going to work.

How should she pass the time? She could not keep walking until six, she would be too tired; so she would find a place where she could sit down and wait.

The sky was gradually getting brighter, and round about her various forms were taking a concrete shape.

At the end of a glade she could see a small hut made of branches and twigs which was used by the game keepers during the winter. She thought that if she could get to the hut she would be hidden there and no one would see her and inquire what she was doing out in the fields at that early hour.

She found a small trail, barely traced, which seemed to lead to the hut. She took it, and although it led her straight in the direction of the little cabin, she had not reached it when the path ended, for it was built upon a small island upon which grew three weeping willows. Around it was a ditch full of water. Fortunately, the trunk of a tree had been thrown across the ditch. Although it was not very straight, and was wet with the morning dew, which made it very slippery, Perrine was not deterred from crossing.

She managed to get across, and soon found herself before the door of the little hut, which she only had to push to open.

Oh, what a pretty nest! The hut was square, and from roof to floor was lined inside with ferns. There was a little opening on each of the four sides, which from without was invisible, but from within one could gain a good view of the surrounding country. On the ground was a thick bed of ferns, and in one of the corners a bench made from the trunk of a tree.

How delightful! And how little it resembled the room she had just left! How much better it would be for her if she could sleep here in the fresh air, sleeping in peace amongst the ferns, with no other noise but the rustling of the leaves and the ripple of the water.

How much better to be here than lying between Mother Françoise's hard sheets, listening to the complaints of La Noyelle and her friends in that dreadful atmosphere which even now seemed to assail her nostrils.

She laid down on the ferns, curled up in a corner against the soft walls covered with reeds, then closed her eyes. Before long she felt a soft numbness creeping over her. She jumped to her feet, fearing that she might drop off to sleep and not awake before it was time for her to go to the factory.

The sun had now risen, and through the aperture facing east a streak of gold entered the hut. Outside the birds were singing, and all over the tiny island, on the pond, on the branches of the weeping willows, was heard a confusion of sounds, twittering and little shrill cries which announced an awakening to life. Looking out of the window, she could see the birds picking at the humid earth with their beaks, snapping at the worms. Over the pond floated a light mist. A wild duck, far prettier than the tame ducks, was swimming on the water, surrounded with her young. She tried to keep them beside her with continual little quacks, but she found it impossible to do so. The ducklings escaped from the mother duck, scurrying off amongst the reeds to search for the insects which came within their reach.

Suddenly a quick blue streak, like lightning, flashed before Perrine's eyes. It was not until it had disappeared that she realized that it was a kingfisher which had just crossed the pond. For a long time, standing quite still for fear a movement might betray her presence and cause the birds to fly away, she stood at the opening looking out at them. How pretty it all was in the morning light, gay, alive, amusing, something new to look upon.

Now and again she saw dark shadows pass capriciously over the pond. The shadows grew larger without apparent cause, covering the pond. She could not understand this, for the sun, which had risen above the horizon, was shining in the sky without a cloud. How did these shadows come?

She went to the door and saw a thick black smoke coming from the factory chimneys.

Work would commence very soon; it was time to leave the hut. As she was about to go she picked up a newspaper from the seat that she had not noticed before in the dim light. The newspaper was dated February 2. Then this thought came to her: This newspaper was on the only spot in the place where one could sit down, and the date of it was several months previous, so then this proved that the hut had been abandoned and no one had passed through the door since last February.

CHAPTER XI. WORK IN THE FACTORY

WHEN she reached the road a loud whistle was heard, shrill and powerful. Almost immediately other whistles replied from the distance. This was the call for the factory hands who lived in Maraucourt, and the other whistles repeated the summons to work from village to village, St. Pipoy, Harcheux, Racour, Flexelles, in all the Paindavoine factories, announcing to the owner of the vast works that everywhere, at the same time, his factories were calling to his employés to be ready for the day's work.

Fearing she might be late she ran as far as the village. There she found all the doors of the houses open. On the thresholds the men were eating their soups or leaning against the walls; others were in the cabarets drinking wine; others were washing at the pump in the yard. No one seemed to be going to work, so evidently it was not time yet, so Perrine thought that there was no occasion for her to hurry.

But before long a louder whistle was blown, and then there was a general movement everywhere; from houses, yards and taverns came a dense crowd, filling the street. Men, women and children went towards the factories, some smoking their pipes, others munching a crust of bread, the greater number chattering loudly. In one of the groups Perrine caught sight of Rosalie in company with La Noyelle. She joined them.

"Why, where have you been?" asked Rosalie in surprise.

"I got up early so as to take a walk," Perrine replied.

"You did? I went to look for you."

"Oh, thank you; but never do that, for I get up very early," said Perrine.

Upon arriving at the factory the crowd went into the various workshops under the watchful eye of a tall thin man who stood near the iron gates, his hand in the pocket of his coat, his straw hat stuck on the back of his head. His sharp eyes scanned everyone who passed.

"That's Skinny," informed Rosalie in a whisper.

Perrine did not need to be told this. She seemed to know at once that this was the foreman Talouel.

"Do I come in with you?" asked Perrine.

"Sure!"

This was a decisive moment for little Perrine, but she controlled her nervousness and drew herself up to her full height. Why should they not take her if they took everyone?

Rosalie drew Perrine out of the crowd, then went up to Talouel.

"Monsieur," she said, "here's a friend of mine who wants a job."

Talouel glanced sharply at the friend.

"In a moment ... we'll see," he replied curtly.

Rosalie, who knew what to do, signed to Perrine to stand aside and wait. At this moment there was a slight commotion at the gates, and the crowd drew aside respectfully to allow Monsieur Paindavoine's carriage to pass. The same young man who had driven him the evening before was now driving. Although everyone knew that their chief, Vulfran Paindavoine, was blind, all the men took off their hats as he passed and the women curtseyed.

"You see he's not the last one to come," said Rosalie, as the phaeton passed through the gates, "but his nephews likely will be late."

The clock struck, then a few late comers came running up. A young man came hurrying along, arranging his tie as he ran.

"Good morning, Talouel," he said; "is uncle here yet?"

"Yes, Monsieur Theodore," said the foreman, "he got here a good five minutes ago."

"Oh!"

"You're not the last, though. Monsieur Casimir is late also. I can see him coming now."

As Theodore went towards the offices his cousin Casimir came up hurriedly.

The two cousins were not at all alike, either in their looks or ways. Casimir gave the foreman a short nod, but did not say a word.

"What can your friend do?" asked Talouel, turning to Rosalie, his hands still in his pockets.

Perrine herself replied to this question.

"I have not worked in a factory before," she said in a voice that she tried to control.

Talouel gave her a sharp look, then turned again to Rosalie.

"Tell Oneux to put her with the trucks. Now be off. Hurry up!"

Thus dismissed, Rosalie hurried Perrine away.

"What are the trucks?" asked little Perrine as she followed her friend through the big courtyard. She wondered, poor child, if she had the strength and the intelligence to do what was required of her.

"Oh, it's easy enough," replied Rosalie, lightly. "Don't be afraid; you've only got to load the trucks."

"Oh!..."

"And when it's full," continued Rosalie, "you push it along to the place where they empty it. You give a good shove to begin with, then it'll go all alone."

As they passed down the corridors they could scarcely hear each other speak for the noise of the machinery. Rosalie pushed open the door of one of the workshops and took Perrine into a long room. There was a deafening roar from the thousand tiny machines, yet above the noise they could hear a man calling out: "Ah, there you are, you loafer!"

"Who's a loafer, pray?" retorted Rosalie. "That ain't me, just understand that, Father Ninepins."

"What have you been doin'?"

"Skinny told me to bring my friend to you to work on the trucks."

The one whom she had addressed in this amiable manner was an old man with a wooden leg. He had lost his leg in the factory twelve years previous, hence his nickname, "Ninepins." He now had charge of a number of girls whom he treated rudely, shouting and swearing at them. The working of these machines needed as much attention of the eye as deftness of hand in lifting up the full spools and replacing them with empty ones, and fastening the broken thread. He was convinced that if he did not shout and swear at them incessantly, emphasizing each curse with a stout bang of his wooden leg on the floor, he would see his machines stop, which to him was intolerable. But as he was a good man at heart, no one paid much attention to him, and besides, the greater part of his cursing was lost in the noise of the machinery.

"Yes, and with it all, your machine has stopped," cried Rosalie triumphantly, shaking her fist at him.

"Go on with you," he shouted back; "that ain't my fault."

"What's your name?" he added, addressing Perrine.

This request, which she ought to have foreseen, for only the night before Rosalie had asked the same question, made her start. As she did not wish to give her real name, she stood hesitating. Old Ninepins thought that she had not heard, and banging his wooden leg on the floor again, he cried:

"I asked you what your name was, didn't I? Eh?"

She had time to collect herself and to recall the one that she had already given to Rosalie.

"Aurelie," she said.

"Aurelie what?" he demanded.

"That is all ... just Aurelie," she replied.

"All right, Aurelie; come on with me," he said.

He took her to a small truck stationed in a far corner and explained what she had to do, the same as Rosalie had.

"Do you understand?" he shouted several times.

She nodded.

And really what she had to do was so simple that she would indeed have been stupid if she had been unable to do it. She gave all her attention to the task, but every now and again old Ninepins called after her:

"Now, don't play on the way." But this was more to warn than to scold her.

She had no thought of playing, but as she pushed her truck with a good regular speed, while not stopping, she was able to see what was going on on the way. One push started the truck, and all she had to do was to see that there were no obstacles in its way.

At luncheon time each girl hurried to her home. Perrine went to the baker's and got the baker to cut her a half a pound of bread, which she ate as she walked the streets, smelling the while the good odor of the soup which came from the open doors before which she passed. She walked slowly when she smelled a soup that she liked. She was rather hungry, and a half a pound of bread is not much, so it disappeared quickly.

Long before the time for her to go back to work she was at the gates. She sat down on a bench in the shade of a tree and waited for the whistle, watching the boys and girls playing, running and jumping. She was too timid to join in their games, although she would like to have done so.

When Rosalie came she went back to her work with her.

Before the day was ended she was so tired that she did indeed merit Ninepins' sharp rebuke.

"Go on! Can't you go faster than that?" he cried.

Startled by the bang from his wooden leg which accompanied his words, she stepped out like a horse under the lash of a whip, but only to slow up the moment she was out of his sight. Her shoulders ached, her arms ached, her head ached. At first it had seemed so easy to push the truck, but to have to keep at it all day was too much for her. All she wanted now was for the day to end. Why could she not do as much as the others? Some of them were not so old as she, and yet they did not appear tired. Perhaps when she was accustomed to the work she would not feel so exhausted.

She reasoned thus as she wearily pushed her loaded truck, glancing at the others with envy as they briskly went on with their work. Suddenly she saw Rosalie, who was fastening some threads, fall down beside the girl who was next to her. At the same time a girlish cry of anguish was heard.

The machinery was stopped at once. All was silent now, the silence only broken by a moan. Boys and girls, in fact everyone, hurried towards Rosalie, despite the sharp words from old Ninepins. "Thunder in Heaven, the machines have stopped. What's the matter?" he cried.

The girls crowded around Rosalie and lifted her to her feet.

"What's the matter?" they asked.

"It's my hand," she murmured; "I caught it in the machine. Oh!..."

Her face was very pale, her lips bloodless. Drops of blood were falling from her crushed hand. But upon examining it, it was found that only two fingers were hurt, one probably broken.

Ninepins, who at first had felt pity for the girl, now began pushing those who surrounded her back to their places.

"Be off; go back to your work," he cried. "A lot of fuss about nothing."

"Yes; it was a lot of fuss for nothing when you broke your leg, wasn't it?" cried out a voice.

He glanced about to see who had spoken, but it was impossible to find out in the crowd. Then he shouted again:

"Get back to your work. Hurry up!"

Slowly they dispersed and Perrine, like the others, was on her way back to her truck, when Ninepins called to her:

"Here, you new one, there; come here! Come on, quicker than that."

She came back timidly, wondering why she was more guilty than the others who had also left their work. But she found that he did not wish to punish her.

"Take that young fool there to the foreman," he said.

"What do you call me a fool for?" cried Rosalie, raising her voice, for already the machines were in motion. "It wasn't my fault, was it?"

"Sure, it was your fault, clumsy." Then he added in a softer tone:

"Does it hurt?"

"Not so very much," replied Rosalie bravely.

"Well, go on home; be off now."

Rosalie and Perrine went out together, Rosalie holding her wounded hand, which was the left, in her right hand.

"Won't you lean on me, Rosalie?" asked little Perrine anxiously. "I am sure it must be dreadful."

"No, I'm all right; thank you," said Rosalie. "At least I can walk."

"Well, then, it isn't much then, is it?" asked Perrine.

"One can't tell the first day. It's later that one suffers. I slipped, that's how it happened."

"You must have been getting tired," said Perrine, thinking of her own feelings.

"Sure, it's always when one is tired that one is caught," said Rosalie. "We are quick and sharp first thing in the morning. I wonder what Aunt Zenobie will say!"

"But it wasn't your fault," insisted Perrine.

"I know that," said Rosalie, ruefully. "Grandmother will believe that, but Aunt Zenobie won't. She'll say it's 'cause I don't want to work."

On their way through the building several men stopped them to ask what was the matter. Some pitied Rosalie, but most of them listened

294

indifferently, as though they were used to such accidents. They said that it was always so: one gets hurt the same as one falls sick; just a matter of chance, each in his turn, you today, and me tomorrow. But there were some who showed anger that such an accident could have occurred.

They came to a small outside building which was used for offices. They had to mount some wide steps which led to a porch. Talouel was standing on the porch, walking up and down with his hands in his pockets, his hat on his head. He seemed to be taking a general survey, like a captain on the bridge.

"What's the matter now?" he cried, angrily, when he saw the two girls.

Rosalie showed him her bleeding hand.

"Wrap your paw up in your handkerchief then," he said, roughly.

With Perrine's aid she got her handkerchief out of her pocket. Talouel strode up and down the porch. After the handkerchief had been twisted around the wounded hand he came over to poor Rosalie and stood towering above her.

"Empty your pockets," he ordered. She looked at him, not understanding.

"I say, take everything out of your pockets," he said again.

She did what she was told, and drew from her pockets an assortment of things—a whistle made from a nut, some bones, a thimble, a stick of liquorice, three cents, and a little mirror.

The bully at once seized the mirror.

"Ah, I was sure of it," he cried. "While you were looking at yourself in the glass a thread broke and your spool stopped. You tried to catch the time lost and that's how it happened."

"I did not look in my glass," said Rosalie.

"Bah! you're all the same. I know you. Now: what's the trouble?"

"I don't know, but my hand is crushed," said poor Rosalie, trying to keep back her tears.

"Well, and what do you want me to do?"

"Father Ninepins told me to come to you," said Rosalie.

"And you ... what's the matter with you?" he asked, turning to Perrine.

"Nothing," she replied, disconcerted.

"Well?"

"Father Ninepins told her to bring me here," said Rosalie.

"Well, she can take you to Dr. Ruchon and let him see it. But I'm going to look into this matter and find out if it is your fault, and if it is ... look out!"

He spoke in a loud, bullying voice which could be heard throughout the offices.

As the two girls were about to go M. Vulfran Paindavoine appeared, guiding himself with his hand along the wall.

"What's it all about, Talouel? What's the matter here?"

"Nothing much, sir," replied the foreman. "One of the girls has hurt her hand."

"Where is she?"

"Here I am, Monsieur Vulfran," said Rosalie, going up to him.

"Why, it's Mother Françoise's granddaughter, Rosalie, isn't it?" asked the blind man.

"Yes, it's me, Monsieur Vulfran," said Rosalie, beginning to cry. Harsh words had hardened her heart, but this tone of pity was too much for poor Rosalie.

"What is the matter with your hand, my poor girl?" asked the blind man.

"Oh, sir, I think my two fingers are broken," she said, "although I am not in much pain."

"Well, why are you crying?" asked M. Vulfran, tenderly.

"Because you speak so kindly to me."

Talouel shrugged his shoulders.

"Now go home at once," said M. Vulfran, "and I'll send the doctor to you."

"Write a note to Dr. Ruchon," he said, turning to Talouel, "and tell him to call at Mother Françoise's house; say that the matter is urgent and he must go there at once."

"Do you want anyone to go with you?" he asked, addressing Rosalie.

"Oh, thank you, Monsieur Vulfran; I have a friend here with me," she replied.

"She can go with you then, and tell your grandmother that you will be paid while you are away."

It was Perrine now who felt like crying, but catching Talouel's glance, she stiffened. It was not until they had passed out of the yard that she betrayed her emotion.

"Isn't Monsieur Vulfran kind?" she said.

"Yes," replied Rosalie; "he would be all right if he were alone, but with Skinny he can't be; he hasn't the time and he has a lot to think about."

"Well, he seemed very kind to you," said little Perrine.

"Oh, yes," Rosalie said, drawing herself up; "I make him think of his son. My mother was Monsieur Edmond's foster sister."

"Does he think of his son?"

"He thinks of nothing else."

Everybody came to their doors as Rosalie and Perrine passed. Rosalie's handkerchief was covered with blood. Most of the people were merely curious, others felt sorry, others were angry, knowing that what had happened to this girl that day might happen the next day, at any moment, to their fathers, husbands, and children. Was not everyone in Maraucourt employed at the factory?

"You come on in with me," said Rosalie, when they reached the house; "then perhaps Aunt Zenobie won't say much."

But Perrine's presence had no effect upon the terrible aunt. Seeing Rosalie arrive at such an unusual hour, and noticing that her hand was wrapped up, she cried out shrilly: "Now, then, you've gone and hurt yourself, you lazy bones. I bet you did it on purpose."

"Oh, I'm goin' to be paid," retorted Rosalie, scornfully.

"You think so, do you?"

"Monsieur Vulfran told me that I should."

But this information did not appease Aunt Zenobie. She continued to scold until Mother Françoise, leaving her store, came to see what was the matter. But the old grandmother, instead of showing anger, put her arms about Rosalie and said: "Oh, my dearie; you've gone and got hurt."

"Just a little, grandmother ... it's my fingers ... but it ain't much."

"We must have Dr. Ruchon."

"Monsieur Vulfran is going to send him here."

Perrine was about to follow them into the house when Aunt Zenobie turned upon her and stopped her.

"What are you coming for?" she asked. "Do you think we need you to look after her?"

"Thank you for coming," called out Rosalie to Perrine.

Perrine had nothing to do but to return to the factory, which she did. But just as she reached the gates a whistle announced that it was closing time.

CHAPTER XII. NEW SHOES

A DOZEN times during the day she had asked herself how she could possibly sleep in that room where she had been almost suffocated. She was sure that she would not be able to sleep any better that night, or the next, or the next.

And if she could not find rest after a hard day's work, whatever would happen to her?

In her little mind she weighed all the consequences of this terrible question. If she had not the strength to do her work she would be sent away from the factory, and that would be the end of all her hopes. She would be ill and there would be no one to help her, and she would have to lie down at the foot of a tree and die.

It is true that unless she wished she was not obliged to occupy the bed that she had paid for, but where would she find another, and what would she say to Rosalie? How could she say in a nice way that what was good for others was not good for her, and when they knew how disgusted she had been, how would they treat her? She might create such ill feeling that she would be forced to leave the factory.

The day had passed without her having come to a decision.

But now that Rosalie had hurt her hand the situation was changed. Poor Rosalie would probably have to stay in bed for several days, and she would not know what happened in the house at the end of the yard. She would not know who slept in the room or who did not; consequently she need fear no questions. And, on the other hand, as none of the girls in the room knew who the new lodger for the night had been, neither would they bother about her; it might very well be someone who had decided to find a lodging elsewhere.

Reasoning thus, she decided quickly that she would go and sleep in her new little home. How good it would be to sleep there—nothing to fear from anyone, a roof to cover her head, without counting the enjoyment of living in a house of one's own.

The matter was quite decided, and after having been to the baker's to buy another half a pound of bread for her supper, instead of returning to Mother Françoise's she again took the road that she had taken early that morning.

She slipped behind the hedge as the factory hands who lived outside Maraucourt came tramping along the road on their way home. She did not wish to be seen by them. While she waited for them to pass she gathered a quantity of rushes and ferns and made a broom. Her new home was clean and comfortable, but with a little attention it could be made more so, and she would pick a lot of dried ferns and make a good soft bed to lie upon.

Forgetting her fatigue, she quickly tied the broom together with some wisps of straw and fastened it to a stick. No less quickly a bunch of ferns was arranged in a mass so that she could easily carry them to her hut.

The road was now deserted as far as she could see. Hoisting the bed of ferns on her back and taking the broom in her hands, she ran down the hill and across the road. When she came to the narrow path she had to slacken her speed, for the ferns caught in the branches and she could not pass without going down on her knees.

Upon arriving at the island, she began at once to do her housework. She threw away the old ferns, then commenced to sweep everywhere, the roof, the walls and the ground.

As she looked out over the pond and saw the reeds growing thickly, a bright idea came to her. She needed some shoes. One does not go about a deserted island in leather shoes. She knew how to plait, and she would make a pair of soles with the reeds and get a little canvas for the tops and tie them on with ribbon.

As soon as she had finished her sweeping she ran out to the pond and picked a quantity of the most flexible reeds and carried them back to the door of her hut and commenced to work. But after she had made a plait of reeds about a yard long she found that this sole that she was making would be too light; because it was too hollow, there would be no solidity, and that before plaiting the reeds they would have to undergo a preparation which in crushing the fibres would transform them into coarse strings.

However, this did not stop her. Now she needed a hammer, of course she could not find one, but what she did find was a big round stone, which served her purpose very well indeed. Then she commenced to beat the reeds. Night came on while she was still at work, and she went to sleep dreaming of the beautiful sandals tied with blue ribbons which she would have, for she did not doubt but that she would succeed with what she had undertaken ... if not the first time, well, then the second or the third ... or the tenth.

By the next evening she had plaited enough to begin the soles, and the following day, having bought a curved awl for the price of one sou, some thread for one sou, a piece of ribbon for the same price, a small piece of rough canvas for four sous, in all seven sous, which was all that she could spend if she did not wish to go without bread on the Saturday, she tried to make a sole like those worn on shoes. The first one that she made was almost round. This was not exactly the shape of the foot. The second one, to which she gave much more attention, seemed to resemble nothing at all; the third was a little better, but finally the fourth, which, with some practice, she had managed to tighten in the center and draw in at the heel, could pass for a sole.

Once more she had proved that with a little perseverance, a little will, one can do what one wants, even if at first it seems impossible. And she had done this with scarcely anything, a few sous, with no tools, with hardly anything at her command. She was really very happy and she considered that her work was very successful.

Now what she needed most to finish her sandals were scissors. They would cost so much to buy she would have to manage without them. Fortunately she had her knife, and with the help of a stone to sharpen the point she could make it fine enough to trim the canvas.

But the cutting of the pieces of canvas she found quite a difficult matter. Finally she accomplished it, and on the following Saturday morning she had the satisfaction of going forth shod in a nice pair of gray canvas shoes, tied with blue ribbons crossed over her stockings.

While she had been working on her shoes (the work had taken four evenings and three mornings beginning at the break of day), she had wondered what she should do with her leather shoes while she was away from the hut. She had no fear that they would be stolen by anyone, for no one came to the place, but then the rats might eat them. So as to prevent this she would put them in a place where the rats could not get at them.

This was a rather difficult matter, for the rats seemed to be everywhere. She had no closet, no box to put them away in. Finally she tied them to the roof with some wisps of straw.

CHAPTER XIII. STRANGE HOUSEKEEPING

ALTHOUGH she was very proud of her shoes, she was rather anxious as to how she would conduct herself while wearing them at work. While she loaded her truck or pushed it along she was continually looking down at her feet.

By doing so she would probably attract the attention of the other girls. This is exactly what did happen. Several of her comrades noticed them and complimented her.

"Where did you buy those shoes?" one asked.

"They are not shoes; they are sandals," corrected Perrine.

"No, they are not; they are shoes," said the girl; "but whatever they are they sure are pretty. Where did you buy them?"

"I made them myself with plaited reeds and four cents worth of canvas," replied Perrine.

"They *are* beautiful."

The success she had made of her shoes decided her to undertake another task. She had thought several times of doing it, but it was much more difficult, or so she thought, and might mean too much expense. She wanted to make a chemise to replace the only one which she possessed. For it was very inconvenient to take off this only garment to wash it and then wait until it was dry to put it on again. She needed two yards of calico, and she wondered how much it would cost. And how would she cut the goods when she had them? These were very difficult questions to answer. She certainly had something to think about.

She wondered if it would not be wiser to begin by making a print dress to replace her waist and skirt, which was worn more than ever now, as she had to sleep in it. It could last a very little while longer. When it was finished, how would she go out? For her daily bread, as much as for the success of her future plans, she must continue to be admitted to the factory.

Yet on the Saturday evening when she had the three francs in her hand which she had earned for the week's work, she could not resist the temptation of a chemise. She still considered a waist and skirt of the utmost utility, but then a chemise also was indispensable, and besides there were many arguments in favor of the chemise—cleanliness in which she had been brought up, self-respect. Finally the chemise won the day. She would mend her waist and skirt; as the material had formerly been very strong, it would still hold a few more darns.

Every day at the luncheon hour she went to Mother Françoise's house to ask news of Rosalie. Sometimes news was given to her, sometimes not, according to whether it was the grandmother or the aunt whom she saw.

On her way to inquire for Rosalie she passed a little store which was divided into two sections. On one side newspapers, pictures and songs were sold, and on the other linens, calicos and prints. Perrine had often looked in this store. How nice it would be to go in and have them cut off as much material as she wished! Sometimes, when she had been looking in the window, pretending to look at the newspapers or a song, she had seen girls from the factory enter and come out shortly after with parcels carefully wrapped up, which they held clasped tightly to them. She had thought then that such pleasure was not for her ... at least not then.

Now she could enter the store if she wished, for she had three silver coins in her hand. She went in.

"What is it you want, mademoiselle?" asked a little old woman politely, with a pleasant smile.

"Will you please tell me what is the price of calico the yard ... the cheapest?" asked Perrine timidly.

"I have it at forty centimes the yard," said the old woman.

Perrine gave a sigh of relief.

"Will you cut me two yards, please?" she said.

"It won't wear very well ... but the sixty centimes...."

"The forty centime one will do, thank you," said little Perrine.

"As you like," said the old woman. "I wouldn't like you to come back after and say...."

"Oh, I wouldn't do that," interrupted Perrine hastily.

The old woman cut off two yards, and Perrine noticed that it was not white nor shiny like the one she had admired in the window.

"Any more?" asked the shopkeeper when she had torn the calico with a sharp, dry rip.

"I want some thread also," said Perrine; "a spool of white, number forty."

Now it was Perrine's turn to leave the store with her little newspaper parcel hugged tightly to her heart. Out of her three francs (sixty centimes) she had spent eighteen, so there still remained forty-two until the following Saturday. She would have to spend twenty sous for bread, so that left her fourteen sous for extras.

302

She ran back all the way to her little island. When she reached her cabin she was out of breath, but that did not prevent her from beginning her work at once. She had some time ago decided upon the shape she would give her chemise. She would make it quite straight, first, because that was the simplest and the easiest way for one who had never cut out anything before and who had no scissors, and secondly, because she could use the string that was in her old one for this new one.

Everything went very well; to begin with, there was no cutting in the straight piece. Perhaps there was nothing to admire in her work but at any rate she did not have to do it over again. But when the time came for shaping the openings for the head and arms then she experienced difficulties! She had only a knife to do the cutting and she was so afraid that she would tear the calico. With a trembling hand she took the risk. At last it was finished, and on Tuesday morning she would be able to go to the factory wearing a chemise earned by her own work, cut and sewn by her own hands.

That day when she went to Mother Françoise's; it was Rosalie who came to meet her with her arm in a sling.

"Are you better?" asked Perrine.

"No, but they let me get up and they said that I could come out in the yard," replied Rosalie.

Perrine was very pleased to see her friend again and asked all kinds of questions, but Rosalie seemed rather reserved. Perrine could not understand this attitude.

"Where are you living now?" asked Rosalie.

Fearing to say where, Perrine evaded a direct answer to this question.

"It was too expensive for me here," she said, "and I had so little money left for food and other things."

"Well, did you find anything cheaper elsewhere?"

"I don't have to pay."

"Oh!..."

She looked narrowly at Perrine, then her curiosity got the better of her.

"Who are you with?" she asked.

Again Perrine could not give a direct answer.

"I'll tell you that later," she said.

"Oh, when you like," replied Rosalie carelessly, "only let me tell you this, if you see Aunt Zenobie in the yard or at the door you had better not come in. She doesn't want to see you here. If you come it is better to come in the evening, then she ... she is busy."

Perrine went to the factory very saddened by this welcome. What had she done that she could not go into the house? All day long she remained under the impression that she had offended them. When evening came and she found herself alone in the cabin having nothing to do for the first time in eight days, she was even more depressed. Then she thought that she would go and walk in the fields that surrounded her little island, for she had not yet had time to do this.

It was a beautiful evening. She wandered around the pond, walking in the high grass that had not been trodden by anyone. She looked across the water at her little home which seemed almost hidden amongst the trees. The birds and beasts could not suspect that it was the work of man behind which he could lie in ambush with his gun.

At that moment she heard a noise at her feet which frightened her and a water hen jumped into the water, terrified. Then looking about her she saw a nest made of grass and feathers in which were ten white eggs, dirty little eggs with small dark spots.

Instead of being placed on the ground amongst the grass the nest was floating on the water. She examined it but without touching it, and noticed that it was made in a way to go up and down according to the flow of the water, and was so surrounded with reeds that neither the current nor the wind could carry it away.

The mother hen, anxious, took up her position at a distance and stayed there. Perrine hid herself in the high grass and waited to see if she would come back to her nest.

As she did not return, she went on with her walk, and again and again the rustling of her dress frightened other birds. The water hens, so lissom in their escape, ran to the floating leaves of the water lilies without going under. She saw birds everywhere.

When an hour later she returned to her little home the hut was hidden half in the shadows of night. It was so quiet and pretty she thought, and how pleased she was that she had shown as much intelligence as these birds ... to make her nest here.

With Perrine, as with many little children, it was the events of the day which shaped her dreams by night. The unhappiness through which she had passed the last few months had often colored her dreams, and many times since her troubles had commenced, she had awakened in the night with the perspiration pouring off her. Her sleep was disturbed with nightmares caused by the miseries she had experienced in the day.

Now since she had been at Maraucourt and had new hopes and was at work, the nightmares had been less frequent and so she was not so sad.

Now she thought of what she was going to do at the factory the next day, of the skirt and waist that she would make, of her underwear.

Now on this particular evening after she had wandered over the fields surrounding her home and had entered her little nest to go to sleep, strange visions passed before her sleepy eyes. She thought that she was walking about the field exploring, and came upon a great big kitchen, a wonderful kitchen like in castles, and there were a number of little dwarfs of the most diabolical shapes, sitting around a big table before a blazing fire; some of them were breaking eggs, others were beating them up until they were white and frothy; and some of these eggs were as large as melons and others were as small as a little pea, and the dwarfs made the most extraordinary dishes from them. They seemed to know the every kind of dish that could be made with eggs,—boiled eggs with cheese and butter; with tomatoes; poached; fried eggs; various omelettes with ham and kidney, jam or rum; the rum set afire and flaming with sparkling lights. And then there were more important dishes still which only the head cooks were handling ... pastries and delicious creams.

Now and again she half woke and she tried to banish the stupid dream but it came again and the elfs still went on doing their fantastic work, so that when the factory whistle sounded she was still watching them prepare some chocolate creams which she could almost taste in her mouth.

Then she knew that what had impressed her most during her walk was not the beauty of the night but simply those eggs which she had seen in the nest, which had told her stomach that for fourteen days she had eaten only bread and water. These eggs had made her dream of the elfs and all those delicious things that they were making; she was hungry for good things and she had found it out through her dream.

Why had she not taken those eggs, or at least some of them, they did not belong to anyone for the duck was wild? Of course as she had no saucepan or frying pan or any kitchen utensils whatever, she could not prepare any of the dishes that she had seen made before her dream eyes. But there, that was the best about eggs, they could be used without any very skillful preparation; a lighted match put to a little heap of dry wood and then she could cook them hard or soft, how she liked, in the hot ashes. And she would buy a saucepan or a pan as soon as possible.

Several times this idea came to her while she was at work that day until finally she decided to buy a box of matches and a cent's worth of salt. As soon as she had made her purchases she ran back to her hut.

She had been too interested in the place where she had discovered the nest not to be able to find it again. The mother was not occupying the nest but she had been there during the day because Perrine saw now that instead of ten eggs there were eleven, which proved that she had not finished laying.

Here was a good chance for her to help herself. In the first place the eggs were fresh, and then if she only took five or six, the duck, who did not know how to count, would not notice that any one had been there.

A short time ago Perrine would not have had any scruples and she would have quickly emptied the nest, without a thought, but the sorrows that she had experienced had made her very thoughtful for the griefs of others; in this same manner her love for Palikare had made her feel an affection for all animals that she had not known in her early childhood.

After she had taken the eggs she wondered where she could cook them; naturally this could not be done in the cabin for the slightest wreath of smoke which would emerge from it would indicate to anyone who saw it that someone was living there.

There was a gypsy camp quite near which she passed by to get to her island, and a little smoke coming from there would attract no attention.

She quickly got together some wood and lighted it; soon she had a fire in the ashes of which she cooked one of her eggs. She lacked an egg cup but what did that matter? A little hole made in a piece of bread could hold the egg. In a few minutes she had the satisfaction of dipping a piece of bread in her egg, which was cooked to perfection. It seemed to her as she took the first mouthful that she had never eaten anything so good.

When she had finished her supper she wondered how she should use the remainder of her eggs. She would have to use them sparingly for she might not be able to get any more for a long time. A hot soup with an egg broken into it would be very good.

As the idea of having some soup came into her head, it was almost immediately followed by the regret that she could not have it. The success of her canvas shoes and her underwear had inspired her with a certain amount of confidence. She had proved that one can do a great deal if one perseveres, but she had not enough confidence to imagine that she could ever make a saucepan for her soup or a metal or wooden spoon, and if she waited until she had the money required to buy these utensils, she would have to content herself with the smell of the soup that came to her as she passed by the open doors.

She was telling herself this as she went to work, but just before she reached the village she saw a heap of rubbish by the side of the road and amongst the debris she noticed some tin cans which had been used for potted meat, fish and vegetables. There were different shapes, some large, some small, some high, some low.

Noticing how shiny they were on the surface, she instinctively stopped; she had not a moment's hesitation. The saucepans, dishes, forks, spoons which she lacked were all here; she could have a whole array of kitchen utensils; she had only to make her choice. With a bound she was across the road; quickly picking out four cans she ran back and hid them behind a hedge so that when evening came she would be able to find them.

When evening came she found her treasures and made for her home.

She did not wish to make a noise on her island any more than she wished smoke to be seen, so at the end of her day's work she went to her gypsy's camp hoping that she might find a tool or something that would serve her for a hammer with which to flatten the tins that were to be used for plates, saucepans, spoons, etc.

She found that it was a very difficult task to make a spoon. It took her no less than three days to do so, and when it was done, she was not at all sure that if she had shown it to anyone, he would have recognized it for a spoon. But she had made something that served her purpose, that was enough; besides, she ate alone and there would be no one to notice her utensils.

Now for the soup for which she longed! All she wanted was butter and sorrel. She would have to buy butter and naturally as she couldn't make milk she would have to buy that also.

The sorrel she would find wild in the fields and she could also find wild carrots and oyster plants. They were not so good as the cultivated vegetables but they would suit her very well indeed.

She not only had eggs and vegetables for her dinner, and her pots and pans, but there were fish in the pond and if she were sharp enough to catch them she would have fish too.

She needed a line and some worms. She had a long piece of string left over from the piece she had bought for her shoes and she had only to spend one sou for some hooks, then with a piece of horse hair she could pick up outside the blacksmith's door, she would have a line good enough to catch several kinds of fish; if the best in the pond passed disdainfully before her simple bait then she would have to be satisfied with little ones.

CHAPTER XIV. A BANQUET IN THE HUT

PERRINE was so busy of an evening that she let an entire week pass before she again went to see Rosalie. However, one of the girls at the factory who lodged with Mother Françoise had brought her news of her friend. Perrine, as well as being busy, had been afraid that she might see that terrible Aunt Zenobie and so she had let the days pass.

Then one evening after work she thought that she would not return at once to her little island. She had no supper to prepare. The night before she had caught some fish and cooked it, and she intended to have it cold for her supper that evening.

Rosalie was alone in the garden sitting under an apple tree. When she saw Perrine she came to the gate, half pleased, half annoyed.

"I thought that you were not coming any more," she said.

"I've been very busy."

"What with?"

Perrine showed Rosalie her shoes. Then she told her how she had made herself a chemise and the trouble she had had in cutting it.

"Couldn't you borrow a pair of scissors from the people in your house?" asked Rosalie in astonishment.

"There is no one in my house who could lend me scissors," replied Perrine.

"Everybody has scissors!"

Perrine wondered if she ought to keep her abode a secret any longer. She was afraid that if she did so she might offend Rosalie, so she decided to tell her.

"Nobody lives in my house," she said smiling.

"Whatever do you mean?" asked Rosalie with round eyes.

"That's so, and that's why, as I wasn't able to borrow a saucepan to cook my soup in and a spoon to eat it with, I had to make them and I can tell you that it was harder for me to make my spoon than to make my shoes."

"You're joking!"

"No, really."

Then she told her everything, how she had taken possession of the cabin, and made her own cooking utensils, and about her search for eggs, and how she fished and cooked in the gypsy's camping ground.

Rosalie's eyes opened wider still in wonder and delight. She seemed to be listening to a wonderful story.

When Perrine told her how she made her first sorrel soup, she clapped her hands.

"Oh, how delicious! How you must have enjoyed it!" she cried. "What fun!"

"Yes, everything is great fun when things go right," said Perrine; "but when things won't go! I worked three days for my spoon. I couldn't scoop it out properly. I spoiled two large pieces of tin and had only one left. And my! how I banged my fingers with the stones that I had to use in place of a hammer!"

"But your soup, that's what I'm thinking of," said Rosalie.

"Yes, it was good."

"You know," said Perrine, "there's sorrel and carrots, watercress, onions, parsnips, turnips, and ever so many things to eat that one can find in the fields. They are not quite the same as the cultivated vegetables, but they are good!"

"One ought to know that!"

"It was my father who taught me to know them."

Rosalie was silent for a moment, then she said:

"Would you like me to come and see you?"

"I should love to have you if you'll promise not to tell anyone where I live," said Perrine, delightedly.

"I promise," said Rosalie, solemnly.

"Well, when will you come?"

"On Sunday I am going to see one of my aunts at Saint-Pipoy; on my way back in the afternoon I can stop...."

Perrine hesitated for a moment, then she said amiably:

"Do better than just call; stay to dinner with me."

Rosalie, like the real peasant that she was, began to reply vaguely in a ceremonious fashion, neither saying yes nor no; but it was quite plain to see that she wished very much to accept the invitation. Perrine insisted.

"Do come; I shall be so pleased," she said. "I am so lonesome."

"Well, really...." began Rosalie.

"Yes, dine with me; that is settled," said Perrine, brightly; "but you must bring your own spoon, because I shall not have the time nor the tin to make another one."

"Shall I bring my bread also? I can...."

"I wish you would. I'll wait for you in the gypsy's ground. You'll find me doing my cooking."

Perrine was very pleased at the thought of receiving a guest in her own home ... there was a menu to compose, provisions to find ... what an affair! She felt quite important. Who would have said a few days before that she would be able to offer dinner to a friend!

But there was a serious side. Suppose she could not find any eggs or catch a fish! Her menu then would be reduced to sorrel soup only. What a dinner!

But fortune favored her. On Friday evening she found some eggs. True, they were only water-hen's eggs, and not so large as the duck's eggs, but then she must not be too particular. And she was just as lucky with her fishing. With a red worm on the end of her line, she managed to catch a fine perch, which was quite sufficient to satisfy hers and Rosalie's appetite. Yet, however, she wanted a dessert, and some gooseberries growing under a weeping willow furnished it. True, they were not quite ripe, but the merit of this fruit is that you can eat it green.

When, late Sunday afternoon, Rosalie arrived at the gypsy camping ground, she found Perrine seated before her fire upon which the soup was boiling.

"I waited for you to mix the yolk of an egg in the soup," said Perrine. "You have only to turn it with your free hand while I gently pour the soup over it; the bread is soaked."

Although Rosalie had dressed herself specially for this dinner, she was not afraid to help. This was play, and it all seemed very amusing to her.

Soon the soup was ready, and it only had to be carried across to the island. This Perrine did.

The cabin door was open, and Rosalie could see before she entered that the place was filled with flowers. In each corner were grouped, in artistic showers, wild roses, yellow iris, cornflowers, and poppies, and the floor was entirely covered with a beautiful soft green moss.

Rosalie's exclamations of delight amply repaid Perrine for all the trouble she had taken.

"How beautiful! Oh, isn't it pretty!" she exclaimed.

On a bed of fresh ferns two large flat leaves were placed opposite each other; these were to serve for plates; and on a very much larger leaf, long and narrow, which is as it should be for a dish, the perch was placed, garnished with a border of watercress. Another leaf, but very small, served as a salt-cellar, also another holding the dessert. Between each dish was a white anemone, its pure whiteness standing out dazzlingly against the fresh verdure.

"If you will sit down...." said Perrine, extending her hand. And when they had taken their seats opposite one another the dinner commenced.

"How sorry I should have been if I hadn't have come," said Rosalie, speaking with her mouth full; "it is so pretty and so good."

"Why shouldn't you have come?"

"Because they wanted to send me to Picquigny for Mr. Bendit; he is ill."

"What's the matter with him?"

"He's got typhoid fever. He's very ill. Since yesterday he hasn't known what he's been talking about, and he doesn't know anybody. And I had an idea about you...."

"Me! What about me?"

"Something you can do...."

"If there is anything I can do for Mr. Bendit I'd be only too willing. He was kind to me; but I'm only a poor girl; I don't understand."

"Give me a little more fish and some more watercress, and I'll explain," said Rosalie. "You know that Mr. Bendit has charge of the foreign correspondence; he translates the English and German letters. Naturally, as he is off his head now, he can't translate. They wanted to get somebody else to replace him, but as this other man might take his place after he is better (that is, if he does get better), M. Fabry and M. Mombleux have taken charge of the work, so that he will be sure to have his job when he's up again. But now M. Fabry has been sent away to Scotland and M. Mombleux is in a fix, because, although he can read German all right, he's not much on English. If the writing isn't very clear he can't make out the letters at all. I heard him saying so at the table when I was waiting on them. So I thought I'd tell him that you can speak English just as good as you can French."

"I spoke French with my father, and English with my mother," said Perrine, "and when we were all three talking together we spoke sometimes one, sometimes the other, mixing two languages without paying attention."

"I wasn't sure whether I should say anything about you or not, but now I will, if you like."

"Why, yes; do, if you think a poor girl like me could be of any use to them."

"'Tain't a question of being a poor girl or a young lady; it's a question of knowing English," said Rosalie.

"I speak it, but to translate a business letter is another thing," said Perrine, doubtfully.

"It'll be all right with M. Mombleux; he knows the business part."

"Well, then, tell him I shall be very pleased if I can do anything for M. Bendit."

"I'll tell him."

The perch, although a large one, had all been eaten, and all the watercress had disappeared. It was now time for the dessert. Perrine got up and replaced the fish plates with smaller leaf plates in the shape of a cup; she had picked the prettiest, with variegated shades, and marked as exquisitely as enameled ware. Then she offered her guest the gooseberries.

"Let me offer you some fruit from my own garden," she said, laughing, as though she were playing at keeping doll's house.

"Where is your garden?"

"Over your head. There is a gooseberry bush growing in the branches of this willow tree which holds up the cabin, so it seems."

"You know you won't be able to live in here much longer," said Rosalie.

"Until the winter, I think."

"Until winter! Why, the bird catchers will need this place pretty soon; that I'm sure."

"Oh! ... Oh, dear ... Oh, dear!"

The day, which had begun so brightly for Perrine, ended sadly. That night was certainly the worst Perrine had passed since she had been on her little island.

Where should she go?

And all her utensils that she had taken such trouble to make; what should she do with them?

CHAPTER XV. AURELIE'S CHANCE

IF ROSALIE had not spoken to Perrine of the near opening of the shooting season for water fowl, Perrine would have stayed on in her cabin unaware of the danger that might come to her. Although this news came as a blow to her, what Rosalie had said about M. Bendit and the translations she might do for M. Mombleux gave her something else to think about.

Yes, her island was charming, and it would be a great grief for her to leave it. And yet here was an opportunity where she could be useful to two valued employés at the factory, and this step would lead to other steps, and it would open doors perhaps through which she could pass later. This was something that she should consider above all else, even above the sorrow of being dispossessed of her little kingdom. It was not for this game—robbing nests, catching fish, picking flowers, listening to the birds sing—that she had endured all the misery and fatigue of her long journey. She had an object in view. She must remember what her mother told her to do, and do it.

She had told Rosalie that she would call at Mother Françoise's house on Monday to see if Mombleux had need of her services. Rosalie came to meet her and said that as no letters had come from England that Monday, there would not be any translations to make that day, but perhaps there would be something for the next day. This was at the luncheon hour, so Perrine returned to the factory. It had just struck two when Ninepin hopped up to her on his wooden leg and told her that she was wanted at the offices at once.

"What for?" she asked in amazement.

"What's that to do with me? They just sent word for you to go to the office ... go on," he said, roughly.

She hurried off. She could not understand. If it was a matter of helping Mombleux with a translation, why should she have to go to the office, where everyone could see her and know that he had had to ask for her help?

She quickly went up the steps, where she saw Talouel standing outside waiting for her.

"Are you the girl who speaks English?" he asked. "Now, no lies, 'cause you speak French without an accent."

"My mother was English and my father was French," replied Perrine, "so I speak both languages."

"Good. You are to go to Saint-Pipoy. Monsieur Paindavoine wants you."

She was so surprised at this news that she stood staring at the manager in amazement.

"Well, stupid?" he said.

As though to excuse herself, she said:

"I was taken aback. I'm a stranger here and I don't know where Saint-Pipoy is."

"You won't be lost; you are to go in the carriage," said the manager. "Here, William...."

M. Paindavoine's horse and carriage, which had been standing in the shade, now drew up.

"Here's the girl," said the manager to a young man. "Take her to M. Paindavoine quickly."

Perrine was already down the steps, and was about to take her seat beside William when he stopped her with a sign of his hand.

"Not here; take the back seat," he said.

There was a narrow seat for one person at the back. She got up into it and they started off at a brisk trot.

When they had left the village behind William, slacking the horse's speed, turned round to Perrine.

"You're going to have a chance to please the boss," he said.

"How so?" asked Perrine.

"He's got some English mechanics come over to put a machine together, and they can't understand each other. He's got M. Mombleux there, who says he can speak English, but if he does it isn't the same English as these Englishmen speak. They keep on jabbering, but don't seem to understand, and the boss is mad. It makes you split your sides to hear 'em. At last M. Mombleux couldn't go on any longer, and to calm the boss he said that he knew of a girl named Aurelie in the factory who spoke English, and the boss made me come off at once for you."

There was a moment's silence; then he turned round again to Perrine.

"If you speak English like M. Mombleux," he said mockingly, "perhaps it'd be better if you didn't go any farther."

"Shall I put you down?" he added with a grin.

"You can go on," said Perrine, quietly.

"Well, I was just thinking for you; that's all," he said.

"Thank you; but I wish to go on, please."

314

Yet in spite of her apparent coolness, little Perrine was very nervous, because, although she was sure of her English, she did not know what sort of English the engineer spoke. As William had said mockingly, it was not the same that M. Mombleux understood. And she fully realized that there would be many technical words that she would not be able to translate. She would not understand, and she would hesitate, and then probably M. Paindavoine would be angry with her, the same as he had been with M. Mombleux.

Above the tops of the poplars she could already see the great smoking chimneys of the factories of Saint-Pipoy. She knew that spinning and weaving were done here, the same as at Maraucourt, and, besides that, it was here that they manufactured red rope and string. But whether she knew that or not, it was nothing that would help her in the task before her.

They turned the bend of the road. With a sweeping glance she could take in all the great buildings, and although these works were not so large as those of Maraucourt, they were nevertheless of considerable importance.

The carriage passed through the great iron gates and soon stopped before the main office.

"Come with me," said William.

He led her into an office where M. Paindavoine was seated talking to the manager of the Saint-Pipoy works.

"Here's the girl, sir," said William, holding his hat in his hand.

"Very well; you can go," said his master.

Without speaking to Perrine, M. Paindavoine made a sign to his manager to come nearer to him. Then he spoke to him in a low voice. The manager also dropped his voice to answer. But Perrine's hearing was keen, and she understood that they were speaking of her. She heard the manager reply: "A young girl, about twelve or thirteen, who looks intelligent."

"Come here, my child," said M. Paindavoine, in the same tone that she had already heard him use to Rosalie, and which was very different from that which he used for his employés.

She felt encouraged and went up to him.

"What is your name?" he asked.

"Aurelie."

"Where are your father and mother?"

"They are both dead."

"How long have you been in my employ?"

"For three weeks."

"Where do you come from?"

"I have just come from Paris."

"You speak English?"

"My mother was English, and I can speak in conversation, and I understand, but...."

"There are no 'buts'; you know or you do not know."

"I don't know the words used in various trades, because they use words that I have never heard, and I don't know the meaning of them," said Perrine.

"You see, Benoist," said M. Paindavoine quickly; "what this little girl says is so; that shows she is not stupid."

"She looks anything but that," answered Benoist.

"Well, perhaps we shall be able to manage somehow," said M. Vulfran. He got up, and placing one arm on the manager, he leaned on his cane with the other.

"Follow us, little girl," he said.

Perrine usually had her eyes about her and noticed everything that happened, but she took no heed where she was going. As she followed in her grandfather's footsteps, she was plunged in thought. What would be the result of this interview with the English mechanics?

They came to a big red brick building. Here she saw Mombleux walking back and forth, evidently in a bad humor, and it seemed to her that he threw her anything but a friendly look.

They went in and were taken up to the first floor. Here in a big hall stood a number of wooden crates bearing a firm's name, "Morton and Pratt, Manchester." On one of the crates the Englishmen were sitting, waiting. Perrine noticed that from their dress they had every appearance of being gentlemen, and she hoped that she would be able better to understand them than if they had been rough workingmen. When M. Vulfran entered they rose.

"Tell them that you can speak English and that they can explain to you," said M. Vulfran.

She did what she was told, and at the first words she had the satisfaction of seeing the Englishmen's faces brighten. It is true she only spoke a few words to begin the conversation, but the pleasant smile they gave her banished all her nervousness.

"They understand her perfectly," said the manager.

"Well, then, ask them," said M. Vulfran, "why they have come a week earlier than the date arranged for their coming, because it so happens that the engineer who was to direct them in their work, and who speaks English, is away for a few days."

Perrine translated the phrase accurately, and one of the men answered at once.

"They say," she said, "that they have been to Cambrai and put up some machinery, and they got through with their work quicker than they thought they would, so they came here direct instead of going back to England and returning again."

"Whose machinery were they working on at Cambrai?" asked M. Vulfran.

"It was for the M. M. and E. Aveline and Company."

"What were the machines?"

The question was put and the reply was given in English, but Perrine hesitated.

"Why do you hesitate?" asked M. Vulfran, impatiently.

"Because it's a word used in the business that I don't know," answered Perrine, timidly.

"Say the word in English."

"Hydraulic mangle."

"That's all right," said M. Vulfran. He repeated the word in English, but with quite a different accent from the English mechanics, which explains why he had not understood them when they had spoken the words.

"You see that Aveline and Company are ahead of us," he said, turning to his manager. "We have no time to lose. I am going to cable to Fabry to return at once; but while waiting we must persuade these young men to get to work. Ask them what they are standing there for, little girl."

She translated the question, and the one who seemed to be the chief gave her a long answer.

"Well?" asked M. Vulfran.

"They are saying some things that are very difficult for me to understand."

"However, try and explain to me."

"They say that the floor is not strong enough to hold their machine, which weighs...."

She stopped to question the workmen in English, who told her the weight.

"Ah, that is it, is it?" said M. Vulfran.

"And when the machine is started going its weight will break the flooring," she continued, turning to M. Vulfran.

"The beams are sixty centimetres in width."

She told the men what M. Vulfran said, listened to their reply, then continued:

"They say that they have examined the flooring, and that it is not safe for this machine. They want a thorough test made and strong supports placed under the floor."

"The supports can be placed there at once, and when Fabry returns a thorough examination will be made. Tell them that. Let them get to work without losing a moment. They can have all the workmen they need ... carpenters and masons, millwrights. They have only to tell you. You have to be at their service, and then you tell Monsieur Benoist what they require."

She translated these instructions to the men, who appeared satisfied when she told them that she was to stay and interpret for them.

"You will stay here," continued M. Vulfran. "Your food will be given to you and also a lodging at the inn. You will have nothing to pay there. And if we are pleased with you, you will receive something extra when Monsieur Fabry returns."

CHAPTER XVI. GRANDFATHER'S INTERPRETER

SHE was an interpreter; that was far better than pushing trucks. When the day's work was over, acting in the capacity of interpreter, she escorted the two Englishmen to the village inn and engaged a room for them and one for herself, not a miserable garret where she would have to sleep with several others, but a real bedroom all to herself. As they could not speak one word of French, the two Englishmen asked her if she would not take her dinner with them. They ordered a dinner that would have been enough for ten men.

That night she slept in a real bed and between real sheets, yet it was a very long time before she could get to sleep. Even when her eyelids grew too heavy to keep open her excitement was so great that every now and then she would start up in bed. She tried to force herself to be calm. She told herself that things would have to take their course, without her wondering all the time if she were going to be happy or not. That was the only sensible thing to do. Things seemed to be taking such a favorable turn she must wait. But the best arguments when addressed to oneself have never made anyone go to sleep, and the better the argument the more likely one is to keep awake.

The next morning, when the factory whistle blew, she went to the door of the room occupied by the two machinists and knocked, and told them it was time to get up.

They paid no heed to the whistle, however, and it was not until they had taken a bath and made an elaborate *toilette*, something unknown to the villagers in those parts, and partaken of a hearty breakfast, consisting of a thick, juicy steak, plenty of buttered toast and several cups of tea, that they showed any readiness to get to their work.

Perrine, who had discreetly waited for them outside, wondered if they would ever be ready. When at last they came out, and she tripped behind them to the factory, her one thought was that her grandfather would surely be there ahead of them.

However, it was not until the afternoon that M. Vulfran arrived. He was accompanied by his youngest nephew, Casimir.

The youth looked disdainfully at the work the machinists had done, which in truth was merely in preparation.

"These fellows won't do much before Fabry returns," he said. "That's not surprising considering the supervision you have given them, uncle."

He said this jeeringly, but instead of taking his words lightly, his uncle reprimanded him severely: "If you had been able to attend to this matter, I should not have been forced to have called in this little girl, who until now has only pushed trucks."

Perrine saw Casimir bite his lip in anger, but he controlled himself and said lightly: "If I had foreseen that I should have to give up a government position for a commercial one, I should certainly have learned English in preference to German."

"It is never too late to learn," replied his uncle in a tone that brooked no further parley.

The quick words on both sides had been spoken in evident displeasure.

Perrine had made herself as small as possible. She had not dared move, but Casimir did not even turn his eyes in her direction, and almost at once he went out, giving his arm to his uncle. Then she was able to give free rein to her thoughts. How severe M. Vulfran was with his nephew, but what a disagreeable, horrid youth was that nephew! If they had any affection for one another it certainly was not apparent. Why was it? Why wasn't this nephew kind to his old uncle, who was blind and broken down with sorrow? And why was the old man so hard with a nephew who was taking the place of his own son?

While she was pondering these questions M. Vulfran returned, this time being led in by the manager, who, having placed him in a seat, began to explain to him the work that the machinists were now engaged upon.

Some minutes later she heard M. Benoist calling: "Aurelie! Aurelie!"

She did not move, for she had forgotten that Aurelie was the name that she had given to herself.

The third time he called: "Aurelie!"

She jumped up with a start as she realized that that was the name by which they knew her. She hurried over to them.

"Are you deaf?" demanded Monsieur Benoist.

"No, sir; I was listening to the machinists."

"You can leave me now," said M. Vulfran to his manager.

When the manager had gone he turned to Perrine, who had remained standing before him.

"Can you read, my child?"

"Yes, sir."

"English as well as French?"

"Yes, both the same."

"But while reading English can you turn it into French?"

"When the phrases are not too difficult; yes, sir."

"The daily news from the papers, do you think you could do that?"

"I have never tried that, because if I read an English paper there is no need for me to translate it for myself, because I understand what it says."

"Well, we will try. Tell the machinists that when they want you they can call you, and then come and read from an English paper some articles that

I wish to have read to me in French. Go and tell the men and then come back and sit down here beside me."

When she had done what she was told, she sat down beside M. Vulfran and took the newspaper that he handed her, "The Dundee News."

"What shall I read?" she asked as she unfolded it.

"Look for the commercial column."

The long black and white columns bewildered poor little Perrine. She was so nervous and her hands trembled so she wondered if she would ever be able to accomplish what she was asked to do. She gazed from the top of one page to the bottom of another, and still could not find what she was seeking. She began to fear that her employer would get impatient with her for being so slow and awkward.

But instead of getting impatient he told her to take her time. With that keen hearing so subtle with the blind, he had divined what a state of emotion she was in. He could tell that from the rustling of the newspaper she held in her hand.

"We have plenty of time," he said, encouragingly; "besides I don't suppose you have ever read a trade journal before."

"No, sir; I have not," she replied.

She continued to scan the sheets, then suddenly she gave a little cry of pleasure.

"Have you found it?"

"Yes, I think so."

"Now look for these words," he said in English: "Linen, Hemp, Jute, Sacks, Twine."

"But, sir, you know English," she cried, involuntarily.

"Five or six words of the trade; that is all, unfortunately," he replied.

When she had found what he required she commenced her translation, but she was so hopelessly slow, hesitating and confused, that in a few moments the beads of perspiration stood out on her forehead and hands from sheer agony, despite the fact that from time to time he encouraged her.

"That will do. I understand that ... go on," he said.

And she continued, raising her voice when the hammering blows from the workmen became too loud.

At last she came to the end of the column.

"Now see if there is any news from Calcutta," said her employer.

She scanned the sheets again.

"Yes, here it is," she said, after a moment; "From our special correspondent."

"That's it. Read!"

"The news that we are receiving from Dacca...."

Her voice shook so as she said this name that Monsieur Vulfran's attention was attracted.

"What's the matter?" he said. "Why are you trembling?"

"I don't know," she said, timidly; "perhaps I am nervous."

"I told you not to mind," he chided. "You are doing very much better than I thought."

She read the cables from Dacca which mentioned a gathering of jute along the shores of the Brahmaputra. Then he told her to look and see if there was a cable from Saint Helena.

Her eyes ran up and down the columns until the words "Saint Helena" caught her eye.

"On the 23rd, the English steamer 'Alma' sailed from Calcutta for Dundee; on the 24th, the Norwegian steamer 'Grundloven' sailed from Naraingaudj for Boulogne."

He appeared satisfied.

"That is very good," he said. "I am quite pleased with you."

She wanted to reply, but afraid that her voice would betray her joy, she kept silent.

"I can see that until poor Bendit is better I can make good use of you," he continued.

After receiving an account of the work that the men had done, and telling them to be as quick as possible, he told Perrine to lead him to the manager's office.

"Have I to give you my hand?" she asked, timidly.

"Why, yes, my child," he replied. "How do you think you can guide me otherwise? And warn me when there is anything in the way, and above all don't be absent-minded."

"Oh, I assure you, sir, you can place every confidence in me," she said with emotion.

"You see that I already have confidence," he replied.

322

She took him gently by the left hand, whilst with his right he held his cane, feeling ahead of him cautiously as he went forward.

They had scarcely left the workshops before they came to the railway tracks, and she thought that she ought to warn him.

"Here are the rails, just here," she said. "Please...."

But he interrupted her.

"That you need not tell me," he said. "I know every bit of the ground round about the works; my head knows it and my feet know it, but it's the unexpected obstacles that we might find on the road that you must tell me about, something that's in the path that should not be. All the ground I know, thoroughly."

It was not only his grounds that he knew, but he knew his people also. When he went through the yards his men greeted him. They not only took their hats off as though he saw them, but they said his name.

"Good morning, sir!... Good morning, Monsieur Vulfran!"

And to a great number he was able to reply by their names: "Good morning, Jacque!" ... "Good morning, Pascal!" He knew the voices of all those who had long been in his employ. When he hesitated, which was rarely, for he knew almost all, he would stop and say: "It's you, is it not?" mentioning the speaker's name.

If he made a mistake he explained why he had done so.

Walking thus, it was a slow walk from the factories to the offices. She led him to his armchair; then he dismissed her.

"Until tomorrow," he said; "I shall want you then."

CHAPTER XVII. HARD QUESTIONS

THE next morning, at the same hour as on the previous day, Monsieur Paindavoine entered the workshops, guided by the manager. Perrine wanted to go and meet him, but she could not at this moment as she was busy transmitting orders from the chief machinist to the men who were working for him—masons, carpenters, smiths, mechanics. Clearly and without repetition, she explained to each one what orders were given to him; then she interpreted for the chief machinist the questions or objections which the French workmen desired to address to him.

Perrine's grandfather had drawn near. The voices stopped as the tap of his cane announced his approach, but he made a sign for them to continue the same as though he were not there.

And while Perrine, obeying him, went on talking with the men, he said quietly to the manager, though not low enough but that Perrine heard:

"Do you know, that little girl would make a fine engineer!"

"Yes," said the manager; "it's astonishing how decided and confident she is with the men."

"Yes, and she can do something else. Yesterday she translated the 'Dundee News' more intelligently than Bendit. And it was the first time that she had read trade journal stuff."

"Does anyone know who her parents were?" asked the manager.

"Perhaps Talouel does; I do not," said Vulfran.

"She is in a very miserable and pitiful condition," said the manager.

"I gave her five francs for her food and lodging."

"I am speaking of her clothes. Her waist is worn to threads; I have never seen such a skirt on anybody but a beggar, and she certainly must have made the shoes she is wearing herself."

"And her face, what is she like, Benoist?"

"Very intelligent and very pretty."

"Hard looking or any signs of vice?"

"No; quite the contrary. She has a very frank, honest look. She has great eyes that look as though they could pierce a wall, and yet at the same time they have a soft, trusting look."

"Where in the world does she come from?"

"Not from these parts, that's a sure thing."

"She told me that her mother was English."

"And yet she does not look English. She seems to belong to quite another race, but she is very pretty; even with the old rags that she is wearing the girl seems to have a strange sort of beauty. She must have a strong character or some power, or why is it that these workmen pay such attention to such a poor little ragged thing?"

And as Benoist never missed a chance to flatter his employer, he added: "Undoubtedly without having even seen her you have guessed all that I have told you."

"Her accent struck me as being very cultured," replied Monsieur Vulfran.

Although Perrine had not heard all that the two men had said, she had caught a few words, which had thrown her into a state of great agitation.

She tried to recover her self-control, for it would never do to listen to what was being said behind her when the machinists and workmen were talking to her at the same time. What would her employer think if in giving her explanations in French he saw that she had not been paying attention to her task.

However, everything was explained to them in a manner satisfactory to both sides. When she had finished, Monsieur Vulfran called to her: "Aurelie!"

This time she took care to reply quickly to the name which in the future was to be hers.

As on the previous day, he made her sit down beside him and gave her a paper to translate for him into French. This time it was not the "Dundee News," but the "Dundee Trade Report Association," which is an official bulletin published on the commerce of jute. So without having to search for any particular article, she read it to him from beginning to end. Then, when the reading was over, as before, he asked her to lead him through the grounds, but this time he began to question her about herself.

"You told me that you had lost your mother. How long ago was that?" he asked.

"Five weeks," she replied.

"In Paris?"

"Yes, in Paris."

"And your father?"

"Father died six months before mother," she said in a low voice.

As he held her hand in his he could feel it tremble, and he knew what anguish she felt as he evoked the memory of her dead parents, but he did not change the subject; he gently continued to question her.

"What did your parents do?"

"We sold things," she replied.

"In Paris? Round about Paris?"

"We traveled; we had a wagon and we were sometimes in one part of the country, sometimes in another."

"And when your mother died you left Paris?"

"Yes, sir."

"Why?"

325

"Because mother made me promise not to stay in Paris after she had gone, but to go North where my father's people live."

"Then why did you come here?"

"When my mother died we had to sell our wagon and our donkey and the few things we had, and all this money was spent during her illness. When I left the cemetery after she was buried all the money I had was five francs thirty-five centimes, which was not enough for me to take the train. So I decided to make the journey on foot."

Monsieur Vulfran's fingers tightened over hers. She did not understand this movement.

"Oh, forgive me; I am boring you," she said. "I am telling you things perhaps that are of no interest."

"You are not boring me, Aurelie," said the blind man. "On the contrary, I am pleased to know, what an honest little girl you are. I like people who have courage, will, and determination, and who do not easily give up. If I like finding such qualities in men, how much more pleasure does it give me to find them in a girl of your age! So ... you started with five francs thirty-five centimes in your pocket?..."

"A knife, a piece of soap," continued little Perrine, "a thimble, two needles, some thread and a map of the roads, that was all."

"Could you understand the map?"

"Yes, I had to know, because we used to travel all over the country. That was the only thing that I kept of our belongings."

The blind man stopped his little guide.

"Isn't there a big tree here on the left?" he asked.

"Yes, with a seat all around it," she replied.

"Come along then; we'll be better sitting down."

When they were seated she went on with her story. She had no occasion to shorten it, for she saw that her employer was greatly interested.

"You never thought of begging?" he asked, when she came to the time when she had left the woods after being overtaken by the terrible storm.

"No, sir; never."

"But what did you count upon when you saw that you could not get any work?"

"I didn't count on anything. I thought that if I kept on as long as I had the strength I might find something. It was only when I was so hungry and so tired that I had to give up. If I had dropped one hour sooner all would have been over."

Then she told him how her donkey, licking her face, had brought her back to consciousness, and how the ragpicker had saved her from starvation. Then passing quickly over the days she had spent with La Rouquerie, she came to the day when she had made Rosalie's acquaintance.

"And Rosalie told me," she said, "that anyone who wants work can get it in your factories. I came and they employed me at once."

"When are you going on to your relations?"

Perrine was embarrassed. She did not expect this question.

"I am not going any further," she replied, after a moment's hesitation. "I don't know if they want me, for they were angry with father. I was going to try and be near them because I have no one else, but I don't know if I shall be welcomed. Now that I have found work, it seems to me that it would be better for me to stay here. What will become of me if they turn me away? I know I shall not starve here, and I am too afraid to go on the road again. I shall not let them know that I am here unless some piece of luck comes my way."

"Didn't your relatives ever try to find out about you?" asked M. Vulfran.

"No, never," replied Perrine.

"Well, then, perhaps you are right," he said. "Yet if you don't like to take a chance and go and see them, why don't you write them a letter? They may not be able to give you a home, so then you could stay here where you'd be sure of earning your living. On the other hand, they may be very glad to have you, and you would have love and protection, which you would not have here. You've learned already that life is very hard for a young girl of your age, and in your position ... and very sad."

"Yes, sir; I know it is very sad," said little Perrine, lifting her beautiful eyes to the sightless eyes of her grandfather. "Every day I think how sad it is, and I know if they would hold out their arms to welcome me I would run into them so quickly! But suppose they were just as cold and hard to me as they were with my father...."

"Had these relations any serious cause to be angry with your father? Did he do anything very bad?"

"I cannot think," said little Perrine, "that my father, who was always so good and kind, and who loved me and mother so much, could have ever been bad. He could not have done anything very wrong, and yet his people must have had, in their opinion, serious reasons for being angry with him, it seems to me."

"Yes, evidently," said the blind man. "But what they have against him they could not hold against you. The sins of the father should not fall upon the children."

"If that could be true!"

She said these words in a voice that trembled so with emotion that the blind man was surprised at the depths of this little girl's feelings.

"You see," he said, "how in the depths of your heart how much you want their love and affection."

"Yes, but how I dread being turned away," she replied.

"But why should you be?" he asked. "Have your grandparents any other children beside your father?"

"No."

"Why shouldn't they be glad that you should come and take the place of the son they have lost? You don't know what it is to be alone in the world."

"Yes, I do ... I know only too well what it is," replied Perrine.

"Youth who has a future ahead is not like old age, which has nothing before it but Death."

She looked at him. She did not take her eyes from his face, for he could not see her. What did his words mean? From the expression of his face little Perrine tried to read the inmost thoughts that stirred this old man's heart.

"Well," he said, after waiting a moment, "what do you think you will do?"

"I hesitate because I feel so bad about it," she said. "If I could only believe that they would be glad to have me and would not turn me away...."

"You know nothing of life, poor little girl," said the old gentleman. "Age should not be alone any more than youth."

"Do you think all old people feel like that?" asked Perrine.

"They may not think that it is so, but they feel it."

"You think so?" she said, trembling, her eyes still fixed on his face.

He did not reply directly, but speaking softly as though to himself, he said:

"Yes, yes; they feel it...."

Then getting up from his seat abruptly, as though to drive away thoughts that made him feel sad, he said in a tone of authority: "Come across to the offices. I wish to go there."

CHAPTER XVIII. SECRETARY TO M. VULFRAN

WHEN would Fabry, the engineer, return? That was the question that Perrine anxiously asked herself, for on that day her role of interpreter to the English machinists would terminate.

That of translator of newspaper articles to M. Vulfran, would that continue until M. Bendit had recovered from his illness? Here was another question that made her even still more anxious.

It was on Thursday, when she reached the factories with the two machinists, that she found Monsieur Fabry in the workshop busy inspecting the work that had already been done. Discreetly she waited at a distance, not taking part in any of the explanations that were being made, but all the same the chief machinist drew her into the conversation.

"Without this little girl's help," he said, "we should have stood here waiting with our arms folded."

Monsieur Fabry then looked at her, but he said nothing, and she on her side did not dare ask him what she had to do now, whether she was to stay at Saint-Pipoy or return to Maraucourt.

She stood there undecided, thinking that as it was M. Vulfran who had sent for her, it would be he who would send her away or keep her.

He came at his usual hour, led by the manager, who gave him an account of the orders that the engineer had given and the observations that he had made. But it appeared that he was not completely satisfied.

"It is a pity that the little girl is not here," he said in annoyance.

"But she is here," replied the manager, making a sign to Perrine to approach.

"Why was it you did not go back to Maraucourt, girl?" he asked.

"I thought that I ought not to leave here until you told me to go back," she replied.

"That was quite right," he said. "You must be here waiting for me when I come...."

He stopped for a second, then went on: "And I shall also need you at Maraucourt. You can go back this evening, and tomorrow be at the office. I will tell you what you will have to do."

When she had interpreted the orders which he wished to give to the machinists, he left, and that day she was not required to read the newspapers.

But what did that matter? Hadn't her grandfather said that on the morrow he would need her at Maraucourt?

"I shall need you at Maraucourt!" She kept repeating these words over and over again as she tramped along the roads over which William had driven her in the trap.

How was she going to be employed? She imagined all sorts of ways, but she could not feel certain of anything, except that she was not to be sent back to push trucks. That was a sure thing; for the rest she would have to wait. But she need not wait in a state of feverish anxiety, for from her grandfather's manner she might hope for the best. If she, a poor little girl, could only have enough wisdom to follow the course that her mother had mapped out for her before dying, slowly and carefully, without trying to hasten events, her life, which she held in her own hands, would be what she herself made it. She must remember this always, in everything she said, every time she had to make a resolution, every time she took a step forward, and each time she took this step she must take it without asking advice of anyone.

On her way back to Maraucourt she turned all this over in her little head. She walked slowly, stopping when she wanted to pick a flower that grew beneath the hedge, or when, in looking over a fence, she could see a pretty one that seemed to be beckoning to her from the meadow. Now and again she got rather excited; then she would quicken her step; then she slowed up again, telling herself that there was no occasion for her to hurry. Here was one thing she had to do—she must make it a rule, make it a habit, not to give way to an impulse. Oh, she would have to be very wise. Her pretty face was very grave as she walked along, her hands full of lovely wild flowers.

She found her island the same as she had left it, each thing in its place. The birds had even shown respect for the berries beneath the willow tree which had ripened in her absence. Here was something for her supper. She had not counted upon having berries.

She had returned at an earlier hour than when she had left the factory, so she did not feel inclined to go to bed as soon as her supper was over. She sat by the pond in the quiet of the evening, watching the night slowly fall.

Although she had been away only a short time, something seemed to have occurred to disturb the quietness of her little shelter. In the fields there was no longer the solemn silence of the night which had struck her on the first days that she had installed herself on the island. Previously, all she could hear in the entire valley, on the pond, in the big trees and the foliage, was the mysterious rustling of the birds as they returned to the nests for the night. Now the silence was disturbed by all kinds of noises— the blow of the forge, the grind of the axle, the swish of a whip, and the murmur of voices.

As she had tramped along the roads from Saint-Pipoy she had noticed that the harvest had commenced in the fields that were most exposed, and soon the mowers would come as far as her little nook, which was shaded by the big trees.

She would certainly have to leave her tiny home; it would not be possible for her to live there longer. Whether she had to leave on account of the harvesters or the bird catchers, it was the same thing, just a matter of days.

Although for the last few days she had got used to having sheets on her bed, and a room with a window, and closed doors, she slept that night on her bed of ferns as though she had never left it, and it was only when the sun rose in the heavens that she awoke.

When she reached the factory, instead of following her companions to where the trucks stood, she made her way to the general offices, wondering what she should do—go in, or wait outside.

She decided to do the latter. If they saw her standing outside the doors, someone would see her and call her in.

She waited there for almost an hour. Finally she saw Talouel, who asked her roughly what she was doing there.

"Monsieur Vulfran told me to come this morning to the office to see him," she said.

"Outside there, is not the office," he said.

"I was waiting to be called in," she replied.

"Come up then."

She went up the steps, following him in.

"What did you do at Saint-Pipoy?" he asked, turning to look at her.

She told him in what capacity M. Vulfran had employed her.

"Monsieur Fabry then had been messing up things?"

"I don't know."

"What do you mean—you don't know? Are you a silly?"

"Maybe I am."

"You're not, and you know it; and if you don't reply it's because you don't want to. Don't forget who is talking to you; do you know what I am here?"

"Yes, the foreman."

"That means the master. And as your master you do as I tell you. I am going to know all. Those who don't obey I fire! Remember that!"

This was indeed the man whom she had heard the factory girls talking about when she had slept in that terrible room at Mother Françoise's. The tyrant who wanted to be everything in the works, not only at Maraucourt, but at Saint-Pipoy, at Bacourt, at Flexelles, everywhere, and who would employ any means to uphold his authority, even disputing it with that of Monsieur Vulfran's.

"I ask you what Monsieur Fabry has been doing?" he asked, lowering his voice.

"I cannot tell you because I do not know myself. But I can tell you what observations Monsieur Vulfran had me interpret for the machinists."

She repeated what she had had to tell the men without omitting a single thing.

"Is that all?"

"That is all."

"Did Monsieur Vulfran make you translate his letters?"

"No, he did not. I only read some articles from the 'Dundee News' and a little paper all through; it was called the 'Dundee Trades Report Association.'"

"You know if you don't tell me the truth, all the truth, I'll get it pretty quick, and then ... Ouste! off you go."

"Why should I not speak the truth?" asked Perrine.

"It's up to you to do so," he retorted. "I've warned you ... remember."

"I'll remember," said Perrine, "I assure you."

"Very good. Now go and sit down on that bench over there. If the boss really needs you he'll remember that he told you to come here this morning. He is busy talking to some of his men now."

She sat on the bench for almost an hour, not daring to move so long as Talouel was near. What a dreadful man! How afraid she was of him! But it would never do to let him see that she was afraid. He wanted her to spy on her employer, and then tell him what was in the letters that she translated for him!

This indeed might well scare her, yet there was something to be pleased about. Talouel evidently thought that she would have the letters to translate; that meant that her grandfather would have her with him all the time that M. Bendit was ill.

While she sat there waiting she caught sight of William several times. When he was not fulfilling the duties of coachman he acted as useful man to M. Vulfran. Each time that he appeared on the scene Perrine thought that he had come to fetch her, but he passed without saying a word to her. He seemed always in a hurry.

Finally some workingmen came out of M. Vulfran's office with a very dissatisfied expression on their faces. Then William came and beckoned to her and showed her into M. Vulfran's office. She found her grandfather seated at a large table covered with ledgers, at the side of which were paper weights stamped with large letters in relief. In this way the blind man was able to find what his eyes could not see.

Without announcing her, William had pushed Perrine inside the room and closed the door after her. She waited a moment, then she thought that she had better let M. Vulfran know that she was there.

"Monsieur," she said, "I am here ... Aurelie."

"Yes," he said, "I recognized your step. Come nearer and listen to me. I am interested in you. You have told me your troubles and I think you have been very courageous. From the translations that you have made for me, and the manner in which you have acted as interpreter for the machinists, I see that you are intelligent. Now that I am blind, I need someone to see for me, to tell me about things I wish to know, and also about things that strike them also. I had hoped that William would have been able to do this for me, but unfortunately he drinks too much and I can't keep him.

"Now, would you like to take the position that he has been unable to hold? To commence with, you will have ninety francs a month. If I am pleased with you I may do more for you."

Overwhelmed with joy, Perrine stood before the blind man unable to say a word.

"Why don't you speak?" he said at last.

"I can't ... I don't know what to say ... to thank you," she said. Her voice broke. "I feel so...."

333

"Yes, yes," he said. "I know how you feel. Your voice tells me that. I am pleased. That is as good as a promise that you will do all you can to give me satisfaction. Now let us change the subject. Have you written to your grandparents?"

"No," said Perrine, hesitatingly; "I ... I did not have any paper."

"Oh, very well. You will be able to find all you need in Monsieur Bendit's office. When you write tell them exactly what position you occupy in my employ. If they have anything better to offer you, they will send for you; if not, they will let you remain here."

"Oh, certainly ... I am sure I shall stay...."

"Yes, I think so. I think it will be best for you. As you will be in the offices, you will be in communication with my employés; you can take my orders to them, and you will also have to go out with me, so in that case you cannot wear your factory clothes, which Monsieur Benoist tells me are rather shabby."

"They are in rags," said Perrine; "but I assure you, sir, it is not because I am lazy or that I don't care...."

"I am sure of that," replied M. Vulfran. "Now, as all that will be changed, you go to the cashier in the counting house, and he will give you a money order. You can go then to Madame Lachaise in the village and get some clothes, some linen, hats and shoes; what you need...."

Perrine was listening as though it were not an old blind man with a grave face that was speaking, but a beautiful fairy who was holding over her her magic wand.

She was silent. Then his voice recalled her to the reality.

"You are free to choose what you like, but bear in mind the choice you make will guide me in acquiring a knowledge of your character. Now you can go and see about your things at once. I shall not need you until tomorrow."

CHAPTER XIX. SUSPICION AND CONFIDENCE

SHE went to the counting house, and after the chief cashier and his clerks had eyed her from head to foot, she was handed the order which M. Vulfran had said was to be given to her. She left the factory wondering where she would find Madame Lachaise's shop.

She hoped that it was the woman who had sold her the calico, because as she knew her already, it would be less embarrassing to ask her advice as to what she should buy, than it would be to ask a perfect stranger. And so much hung on the choice she would make; her anxiety increased as she thought of her employer's last words: "the choice you make will guide me in acquiring a knowledge of your character."

She did not need this warning to keep her from making extravagant purchases, but then on the other hand, what she thought would be the right things for herself, would her employer consider suitable? In her fancy she had worn beautiful clothes, and when she was quite a little girl she had been very proud to display her pretty things, but of course dresses on this order would not be fitting for her now. The simplest that she could find would be better.

Who would have thought that the unexpected present of new clothes could have filled her with so much anxiety and embarrassment. She knew that she ought to be filled with joy and yet here she was greatly worried and hesitating.

Just near the church she found Mme. Lachaise's shop. It was by far the best shop in Maraucourt. In the window there was a fine display of materials, ribbons, lingerie, hats, jewels, perfumes, which aroused the envy and tempted the greed of all the frivolous girls throughout the surrounding villages. It was here where they spent their small earnings, the same as their fathers and husbands spent theirs at the taverns.

When Perrine saw this display of finery she was still more perplexed and embarrassed. She entered the shop and stood in the middle of the floor, for neither the mistress of the establishment nor the milliners who were working behind the counter seemed to think that the ragged little girl required any attention. Finally Perrine decided to hold out the envelope containing the order that she held in her hand.

"What is it you want, little girl?" demanded Madame Lachaise.

As she still held out the envelope the mistress of the store caught sight of the words Maraucourt Factories, Vulfran Paindavoine in one of the corners. The expression of her face changed at once, her smile was very pleasant now.

"What do you wish, Mademoiselle?" she asked, leaving her desk and drawing forward a chair for Perrine. Perrine told her that she wanted a dress, some underlinen, a pair of shoes and a hat.

"We can supply you with all those," said Madame Lachaise, "and with goods of the very best quality. Would you like to commence with the dress? Yes. Very well then, I will show you some materials."

But it was not materials that Perrine wished to see; she wanted a ready-made dress. Something that she could put on at once, or at least something that would be ready for her to wear the next day when she went out with Monsieur Paindavoine.

"Ah, you are going out with Monsieur Vulfran?" said Madame Lachaise quickly; her curiosity was strung to its highest pitch at this statement. She wondered what the all powerful master of Maraucourt could have to do with this ragged little girl and she did not hesitate to ask.

But instead of replying to her question Perrine continued to explain that she wanted to see some black dresses as she was in mourning.

"You want a dress so as to be able to attend a funeral then?"

"No, it is not for a funeral," said Perrine.

"Well, you understand, Mademoiselle, if I know what you require the dress for I shall be able to know what style, material, and price it should be."

"I want the plainest style," said little Perrine timidly, "and the lightest but best wearing material, and the lowest price."

"Very good, very good," replied Madame Lachaise, "they will show you something. Virginie, attend to Mademoiselle."

How her tone had changed! her manner also. With great dignity Madame Lachaise went back to her seat at the desk, disdaining to busy herself with a customer who had such small desires. She was probably one of the servant's daughters, for whom Monsieur Vulfran was going to buy a mourning outfit; but which servant?

However as Virginie brought forward a cashmere dress trimmed with passementerie and jet, she thought fit to interfere.

"No, no, not that," she said. "That would be beyond the price. Show her that black challis dress with the little dots. The skirt will be a trifle too long and the waist too large, but it can easily be made to fit her, besides we have nothing else in black."

Here was a reason that dispensed with all others, but even though it was too large, Perrine found the skirt and waist that went with it very pretty, and the saleslady assured her that with a little alteration is would suit her beautifully, and of course she had to believe her.

The choice for the stockings and undergarments was easier because she wanted the least expensive, but when she stated that she only wanted to purchase two pairs of stockings and two chemises, Mlle. Virginie became just as disdainful as her employer, and it was as though she was conferring a favor that she condescended to try some shoes on Perrine, and the black straw hat which completed the wardrobe of this little simpleton.

Could anyone believe that a girl would be such an idiot! She had been given an order to buy what she wanted and she asked for two pairs of stockings and two chemises. And when Perrine asked for some handkerchiefs, which for a long time had been the object of her desires, this new purchase, which was limited to three handkerchiefs, did not help to change the shopkeeper's or the saleslady's contempt for her.

"She's nothing at all," they murmured.

"And now shall we send you these things?" asked Mme. Lachaise.

"No, thank you," said Perrine, "I will call this evening and fetch them when the alterations are made."

"Well, then, don't come before eight o'clock or after nine," she was told.

Perrine had a very good reason for not wishing to have the things sent to her. She was not sure where she was going to sleep that night. Her little island was not to be thought of. Those who possess nothing can dispense with doors and locks, but when one has riches ... for despite the condescension of the shopkeeper and her assistant, these were riches to Perrine and needed to be guarded. So that night she would have to take a lodging and quite naturally she thought of going to Rosalie's grandmother. When she left Madame Lachaise's shop, she went on her way to Mother Françoise's to see if she could accommodate her and give her what she desired; that was a tiny little room that would not cost much.

As she reached the gate she met Rosalie coming out, walking quickly.

"You're going out?" cried Perrine.

"Yes, and you ... so you are free then?"

In a few hurried words they explained.

Rosalie, who was going on an important errand to Picquigny, could not return to her grandmother's at once, as she would have liked, so as to make the best arrangements that she could for Perrine; but as Perrine had nothing to do for that day, why shouldn't she go with her to Picquigny; and they would come back together; it would be a pleasure trip then.

They went off gaily, and Rosalie accomplished her errand quickly, then their pleasure trip commenced. They walked through the fields, chatting and laughing, picked flowers, then rested in the heat of the day under the shadows of the great trees. It was not until night that they arrived back in Maraucourt. Not until Rosalie reached her grandmother's gate did she realize what time it was.

"What will Aunt Zenobie say?" she said half afraid.

"Oh well...." began Perrine.

"Oh well, I don't care," said Rosalie defiantly, "I've enjoyed myself ... and you?"

"Well, if you who have people to talk to every day have enjoyed yourself, how much more have I who never have anybody to talk to," said Perrine ruefully.

"I've had a lovely time," she sighed.

"Well, then we don't care what anybody says," said Rosalie bravely.

Fortunately, Aunt Zenobie was busy waiting on the boarders, so the arrangements for the room was made with Mother Françoise, who did not drive too hard a bargain and that was done quickly and promptly. Fifty francs a month for two meals a day; twelve francs for a little room decorated with a little mirror, a window, and a dressing table.

At eight o'clock Perrine dined alone in the general dining room, a table napkin on her lap. At eight-thirty she went to Madame Lachaise's establishment to fetch her dress and other things which were quite ready for her. At nine o'clock, in her tiny room, the door of which she locked, she went to bed, a little worried, a little excited, a little hesitating, but, in her heart of hearts full of hope.

Now we should see.

What she did see the next morning when she was called into M. Vulfran's office after he had given his orders to his principal employés, was such a severe expression on his face that she was thoroughly disconcerted; although the eyes that turned towards her as she entered his room were devoid of look, she could not mistake the expression on this face that she had studied so much.

Certainly it was not the kind look of a benefactor, but quite the reverse: it was an expression of displeasure and anger that she saw.

What had she done wrong that he should be angry; with her?

She put this question to herself but she could find no reply to it; perhaps she had spent too much at Madame Lachaise's and her employer had judged her character from these purchases. And in her selection she had tried to be so modest and economical. What should she have bought then? or rather what should she not have bought?

But she had no more time to wonder, for her employer was speaking to her in a severe tone:

"Why did you not tell me the truth?" he said.

"In what have I not told the truth?" she asked in a frightened voice.

"In regard to your conduct since you came to this village."

"But I assure you, Monsieur, I have told you the truth."

"You told me that you lodged at Mother Françoise's house. And when you left there where did you go? I may as well tell you that yesterday Zenobie, that is Françoise's daughter, was asked to give some information, some references of you, and she said that you only spent one night in her mother's house, then you disappeared, and no one knew what you did from that night until now."

Perrine had listened to the commencement of this cross examination in afright, but as Monsieur Vulfran went on she grew braver.

"There is someone who knows what I did after I left the room I used at Mother Françoise's," she said quietly.

"Who?"

"Rosalie, her granddaughter, knows. She will tell you that what I am now going to tell you, sir, is the truth. That is, if you think my doings are worth knowing about."

"The position that you are to hold in my service demands that I know what you are," said Monsieur Vulfran.

"Well, Monsieur, I will tell you," said little Perrine. "When you know you can send for Rosalie and question her without me seeing her, and then you will have the proof that I have not deceived you."

"Yes, that can be done," he said in a softened voice, "now go on...."

She told her story, dwelling on the horror of that night in that miserable room, her disgust, how she was almost suffocated, and how she crept outside at the break of dawn too sick to stay in that terrible garret one moment longer.

"Cannot you bear what the other girls could?" asked her employer.

"The others perhaps have not lived in the open air as I have," said Perrine, her beautiful eyes fixed on her grandfather's face. "I assure you I am not hard to please. We were so poor that we endured great misery. But I could not stay in that room. I should have died, and I don't think it was wrong of me to try to escape death. I could not live if I had to sleep there."

"Why! can that room be so unhealthy, so unwholesome as that?" mused Monsieur Vulfran.

"Oh, sir," cried Perrine, "if you could see it you would never permit your work girls to live there, never, never."

"Go on with your story," he said abruptly.

She told him how she had discovered the tiny island and how the idea had come to her to take possession of the cabin.

"You were not afraid?" he asked.

"I am not accustomed to being afraid," she said, with a wan little smile flitting across her beautiful face.

"You are speaking of that cabin in the valley there a little to the side of the road to Saint-Pipoy, on the left, are you not?" asked Monsieur Vulfran.

"Yes, Monsieur."

"That belongs to me and my nephews use it. Was it there that you slept?"

"I not only slept there, but I worked there and I ate there, and I even gave a dinner to Rosalie, and she can tell you about it," said little Perrine eagerly, for now that she had told him her story she wanted him to know everything. "I did not leave the cabin until you sent for me to go to Saint-Pipoy, and then you told me to stay there so as to be on hand to interpret for the machinists. And now tonight I have taken a lodging again at Mother Françoise's, but now I can pay for a room all to myself."

"Were you rich then, that you were able to invite a friend to dinner?" asked the blind man.

"If I only dare tell you," said Perrine timidly.

"You can tell me everything," said the blind man.

"I may take up your time just to tell you a story about two little girls?" asked little Perrine.

340

"Now that I cannot use my time as I should like," said the blind man sadly, "it is often very long, very long ... and empty."

A shade passed over her grandfather's face. He had so much; there were men who envied him—and yet how sad and barren was his life. When he said that his days were "empty" Perrine's heart went out to him. She also, since the death of her father and mother, knew what it was for the days to be long and empty, nothing to fill them but the anxiety, the fatigue, and the misery of the moment. No one to share them with you, none to uphold you, or cheer you. He had not known bodily fatigue, privations and poverty. But they are not the only trials to be borne, there are other sorrows in this world from which one suffers. And it was those other sorrows that had made him say those few words in such a sad, sad tone; the memory of which made this old blind man bend his head while the tears sprang into his sightless eyes. But no tears fell. Perrine's eyes had not left his face; if she had seen that her story did not interest him, she would have stopped at once, but she knew that he was not bored. He interrupted her several times and said:

"And you did that!"

Then he questioned her, asking her to tell him in detail what she had omitted for fear of tiring him. He put questions to her which showed that he wished to have an exact account, not only of her work, but above all to know what means she had employed to replace all that she had been lacking.

"And that's what you did?" he asked again and again.

When she had finished her story, he placed his hand on her head: "You are a brave little girl," he said, "and I am pleased to see that one can do something with you. Now go into your office and spend the time as you like; at three o'clock we will go out."

CHAPTER XX. THE SCHEMERS

MR. BENDIT'S office which Perrine occupied was a tiny place whose sole furniture consisted of a table and two chairs, a bookcase in blackwood, and a map of the world.

Yet with its polished pine floor, and a window with its red and white shade, it appeared very bright to Perrine. Not only was the office assigned to her cheerful, but she found that by leaving the door open she could see and occasionally hear what was going on in the other offices.

Monsieur Vulfran's nephews, Theodore and Casimir, had their rooms on the right and on the left of his; after theirs came the counting house, then lastly, there was Fabry, the engineer's, office. This one was opposite hers. Fabry's office was a large room where several draughtsmen were standing up before their drawings, arranged on high inclined desks.

Having nothing to do and not liking to take M. Bendit's chair, Perrine took a seat by the door. She opened one of the dictionaries which were the only kind of books the office contained. She would have preferred anything else but she had to be contented with what was there.

The hours passed slowly, but at last the bell rang for luncheon. Perrine was one of the first to go out. On the way she was joined by Fabry and Mombleux. They also were going to Mother Françoise's house.

"So then you are a comrade of ours, Mademoiselle," said Mombleux, who had not forgotten his humiliation at Saint-Pipoy, and he wanted to make the one who was the cause of it pay for it.

She felt the sarcasm of his words and for a moment she was disconcerted, but she recovered herself quickly.

"No, Monsieur," she said quietly, "not of yours but of William's."

The tone of her reply evidently pleased the engineer, for turning to Perrine he gave her an encouraging smile.

"But if you are replacing Mr. Bendit?" said Mombleux obstinately.

"Say that Mademoiselle is keeping his job for him," retorted Fabry.

"It's the same thing," answered Mombleux.

"Not at all, for in a week or two, when he'll be better, he'll come back in his old place. He certainly would not have had it if Mademoiselle had not been here to keep it for him."

"It seems to me that you and I also have helped to keep it for him," said Mombleux.

"Yes, but this little girl has done her share; he'll have to be grateful to all three of us," said Fabry, smiling again at Perrine.

If she had misunderstood the sense of Mombleux's words, the way in which she was treated at Mother Françoise's would have enlightened her. Her place was not set at the boarders' table as it would have been if she had been considered their equal, but at a little table at the side. And she was served after everyone else had taken from the dishes what they required.

But that did not hurt her; what did it matter to her if she were served first or last, and if the best pieces had already been taken. What interested her was that she was placed near enough to them to hear their conversation. She hoped that what she heard might guide her as to how she should act in the midst of the difficulties which confronted her.

These men knew the habits of M. Vulfran, his nephews, and Talouel, of whom she stood so much in fear; a word from them would enlighten her and she might be shown a danger which she did not even suspect, and if she was aware of it she could avoid it. She would not spy upon them. She would not listen at doors. When they were speaking they knew that they were not alone. So she need have no scruples but could profit by their remarks.

Unfortunately on that particular morning they said nothing that interested her; their talk was on insignificant matters. As soon as she had finished her meal she hurried to Rosalie, for she wanted to know how M. Vulfran had discovered that she had only slept one night at her grandmother's house.

"It was that Skinny who came here while you were at Picquigny," said Rosalie, "and he got Aunt Zenobie to talk about you; and you bet it isn't hard to make Aunt Zenobie talk especially when she gets something for doing so. She told him that you had spent only one night here and all sorts of other things besides."

"What other things?"

"I don't know because I was not there, but you can imagine the worst, but fortunately it has not turned out badly for you."

"No, on the contrary it has turned out very well, because M. Vulfran was amused and interested when I told him my story."

"I'll tell Aunt Zenobie, that'll make her mad."

"Oh, don't put her against me."

"Put her against you; oh, there's no danger of that now. She knows the position that M. Vulfran has given you, you won't have a better friend ...

seemingly. You'll see tomorrow. Only if you don't want that Skinny to know your business, don't tell anything to her."

"That I won't."

"Oh, she's sly enough."

"Yes, but now you've warned me...."

At three o'clock as arranged, M. Vulfran rang for Perrine and they drove off in the phaeton to make the customary round of the factories, for he did not let a single day pass without visiting the different buildings.

Although he could not see he could at least be seen, and when he gave his orders it was difficult to believe that he was blind; he seemed to know everything that was going on.

That day they began at the village of Flexelles. They stayed some time in the building and when they came out William was not to be seen. The horse was tied to a tree and William, the coachman, had disappeared. As soon as his employer had gone into his factories, William of course, as usual, had hurried to the nearest wine shop ... meeting a boon companion there he had forgotten the hour.

M. Vulfran sent one of his men off to search for his recalcitrant coachman. After waiting several minutes, the blind man became very angry. Finally William, with head held high, came staggering along.

"I can tell by the sound of his footsteps that he is drunk, Benoist," said M. Vulfran, addressing his manager, who stood beside him. "I am right, am I not?"

"Yes, sir ... nothing can be hidden from you. He is drunk...."

William began to apologize.

"I've just come from...." he began, but his employer cut him short.

"That is enough," said M. Vulfran, sternly. "I can tell by your breath and the way you walk that you are drunk."

"I was just going to say, sir," began William again, as he untied the horse, but at that moment he dropped the whip and stooping down, he tried three times to grasp it. The manager looked grave.

"I think it would be better if I drove you to Maraucourt," he said. "I am afraid you would not be safe with William."

"Why so?" demanded William insolently.

"Silence," commanded M. Vulfran, in a tone that admitted of no reply. "From this moment you can consider yourself dismissed from my service."

"But, sir, I was going to say...."

With an uplifted motion of his hand M. Vulfran stopped him and turned to his manager.

"Thank you, Benoist," he said, "but I think this little girl can drive me home. Coco is as quiet as a lamb, and she can well replace this drunken creature."

He was assisted into the carriage, and Perrine took her place beside him. She was very grave, for she felt the responsibility of her position.

"Not too quickly," said M. Vulfran, when she touched Coco with the end of her whip.

"Oh, please, sir, I don't want to go quickly, I assure you," she said, nervously.

"That's a good thing; let her just trot."

There was a great surprise in the streets of Maraucourt when the villagers saw the head of the firm seated beside a little girl wearing a hat of black straw and a black dress, who was gravely driving old Coco at a straight trot instead of the zigzag course that William forced the old animal to take in spite of herself. What was happening? Where was this little girl going? They questioned one another as they stood at the doors, for few people in the village knew of her and of the position that M. Vulfran had given her.

When they arrived at Mother Françoise's house, Aunt Zenobie was leaning over the gate talking to two women. When she caught sight of Perrine she stared in amazement, but her look of astonishment was quickly followed by her best smile, the smile of a real friend.

"Good day, Monsieur Vulfran! Good day, Mademoiselle Aurelie!" she called out.

As soon as the carriage had passed she told her neighbors how she had procured the fine position for the young girl who had been their boarder. She had recommended her so highly to Skinny.

"She's a nice girl, though," she added, "and she'll not forget what she owes us. She owes it all to us."

If the villagers had been surprised to see Perrine driving M. Vulfran, Talouel was absolutely stunned.

"Where is William?" he cried, hurrying down the steps of the veranda to meet his employer.

"Sent off for continual drunkenness," said M. Vulfran, smiling.

345

"I had supposed that you would take this step eventually," said Talouel.

"Exactly," replied his employer briefly.

Talouel had established his power in the house by these two words, "I suppose." His aim was to persuade his chief that he was so devoted to his interests that he was able to foresee every wish that he might have. So he usually began with these words, "I suppose that you want...."

He had the subtlety of the peasant, always on the alert, and his quality for spying made him stop at nothing to get the information he desired. M. Vulfran usually made the same reply when Talouel had "supposed" something.

"Exactly," the blind man would say.

"And I suppose you find," continued Talouel, as he helped his employer to get down, "that the one who has replaced him deserves your trust?"

"Exactly," said the blind man again.

"I'm not astonished," added the crafty Talouel. "The day when Rosalie brought her here I thought there was something in her, and I was sure you would soon find that out."

As he spoke he looked at Perrine, and his look plainly said: "You see what I've done for you. Don't forget it, and be ready to do me a service."

A demand of payment on this order was not long in coming.

A little later, stopping before the door of the office in which Perrine sat, he said in a low voice from the doorway:

"Tell me what happened with William."

Perrine thought that if she frankly replied to his question she would not be revealing any serious matter, so she related exactly what had occurred.

"Ah, good," he said, more at ease. "Now, if he should come to me and ask to be taken back I'll settle with him."

Later on Fabry and Mombleux put the same question to her, for everyone now knew that little Perrine had had to drive the chief home because his coachman had been too drunk to hold the reins.

"It's a miracle that he hasn't upset the boss a dozen times," said Fabry, "for he drives like a crazy creature when he's drunk. He should have been sent off long ago."

"Yes, and he would have been," said Mombleux, smiling, "if certain ones who wanted his help had not done all they could to keep him."

Perrine became all attention.

"They'll make a face when they see that he's gone, but I'll give William his due: he didn't know that he was spying."

They were silent while Zenobie came in to change the plates. They had not thought that the pretty little girl in the corner was listening to their conversation. After Zenobie had left the room they went on with their talk.

"But what if the son returns?" asked Mombleux.

"Well, most of us want him back, for the old man's getting old," said Fabry; "but perhaps he's dead."

"That might be," agreed Mombleux. "Talouel's so ambitious he'd stop at nothing. He wants to own the place, and he'll get it if he can."

"Yes, and who knows? Maybe he had a hand in keeping M. Edmond away. Neither of us were here at the time, but you might be sure that Talouel would work out things to his own interests."

"I hadn't thought of that."

"Yes, and at that time he didn't know that there'd be others to take the place of M. Edmond. I'm not sure what he's scheming to get, but it's something big."

"Yes, and he's doing some dirty work for sure, and only think, when he was twenty years old he couldn't write his own name."

Rosalie came into the room at this moment and asked Perrine if she would like to go on an errand with her. Perrine could not refuse. She had finished her dinner some time ago, and if she remained in her corner she would soon awaken their suspicions.

It was a quiet evening. The people sat at their street doors chatting. After Rosalie had finished her errand she wanted to go from one door to another to gossip, but Perrine had no desire for this, and she excused herself on the plea of being tired. She did not want to go to bed. She just wanted to be alone, to think, in her little room, with the door closed. She wanted to take a clear account of the situation in which she now found herself.

When she heard Fabry and Mombleux speaking of the manager she realized how much she had to fear this man. He had given her to understand that he was the master, and as such it was his right to be informed of all that happened. But all that was nothing compared with what had been revealed to her in the conversation that she had just heard.

She knew that he wished to exercise his authority over everyone. But she had not known that his ambition was to take her grandfather's place some day. This man was scheming to replace the all-powerful master of the Maraucourt factories; for years he had plotted with this object in view. All this she had just learned. The two men whose conversation she had overheard were in a position to know the facts. And this terrible man, now that she had replaced William, intended that she should spy upon his employer.

What should she do? She was only a little girl, almost a child, and there was no one to protect her. What should she do?

She had asked herself this question before, but under different circumstances. It was impossible for her to lie down, so nervous and excited was she at what she had heard.

Perhaps this dreadful man had schemed to keep her dear dead father away from his home, and he was still working in an underhanded way for what? Was he trying to get out of the way the two nephews who would replace his master? If he had the power to do this, what might he not do to her if she refused to spy for him?

She spent the greater part of the night turning these questions over in her little head. At last, tired out with the difficulties which confronted her, she dropped her curly head on the pillow and slept.

CHAPTER XXI. LETTERS FROM DACCA

THE first thing that M. Vulfran did upon reaching his office in the morning was to open his mail. Domestic letters were arranged in one pile and foreign letters in another. Since he had gone blind his nephews or Talouel read the French mail aloud to him; the English letters were given to Fabry and the German to Mombleux.

The day following the conversation between Fabry and Mombleux which had caused Perrine so much anxiety, M. Vulfran, his nephews and the manager were occupied with the morning's mail. Suddenly Theodore exclaimed:

"A letter from Dacca, dated May 29."

"In French?" demanded M. Vulfran.

"No, in English."

"What signature?"

"It's not very clear ... looks like Field. Fildes ... preceded by a word that I can't make out. There are four pages. Your name occurs in several places, uncle. Shall I give it to Fabry?"

348

Simultaneously, Theodore and Talouel cast a quick look at M. Vulfran, but catching each other in this act, which betrayed that each was intensely curious, they both assumed an indifferent air.

"I'm putting the letter on your table, uncle," said Theodore.

"Give it to me," replied M. Vulfran.

When the stenographer had gone off with the replies to the various letters, M. Vulfran dismissed his manager and his two nephews and rang for Perrine.

She appeared immediately.

"What's in the letter?" he asked.

She took the letter that he handed to her and glanced at it. If he could have seen her he would have noticed that she had turned very pale and that her hands trembled.

"It is an English letter, dated May 29, from Dacca," she replied.

"From whom?"

"From Father Fields."

"What does it say?"

"May I read a few lines first, please ... before I tell you?"

"Yes, but do it quickly."

She tried to do as she was told, but her emotion increased as she read ... the words dancing before her eyes.

"Well?" demanded M. Vulfran, impatiently.

"It is difficult to read," she murmured, "and difficult to understand; the sentences are very long."

"Don't translate literally; just tell me what it is about."

There was another long pause; at last she said:

"Father Fields says that Father Leclerc, to whom you wrote, is dead, and that before dying he asked him to send this reply to you. He was unable to communicate with you before, as he had some difficulty in getting together the facts that you desired. He excuses himself for writing in English, as his knowledge of French is very slight."

"What information does he send?" asked the blind man.

"I have not come to that yet, sir," replied Perrine.

Although little Perrine gave this reply in a very gentle voice, the blind man knew that he would gain nothing by hurrying her.

349

"You are right," he said; "not being in French, you must understand it thoroughly before you can explain it to me. You'd better take the letter and go into Bendit's office; translate it as accurately as you can, writing it out so that you can read it to me. Don't lose a minute. I'm anxious to know what it contains."

He called her back as she was leaving.

"This letter relates to a personal matter," he said, "and I do not wish anyone to know about it ... understand ... no one. If anyone dares question you about it, you must say nothing, nor give them any inkling of what it is about. You see what confidence I place in you. I hope that you will prove yourself worthy of my trust. If you serve me faithfully, you may be sure that you will be taken care of."

"I promise you, sir, that I'll deserve your trust," said Perrine, earnestly.

"Very well; now hurry."

But hurry she could not. She read the letter from beginning to end, then re-read it. Finally she took a large sheet of paper and commenced to write:

"Dacca, May 29.

"Honored Sir:

"It is with great grief that I inform you that we have lost our Reverend Father Leclerc, to whom you wrote for certain important information. When dying he asked me to send a reply to your letter, and I regret that it could not have been sent earlier, but after a lapse of twelve years I have had some difficulty in getting the facts that you desire, and I must ask pardon for sending the information I now have in English, as my knowledge of French is very slight...."

Perrine, who had only read this far to M. Vulfran, now stopped to read and correct what she had done. She was giving all her attention to her translation when the office door was opened by Theodore Paindavoine. He came into the room, closing the door after him, and asked for a French and English dictionary.

This dictionary was opened before her. She closed it and handed it to him.

"Are you not using it?" he asked, coming close to her.

"Yes, but I can manage without it," she replied.

"How's that?"

"I really only need it to spell the French words correctly," she said, "and a French dictionary will do as well."

350

She knew that he was standing just at the back of her, and although she could not see his eyes, being afraid to turn round, she felt that he was reading over her shoulder.

"Ah, you're translating that letter from Dacca?" he said.

She was surprised that he knew about this letter which was to be kept a secret. Then she realized that he was questioning her, and that his request for a dictionary was only a pretext. Why did he need an English dictionary if he could not understand a word of English?

"Yes, monsieur," she said.

"Is the translation coming along all right?" he asked.

She felt that he was bending over her, that his eyes were fixed on what she had translated. Quickly she moved her paper, turning it so that he could only see it sideways.

"Oh, please, sir," she exclaimed; "don't read it. It is not correct ... it is all confused. I was just trying."

"Oh, never mind that."

"Oh, but I do mind. I should be ashamed to let you see this."

He wanted to take the sheet of paper, but she put both her small hands over it. She determined to hold her own even with one of the heads of the house.

Until then he had spoken pleasantly to her.

"Now give it to me," he said briefly. "I'm not playing schoolmaster with a pretty little girl like you."

"But, sir, it is impossible; I can't let you see it," she said obstinately.

Laughingly he tried to take it from her, but she resisted him.

"No, I will not let you have it," she said with determination.

"Oh, this is a joke!" replied Theodore.

"It is not a joke; I am very serious," said little Perrine. "Monsieur Vulfran forbade me to let anyone see this letter. I am obeying him."

"It was I who opened it."

"The letter in English is not the translation."

"Oh, my uncle will show me this wonderful translation presently," he replied.

"If your uncle shows it, very well; but that won't be me showing it. He gave me his orders and I must obey him."

He saw by her resolute attitude that if he wanted the paper he would have to take it from her by force. But then, if he did so, she would probably call out. He did not dare go as far as that.

"I am delighted to see how faithfully you carry out my uncle's orders, even in trivial things," he said, sarcastically, leaving the room.

When he had gone and closed the door Perrine tried to go on with her work, but she was so upset she found it impossible to do so. She knew that Theodore was not delighted, as he had said, but furious. If he intended to make her pay for thwarting his will, how could she defend herself against such a powerful enemy? He could crush her with the first blow and she would have to leave.

The door was again opened and Talouel, with gliding step, came into the room. His eyes fell at once on the letter.

"Well, how is the translation of that letter from Dacca coming along?" he asked.

"I have only just commenced it," replied Perrine timidly.

"M. Theodore interrupted you just now. What did he want?"

"A French and English dictionary."

"What for? He doesn't know English."

"He did not tell me why he wanted it."

"Did he want to know what was in the letter?" asked Talouel.

"I had only commenced the first phrase," said Perrine, evasively.

"You don't ask me to believe that you have not read it?"

"I have not yet translated it."

"I ask you if you have read it."

"I cannot reply to that."

"Why not?"

"Because M. Vulfran has forbidden me to speak of this letter."

"You know very well that M. Vulfran and I are as one. All of his orders pass by me; all favors that he bestows are also passed by me. I have to know all that concerns him."

"Even his personal affairs?"

"Does that letter relate to personal affairs then?" asked Talouel.

She realized that she had let herself be caught.

"I did not say that," she said. "I said that in case it was a personal letter, ought I to let you know the contents?"

"I certainly should know," said Talouel, "if it relates to personal affairs. Do you know that he is ill from worrying over matters which might kill him? If he now received some news that might cause him great sorrow or great joy, it might prove fatal to him. He must not be told anything suddenly. That is why I ought to know beforehand anything that concerns him, so as to prepare him. I could not do that if you read your translation straight off to him."

He said this in a suave, insinuating voice, very different from his ordinary rough tones.

She was silent, looking up at him with an emotion which made her very pale.

"I hope that you are intelligent enough to understand what I am telling you," he continued. "It is important for us, for the entire town, who depend upon M. Vulfran for a livelihood, to consider his health. See what a good job you have now with him; in time it will be much better. We, every one of us, must work for his good. He looks strong, but he is not so strong as he appears, so much sorrow has undermined his health; and then the loss of his sight depresses him terribly. He places every confidence in me, and I must see that nothing hurts him."

If Perrine had not known Talouel she might have been won by his words; but after what she had heard the factory girls say about him, and the talk that she had overheard between Fabry and Mombleux, who were men able to judge character, she felt that she could not believe in him. He was not sincere. He wanted to make her talk, and he would attempt any deceit and hypocrisy to gain his object.

M. Vulfran had told her that if she were questioned she must not let anyone know the contents of the letter. Evidently he had foreseen what might happen. She must obey him.

Talouel, leaning on her desk, fixed his eyes on her face. She needed all her courage; it seemed as though he were trying to hypnotize her. In a hoarse voice which betrayed her emotion, but which did not tremble, however, she said:

"Monsieur Vulfran forbade me to speak of this letter to anyone."

Her determined attitude made him furious, but controlling himself, he leaned over her again and said gently, but firmly: "Yes, of course; but then I'm not anyone. I am his other self."

She did not reply.

"Are you a fool?" he cried at last in a stifled voice.

"Perhaps I am," she said.

"Well, then, understand," he said, roughly, "you'd better show some intelligence if you want to hold this job that M. Vulfran has given you. If you haven't any intelligence you can't hold the job, and instead of protecting you, as I intended, it will be my duty to pack you off ... fire you! Understand?"

"Yes, sir."

"Well, think about it; think what your position is today and think what it will be tomorrow, turned out in the streets; then let me know what you decide to do. Tell me this evening."

Then as she showed no signs of weakening, he went out of the room with the same gliding step with which he had entered.

CHAPTER XXII. A CABLE TO DACCA

M. VULFRAN was waiting for her. She had no time to think over what Talouel had threatened. She went on with her translation, hoping that her emotion would die down and leave her in a state better able to come to a decision as to what she should do. She continued to write:

"So much time has elapsed since the marriage of your son, M. Edmond Paindavoine, that I have had some difficulty in getting together the facts. It was our own Father Leclerc who performed this marriage.

"The lady who became your son's wife was endowed with the finest womanly qualities. She was upright, kind, charming; added to these qualities, she was gifted with remarkable personal charms. The time is past when all the knowledge the Hindu woman possessed consisted in the art of being graceful and the science of etiquette of their social world. Today the Hindu woman's mind is cultivated to a remarkable degree. Your son's wife was a highly educated girl. Her father and mother were of the Brahmin faith, but Father Leclerc had the joy of converting them to our own religion. Unfortunately, when a Hindu is converted to our religion he loses his caste, his rank, his standing in social life. This was the case with the family whose daughter married your son. By becoming Christians, they became to a certain extent outcasts.

"So you will quite understand that being cast off by the all-powerful Hindu world, this charming girl, who was now a Christian, should turn and take her place in European society. Her father went into partnership with a well-known French exporter, and the firm was known as Doressany (Hindu) & Bercher (French).

"It was in the home of Madame Bercher that your son met Marie Doressany and fell in love with her. Everybody spoke in the highest praise of this young lady. I did not know her, for I came to Dacca after she left. Why there should have been any obstacle to this union I cannot say. That is a matter I must not discuss. Although there were, however, objections, the marriage took place and in our own Chapel. The Reverend Father Leclerc bestowed the nuptial blessing upon the marriage of your son and Marie Doressany. This marriage was recorded in our registers, and a copy of it can be sent to you if you wish.

"For four years your son Edmond lived at the home of his wife's parents. There a little girl was born to the young couple. Everyone who remembers them speaks of them, as a model couple, and like all young people, they took part in the social pleasures of their world.

"For some time the firm of Doressany & Bercher prospered, then hard times came, and after several bad seasons the firm was ruined. M. and Mme. Doressany died at some months' interval, and Monsieur Bercher with his family returned to France. Your son then traveled to Dalhousie as collector of plants and antiquities for various English houses. He took with him his young wife and his little girl, who was about three years old.

"He did not return to Dacca, but I learn from one of his friends to whom he has written several times, and from Father Leclerc, who wrote regularly to Mme. Paindavoine, that they had a villa at Dehra. They selected this spot to live in as it was the center of his voyages; he traveled between the Thiberian frontier and the Himalayas.

"I do not know Dehra, but we have a mission in this town, and if you think it might help in our researches I shall be pleased to send you a letter for one of the Fathers whose help might be useful in this matter...."

At last the letter was finished. The moment she had translated the last word, without even waiting to write the polite ending, she gathered up her sheets and went quickly to M. Vulfran's office. She found him walking back and forth the length of the room, counting his steps as much to avoid bumping against the wall as to curb his impatience.

"You have been very slow," he said.

"The letter was long and difficult," she replied.

"And you were interrupted, were you not? I heard the door of your office open and close twice."

Since he put the question to her, she thought that she ought to reply truthfully. It would solve the problem that had caused her so much anxiety.

"Monsieur Theodore and Monsieur Talouel came into the office," she said.

"Ah!..."

He seemed as though he wanted to say more, but refrained.

"Give me the letter first," he said, "and we'll see to the other matter after. Sit down beside me and read slowly. Don't raise your voice."

She read. Her voice was somewhat weak.

As she read the blind man murmured to himself from time to time: "Model couple" ... "social pleasures" ... "English houses" ... "which?" ... "One of his friends" ... "Which friend?"

When she had finished there was a silence. Finally M. Vulfran spoke:

"Can you translate into English as well as you translate English into French?" he asked.

"I can do it if the phrases are not too difficult," she replied.

"A cable?"

"Yes, I think so."

"Well, sit down at that little table and write."

He dictated in French:

"Father Fields' Mission, Dacca:

"Thanks for letter. Please send by cable, reply prepaid, twenty words ... name of friend who received last news, date of letter. Send also name of the Reverend Father at Dehra. Inform him that I shall write him immediately. Paindavoine."

"Translate that into English and make it shorter rather than longer, if possible. At one franc sixty centimes a word, we must not waste words. Write very clearly."

The translation was quickly made.

"How many words?" he asked.

"In English ... thirty-seven."

He made the calculation for the message and for the return answer.

"Now," he said to Perrine, giving her the money, "take it yourself to the telegraph office, hand it in and see that no mistakes are made by the receiver."

As she crossed the veranda she saw Talouel, who, with his hands thrust in his pockets, was strolling about as though on the lookout for all that passed in the yards as well as in the offices.

"Where are you going?" he demanded.

"To the cable office with a message," replied Perrine. She held the paper in one hand and the money in the other. He took the paper from her, snatching it so roughly that if she had not let it go he would have torn it. He hastily opened it. His face flushed with anger when he saw that the message was written in English.

"You know that you've got to talk with me later on, eh?" he said.

"Yes, sir."

She did not see M. Vulfran again before three o'clock, when he rang for her to go out. She had wondered who would replace William, and she was very surprised when M. Vulfran told her to take her seat beside him, after having sent away the coachman who had brought old Coco around.

"As you drove him so well yesterday, there is no reason why you should not drive him well today," said M. Vulfran. "Besides, I want to talk to you, and it is better for us to be alone like this."

It was not until they had left behind the village, where their appearance excited the same curiosity as the evening before, and were going at a gentle trot along the lanes, that M. Vulfran began to talk. Perrine would like to have put off this moment; she was very nervous.

"You told me that M. Theodore and Talouel came into your office?" said the blind man.

"Yes, sir."

"What did they want?"

She hesitated. Her little face wore a very worried look.

"Why do you hesitate?" asked the blind man. "Don't you think that you ought to tell me everything?"

"Yes, indeed," said Perrine, fervently. Was this not the best way to solve her difficulties? She told what had happened when Theodore had come into the office.

"Was that all?" asked M. Vulfran, when she stopped.

"Yes, sir; that was all."

"And Talouel?"

Again she told exactly what had occurred, only omitting to tell him that Talouel had said that a sudden announcement of news, good or bad, might prove fatal to him. She then told him what had passed regarding the cable; and also that Talouel said he was going to talk with her after work that same day.

As she talked she had let old Coco go at her own will, and the old horse, taking advantage of her freedom, shambled along calmly from one side of the road to the other, sniffing the odor of the warm hay that the breeze wafted to his nostrils.

When Perrine stopped talking her grandfather remained silent for some time. Knowing that he could not see her, she fixed her eyes on his face and she read in his expression as much sadness as annoyance.

"No harm shall come to you," he said at last. "I shall not mention what you have told me, and if anyone wants to take revenge on you for opposing their attempts I shall be near to protect you. I thought something like this would happen, but it will not occur a second time. In the future you will sit at the little table that is in my office. I hardly think that they'll try to question you before me. But as they might try to do so after you leave off work, over at Mother Françoise's where you eat, I shall take you to my home to live with me. You will have a room in the chateau, and you will eat at my table. As I am expecting to have some correspondence with persons in India, and I shall receive letters in English and cables, you alone will know about them. I must take every precaution, for they will do their utmost to make you talk. I shall be able to protect you if you are by my side; besides, this will be my reply to those who try to force you to speak, as well as a warning if they still try to tempt you. Then, also, it will be a reward for you."

Perrine, who had been trembling with anxiety when M. Vulfran commenced to speak, was now so overcome with joy that she could find no words with which to reply.

"I had faith in you, child," continued the old man, "from the moment I knew what struggle you had made against poverty. When one is as brave as you, one is honest. You have proved to me that I have not made a mistake, and that I can be proud of you. It is as though I have known you for years. I am a very lonely and unhappy man. What is my wealth to me? It is a heavy burden if you have not the health to enjoy it. And yet there are those who envy me. There are seven thousand men and women who depend upon me for a living. If I failed there would be misery and hunger and perhaps death for many. I must keep up for them. I must uphold the honor of this house which I have built up, little by little. It is my joy, my pride ... and yet ... I am blind!"

The last words were said with such bitterness that Perrine's eyes filled with tears. The blind man continued: "You ought to know from village talk and from the letter that you translated that I have a son. My son and I disagreed. We parted; there were many reasons for us doing so. He then married against my wishes and our separation was complete. But with all this my affection for him has not changed. I love him after all these years of absence as though he were still the little boy I brought up, and when I think of him, which is day and night, it is the little boy that I see with my sightless eyes. My son preferred that woman to his own father. Instead of coming back to me he preferred to live with her because I would not, or could not, receive her. I hoped that he would give in, but he thought probably that I in time would give in. We have both the same characters. I have had no news from him. After my illness, of which I am sure he knew, for I have every reason to believe that he has been kept informed of all that happens here, I thought that he would come back to me, but he has not returned. That wretched woman evidently holds him back. She is not content with having taken him from me, she keeps him ... the wretch...."

The blind man stopped. Perrine, who had been hanging on his words, had scarcely breathed, but at the last words she spoke.

"The letter from Father Fields said that she was a lady, honorable and upright. He does not speak of her as a wretch."

"What the letter says cannot go against facts," said the blind man, obstinately. "The main fact which has made me hate her is that she keeps my son from me. A creature of her kind should efface herself and let him return and take up again the life which is his. It is through her that we are parted. I have tried to find him, but I cannot. He must come back and take his place. You may not understand all I tell you, my child, but when I die my whole fortune must go to my son. He is my heir. When I die who will take my place if he is not here? Can you understand what I am saying, little girl?" said the old man, almost entreatingly.

"I think so, sir," said Perrine gently.

"But there, I don't wish you to understand entirely. There are those around me who ought to help me. There are certain ones who do not want my boy to return; it is to their interest that he should not come back, so they try to think that he is dead. My boy dead! Could he be? Could God strike me such a terrible blow? They try to believe it, but I will not. No, I will not! It can't be! Oh, what should I do if my boy was dead!"

Perrine's eyes were no longer fixed on the blind man's face; she had turned her face from him as though he could see her own.

"I talk to you frankly, little girl," continued the old man, "because I need your help. They are going to try and tempt you again to spy for them. I have warned you; that is all that I can do."

They could now see the factory chimneys of Fercheux. Still a few more rods and they came to the village. Perrine, who was trembling, could only find words to say in a broken voice: "Monsieur Vulfran, you may trust me. I will serve you faithfully with all my heart."

CHAPTER XXIII. GRANDFATHER'S COMPANION

THAT evening, when the tour of the factories was over, instead of returning to his office as was his custom, M. Vulfran told Perrine to drive straight to the chateau.

For the first time she passed through the magnificent iron gates, a masterpiece of skill that a king had coveted, so it was said, these wonderful iron gates which one of France's richest merchants had bought for his chateau.

"Follow the main driveway," said M. Vulfran.

For the first time also she saw close to the beautiful flowers and the velvety lawns which until then she had only seen from a distance. The beautiful blossoms, red and pink masses, seemed like great splashes on the verdure. Accustomed to take this road, old Coco trotted along calmly, and as there was no occasion to guide her, Perrine was able to gaze right and left of her and admire the flowers, plants and shrubs in all their beauty. Although their master could not see them as formerly, the same attention and skill was showered upon them.

Of her own accord, Coco stopped before the wide steps where an old servant, warned by the lodge-keeper's bell, stood waiting.

"Are you there, Bastien?" asked M. Vulfran, without getting down.

"Yes, sir."

"Then take this young girl to the butterfly room, which is to be hers in the future. See that everything is given to her that she needs. Set her plate opposite to mine at table. Now send Felix to me. I want him to drive me to the office."

Perrine thought that she was dreaming.

"We dine at eight o'clock," said M. Vulfran. "Until then you are free to do as you like."

She got out of the carriage quickly and followed the old butler. She was so dazed that it was as though she had suddenly been set down in an enchanted palace.

And was not this beautiful chateau like a palace? The monumental hall, from which rose a wonderful stairway of white marble, up which ran a crimson carpet, was a delight to the eyes. On each landing exquisite flowers and plants were grouped artistically in pots and jardinieres. Their perfume filled the air.

Bastien took her to the second floor, and without entering opened the door of a room for her.

"I'll send the chambermaid to you," he said, leaving her.

She passed through a somber little hall, then found herself in a very large room draped with ivory colored cretonne patterned with butterflies in vivid shades. The furniture was ivory colored wood, and the carpet gray, with clusters of wild flowers, primrose, poppies, cornflowers and buttercups.

How pretty and dainty it was!

She was still in a dream, pushing her feet into the soft carpet, when the maid entered.

"Bastien told me that I was to be at your service, mademoiselle," she said.

Here stood a chambermaid in a clean light dress and a muslin cap at her service ... she who only a few days before had slept in a hut on a bed of ferns with rats and frogs scampering about her.

"Thank you," she said at last, collecting her wits, "but I do not need anything ... at least I think not."

"If you like I will show you the apartment," said the maid.

What she meant by "show the apartment" was to throw open the doors of a big wardrobe with glass doors, and a closet, then to pull out the drawers of the dressing table in which were brushes, scissors, soaps and bottles, etc. That done, she showed Perrine two knobs on the wall.

"This one is for the lights," she said, flashing on the electric light, "and this one is the bell if you need anything.

"If you need Bastien," she explained, "you have to ring once, and if you need me, ring twice."

How much had happened in a few hours! Who would have thought when she took her stand against Theodore and Talouel that the wind was going to blow so favorably in her direction. How amusing it was ... their ill feeling towards her had itself brought her this good luck.

"I suppose that young girl did something foolish?" said Talouel, meeting his employer at the foot of the steps. "I see she has not returned with you."

"Oh, no; she did not," replied M. Vulfran.

"But if Felix drove you back?..."

"As I passed the chateau I dropped her there so that she would have time to get ready for dinner."

"Dinner? Oh, I suppose...."

He was gasping with amazement, and for once he could not say what he did suppose.

"You do nothing but 'suppose'," said M. Vulfran, tartly. "I may as well tell you that for a long time I have wanted someone intelligent to be near me, one who is discreet and whom I can trust. This young girl seems to have these qualities. I am sure that she is intelligent, and I have already had the proof that I can trust her."

M. Vulfran's tone was significant. Talouel could not misunderstand the sense of his words.

"I am taking her to live with me," continued M. Vulfran, "because I know that there are those who are trying to tempt her. She is not one to yield, but I do not intend that she should run any risk at their hands."

These words were said with even greater significance.

"She will stay with me altogether now," continued M. Vulfran. "She will work here in my office; during the day she will accompany me; she will eat at my table. I shall not be so lonesome at my meals, for her chatter will entertain me."

"I suppose she will give you all the satisfaction that you expect," remarked Talouel suavely.

"I suppose so also," replied his employer, very drily.

Meanwhile Perrine, leaning with her elbows on the window sill, looked out dreamily over the beautiful garden, at the factories beyond the village with its houses and church, the meadows in which the silvery water glistened in the oblique rays of the setting sun; and then her eyes turned in the opposite direction, to the woods where she had sat down the day she had come, and where in the evening breeze she had seemed to hear the soft voice of her mother murmuring, "I know you will be happy."

Her dear mother had foreseen the future, and the big daisies had also spoken true. Yes, she was beginning to be happy. She must be patient and all would come right in time. She need not hurry matters now. There was no poverty, no hunger or thirst, in this beautiful chateau where she had entered so quickly.

When the factory whistle announced the closing hour she was still standing at her window, deep in thought. The piercing whistle recalled her from the future to the present.

Along the white roads between the fields she saw a black swarm of workers, first a great compact mass, then gradually it grew smaller, as they dwindled off in different directions in groups towards their homes.

Old Coco's gentle trot was soon heard on the drive, and Perrine saw her blind grandfather returning to his home.

She gave herself a real wash with eau de Cologne as well as soap, a delicious perfume soap. It was not until the clock on the mantle shelf struck eight that she went down.

She wondered how she would find the dining room. She did not have to look for it, however. A footman in a black coat, who was standing in the hall, showed her the way. Almost immediately M. Vulfran came in. No one guided him. He seemed to have no difficulty in finding his way to his seat.

A bowl of beautiful orchids stood in the middle of the table, which was covered with massive silver and cut glass, which gleamed in the lights that fell from the crystal chandelier.

For a moment she stood behind her chair, not knowing what to do. M. Vulfran seemed to sense her attitude.

"Sit down," he said.

The dinner was served at once. The servant who had shown her the way to the dining room put a plate of soup before her, while Bastien brought another to his master which was full to the brim.

If she had been dining there alone with M. Vulfran she would have been quite at her ease, but the inquisitive glances the servants cast at her made her feel deeply embarrassed. Probably they were wondering how a little tramp like her would eat.

Fortunately, however, she made no mistakes.

The dinner was very simple—soup, roast lamb, green peas and salad—but there was abundance of dessert ... two or three raised stands of delicious fruit and cakes.

"Tomorrow, if you like, you may go and see the hot houses where these fruits are grown," said M. Vulfran.

Perrine thanked him and said she would like to.

She had commenced by helping herself discreetly to some cherries. M. Vulfran wished her also to take some apricots, peaches and grapes.

"Take all you want," he said. "At your age I should have eaten all the fruit that is on the table ... if it had been offered to me."

Bastien selected an apricot and peach and placed them before Perrine as he might have done for an intelligent monkey, just to see how the "little animal" would eat.

But despite the delicious fruit, Perrine was very pleased when the dinner came to an end. She hoped that the next day the servants would not stare so much.

"Now you are free until tomorrow," said M. Vulfran, rising from his seat. "It is moonlight, and you can go for a stroll in the garden, or read in the library, or take a book up to your own room."

She was embarrassed, wondering if she ought not to tell M. Vulfran that she would do as he wished. While she stood hesitating she saw Bastien making signs to her which at first she did not understand. He held an imaginary book in one hand and appeared to be turning the pages with the other, then glanced at M. Vulfran and moved his lips as though he were reading. Suddenly Perrine understood. She was to ask if she might read to him.

"But don't you need me, sir?" she said, timidly. "Would you not like me to read to you?"

Bastien nodded his head in approval. He seemed delighted that she had guessed what he had tried to explain.

"Oh, you need some time to yourself," replied M. Vulfran.

"I assure you that I am not at all tired," said Perrine.

"Very well, then," said the blind man; "follow me into the study."

364

The library was a big somber room separated from the dining room by the hall. There was a strip of carpet laid from one room to the other, which was a guide for the blind man. He now walked direct to the room opposite.

Perrine had wondered how he spent his time when he was alone, as he could not read. From the appearance of the room one could not guess, for the large table was covered with papers and magazines. Before the window stood a large Voltaire chair, upholstered in tapestry. The chair was rather worn. This seemed to indicate that the blind man sat for long hours face to face with the sky, the clouds of which he could never see.

"What could you read to me?" he asked Perrine.

"A newspaper," she said, "if you wish. There are some on the table."

"The less time one gives to the newspapers the better," he replied. "Do you like books on travels?"

"Yes, sir; I do," she said.

"I do, too," he said. "They amuse one as well as instruct one."

Then, as though speaking to himself, as though unaware of her presence, he said softly: "Get away from yourself. Get interested in another life than your own."

"We'll read from 'Around the World'," he said. He led her to a bookcase which contained several volumes on travels and told her to look in the index.

"What shall I look for?" she asked.

"Look in the I's ... for the word India."

Thus he was following his own thoughts. How could he live the life of another? His one thought was of his son. He now wanted to read about the country where his boy lived.

"Tell me what you find," he said.

She read aloud the various headings concerning India. He told her which volume to take. As she was about to take it she stood as though transfixed, gazing at a portrait hanging over the fireplace which her eyes, gradually becoming accustomed to the dim light, had not seen before.

"Why are you silent?" he asked.

"I am looking at the portrait over the mantel shelf," she said, in a trembling voice.

"That was my son when he was twenty," said the old gentleman; "but you can't see it very well. I'll light up."

He touched the electric knob and the room was flooded with light. Perrine, who had taken a few steps nearer, uttered a cry and let the book of travels fall to the floor.

"What is the matter?" he asked.

She did not reply, but stood there with her eyes fixed on the picture of a fair young man dressed in a hunting suit leaning with one hand on a gun and the other stroking the head of a black spaniel.

There was silence in the room, then the blind man heard a little sob.

"Why are you crying?" he asked.

Perrine did not reply for a moment. With an effort she tried to control her emotion.

"It is the picture ... your son ... you are his father?" she stammered.

At first he did not understand, then in a voice that was strangely sympathetic he said:

"And you ... you were thinking of your father, perhaps?"

"Yes, yes, sir; I was."

"Poor little girl," he murmured.

CHAPTER XXIV. GETTING AN EDUCATION

THE next morning, when Theodore and Casimir entered their uncle's office to attend to the correspondence, they were amazed to see Perrine installed at her table as though she were a fixture there.

Talouel had taken care not to tell them, but he had contrived to be present when they entered so as to witness their discomfiture. The sight of their amazement gave him considerable enjoyment. Although he was furious at the way this little beggar girl had imposed, as he thought, upon the senile weakness of an old man, it was at least some compensation to know that the two nephews felt the same astonishment and indignation that he had.

Evidently they did not understand her presence in this sacred office, where they themselves only remained just the time necessary to report on the business of which they were in charge.

Theodore and Casimir looked in dismay at one another, but they did not dare ask questions. Talouel left the room the same time as they.

"You were surprised to see that girl in the boss' office, eh?" he said, when they got outside.

They did not deign to reply.

"If you had not come in late this morning, I should have let you know that she was there, and then you would not have looked so taken back. She noticed how surprised you were."

He had managed to give them two little knocks: First, there was a gentle scolding for them being late; secondly, he had let them see that he, a foreman, had noticed that they had been unable to hide their discomfiture and that the girl had noticed it, too. And they were M. Vulfran's nephews! Ah! ha!

"M. Vulfran told me yesterday that he had taken that girl to live at the chateau with him, and that in the future she would work in his office."

"But who is the girl?"

"That's what I'd like to know. I don't think your uncle knows either. He told me he wanted someone to be with him whom he could trust."

"Hasn't he got us?" asked Casimir.

"That is just what I said to him. I mentioned you both, and do you know what he replied?"

He wanted to pause to give more effect to his words, but he was afraid that they would turn their backs upon him before he had said what he wanted.

"'Oh, my nephews,' he said, 'and what are they?' From the tone in which he said those few words I thought it better not to reply," continued Talouel. "He told me then that he intended to have that girl up at the chateau with him because there was someone trying to tempt her to tell something that she should not tell. He said he knew that she could be trusted, but he said he didn't like others that he could not trust to put the girl in such a position. He said she had already proved to him that she could be trusted. I wonder who he meant had tried to tempt her?

"I thought it my duty to tell you this, because while M. Edmond is away you two take his place," added Talouel.

He had given them several thrusts, but he wanted to give them one last sharp knock.

"Of course, M. Edmond might return at any moment," he said. "I believe that your uncle is on the right track at last. He has been making inquiries, and from the looks of things I think we shall have him back soon."

"What have you heard? Anything?" asked Theodore, who could not restrain his curiosity.

"Oh, I keep my eyes open," said Talouel, "and I can tell you that that girl is doing a lot of translating in the way of letters and cables that come from India."

At that moment he looked from a window and saw a telegraph boy strolling up to the office.

"Here is another cable coming," he said. "This is a reply to one that has been sent to Dacca. It must be very annoying for you not to be able to speak English. You could be the first to announce to the boss that your cousin will be coming back. Now that little tramp will be the one to do it."

Talouel hurried forward to meet the telegraph boy.

"Say, you don't hurry yourself, do you?" he cried.

"Do you want me to kill myself?" asked the boy, insolently.

He hurried with the message to M. Vulfran's office.

"Shall I open it, sir?" he asked eagerly.

"Yes, do," said M. Vulfran.

"Oh, it is in English," replied Talouel, as he looked at the missive.

"Then Aurelie must attend to it," said M. Vulfran, and with a wave of his hand dismissed the manager.

As soon as the door had closed Perrine translated the cable.

It read: "Friend Leserre, a French merchant. Last news from Dehra five years. Wrote Father Makerness according to your wish."

"Five years," cried M. Vulfran. Then, as he was not the sort of man to waste time in regrets, he said to Perrine: "Write two cables, one to M. Leserre in French and one to Father Makerness in English."

She quickly wrote the cable that she had to translate into English, but she asked if she could get a dictionary from Bendit's office before she did the one in French.

"Are you not sure of your spelling?" asked M. Vulfran.

"No, I am not at all sure," she replied, "and I should not like them at the office to make fun of any message that is sent by you."

"Then you would not be able to write a letter without making mistakes?"

"No, I know I should make a lot of mistakes. I can spell French words all right at the commencement, but the endings I find very difficult. I find it much easier to write in English, and I think I ought to tell you so now."

"Have you never been to school?"

"No, never. I only know what my father and mother taught me. When we stopped on the roads they used to make me study, but I never studied very much."

"You are a good girl to tell me so frankly. We must see to that, but for the moment let us attend to what we have on hand."

It was not until the afternoon, when they were driving out, that he again referred to her spelling.

"Have you written to your relations yet?" he asked.

"No, sir."

"Why not?"

"Because I would like nothing better than to stay here with you, who are so kind to me," she said.

"Then you don't want to leave me?" asked the blind man.

"No, I want to help you all I can," said Perrine softly.

"Very well, then you must study so as to be able to act as a little secretary for me. Would you like to be educated?"

"Indeed I would! And I will work so hard," said Perrine.

"Well, the matter can be arranged without depriving myself of your services," said M. Vulfran; "there is a very good teacher here and I will ask her to give you lessons from six to eight in the evenings. She is a very nice woman; there are only two things against her; they are her height and her name; she is taller than I am, and her shoulders are much broader than mine. Her name is Mademoiselle Belhomme. She is indeed a *bel homme*, for although she is only forty her shoulders and figure are more massive than any man's I know ... I must add that she has not a beard."

Perrine smiled at this description of the teacher that she was to have.

After they had made a tour of the factories they stopped before a girl's school and Mlle. Belhomme ran out to greet M. Vulfran. He expressed a wish to get down and go into the school and speak with her. Perrine, who followed in their footsteps, was able to examine her. She was indeed a giant, but her manner seemed very womanly and dignified. At times her manner was almost timid and did not accord at all with her appearance.

Naturally she could not refuse anything the all-powerful master of Maraucourt asked, but even if she had had any reasons to refuse M. Vulfran's request the little girl with the beautiful eyes and hair pleased her very much.

"Yes," she said to M. Vulfran, "we will make her an educated girl. Do you know she has eyes like a gazelle. I have never seen a gazelle, but I should imagine their great brown eyes are like hers. They are wonderful...."

The next day when M. Vulfran returned to his home at the dinner hour he asked the governess what she thought of her new pupil. Mlle. Belhomme was most enthusiastic in her praise of Perrine.

"Does she show any intelligence?" asked M. Vulfran.

"Why she is wonderfully intelligent," replied Mlle. Belhomme; "it would have been such a calamity if she had remained without an education...."

M. Vulfran smiled at Mlle. Belhomme's words.

"What about her spelling?" he asked.

"Oh, that is very poor but she'll do better. Her writing is fairly good but, of course, she needs to study hard. She is so intelligent it is extraordinary. So as to know exactly what she knew in writing and spelling I asked her to write me an account of Maraucourt. In twenty to a hundred lines I asked her to describe the village to me. She sat down and wrote. Her pen flew over the paper; she did not hesitate for words; she wrote four long pages;

she described the factories, the scenery, every thing clearly and in detail. She wrote about the birds and the fishes over near the pond, and about the morning mists that cover the fields and the water. Then of the calm, quiet evenings. Had I not seen her writing it I should have thought that she had copied it from some good author. Unfortunately the spelling and writing is very poor but, as I said, that does not matter. That is merely a matter of a few months, whilst all the lessons in the world would not teach her how to write if she had not been gifted with the sense of feeling and seeing in such a remarkable manner; that she can convey to others what she feels and sees. If you have time to let me read it to you, you will see that I have not exaggerated."

The governess read Perrine's narrative to him. He was delighted. He had wondered once or twice if he had been wise in so promptly befriending this little girl and giving her a place in his home. It had appeared to him strange the sudden fancy that he had taken to her.

He told Mlle. Belhomme how her little pupil had lived in a cabin in one of the fields, and how, with nothing except what she found on hand, she contrived to make kitchen utensils and shoes, and how she had made her meals of the fish, herbs and fruit that she found.

Mlle. Belhomme's kind face beamed as the blind man talked. She was greatly interested in what he told her. When M. Vulfran stopped the governess remained silent, thinking.

"Don't you think," she said at last, "that to know how to create the necessities that one needs is a master quality to be desired above all?"

"I certainly do, and it was precisely because that child could do that that I first took an interest in her. Ask her some time to tell you her story and you will see that it required some energy and courage for her to arrive where she is now."

"Well, she has received her reward since she has been able to interest you."

"Yes, I am interested, and already attached to her. I am glad that you like her, and I hope that you will do all that you can with her."

Perrine made great progress with her studies. She was interested in everything her governess had to tell her, but her beautiful eyes betrayed the greatest interest when Mlle. Belhomme talked of her grandfather. Many times Perrine had spoken of M. Vulfran's illness to Rosalie, but she had only received vague replies to her queries; now, from her governess, she learned all the details regarding his affliction.

Like everyone at Maraucourt, Mlle. Belhomme was concerned with M. Vulfran's health, and she had often spoken with Dr. Ruchon so she was in a position to satisfy Perrine's curiosity better than Rosalie could.

Her grandfather had a double cataract. It was not incurable; if he were operated upon he might recover his sight. The operation had not yet been attempted because his health would not allow it.... He was suffering from bronchial trouble, and if the operation was to be a success he would have to be in a perfect state of health. But M. Vulfran was imprudent. He was not careful enough in following the doctor's orders. How could he remain calm, as Dr. Ruchon recommended, when he was always worked up to a fever of anxiety over the continued absence of his son. So long as he was not sure of his son's fate, there was no chance for the operation and it was put off. But ... would it be possible to have it later? That the oculists could not decide. They were uncertain, so long as the blind man's health continued in this precarious state.

But when Mlle. Belhomme saw that Perrine was also anxious to talk about Talouel and the two nephews and their hopes regarding the business she was not so communicative. It was quite natural that the girl should show an interest in her benefactor, but that she should be interested in the village gossip was not permissible. Certainly it was not a conversation for a governess and her pupil.... It was not with talks of this kind that one should mould the character of a young girl.

Perrine would have had to renounce all hope of getting any information from her governess if Casimir's mother, Madame Bretoneux, had not decided to come to the chateau on a visit. This coming visit opened the lips of Mlle. Belhomme, which otherwise would certainly have remained closed.

As soon as the governess heard that Mme. Bretoneux was coming she had a very serious talk with her little pupil.

"My dear child," she said, lowering her voice, "I must give you some advice; I want you to be very reserved with this lady who is coming here tomorrow."

"Reserved, about what?" asked Perrine in surprise.

"Monsieur Vulfran did not only ask me to take charge of your education but to take a personal interest in you; that is why I give you this advice."

"Please, Mademoiselle, explain to me what I ought to do," said Perrine; "I don't understand at all what this advice means, and I am very nervous."

"Although you have not been very long at Maraucourt," said Mlle. Belhomme, "you must know that M. Vulfran's illness and the continued absence of his son is a cause of anxiety to all this part of the country."

"Yes, I have heard that," answered Perrine.

"What would become of all those employed in the works, seven thousand, and all those who are dependent on these seven thousand if Monsieur Vulfran should die and his son not return? Will he leave his fortune and works to his nephews, of which he has no more confidence in one than the other, or to one who for twenty years has been his right hand and who, having managed the works with him is, perhaps more than anyone else, in a position to keep his hold on them?

"When M. Vulfran took his nephew Theodore into the business everyone thought that he intended to make him his heir. But later, when Monsieur Casimir left college and his uncle sent for him, they saw that they had made a mistake and that M. Vulfran had not decided to leave his business to these two boys. His only wish was to have his son back for, although they had been parted for ten years, he still loved him. Now no one knew whether the son was dead or alive. But there were those who wished that he was dead so that they themselves could take M. Vulfran's place when he died.

"Now, my dear child," said the governess, "you understand you live here in the home of M. Vulfran and you must be very discreet in this matter and not talk about it to Casimir's mother. She is working all she can for her son's interest and she will push anyone aside who stands in his way. Now, if you were on too good terms with her you would be on bad terms with Theodore's mother, and the other way about. Then, on the other hand, should you gain the good graces of both of them you would perhaps have reason to fear one from another direction. That is why I give you this little advice. Talk as little as possible. And if you are questioned, be careful to make replies as vague as possible. It is better sometimes to be looked upon rather as too stupid than too intelligent. This is so in your case ... the less intelligent you appear, the more intelligent you will really be."

CHAPTER XXV. MEDDLING RELATIVES

THIS advice, given with every kindness, did not tend to lessen Perrine's anxiety. She was dreading Madame Bretoneux's visit on the morrow.

Her governess had not exaggerated the situation. The two mothers were struggling and scheming in every possible way, each to have her son alone inherit one day or another the great works of Maraucourt and the fortune which it was rumored would be more than a hundred million francs.

The one, Mme. Stanislaus Paindavoine, was the wife of M. Vulfran's eldest brother, a big linen merchant. Her husband had not been able to give her the position in society which she believed to be hers, and now she hoped that, through her son inheriting his uncle's great fortune, she would at last be able to take the place in the Parisian world which she knew she could grace.

The other, Madame Bretoneux was M. Vulfran's married sister who had married a Boulogne merchant, who in turn had been a cement and coal merchant, insurance agent and maritime agent, but with all his trades had never acquired riches. She wanted her brother's wealth as much for love of the money as to get it away from her sister-in-law, whom she hated.

While their brother and his only son had lived on good terms, they had had to content themselves with borrowing all they could from him in loans which they never intended to pay back; but the day when Edmond had been packed off to India, ostensibly to buy jute but in reality as a punishment for being too extravagant and getting into debt, the two women had schemed to take advantage of the situation. On each side they had made every preparation so that each could have her son alone, at any moment, take the place of the exile.

In spite of all their endeavors the uncle had never consented to let the boys live with him at the chateau. There was room enough for them all and he was sad and lonely, but he had made a firm stand against having them with him in his home.

"I don't want any quarrels or jealousy around me," he had always replied to the suggestions made.

He had then given Theodore the house he had lived in before he built the chateau and another to Casimir that had belonged to the late head of the counting house whom Mombleux had replaced.

So their surprise and indignation had been intense when a stranger, a poor girl, almost a child, had been installed in the chateau where they themselves had only been admitted as guests.

What did it mean?

Who was this little girl?

What had they to fear from her?

Madame Bretoneux had put these questions to her son but his replies had not satisfied her. She decided to find out for herself, hence her visit.

Very uneasy when she arrived, it was not long before she felt quite at ease again so well did Perrine play the part that mademoiselle had advised her.

Although M. Vulfran had no wish to have his nephews living with him he was very hospitable and cordial to their parents when they came to visit him. On these occasions the beautiful mansion put on its most festive appearance; fires were lighted everywhere; the servants put on their best liveries; the best carriages and horses were brought from the stables, and in the evening the villagers could see the great chateau lighted up from ground floor to roof.

The victoria, with the coachman and footman, had met Mme. Bretoneux at the railway station. Upon her getting out of the carriage Bastien had been on hand to show her to the apartment which was also reserved for her on the first floor.

M. Vulfran never made any change in his habits when his relations came to Maraucourt. He saw them at meal times, spent the evenings with them, but no more of his time did he give them. With him business came before everything; his nephew, the son of whichever one happened to be visiting there, came to luncheon and dinner and remained the evening as late as he wished, but that was all.

M. Vulfran spent his hours at the office just the same and Perrine was always with him, so Madame Bretoneux was not able to follow up her investigations on the "little tramp" as she had wished.

She had questioned Bastien and the maids; she had made a call on Mother Françoise and had questioned her carefully, also Aunt Zenobie and Rosalie, and she had obtained all the information that they could give her; that is, all they knew from the moment of her arrival in the village until she went to live in the great house as a companion to the millionaire. All this, it seemed, was due exclusively to her knowledge of English.

She found it a difficult matter, however, to talk to Perrine alone, who never left M. Vulfran's side unless it was to go to her own room. Madame Bretoneux was in a fever of anxiety to see what was in the girl and discover some reason for her sudden success.

At table Perrine said absolutely nothing. In the morning she went off with M. Vulfran; after she had finished luncheon she went at once to her own room. When they returned from the tour of the factories she went at once to her lessons with her governess; in the evening, upon leaving the table, she went up again to her own room. Madame Bretoneux could not get the girl alone to talk with her. Finally, on the eve of her departure, she decided to go to Perrine's own room. Perrine, who thought that she had got rid of her, was sleeping peacefully.

A few knocks on the door awoke her. She sat up in bed and listened. Another knock.

She got up and went to the door.

"Who is there?" she asked, without opening it.

"Open the door, it is I ... Madame Bretoneux," said a voice.

Perrine turned the lock. Madame Bretoneux slipped into the room while Perrine turned on the light.

"Get into bed again," said Madame Bretoneux, "we can talk just as well."

She took a chair and sat at the foot of the bed so that she was full face with Perrine.

"I want to talk with you about my brother," she began. "You have taken William's place and I want to tell you a few things that you should do; for William, in spite of his faults, was very careful of his master's health. You seem a nice little girl and very willing, and I am sure if you wish you could do as much as William. I assure you that we shall appreciate it."

At the first words Perrine was reassured; if it was only of M. Vulfran's health that she wanted to speak she had nothing to fear.

"I think you are a very intelligent girl," said Mme. Bretoneux with a flattering, ingratiating smile.

At these words and the look which accompanied them Perrine's suspicions were aroused at once.

"Thank you," she said, exaggerating her simple child-like smile, "all I ask is to give as good service as William."

"Ah, I was sure we could count on you," said Mme. Bretoneux.

"You have only to say what you wish, Madame," said little Perrine, looking up at the intruder with her big innocent eyes.

"First of all you must be very attentive about his health; you must watch him carefully and see that he does not take cold. A cold might be fateful; he would have pulmonary congestion and that would aggravate his bronchitis. Do you know if they could cure him of his bronchial trouble they could operate upon him and give him back his sight? Think what happiness that would be for all of us."

"I also would be happy," replied Perrine.

"Those words prove that you are grateful for what he has done for you, but, then, you are not of the family."

Perrine assumed her most innocent air.

"Yes, but that does not prevent me from being attached to M. Vulfran," she said, "believe me, I am."

"Of course," answered Mme. Bretoneux, "and you can prove your devotion by giving him the care which I am telling you to give him. My brother must not only be protected from catching cold, but he must be guarded against sudden emotions which might, in his state of health, kill him. He is trying to find our dear Edmond, his only son. He is making inquiries in India...."

She paused, but Perrine made no reply.

"I am told," she went on, "that my brother gets you to translate the letters and cables that he receives from India. Well, it is most important that if there be bad news that my son should be informed first. Then he will send me a telegram, and as it is not far from here to Boulogne I will come at once to comfort my poor brother. The sympathy of a sister is deeper than that of a sister-in-law, you understand."

"Certainly, Madame, I understand; at least I think so," said Perrine.

"Then we can count on you?"

Perrine hesitated for a moment, but as she was forced to give a reply she said:

"I shall do all that I can for M. Vulfran."

"Yes, and what you do for him will be for us," continued Mme. Bretoneux, "the same as what you do for us will be for him. And I am going to show you that I am not ungrateful. What would you say if I gave you a very nice dress?"

Perrine did not want to say anything, but as she had to make some reply to the question she put it into a smile.

"A very beautiful dress to wear in the evening," said Mme. Bretoneux.

"But I am in mourning," answered Perrine.

"But being in black does not prevent you from wearing a lovely dress. You are not dressed well enough to dine at my brother's table. You are very badly dressed—dressed up like a clever little dog."

Perrine replied that she knew she was not well dressed but she was somewhat humiliated to be compared with a clever little dog, and the way the comparison was made was an evident intention to lower her.

"I took what I could find at Mme. Lachaise's shop," she said in self-defense.

"It was all right for Mme. Lachaise to dress you when you were a little factory girl, but now, that it pleases my brother to have you sit at the table with him, we do not wish to blush for you. You must not mind us making fun of you, but you have no idea how you amused us in that dreadful waist you have been wearing...."

Mme. Bretoneux smiled as though she could still see Perrine in the hideous waist.

"But there," she said brightly, "all that can be remedied; you are a beautiful girl, there is no denying that, and I shall see that you have a dinner dress to set off your beauty and a smart little tailored costume to wear in the carriage, and when you see yourself in it you will remember who gave it you. I expect your underwear is no better than your waist. Let me see it...."

Thereupon, with an air of authority, she opened first one drawer, then another, then shut them again disdainfully with a shrug of her shoulders.

"I thought so," she said, "it is dreadful; not good enough for you."

Perrine felt suffocated; she could not speak.

"It's lucky," continued Mme. Bretoneux, "that I came here, for I intend to look after you."

Perrine wanted to refuse everything and tell this woman that she did not wish her to take care of her, but remembered the part she had to play. After all, Mme. Bretoneux's intentions were most generous; it was her words, her manner, that seemed so hard.

"I'll tell my brother," she continued, "that he must order from a dressmaker at Amiens, whose address I will give him, the dinner dress and the tailor suit which is absolutely necessary, and in addition some good underwear. In fact, a whole outfit. Trust in me and you shall have some pretty things, and I hope that they'll remind you of me all the time. Now don't forget what I have told you."

CHAPTER XXVI. PAINFUL ARGUMENTS

AFTER the talk his mother had had with Perrine, Casimir, by his looks and manner, gave her every opportunity to confide in him. But she had no intention of telling him about the researches that his uncle was having made both in India and in England. True, they had no positive news of the exile; it was all vague and contradictory, but the blind man still hoped on. He left no stone unturned to find his beloved son.

Mme. Bretoneux's advice had some good effect. Until then Perrine had not taken the liberty of having the hood of the phaeton pulled up, if she thought the day was chilly, nor had she dared advise M. Vulfran to put on an overcoat nor suggest that he have a scarf around his neck; neither did she dare close the window in the study if the evening was too cool, but from the moment that Mme. Bretoneux had warned her that the damp mists and rain would be bad for him she put aside all timidity.

Now, no matter what the weather was like, she never got into the carriage without looking to see that his overcoat was in its place and a silk scarf in the pocket; if a slight breeze came up she put the scarf around his neck or helped him into his coat. If a drop of rain began to fall she stopped at once and put up the hood. When she first walked out with him, she had gone her usual pace and he had followed without a word of complaint. But now that she realized that a brisk walk hurt him and usually made him cough or breathe with difficulty, she walked slowly; in every way she devised means of going about their usual day's routine so that he should feel the least fatigue possible.

Day by day the blind man's affection for little Perrine grew. He was never effusive, but one day while she was carefully attending to his wants he told her that she was like a little daughter to him. She was touched. She took his hand and kissed it.

"Yes," he said, "you are a good girl." Putting his hand on her head, he added: "Even when my son returns you shall not leave us; he will be grateful to you for what you are to me."

"I am so little, and I want to be so much," she said.

"I will tell him what you have been," said the blind man, "and besides he will see for himself; for my son has a good kind heart."

Often he would speak in these terms, and Perrine always wanted to ask him how, if these were his sentiments, he could have been so unforgiving and severe with him, but every time she tried to speak the words would not come, for her throat was closed with emotion. It was a serious matter for her to broach such a subject, but on that particular evening she felt encouraged by what had happened. There could not have been a more opportune moment; she was alone with him in his study where no one came unless summoned. She was seated near him under the lamplight. Ought she to hesitate longer?

She thought not.

"Do you mind," she said, in a little trembling voice, "if I ask you something that I do not understand? I think of it all the time, and yet I have been afraid to speak."

"Speak out," he said.

"What I cannot understand," she said timidly, "is that loving your son as you do, you could be parted from him."

"It is because you are so young you do not understand," he said, "that there is duty as well as love. As a father, it was my duty to send him away; that was to teach him a lesson. I had to show him that my will was stronger than his. That is why I sent him to India where I intended to keep him but a short while. I gave him a position befitting my son and heir. He was the representative of my house. Did I know that he would marry that miserable creature? He was mad!"

"But Father Fields said that she was not a miserable creature," insisted Perrine.

"She was or she would not have contracted a marriage that was not valid in France," retorted the blind man, "and I will not recognize her as my daughter."

He said this in a tone that made Perrine feel suddenly cold. Then he continued abruptly: "You wonder why I am trying to get my son back now, if I did not want him back after he had married. Things have changed. Conditions are not the same now as then. After fourteen years of this so-called marriage my son ought to be tired of this woman and of the miserable life that he has been forced to live on account of her. Besides conditions for me have also changed. My health is not what it was, and I am blind. I cannot recover my sight unless I am operated upon and I must be in a calm state favorable to the success of this operation. When my son learns this do you think he will hesitate to leave this woman? I am willing to support her and her daughter also. I am sure many times he has thought of Maraucourt and wanted to return. If I love him I know that he also loves me. When he learns the truth he will come back at once, you will see."

"Then he would have to leave his wife and daughter?"

"He has no wife nor has he a daughter," said the old man sternly.

"Father Fields says that he was married at the Mission House by Father Leclerc," said Perrine.

"This marriage was contracted contrary to the French law," said M. Vulfran.

"But was it not lawful in India?" asked Perrine.

"I will have it annulled in Rome," said the blind man.

"But the daughter?"

"The law would not recognize that child."

"Is the law everything?"

"What do you mean?"

"I mean that it is not the law that makes one love or not love one's parents or children. It was not the law that made me love my poor father. I loved him because he was good and kind and he loved me. I was happy when he kissed me, and smiled at me. I loved him and there was nothing that I liked better than to be with him. He loved me because I was his little girl and needed his affection; he loved me because he knew that I loved him with all my heart. The law had nothing to do with that. I did not ask if it was the law that made him my father. It was our love that made us so much to each other."

"What are you driving at?" asked M. Vulfran.

"I beg your pardon if I have said anything I should not say, but I speak as I think and as I feel."

"And that is why I am listening to you," said the blind man; "what you say is not quite reasonable, but you speak as a good girl would."

"Well, sir, what I am trying to say is this," said Perrine boldly; "if you love your son and want to have him back with you, he also loves his daughter and wants to have her with him."

"He should not hesitate between his father and his daughter," said the old man; "besides, if the marriage is annulled, she will be nothing to him. He could soon marry that woman off again with the dowry that I would give her. Everything is changed since he went away. My fortune is much larger.... He will have riches, honor and position. Surely it isn't a little half-caste that can keep him back."

"Perhaps she is not so dreadful as you imagine," said Perrine.

"A Hindu."

"In the books that I read to you it says that the Hindus are more beautiful than the Europeans," said Perrine.

"Travelers' exaggerations," said the old man scoffingly.

"They have graceful figures, faces of pure oval, deep eyes with a proud look. They are patient, courageous, industrious; they are studious...."

"You have a memory!"

"One should always remember what one reads, should not one?" asked Perrine. "It does not seem that the Hindu is such a horrible creature as you say."

"Well, what does all that matter to me as I do not know her?"

"But if you knew her you might perhaps get interested in her and learn to love her."

"Never! I can't bear to think of her and her mother!..."

"But if you knew her you might not feel so angry towards her."

He clenched his fist as though unable to control his fury, but he did not stop her.

"I don't suppose that she is at all like you suppose," said Perrine; "Father Fields is a good priest and he would not say what was not true, and he says that her mother was good and kind and a lady...."

"He never knew her; it is hearsay."

"But it seems that everyone holds this opinion. If she came to your house would you not be as kind to her as you have been to me, ... a stranger?"

"Don't say anything against yourself."

"I do not speak for or against myself, but what I ask is for justice. I know if that daughter, your granddaughter, came here she would love you with all her heart."

She clasped her hands together and looked up at him as though he could see her; her voice shook with emotion.

"Wouldn't you like to be loved by your granddaughter?" she asked pleadingly.

The blind man rose impatiently.

"I tell you she can never be anything to me," he cried. "I hate her as I hate her mother. The woman took my son from me and she keeps him from me. If she had not bewitched him he would have been back long before this. She has been everything to him while I, his father, have been nothing."

He strode back and forth, carried away with his anger. She had never seen him like this. Suddenly he stopped before her.

"Go to your room," he said almost harshly, "and never speak of those creatures to me again; besides, what right have you to mix up in this? Who told you to speak to me in such a manner?"

For a moment she was dumbfounded, then she said:

"Oh, no one, sir, I assure you. I just put myself into your little granddaughter's place, that is all."

He softened somewhat, but he continued still in a severe voice: "In the future do not speak on this subject; you see it is painful for me and you must not annoy me."

"I beg your pardon," she said, her voice full of tears; "certainly I ought not to have spoken so."

CHAPTER XXVII. THE BLIND MAN'S GRIEF

MONSIEUR VULFRAN advertised in the principal newspapers of Calcutta, Dacca, Bombay and London for his son. He offered a reward of forty pounds to anyone who could furnish any information, however slight it might be, about Edmond Paindavoine. The information must, however, be authentic. Not wishing to give his own address, which might have brought to him all sorts of correspondence more or less dishonest, he put the matter into the hands of his banker at Amiens.

Numerous letters were received, but very few were serious; the greater number came from detectives who guaranteed to find the person they were searching for if the expenses for the first steps necessary could be sent them. Other letters promised everything without any foundation whatever upon which they based their promises. Others related events that had occurred five, ten, twelve years previous; no one kept to the time stated in the advertisement, that was the last three years.

Perrine read or translated all these letters for the blind man. He would not be discouraged at the meagre indications sent him.

"It is only by continued advertising that we shall get results," he said always. Then again he advertised.

Finally, one day a letter from Bosnia gave them some information which might lead to something. It was written in bad English, and stated that if the advertiser would place the forty pounds promised with a banker at Serajevo the writer would furnish authentic information concerning M. Edmond Paindavoine going back to the month of November of the preceding year. If this proposition was acceptable, the reply was to be sent to N. 917, General Delivery, Serajevo.

This letter seemed to give M. Vulfran so much relief and joy that it was a confession of what his fears had been.

For the first time since he had commenced his investigations, he spoke of his son to his two nephews and Talouel.

"I am delighted to tell you that at last I have news of my son," he said. "He was in Bosnia last November."

There was great excitement as the news was spread through the various towns and villages. As usual under such circumstances, it was exaggerated.

"M. Edmond is coming back. He'll be home shortly," went from one to another.

"It's not possible!" cried some.

"If you don't believe it," they were told, "you've only to look at Talouel's face and M. Vulfran's nephews."

Yet there were some who would not believe that the exile would return. The old man had been too hard on him. He had not deserved to be sent away to India because he had made a few debts. His own family had cast him aside, so he had a little family of his own out in India. Why should he come back? And then, even if he was in Bosnia or Turkey, that was not to say that he was on his way to Maraucourt. Coming from India to France, why should he have to go to Bosnia? It was not on the route.

This remark came from Bendit, who, with his English cool-headedness, looked at things only from a practical standpoint, in which sentiment played no part. He thought that just because everyone wished for the son and heir to return, it was not enough to bring him back. The French could wish a thing and believe it, but he was English, he was, and he would not believe that he was coming back until he saw him there with his own eyes!

Day by day the blind man grew more impatient to see his son. Perrine could not bear to hear him talk of his return as a certainty. Many times she tried to tell him that he might be disappointed. One day, when she could bear it no longer, she begged him in her sweet voice not to count too much upon seeing his son for fear something might still keep him away.

The blind man asked her what she meant.

"It is so terrible to hear the worst when one has been expecting the best," she said brokenly. "If I say this it is because that is just what happened to me. We had thought and hoped so much when my father was ill that he would get better, but we lost him, and poor mama and I did not know how to bear it. We would not think that he might die."

"Ah, but my boy is alive, and he will be here soon. He will come back to me very soon," said the old man in a firm voice.

The next day the banker from Amiens called at the factory. He was met at the steps by Talouel, who did all in his power to get the first information which he knew the banker was bringing. At first his attitude was very obsequious, but when he saw that his advances were repulsed, and that the visitor insisted upon seeing his employer at once, he pointed rudely in the direction of M. Vulfran's office and said:

"You will find him over there in that room," and then turned and went off with his hands in his pockets.

The banker knocked on the door indicated.

"Come in," called out M. Vulfran, in answer to his knock.

"What, you ... you at Maraucourt!" he exclaimed when he saw his visitor.

"Yes, I had some business to attend to at Picquigny, and I came on here to bring you some news received from Bosnia."

Perrine sat at her little table. She had gone very white; she seemed like one struck dumb.

"Well?" asked M. Vulfran.

"It is not what you hoped, what we all hoped," said the banker quietly.

"You mean that that fellow who wrote just wanted to get hold of the forty pounds."

"Oh, no; he seems an honest man...."

"Then he knows nothing?"

"He does, but unfortunately his information is only too true."

"Unfortunately!" gasped the blind man. This was the first word of doubt that he had uttered. "You mean," he added, "that they have no more news of him since last November?"

385

"There is no news since then. The French Consul at Serajevo, Bosnia, has sent me this information:

"'Last November your son arrived at Serajevo practising the trade of a strolling photographer....'"

"What do you mean?" exclaimed M. Vulfran. "A strolling photographer!... My son?"

"He had a wagon," continued the banker, "a sort of caravan in which he traveled with his wife and child. He used to take pictures on the market squares where they stopped...."

The banker paused and glanced at some papers he held in his hand.

"Oh, you have something to read, haven't you?" said the blind man as he heard the paper rustle. "Read, it will be quicker."

"He plied the trade of a photographer," continued the banker, consulting his notes, "and at the beginning of November he left Serajevo for Travnik, where he fell ill. He became very ill...."

"My God!" cried the blind man. "Oh, God...."

M. Vulfran had clasped his hands; he was trembling from head to foot, as though a vision of his son was standing before him.

"You must have courage," said the banker, gently. "You need all your courage. Your son...."

"He is dead!" said the blind man.

"That is only too true," replied the banker. "All the papers are authentic. I did not want to have any doubt upon the matter, and that was why I cabled to our Consul at Serajevo. Here is his reply; it leaves no doubt."

But the old man did not appear to be listening. He sat huddled up in his big chair, his head drooped forward on his chest. He gave no sign of life. Perrine, terrified, wondered if he were dead.

Then suddenly he pulled himself together and the tears began to run down his wrinkled cheeks. He brushed them aside quickly and touched the electric bell which communicated with Talouel's and his nephew's offices.

The call was so imperative that they all ran to the office together.

"You are there?" asked the blind man; "Talouel, Theodore and Casimir?"

All three replied together.

"I have just learned of the death of my son," said their employer. "Stop work in all the factories immediately. Tomorrow the funeral services will be held in the churches at Maraucourt, Saint-Pipoy and all the other villages."

"Oh, uncle!" cried both the nephews.

He stopped them with uplifted hand.

"I wish to be alone ... leave me," was all he said.

Everyone left the room but Perrine. She alone remained.

"Aurelie, are you there?" asked the blind man.

She replied with a sob.

"Let us go home," he said.

As was his habit, he placed his hand on her shoulder, and it was like this that they passed through the crowd of workers who streamed from the factory. As they stood aside for him to pass, all who saw him wondered if he would survive this blow. He, who usually walked so upright, was bent like a tree that the storm has broken.

Could he survive this shock? Perrine asked herself this question with even greater agony, for it was she and she alone who knew how his great frame was trembling. His shaking hands grasped her shoulder convulsively, and without him uttering one word little Perrine knew how deeply her grandfather was smitten.

After she had guided him into his study he sent her away.

"Explain why I wish to be left alone. No one is to come in here. No one is to speak to me...."

"And I refused to believe you," he murmured as she was leaving him.

"Oh, please; if you will let me...."

"Leave me," he said roughly.

Perrine closed the door softly.

CHAPTER XXVIII. AN UNRESPECTED FUNERAL

THERE was considerable bustle and excitement at the chateau all that evening. First M. and Mme. Stanislas Paindavoine, who had received a telegram from Theodore, arrived. Then M. and Mme. Bretoneux, sent for by Casimir, came. After that came Mme. Bretoneux's two daughters, their husbands and children. No one wished to miss the funeral service for poor dear Edmond.

Besides, this was the decisive moment for clever manoeuvring. What a disaster if this big industry should fall into the hands of one so incapable as Theodore! What a misfortune if Casimir took charge! Neither side thought that a partnership could be possible, and the two cousins share alike. Each wanted all for himself.

Both Mme. Bretoneux and Mme. Paindavoine had ignored Perrine since their arrival. They had given her to understand that they did not require her services any longer.

She sat in her room hoping that M. Vulfran would send for her so that she could help him into the church, as she had done every Sunday since William had gone. But she waited in vain. When the bells, which had been tolling since the evening before, announced mass, she saw him get up into his carriage leaning on his brother's arm, while his sister and sister-in-law, with the members of their families, took their places in other carriages.

She had no time to lose, for she had to walk. She hurried off.

After she had left the house over which Death had spread its shroud, she was surprised to notice as she hastened through the village that the taverns had taken on their Sunday air. The men drank and laughed and the women chatted at their doors, while the children played in the street. Perrine wondered if none of them were going to attend the service.

Upon entering the church, where she had been afraid that she would not find room, she saw that it was almost empty. The bereaved family sat in the choir; here and there was some village authority, a tradesman and the heads of the factories. Very few of the working men and women were present; they had not thought to come and join their prayers to those of their employer.

Perrine took a seat beside Rosalie and her grandmother, who was in deep mourning.

"Alas! my poor little Edmond," murmured the old nurse, wiping her eyes. "What did M. Vulfran say?"

But Perrine was too overcome to reply. The services commenced.

As she left the church, Mlle. Belhomme came up to her, and, like Françoise, wanted to question her about M. Vulfran. Perrine told her that he had not spoken to her since the evening before.

"As I saw him kneeling there so crushed and broken for the first time, I was pleased that he was blind," said the governess sadly.

"Why?" asked Perrine.

"Because he could not see how few people came to the church. What indifference his men have shown! If he could have seen that empty church it would have added to his grief."

"I think he must have known how few there were there," said Perrine. "His ears take the place of his eyes, and that empty silence could not deceive him."

"Poor man," murmured Mlle. Belhomme; "and yet...."

She paused. Then, as she was not in the habit of holding anything back, she went on: "And yet it will be a great lesson to him. You know, my child, you cannot expect others to share your sorrows if you are not willing to share theirs.

"M. Vulfran gives his men what he considers their due," she continued, in a lower voice. "He is just, but that is all. He has never been a father to his men. He is all for business, business only. What a lot of good he could have done, however, not only here, but everywhere, if he had wished, by setting an example. Had he been more to his men you may be sure that the church would not have been as empty as it was today."

Perhaps that was true, but how it hurt Perrine to hear this from the lips of her governess, of whom she was so fond. If anyone else had said so she might not have felt it so deeply. Yes, undoubtedly it was too true.

They had been walking as they talked, and had now reached the schools where Mlle. Belhomme lived.

"Come in and we'll have luncheon together," she said. She was thinking that her pupil would not be allowed to take her accustomed place at the family table.

"Oh, thank you," said Perrine; "but M. Vulfran might need me."

"Well, in that case you had better go back," said Mlle. Belhomme.

When she reached the chateau she saw that M. Vulfran had no need of her, that he was not even thinking of her. Bastien, whom she met on the stairs, told her that when he came back from the church he had gone to his own room and locked himself in, forbidding anyone to enter.

"He won't even sit down on a day like this with his family," said Bastien, "and they are all going after luncheon. I don't think he even wants to say goodbye to them. Lord help us! What will become of us? Oh, poor master!"

"What can I do?" asked Perrine.

"You can do a great deal. The master believes in you, and he's mighty fond of you."

"Mighty fond of me?" echoed Perrine.

"Yes, and it's as I says it," said the butler. "He likes you a whole lot."

As Bastien had said, all the family left after luncheon. Perrine stayed in her room, but M. Vulfran did not send for her. Just before she went to bed, Bastien came to tell her that his master wished her to accompany him the next morning at the usual hour.

"He wants to get back to work, but will he be able?" said the old butler. "It will be better for him if he can. Work means life for him."

The next day at the usual hour Perrine was waiting for M. Vulfran. With bent back he came forward, guided by Bastien. The butler made a sign to her that his master had passed a bad night.

"Is Aurelie there?" asked the blind man in a changed voice, a voice low and weak, like that of a sick child.

Perrine went forward quickly.

"I am here, M. Vulfran," she said.

"Let us get into the carriage, Aurelie," he said.

As soon as he had taken his place beside Perrine his head drooped on his chest. He said not a word.

At the foot of the office steps Talouel was there ready to receive him and help him to alight.

"I suppose you felt strong enough to come?" he said, in a sympathetic voice which contrasted with the flash in his eyes.

"I did not feel at all strong, but I came because I thought that I ought to come," said his employer.

"That is what I meant ... I...."

M. Vulfran stopped him and told Perrine to guide him to his office.

The mail, which had accumulated in two days, was read, but the blind man made no comments on the correspondence. It was as though he were deaf or asleep. The heads of the factory then came in to discuss an important question that had to be settled that day. When the immediate business was settled Perrine was left alone with the blind man. He was silent.

Time passed; he did not move. She had often seen him sit still, but on such occasions, from the expression on his face, she had known that he was following his work as though he were watching with his eyes. He listened to the whistle of the engines, the rolling of the trucks; he was attentive to every sound and seemed to know exactly what was going on, but now he seemed as though he were turned into a statue. There was no expression in his face and he was so silent. He did not seem to be breathing. Perrine was overcome by a sort of terror. She moved uneasily in her chair; she did not dare speak to him.

Suddenly he put his two hands over his face and, as though unaware that anyone was present, he cried: "My God! my God! you have forsaken me! Oh, Lord, what have I done that you should forsake me!"

Then the heavy silence fell again. Perrine trembled when she heard his cry, although she could not grasp the depth of his despair.

Everything that this man had attempted had been a success; he had triumphed over his rivals; but now, with one blow, that which he wanted most had been snatched from him. He had been waiting for his son; their meeting, after so many years of absence, he had pictured to himself, and then....

Then what?

"My God," cried the blind man again, "why have you taken him from me?"

CHAPTER XXIX. THE ANGEL OF REFORM

AS THE days passed M. Vulfran became very weak. At last he was confined to his room with a serious attack of bronchitis, and the entire management of the works was given over to Talouel, who was triumphant.

When he recovered he was in such a state of apathy that it was alarming. They could not rouse him; nothing seemed to interest him, not even his business. Previously they had feared the effect a shock would have on his system, but now the doctors desired it, for it seemed that only a great shock could drag him out of this terrible condition. What could they do?

After a time he returned to his business, but he scarcely took account of what Talouel had done during his absence. His manager, however, had been too clever and shrewd to take any steps that his employer would not have taken himself.

Every day Perrine took him to his various factories, but the drives were made in silence now. Frequently he did not reply to the remarks she made from time to time, and when he reached the works he scarcely listened to what his men had to say.

"Do what you think best," he said always. "Arrange the matter with Talouel."

How long would this apathy last?

One afternoon, when old Coco was bringing them back to Maraucourt, they heard a bell ringing.

"Stop," he said; "I think that's the fire alarm."

Perrine stopped the horse.

"Yes, it's a fire," he said, listening. "Do you see anything?"

"I can see a lot of black smoke over by the poplars on the left," replied Perrine.

"On the left? That is the way to the factory."

"Yes; shall I drive that way?" asked Perrine.

"Yes," replied M. Vulfran, indifferently.

It was not until they reached the village that they knew where the fire was.

"Don't hurry, M. Vulfran," called out a peasant; "the fire ain't in your house. It's La Tiburce's house that's on fire."

La Tiburce was a drunken creature who minded little babies who were too young to be taken to the crèche. She lived in a miserable tumble-down house near the schools.

"Let us go there," said M. Vulfran.

They had only to follow the crowd, for the people, when they saw the flames and smoke rising, were running excitedly to the spot where the fire was. Before reaching the scene Perrine had to stop several times for fear of running someone down. Nothing in the world would have made the people get out of their way. Finally M. Vulfran got out of the carriage and, guided by Perrine, walked through the crowd. As they neared the entrance to the house, Fabry, wearing a helmet, for he was chief of the firemen, came up to them.

"We've got it under control," he said, "but the house is entirely burnt, and what's worse, several children, five or six, perhaps, are lost. One is buried beneath, two have been suffocated, and we don't know where the other three are."

"How did it happen?" asked M. Vulfran.

"La Tiburce was asleep, drunk. She is still in that condition. The biggest of the children were playing with the matches. When the fire began to flare up some of the children got out, and La Tiburce woke up. She is so drunk she got out herself but left the little ones in the cradle."

The sound of cries and loud talking could be heard in the yard. M. Vulfran wanted to go in.

"Don't go in there, sir," said Fabry. "The mothers whose two children were suffocated are carrying on pretty badly."

"Who are they?"

"Two women who work in your factory."

"I must speak to them."

Leaning on Perrine's shoulder, he told her to guide him. Preceded by Fabry, who made way for them, they went into the yard where the firemen were turning the hose on the house as the flames burst forth in a crackling sound.

In a far-off corner several women stood round the two mothers who were crying. Fabry brushed aside the group. M. Vulfran went up to the bereaved parents, who sat with their dead children on their knees. Then one of the women, who thought perhaps that a supreme help had come, looked up with a gleam of hope in her eyes. When she recognized M. Vulfran she raised her arm to him threateningly.

"Ah," she cried, "come and see for yourself what they do to our babies while we are sweating and killing ourselves for you. Can you give us back their lives? Oh, my little boy."

She burst into sobs as she bent over her child.

M. Vulfran hesitated for a moment; then he turned to Fabry and said:

"You are right; let us go."

They returned to the offices. After a time Talouel came to tell his employer that out of the six children that they had thought were dead, three had been found in the homes of neighbors, where they had been carried when the fire first broke out. The burial for the other three tiny victims was to take place the next day.

When Talouel had gone, Perrine, who had been very thoughtful, decided to speak to M. Vulfran.

"Are you not going to the burial service of these little babies?" she asked. Her trembling voice betrayed her emotion.

"Why should I go?" asked M. Vulfran.

"Because that would be the most dignified answer you could give to what that poor woman said."

"Did my work people come to the burial service of my son?" asked M. Vulfran, coldly.

"They did not share your sorrow," said Perrine gravely, "but if you share theirs now they will be touched."

"You don't know how ungrateful the workingman is."

"Ungrateful! For what? The money they receive? They consider that they have a right to the money they earn. It is theirs. Would they show ingratitude if an interest was taken in them, if a little friendly help was given them? Perhaps it would not be the same, do you think so? Friendship creates friendship. One often loves when one knows one is loved, and it seems to me that when we are friendly to others, we make friends ourselves. It means so much to lighten the burdens of the poor, but how much more is it to lighten their sorrows ... by helping to share them."

It seemed to her that she had still so much to say on this subject, but M. Vulfran did not reply. He did not even appear to be listening to her, and she was afraid to say more. Later she might make another attempt.

As they left the office M. Vulfran turned to Talouel, who was standing on the steps, and said:

"Tell the priest to arrange a suitable burial for the three children. It will be at my expense and I shall be there."

Talouel jumped.

"And let everyone know," continued M. Vulfran, "that all who wish to go to the church tomorrow, can take the time off. This fire is a great misfortune."

"We are not responsible for it," said Talouel.

"Not directly ... no," said M. Vulfran.

Perrine had another surprise the next morning. After the mail had been opened and the replies dictated, M. Vulfran detained Fabry and said: "I want you to start for Rouen. I think you can spare the time. I have heard that they have built a model crèche there. It is not built by the town, but someone has had it built to the memory of one whom they have lost. I want you to see how this is made. Study it in all its details—the construction, heating and ventilation and the expense of keeping it up. In three months we must have a crèche at the entrance of all my factories. I don't want such a calamity as that which occurred yesterday to take place again. I rely upon you and the responsibility is upon you now."

That evening Perrine told the great news to her governess, who was delighted. While they were talking about it, M. Vulfran came into the room.

"Mademoiselle," he said, "I have come to ask a favor of you in the name of all the village. It is a big favor. It may mean a great sacrifice on your part. This is it."

In a few words he outlined the request he had to make. It was that mademoiselle should send in her resignation at the schools and take charge of the five crèches which he was going to build. He knew of no one who was capable of taking on their shoulders such a big burden. He would donate a crèche to each village and endow it with sufficient capital to keep up its maintenance.

Although Mlle. Belhomme loved to teach, and it would be indeed a sacrifice for her to give up her school, she felt, after she had talked with the blind man, that it was here where her duty lay. It was indeed a great work that she was called upon to do, and she would enter upon her task with all the enthusiasm of which her big heart was capable.

"This is a great thing you are doing, Monsieur Vulfran," she said, with tears in her eyes, "and I will do all I can to make this work a success."

"It is your pupil one must thank for it," said the blind man, "not I. Her words and suggestions have awakened something in my heart. I have stepped out on a new road. I am only at the first steps. It is nothing compared with what I intend to do."

"Oh, please," said Perrine, her eyes bright with delight and pride, "if you still want to do something...."

"What is it?" he asked with a smile.

"I want to take you somewhere ... tonight."

"What do you mean? Where do you want to take me?" asked the blind man, mystified.

"To a place where your presence only for a few moments will bring about extraordinary results," said Perrine.

"Well, can't you tell me where this mysterious place is?" asked M. Vulfran.

"But if I tell you, your visit will not have the same effect. It will be a failure. It will be a fine evening and warm, and I am sure that you will not take cold. Please say you will go!"

"I think one could have confidence in her," said Mademoiselle Belhomme, "although her request seems a little strange and childish."

"Well," said M. Vulfran, indulgently, "I'll do as you wish, Aurelie. Now at what hour are we to start on this adventure?"

"The later it is the better it will be," said Perrine.

During the evening he spoke several times of the outing they were to have, but Perrine would not explain.

"Do you know, little girl, you have aroused my curiosity?" he said at last.

"I am glad you are interested," she said gravely. "There is so much that can be done in the future. Do not look back to the past any more."

"The future is empty for me," said the blind man bitterly.

"Oh, no; it is not," said Perrine, lifting her lovely face to his. Her eyes were shining with a beautiful light. "It will not be empty if you think of others. When one is a child, and not very happy, one often thinks that if a wonderful fairy came to them, of what beautiful things they would ask. But if one is the fairy, or rather the magician oneself, and can do all the wonderful things alone, wouldn't it be splendid to use one's power?..."

The evening passed. Several times the blind man asked if it were not time to start, but Perrine delayed as long as possible.

At last she said that she thought they could start. The night was warm, no breeze, no mists. The atmosphere was a trifle heavy and the sky dark.

When they reached the village it was all quiet. All seemed to sleep. Not a light shone from the windows.

The dark night made no difference to the blind man. As they walked along the road from the chateau he knew exactly where he was.

"We must be nearing Françoise's house," he said, after they had walked a little distance.

"That is just where we are going," said Perrine. "We are there now. Let me take your hand and guide you, and please don't speak. We have some stairs to go up, but they are quite easy and straight. When we get to the top of these stairs I shall open a door and we shall go into a room for just one moment."

"What do you want me to see ... when I can't see anything?" he said.

"There will be no need for you to see," replied Perrine.

"Then why come?"

"I want you here," said Perrine earnestly. "Here are the stairs. Now step up, please."

They climbed up the stairs and Perrine opened a door and gently drew M. Vulfran inside a room and closed the door again.

They stood in a suffocating, evil-smelling room.

"Who is there?" asked a weary voice.

Pressing his hand, Perrine warned M. Vulfran not to speak.

The same voice spoke:

"Get into bed, La Noyelle. How late you are."

This time M. Vulfran clasped Perrine's hand in a sign for them to leave the place.

She opened the door and they went down, while a murmur of voices accompanied them. When they reached the street M. Vulfran spoke: "You wanted me to know what that room was the first night when you slept there?"

"I wanted you to know what kind of a place all the women who work for you have to sleep in. They are all alike in Maraucourt and the other villages. You have stood in one of these dreadful rooms; all the others are like it. Think of your women and children, your factory hands, who are breathing that poisoned air. They are slowly dying. They are almost all weak and sick."

M. Vulfran was silent. He did not speak again, neither did Perrine. When they entered the hall he bade her good night, and guided by Bastien, he went to his own room.

CHAPTER XXX. GRANDFATHER FINDS PERRINE

ONE year had passed since Perrine had arrived at Maraucourt on that radiant Sunday morning. What a miserable lonely little girl she had been then.

The day was just as radiant now, but what a change in Perrine, and, be it said, in the whole village also. She was now a lovely girl of fifteen. She knew she was loved and loved for herself, and this is what gave the deep look of happiness to her eyes.

And the village! No one would have recognized it now. There were new buildings, pretty cottages, and a hospital commanding a view of the surrounding country. Near the factories were two handsome red brick buildings. These were the crèches where the little children, whose mothers were working in the factories, were kept. All the little children had their meals there, and many of them slept there. It was a home for them.

M. Vulfran had bought up all the old houses, the tumble-down hovels and huts, and had built new cottages in their places. There was a large restaurant built where the men and women could get a dinner for eleven cents, the meal consisting of a soup, stew or roast, bread and cider.

Every little cottage, for which the tenant paid one hundred francs a year, had its own tiny garden in which to grow vegetables for the family.

In the road leading to the chateau there was now a fine recreation ground, which was greatly patronized after the factories had closed. There were merry-go-rounds, swings, bowling alleys and a stand for the musicians who played every Saturday and Sunday, and of course on every holiday. This public park of amusement was used by the people of all five villages. Monsieur Vulfran had thought it better to have one place of reunion and recreation. If his people all met together to enjoy their leisure hours, it would establish good relations and a bond of friendship between them. At the end of the grounds there was a fine library with a reading and writing room.

M. Vulfran's relations thought that he had gone mad. Did he intend to ruin himself? That is to say, ruin them? Some steps ought to be taken to prevent him from spending his fortune in this manner. His fondness for that girl was a proof that he was losing his mind. That girl did not know what she was doing! All their animosity was centered on her. What did it matter to her that his fortune was being thrown away? But if Perrine had all the relations against her, she knew that she had M. Vulfran's friendship, and the family doctor, Doctor Ruchon, Mlle. Belhomme and Fabry all adored her. Since the doctor had seen that it was the "little girl" who had been the means of his patient exerting this wonderful moral and intellectual energy, his attitude to her expressed the greatest respect and affection. In the doctor's eyes, Perrine was a wonderful little girl.

"She can do a great deal more than I can," he said, shaking his gray head.

And Mlle. Belhomme, how proud she was of her pupil! As to Fabry, he was on the best of terms with her. He had been so closely connected with her in the good work that had been done, for Fabry had superintended everything.

It was half-past twelve. Fabry had not yet arrived. M. Vulfran, usually so calm, was getting impatient. Luncheon was over and he had gone into his study with Perrine; every now and again he walked to the window and listened.

"The train must be late," he murmured.

Perrine wanted to keep him away from the window, for there were many things going on outside in the park about which she did not wish him to know. With unusual activity, the gardeners were putting great pots of flowers on the steps and in front of the house. Flags were flying from the recreation grounds, which could be seen from the windows.

At last the wheels of a carriage were heard on the drive.

"There's Fabry," said M. Vulfran. His voice expressed anxiety, but pleasure at the same time.

Fabry came in quickly. He also appeared to be in a somewhat excited state. He gave a look at Perrine which made her feel uneasy without knowing why.

"I got your telegram," said M. Vulfran, "but it was so vague. I want to be sure. Speak out."

"Shall I speak before mademoiselle?" asked Fabry, glancing at Perrine.

"Yes, if it is as you say."

It was the first time that Fabry had asked if he could speak before Perrine. In the state of mind in which she was suddenly thrown, this precaution only made her the more anxious.

"The person whom we had lost trace of," said Fabry, without looking at Perrine, "came on to Paris. There she died. Here is a copy of the death certificate. It is in the name of Marie Doressany, widow of Edmond Vulfran Paindavoine."

With trembling hands the blind man took the paper.

"Shall I read it to you?" asked Fabry.

"No, if you have verified the names we will attend to that later. Go on."

"I not only got the certificate; I wanted to question the man whom they call Grain-of-Salt. She died in a room in his house. Then I saw all those who were present at the poor woman's funeral. There was a street singer called the Baroness and an old shoemaker called Carp. It was the miserable existence which she had been forced to live that had finally killed her. I even saw the doctor who attended her, Dr. Cendrier. He wanted her to go to the hospital, but she would not be parted from her daughter. Finally, to complete my investigations, they sent me to a woman who buys rags and bones. Her name is La Rouquerie. I could not see her until yesterday, as she had been out in the country."

Fabry paused. Then for the first time he turned to Perrine and bowed respectfully.

"I saw Palikare, mademoiselle," he said. "He is looking very well."

Perrine had risen to her feet. For some moments she stood listening, dazed. Then her eyes filled with tears.

"I then had to find out what had become of the little daughter," continued Fabry. "This ragpicker told me that she had met her in the Chantilly woods and that she was dying of hunger. It was her own donkey that she sold to the ragpicker who found her."

"Tell me," cried M. Vulfran, turning his sightless eyes towards Perrine, who was trembling from head to foot, "why this little girl did not say who she was? You understand how deeply a little girl can feel, so can you explain this?"

Perrine took a few steps towards him.

"Tell me why she does not come into my arms ... her grandfather's arms."

"Oh, grandpapa," cried Perrine, throwing her arms about his neck.

CHAPTER XXXI. THE GRATEFUL PEOPLE

FABRY had left the room, leaving the grandfather and his granddaughter together. For a long time the old man and the girl sat with their arms about each other. They only spoke now and again, just to exchange a word of affection.

"My little granddaughter ... my boy's little girl," murmured the blind man, stroking her curls.

"My grandpapa," murmured Perrine, rubbing her soft cheek against his.

"Why didn't you tell me who you were?" he asked at last.

"But didn't I try several times?" replied Perrine. "Do you remember what you said to me the last time I spoke of dear mother and myself. You said: 'Understand, never speak to me again of those wretched creatures.'"

"But could I guess that you were my granddaughter?" he said.

"If I had come straight to you, don't you think you would have driven me away and not have listened to me?" asked Perrine.

"Ah," said the blind man, sadly, "who knows what I would have done!"

"I thought so," said Perrine, "and I thought it best not to let you know me until, like mama said, 'you would get to love me.'"

"And you have waited so long, and you had so many proofs of my affection."

"But was it the affection of a grandfather? I did not dare think so," said Perrine.

"When I began to suspect that you were my son's child, I then quickly got positive proofs, and I gave you every chance to tell me that you were. Finally I employed Fabry, who, with his investigations, forced you to throw yourself into my arms. If you had spoken sooner, my little darling, you would have spared me many doubts."

"Yes," said Perrine sweetly, "but we are so happy now, and doesn't that prove that what I did was all for the best?"

"Well, all is well. We will leave it at that. Now tell me all about your father ... my boy."

"I cannot speak to you of my father without speaking of my mother," said Perrine gravely. "They both loved me so much, and I loved them just the same."

"My little girl," said the blind man, "what Fabry has just told me of her has touched me deeply. She refused to go to the hospital where she might have been cured because she would not leave you alone in Paris...."

"Oh, yes; you would have loved her," cried Perrine; "my darling mother."

"Talk to me about her," said the old man, "about them both."

"Yes," said Perrine; "I will make you know her and then you will love her."

Perrine told about their life before they lost all their money; then about their travels through the various countries and the wanderings over the mountains; then of her father's illness and his death, and how she and her sick mother journeyed through France with the hope that they could reach Maraucourt in time before the sick woman died.

While they were talking they could hear vague sounds outside in the garden.

"What is the matter out there?" asked M. Vulfran. Perrine went to the window. The lawns and drive were black with a crowd of men, women and children. They were dressed in their Sunday clothes; many of them carried banners and flags. This crowd, between six and seven thousand people, reached outside the grounds to the public park, and the murmur of their voices had reached the ears of the blind man and had turned his attention from Perrine's story, great though it was.

"What is it?" he asked.

"It is your birthday today," said Perrine, smiling, "and all your men are here to celebrate it and to thank you for all you have done for them and their families."

"Oh!...."

The blind man walked to the window as though he could see them. He was recognized and a murmur ran through the crowd.

"*Mon Dieu*," he murmured, "how terrible they would be if they were against us." For the first time he realized the strength of the masses which he controlled.

"Yes," said Perrine, "but they are with us because we are with them."

"Yes, little girl, and it is all due to you," he replied. "This is very different from the day when the service for your dear father was held in that empty church."

"Yes, they are all here now," said Perrine, "and this is the Order of the Day, grandpapa dear: I am to guide you to the steps exactly at two o'clock. From there everyone will be able to see you. A man representing each village where you have your factories will come up the steps, and fatherly old Gathoye in the name of all is to make a speech."

At this moment the clock struck two.

"Now give me your hand, grandpapa, dear," said Perrine.

They reached the top of the steps and a great cheer broke out. Then the dear old Gathoye, who was the oldest employé, came forward alone. He was followed by the five delegates. Ten times the old man had been made to go over his speech that morning.

"Monsieur Vulfran, sir," he began, "it is to wish you ... it is to congratulate you ... to congratulate you on...."

Here he stopped short and began gesticulating with his hands, and the crowd, who saw his eloquent gestures, thought that he making an elaborate speech.

After some vain efforts, during which he scratched his head several times, he said: "This is how it is: I had a fine speech all ready, but I've gone and forgot all I got to say. I had to congratulate you and thank you in the name of all from the bottom of our hearts...."

He raised his hand solemnly.

"I swear that's so on the faith of your oldest employé, Gathoye."

Although the speech was very incoherent, nevertheless it touched M. Vulfran deeply. With his hand on Perrine's shoulder, he moved forward to the balustrade. There all could see him from below.

"My friends," he called out in a loud voice, "your sincere kind wishes give me the greatest pleasure, all the more so as you bring them to me on the happiest day of my life, the day when I have found my little granddaughter, the daughter of my only son whom I have lost. You know her; you have seen her at the factory. She will go on with the work we have already begun, and I promise you that your future, and your children's future, is in good hands."

Thereupon he leaned down towards Perrine and before she could protest he lifted her up in his arms that were still strong, and presented her to the crowd, then kissed her tenderly.

Then a deafening cheer rang out. It was continued for several minutes. Cheers came from the mouths of seven thousand men, women and children. Then, as the Order of the Day had been previously arranged, a line was formed and in single file they passed before their old chief and his granddaughter. With a bow and a hearty wish each man passed by.

"Ah, grandpapa, if you could only see their kind faces!" cried Perrine.

But there were some faces that were not exactly radiant. The two nephews certainly looked very glum when, after the ceremony, they came up to their cousin to offer their congratulations.

"As for me," said Talouel, who did not mean to lose any time in paying court to the young heiress, "I had always supposed...."

The excitement of the day proved too much for M. Vulfran. The doctor was called in.

"You can understand, doctor," said the blind man anxiously, "how much I want to see my little granddaughter. You must get me into a state so that I can have this operation."

"That is just it," said the doctor cheerily, "you must not have all this excitement. You must be perfectly calm. Now that this beautiful weather has come, you must go out, but you must keep quiet, and I guarantee that as soon as your cough has gone we shall be able to have a successful operation."

And the doctor's words came true. A month after M. Vulfran's birthday two specialists came down from Paris to perform the operation.

When they wished to put him under an anesthetic he refused.

"If my granddaughter will have the courage to hold my hand," he said, "you will see that I will be brave. Is it very painful?"

They would use cocaine to alleviate the pain.

The operation was over. Then came five or six days of waiting. The patient was kept in a dark room. Then at last the grandfather was allowed to see his little granddaughter.

"Ah, if I had only had my eyes," he cried as he gazed at Perrine's beautiful little face, "I should have recognized her at the first glance. What fools! Couldn't anyone have seen the likeness to her father? This time Talouel would have been right if he had said that he 'supposed'...."

They did not let him use his eyes for long. Again the bandage was put on and was kept on for thirty days. Then one of the oculists who had remained at the chateau went up to Paris to select the glasses which would enable him to read and see at a distance.

What M. Vulfran desired most, now that he had seen Perrine's sweet face, was to go out and see his works, but this needed great precaution, and the trip had to be postponed for a time, for he did not wish to be closed up in a landau with the windows up, but to use his old phaeton and be driven by Perrine and show himself with her everywhere. For that they had to wait for a warm, sunny day.

At last the day they wanted came. The sky was blue, the air soft and warm. After luncheon Perrine gave the order to Bastien for the phaeton with old Coco to be at the door.

"Yes, at once, mademoiselle," he said with a smile.

Perrine was surprised at the tone of his reply and his smile; but she paid no more attention to it, as she was busy fussing about her grandfather so that he would not take cold.

Presently Bastien came to say that the phaeton was ready. Perrine's eyes did not leave her grandfather as he walked forwards and down the steps alone. When they reached the last step a loud bray made her start. She looked up.

There stood a donkey harnessed to a phaeton! A donkey, and that donkey was like Palikare, a Palikare shiny and glossy, with polished shoes and adorned with a beautiful yellow harness with blue tassels. The donkey, with his neck stretched out, continued to bray. In spite of the groom's hold upon him he turned and tried to get to Perrine.

"Palikare!" she cried.

She flew to him and flung her arms around his neck.

"Oh, grandpapa, what a lovely surprise!" she cried, dancing around her dear Palikare.

"You don't owe it to me," said her grandfather. "Fabry bought it from that ragpicker to whom you sold it. The office staff offer it as a gift to their old comrade."

"Oh, hasn't Monsieur Fabry got a good, kind heart!" cried Perrine.

"Yes, he thought of it, but your cousins did not," said M. Vulfran. "I have ordered a pretty cart from Paris for him. This phaeton is not the thing for him."

They got up into the carriage and Perrine took the reins delightedly.

"Where shall we go first, grandpapa?" she asked.

"Why, to the log cabin," he said. "Don't you think I want to see the little nest where you once lived, my darling?"

He referred to the cabin on the island where she had lived for a time the preceding year. It remained fondly in his mind. She drove on to the entrance and helped her grandfather alight at the path.

The cabin seemed just the same as when Perrine left it.

"How strange," said M. Vulfran, "that only a few steps from a great industrial center you were able to live the life of a savage here."

"In India we led a real savage life," said Perrine. "Everything around us belonged to us there, but here, I had no right to this and I was often very afraid."

After M. Vulfran had inspected the little log hut he wanted to see the crèche at Maraucourt.

He thought that he would easily recognize it, as he had so often discussed the plans with Fabry, but when he found himself at the entrance, and was able to see at a glance all the other rooms, the dormitory where the little babies were asleep in their rose and blue cribs according to the sex, the playroom where those who could walk were playing, the kitchen, the lavatory, he was surprised and delighted.

Using large glass doors, the architect had cleverly made his plans so that from the first room the mothers could see all that went on in the other rooms where they were not allowed to enter.

In the nursery the children sprang forward and jumped upon Perrine, showing her the playthings that they had in their hands.

"I see that you are known here," said M. Vulfran.

"Known!" replied Mlle. Belhomme, greeting them. "She is loved by all; she is a little mother to them, and no one can play like she can."

M. Vulfran put his arms affectionately around his granddaughter as they went on to the carriage.

They returned home slowly as evening fell. Then as they passed from one hill to another, they found themselves overlooking the surrounding country, where new roofs and tall chimneys could be seen everywhere.

M. Vulfran took Perrine's hand.

"All that is your work, child," he said; "I only thought of business. See what you have done. But so that this can all be continued in the years to come, we shall have to find you a husband, one who will be worthy of you, who will work for us. We will not ask anything more of him. I think one day we shall find the right man and we shall all be happy ... en famille...."

THE END